"Crystal Caudill's debut novel captivated me from word one, and her follow-up offering did exactly the same. Even if all it offered was a swoony romance and riveting historical suspense, that would be enough to keep readers glued to the pages. And yet it's also full of emotional depth, complicated family dynamics, and tender redemption. *Counterfeit Hope* does more than entertain—it wraps the reader in grace. A fantastic sophomore novel from a fresh voice in the genre!"

CARRIE SCHMIDT, blogger at ReadingIsMySuperPower.org and author of *Getting Past the Publishing Gatekeepers*

"Caudill has penned a riveting sophomore novel in *Counterfeit Hope*. From the first page, the story draws you in with characters who engage all your emotions and a fast-paced plot that carries the story just right. Another novel for the keeper shelf!"

MISTY M. BELLER, *USA Today* best-selling author of the Call of the Rockies series

"A round of applause for Crystal Caudill and the fabulous story she penned. The rich, well-developed characters, the plot twists, and Crystal's unique voice made it a very enjoyable read and kept me on the edge of my seat just waiting to see what would happen from the beginning. I would highly recommend it for any lover of historical fiction."

LIZ TOLSMA, best-selling author of *What I Would Tell You* and *A Picture of Hope*

"A gripping story of pain, forgiveness and hope. I had a hard time putting this book down! *Counterfeit Hope* is reminiscent of Francine Rivers's *Redeeming Love*, and I appreciate the Crystal Caudill's gentle handling of such sensitive topics. I was thoroughly moved throughout the tale and highly recommend this story and series!"

ANGELA K. COUCH, author of *A Rose for the Resistance* and *Where Wild Roses Bloom*

COUNTERFEIT
HOPE

HIDDEN HEARTS OF THE GILDED AGE
Counterfeit Love
Counterfeit Hope
Counterfeit Faith

HIDDEN HEARTS
OF THE GILDED AGE
- TWO -

COUNTERFEIT
HOPE

CRYSTAL CAUDILL

KREGEL
PUBLICATIONS

Counterfeit Hope
© 2023 by Crystal Caudill

Published by Kregel Publications, a division of Kregel Inc., 2450 Oak Industrial Dr. NE, Grand Rapids, MI 49505. www.kregel.com.

The persons and events portrayed in this work are the creations of the author, and any resemblance to persons living or dead is purely coincidental.

Scripture quotations are from the King James Version.

Library of Congress Cataloging-in-Publication Data
Names: Caudill, Crystal, author.
Title: Counterfeit hope : hidden hearts of the gilded age / Crystal Caudill.
Description: Grand Rapids, MI : Kregel Publications, [2023] | Series: Hidden hearts of the gilded age ; book 2
Subjects: LCGFT: Christian fiction. | Novels.
Classification: LCC PS3603.A89866 C679 2022 (print) | LCC PS3603.
A89866 (ebook) | DDC 813/.6--dc23/eng/20220812
LC record available at https://lccn.loc.gov/2022037003
LC ebook record available at https://lccn.loc.gov/2022037004

ISBN 978-0-8254-4741-9, print
ISBN 978-0-8254-7798-0, epub
ISBN 978-0-8254-6949-7, Kindle

Printed in the United States of America
23 24 25 26 27 28 29 30 31 32 / 5 4 3 2 1

To God: May it all be for Your glory.

To Malaki:
You're my baby. You're my boy.
You're my pride, and you're my joy.
No matter what hardship this life brings, may you always know
the love and hope of Christ in your life.
I love you.

"For we are saved by hope: but hope that is seen is not hope: for what a man seeth, why doth he yet hope for? But if we hope for that we see not, then do we with patience wait for it."

ROMANS 8:24–25

LETTER TO THE READER

Dear Reader,

The story you are about to read contains a heroine who is created by God but broken by the world. Lu Thorne is a former prostitute, a thief, a person who is suffering abuse, and a widowed mother who is stuck in a criminal family that won't let her and her son leave. You will see what her life is like and the struggles she faces, including some instances of abuse. I tried to handle it with a light touch, but for those who are triggered by such events, I want you to have the warning. Skip over those parts if necessary, but I urge you to continue reading. Lu's story is one God led me to write and one I have bathed in prayer. She does find hope and redemption, but like most of us, it isn't an easy road. Thankfully, God doesn't leave us to walk this journey alone.

I like to assume my readers are personally familiar with who Jesus is and the hope He provides, but I know that's not always true. If you want to learn more about who Jesus is and how much He loves YOU—yes, you—then I invite you to visit crystalcaudill.com/hope, or email me at crystal@crystalcaudill.com. Romance stories are good, but the greatest romance ever told was God's love story for you.

With prayers and sisterly love,
Crystal Caudill

CHAPTER 1

Landkreis, Indiana
August 18, 1884

THIS WAS THE LAST TIME. After tonight, she and Oscar would be free from the den of thieves they called family.

Bill's bar mates hooted and hollered as Lu Thorne sidled up to the drunkard and leaned in to kiss his bearded cheek. She filched his coin purse quicker than he could turn his head to catch her lips and left him with a mouthful of hair instead. After months of lightening his pockets, the man ought to know better than to allow her within arm's reach. Still, Bill never failed to be distracted by the low cut of her bodice, her bare arms, or her ankle-baring skirts. Beauty had long been her greatest weapon and biggest curse.

"One of these days I'm gonna get that kiss, Lu."

She tucked the purse into a hidden pocket and stepped away. "Ain't today, sugar."

"Aw, let me have another go. I'll be quicker this time."

"Can't. Ma Frances's rules. Gotta give the others their chance."

"But who'll reward me for my hard work?" Bill's bottom lip pouted as his hands reached out to caress the curve of her waist.

How about his faithful wife or the nine kids he left near starving at home?

She smiled instead of toppling his chair. A lifetime of dealing with men like him told her he'd not learn a lesson from the act. "How about a drink?"

"I suppose that'll do"—his gaze swept the full length of her—"unless you want to offer me something better."

Not even if he was breathing his last. "Horace"—she turned to the bartender—"pour him a shot from the bottom right." The cheap stuff ought to sour Bill's stomach and send him packing. "It'll be on the house."

Horace paused his reach for the bottle. "I don't give free drinks."

Oh, he was a bold one tonight. He should know better than anyone that opposing any member of the Thorne gang equaled trouble. One word to either of her brothers-in-law and he'd regret that boldness for the rest of his life. Though given the ill temper Clint was in, Horace wouldn't even last the night.

"That so?" She leaned an elbow on the counter and stared him down.

Horace's jaw worked side to side for a moment before he grabbed the bottle and thunked it on the counter.

"Thank you."

He ignored her as he filled a glass halfway.

Well did she understand the bitterness of forced compliance, but Horace only had to suffer it on occasion. She'd spent an entire lifetime under the thumb of one master or another. Tonight was no different.

But tomorrow will be.

Lu tempered her smile as Bill gulped his free drink. Membership in the Thorne gang may not have been a choice for her, but that didn't mean she had to stay. Not now that US Marshal Walt Kinder offered an escape from the matriarch's claws. After Walt smuggled her and her five-year-old son to Newburgh, they'd give him the slip and disappear forever. It was a risk to double-cross the US Marshal, but testifying against the Thorne family equaled a surefire death sentence. Their only safe future lay in a town where nobody knew them. A place where she could become one of those new creatures Pastor Newcomb talked about and give Oscar the life she'd never had. An honorable one.

Tomorrow couldn't come soon enough.

She patted Bill's shoulder and continued her routine of visiting the saloon's patrons. Despite the number of passers-through, the picking was dismal. The two coin purses and spattering of coins would never be enough to satisfy Ma Frances's demand for stolen goods, provide for her and Oscar's future, and support Bill's and Widow Zachary's families. In truth, Bill's family could survive without Lu's help. They had for years before her arrival. But it was her fault that Widow Zachary's husband died. Lu couldn't leave the woman and her daughter without the means to flee Landkreis and the constant harassment of the Thornes. The former sheriff's widow had no means to get the funds herself. Lu could steal whatever she and Oscar needed while on the run. One day she'd be able to abandon this life of theft completely, but for now it would have to suffice that she and Oscar were leaving Landkreis and Widow Zachary would have the means to do so too. If Lu was going to help the Zacharys, and herself, she needed a fresh mark.

She examined the rows of stained tables sprinkled with patrons in various states of stupor, and a thundercloud of truth washed away what remained of her hope for a bountiful evening. Every man here already had their pockets lightened tonight. So much for this being her last time picking pockets.

She pivoted toward the exit as the door swung open.

Two weary travelers entered and claimed standing spots at the bar's end. Lu blinked. Pastor Newcomb spoke of God's providence, but even she knew better than to think that extended to people like her. Especially given the fact that she was responsible for the church's fiery demise. Yet, was it possible God had provided for her in this moment? She scoffed. That preacher's nonsense was getting to her. God wouldn't provide someone to steal from. This was a coincidence.

She adjusted her dress to accentuate all the right parts while she evaluated the two men. The shorter one with dark hair, mutton chops, and mustache looked to be a dour, unfriendly sort. His ratty suit with more patches than original material proved him miserly. Likely what little he did carry would be hidden in his socks.

He set a leather doctor's bag on the ground and addressed Horace. "Coffee."

Did the man mistake where he was? The poor doc wouldn't last long in town, nor was he likely to be enticed by her.

Though coated in a good layer of dust, the taller dandy held more promise. Here was a man concerned about the opinion of others. Dark blond hair curled despite the obvious use of pomade, giving his face a boyish appeal that not even his sideburns could age. His tailored sack suit with checkered material, long silver fob, and silk broadcloth vest screamed wealth unheard of in Landkreis. When he leaned against the wall to cross his ankles and fold his arms in a lackadaisical pose, the now-visible outline of a hefty wallet in his coat pocket affirmed she and Oscar could start life out right with what he carried. Wealth alone didn't make a good mark, but by the way he considered each serving girl, he was a lady's man on the prowl. When Pretty Boy's eyes landed on her, a full-toothed smile declared his approval. He'd found his mark, and she'd found hers.

Lu sauntered over, placing a hand on her hip and pulling her shoulders back. If he wanted a show, she knew how to give it. His gaze dipped to the low cut of her bodice then snapped to her face. Red crept up his neck and his throat bobbed. Oh, he was greener than she expected. Far too easy to distract. Such a pity. She would've enjoyed one last challenge to her skill.

"Y'all new in town?" She thickened her natural accent as she gave both men a saucy grin.

Doc looked away, but Pretty Boy twisted toward her. "Fresh off the horse and looking for a place to stay."

"Sorry, sugar. I heard the hotel is full up, but I bet I could persuade Horace to open a room above stairs"—she leaned in—"for the right price, of course."

This was usually the part where her mark's face lit up and he took the liberty to touch her, but Pretty Boy remained motionless and focused on her face. Had she misjudged what type of entertainment he sought?

"We're not staying here."

The objection came from behind, so she shifted to give Doc the most advantageous view. Even misers succumbed to her on occasion. "Are you sure? I could get you a great deal."

Doc stared at the rear wall like she was too vile to even lay eyes upon. "We're not interested. Go find someone else to pawn your goods to."

Heat roiled through her and raised her hackles. She'd be more than happy to never "pawn her goods" again, but her son deserved a better future.

"Don't pay him any mind," Pretty Boy smoothed over. "We're looking for long-term boarding."

She turned her back on Doc, purposely butting him with her bustle, and traced a finger up Pretty Boy's vest. All she needed was for him to want her touch long enough to snag his wallet. "I know Ma Frances has a couple of empty rooms she'd be willing to rent. I can make introductions."

A confident smile returned to his face. "And how is that possible if we've never been properly introduced?"

Finally, she was getting somewhere. "My friends call me Lu."

"And your enemies?"

Lu ignored Doc's comment and leaned into Pretty Boy until he likely couldn't tell the difference between the press of her body and the dig of the counter holding his coat slightly open. "And what do your friends call you, besides handsome?"

His throat bobbed again, and he seemed frozen against response to her unabashed attention. The poor man was too easy to manipulate. She rubbed one hand along his chest, while the other stole into his coat pocket. Her fingers brushed the soft leather just as the billy noodle decided to go church-boy on her. He pushed her off him, and she stepped back with a stumble, hiding the wallet in her largest skirt pocket.

"That's enough." Mortification painted his face. "I'm not that kind of man."

"My mistake. I'll let you be, then." She had what she needed.

Doc blocked her retreat. "Not before you return Joe's wallet."

"Excuse me?" He had to be guessing. No one had ever caught her before.

Pretty Boy—Joe—patted his pockets and then more frantically searched for the missing item. "It's not here."

"Of course it's not." Doc widened his stance and tucked his chin like a charging bull. "You have three seconds to return it, or we'll hand you over to the sheriff."

"Is that all? By all means, Doc." She lifted her wrists as if the man might carry his own fetters and smiled. "But you have to take me yourself."

Momentary surprise dropped into visible mental calculations.

Whatever decision he arrived at, she'd be fine. Ever since her brother-in-law Clint shot Sheriff Zachary and took over his position, the only crimes that resulted in punishment in this town were crimes against the Thorne family. The Stendal police were too scared to act. If Doc did summon the sheriff, Clint might delay her for a little while by playing his own game of "kiss the girl," but she'd tolerate it knowing it was the last time.

After several long moments, Doc spoke. "Then I propose a trade. My friend's wallet for your stolen goods." He pulled out not one, but two of her filched coin purses.

Impossible. She'd felt nothing, not even the lightening of her skirts. It had to be a trick. No one out-pickpocketed her. He must carry two with him. After all, she hadn't really looked at the bags she'd stolen. She discreetly patted the spot where the purses should've been, but the material gave with no resistance.

She tensed. He'd actually done it. "How?"

"Distraction is an art of the trade, and you did that well enough for the both of us." Arrogance curled his lips.

Doctor, my foot. Even confidence man was too polite a term. Once the Thorne family discovered they had competition in town, they'd tear him to bits. The right thing to do would be to warn him, but he was a smart man, by all appearances. He'd figure it out. The risk of losing her tomorrow wasn't worth engaging in war today.

She pulled the wallet from her pocket and held it aloft while extending her other hand. "On the count of three."

Doc nodded.

"One. Two. Three." The purses dropped into her hand. "I hope I never see your sorry faces again."

Doc passed the wallet to his friend. "The feeling is mutual."

For dramatic effect, she huffed and then stomped out the door. Once it slammed on her back, she darted to the tree line. Sweet victory! Doc might have bested her initially, but he didn't know he worked against "Lightning Lu." She pulled a thick stack of banknotes from her pocket. Pretty Boy's stash would allow her to return all of Bill's money to his wife, provide for Widow Zachary, satisfy Ma Frances's demands, *and* leave herself a tidy sum for starting a new life with Oscar. Now to tie up a few loose ends and then head home.

Tomorrow and freedom were almost here.

Andrew Darlington stared at the closed saloon door, still envisioning the fierce blue-gray eyes framed by waves of black hair. That woman was dangerous and quite possibly the best pickpocket he'd ever seen work solo. She'd wielded the gift of beauty God gave her like a weapon and skewered Josiah alive. Had Andrew not once shared her skill of picking pockets, he would've mistaken her flash of movement as an attempt to catch her fall.

"Lu stole my money!" Josiah Isaacs tossed his long leather wallet onto the counter.

Andrew picked it up and lifted the flap. Not a single bill remained. Impressive. It required considerable dexterity and skill to remove the banknotes without notice while being watched. He squelched his traitorous smile. The skill of a thief, no matter how profound, should not earn his admiration. He was a man of the law, albeit undercover.

Thieves, no matter their sex or physical appeal, deserved to go to jail, and it was his duty to send them there.

"Guess you're paying, *Doc.*" Josiah dropped onto the barstool with a grunt. "That's all I brought with me for expenses."

"I told you to keep some reserved in your socks."

The bartender poured two mugs of coffee as he eyed the empty wallet. "Looks like you met the welcomin' committee. Lu has a special fondness for visitors."

Josiah leaned forward. "Any idea where I can find her and retrieve my money?"

If he'd done as Andrew suggested in the first place, the man wouldn't be needing to avoid a reprimand from their district superior. The Secret Service audited expenses down to the penny. Captain Abbott was a fair man, but Josiah's allowance of a woman to turn his head to fluff would not go well.

"Everyone in town knows where to find Lu and her rotten family." The bartender plunked the coffeepot on the corner stove. "Best gallop out of town and forget about that money."

"Wish we could, but we're here to do business with Eli and Walt Kinder. We plan on staying a while." Months, maybe even a year, if Andrew guessed correctly.

Normal counterfeiting cases usually took at least that amount of time, and this was no normal case. Already the surrounding counties had suffered for months under the tyranny of cutthroat bandits and the cowardice of local authorities who refused to take action.

When US Marshal Walt Kinder infiltrated the Landkreis community with the help of his brother, Eli, they had found that the rumors paled in comparison to the true magnitude of the situation. Illegal whiskey manufacturing, coordinated bank and train robberies, and thousands of dollars of counterfeit coins all stemmed from one network of criminals. Given the extensiveness of the counterfeiting, the US Marshals had asked the Secret Service to partner with them—a rare concession given the decades-old tensions between the agencies. Even at this point in the case, and even with Walt's informant willing to testify, it would take much more time to discover all those involved and gather the needed evidence.

"The Kinders are good folk. Fair prices and friendly to boot. I'm Horace."

Andrew extended his hand. "You can call me Doc Andrew."

"Joe."

Horace shook their hands before casting a glance toward the other patrons in the room. Satisfied, he leaned closer. "Word of warning, don't upset anyone in the Thorne family, and that goes for Lu too."

A strangling dread tightened Andrew's throat. "Did you say Thorne?"

"Yeah. The whole family's a bunch of ruffians. Showed up last November, robbed the Stendal hotel, and killed the sheriff. After buryin' one of their own, they made Landkreis home. Lu's the best of 'em. She only steals from you. The rest'll cut your throat or shoot ya if you cross hairs with 'em." Horace shook his head, lines creasing from the corner of his mouth. "My boy stood up to 'em once and was fair near beat to death with a set of lead knuckles. Ain't never been the same since."

Thorne was a common enough name. The likelihood of it being the same Thornes bordered impossible. "Did you report the attack?"

"Won't do no good round here. The sheriff's Lu's brother-in-law."

Not surprising considering Lu's response to his earlier threat. "Good to know. We need long-term boarding. What do you know about Ma Frances's place?"

"Didn't you listen to a word I said? You don't want nothin' to do with those Thornes. You'd be better off travelin' back and forth from Stendal."

"What's the name of the other family members?" Alarm clawed at Andrew's composure as Horace unfolded the nightmare.

"Cyrus is the oldest, similar build and appearance to yourself, 'cept mangier. Clint's the sheriff now that he killed the last one. He's a stout fellow with strength enough to wrestle a bull and win. Priscill's his wife, but you ain't likely to see her much. You met Lu. She's got a son—Oscar, I think. Frances Thorne looks like anyone's favorite grandma, but don't believe it. Oh, and watch doin' business at Grossman's. He ain't family but might as well be."

No mention of Irvine or Richard Thorne, but there was no mistaking it. It was the same family. *His* family, or former family anyway. Andrew gripped the mug. He couldn't tip his hand to Horace. Or to Josiah. After the corrupt dealings of operatives during the previous couple of decades, the Secret Service had strict guidelines about who they hired. Middle-class men with a spotless record. Discovering Andrew's bit of criminal history would get him fired.

"Thanks, that's been helpful. Hey, Doc"—Josiah nodded toward Horace—"pay the man so he can get back to work."

Andrew fished out a coin for payment and sent up a wordless prayer. Of all the cases to be assigned, of all the criminals to face, it had to be them.

Once Horace was out of earshot, Josiah leaned back and folded his hands over his stomach. "Well, that was informative and convenient. Guess we know who to go to for gossip. How long do you think it will take us to make an in with the Thornes?"

Forever, if he could help it.

A curse exploded from the other side of the bar. "She done it again!"

"Quit your squallerin'. I saw Clint patrolling the streets before I came in. You'd have lost your money either way."

Andrew stared into the black sludge that masqueraded as coffee. He'd sworn long ago to rid the country of criminals like his former family. Now God had brought him full circle. Arresting the Thornes would prove once and for all he'd risen above his past and become something they never could be. Honorable. Respected. A hero.

He couldn't hide in the gray areas of omitted information. If there were any hope of maintaining his reputation and the prestige of being a Secret Service operative, he'd have to confess his past to his superiors. Allow them to scrutinize everything he'd ever said or done. It was a risk, but God willing, they'd see what his extraordinary adoptive parents, the Darlingtons, had. Criminals could reform.

"Cat got your tongue?" Josiah asked. "Or are you too scared to venture a guess and be wrong?"

"You just worry about assisting Walt with his informant." Andrew stood. "I'll figure out the rest."

By God's grace, this case would not be the end of his career, but a chance to right all the wrongs of his past life.

CHAPTER 2

THE CLOUDLESS, MOON-FILLED NIGHT ILLUMINATED Lu's return to town. Not that anyone would question her late-night walk through the countryside. Most people assumed she worked as one of Molly's girls on occasion, an assumption wholly unfounded but not unusable. The fewer questions asked, the more likely her real secret would never reach the Thorne family's ears. Although after tonight, it wouldn't matter.

Come morning, Bill's wife would find her hidden jar in the chicken coop fuller one last time. A few extra families had even benefited from the bounty Pretty Boy provided. Lu's only failure came in providing for Widow Zachary. Once again Widow Zachary had refused to accept "blood money" from the woman whose family murdered her husband. The ever-present noose of guilt cinched tighter around Lu's neck. Had she not lied to protect herself and hide the truth of her husband Irvine's death, Sheriff Zachary might still be alive and his wife and daughter not condemned to poverty.

Or worse, forced to become one of Molly's girls.

Lu shuddered.

Maybe she should reconsider losing Walt Kinder and testify against the Thornes after all. If the trials were as successful as he promised they would be, they'd never torment the Zacharys in retribution for Irvine's death again. Lu could discard guilt's noose and become Luella Preston, a mother who provided Oscar a safe home, acceptance in the community, friends with other children, and an education. She'd never have to look at her son and worry when she'd lose the battle for his innocence.

Truth shattered her fantasy. A trial changed nothing. The Zacharys would still be in the same position of poverty. Worse still, questions might arise about Irvine's death and reveal Lu's secret. Then no agreement would save her. At best, Oscar would be tossed into an orphanage. More likely, he'd end up with whatever Thorne wriggled their way out of sentencing—probably Ma Frances, given her wily ways—and raised to become the criminal Lu feared. No, testifying wasn't an option. Too much could go wrong. Once she and Oscar made their escape, she would send money back to Widow Zachary. The woman wouldn't be able to refuse it that way.

Lu cut past the tack shop, through the treed border, and across the fallow fields toward the Thorne family house. The only way to provide for both the Zacharys and Oscar meant continuing with her original plan—escaping with Walt Kinder tonight and then deserting him when she and Oscar were far from Ma Frances's reach.

Light filtered through the front parlor window of the barn-shaped house, and Lu stopped to gather her wits. Though the house was cozy on the outside with its matching rockers on a wooden veranda and wreath of silk flowers on the door, the woman who reigned inside was cold and calculating. If Ma Frances suspected anything amiss, even an out-of-place smile, her and Oscar's freedom would be at risk. Best to smother all thoughts of the future and focus on displaying the submissive daughter-in-law Ma Frances required.

Inside, the sweet aroma of forbidden baked treats filled her nose and tantalized her tongue. Ma Frances must have decided to spoil Oscar with dessert again. Lu smirked. Maintaining her appeal to men meant keeping a trim waist, and imbibing on sweets would do her no favors, but beginning tomorrow, she could be as ugly as a possum. A tiny bite now wouldn't hurt. She walked through the parlor to the empty kitchen.

Perfect. An elderberry pie with a large wedge already missing sat on the table. She pinched off a bit of a mushy berry and flaky crust, then called up the stairs. "Oscar, I'm home."

The pitter-patter of running feet didn't come. Odd. He must've fallen asleep. That boy could sleep through a tornado if given the chance. After this bite, she'd go up and carry him to their new future. Cradling her hand to catch the drippings, she lifted the morsel to her mouth.

"Stop!" Ma Frances swept from the back veranda into the kitchen, countenance as dark as her mourning gown.

Lu froze with the bite halfway to her lips. Couldn't the woman allow one nibble? It wasn't as if she'd gain a hundred pounds.

"What have you told Walt Kinder about our operations?"

Lu dropped her hand and sweat beaded between her shoulders. Ma Frances couldn't know her plan with Walt. They'd been too careful. Even his windbag brother Eli remained unaware of her role. Lu forced a calm she didn't feel. "I didn't say nothing. He's just another mark at the saloon."

"He's a traitor. Tell me everything you've ever told him." Ma Frances grabbed her wrist and shook, flinging the bit of berry and crust across the room.

"Same thing I tell every man. That he's handsome and every girl's dream."

Ma Frances released Lu's wrist with a disgusted huff. "I should know you've only one thing on your mind. Once a harlot, always a harlot."

A wave of prickles set Lu's hairs standing on end. Her former profession had been forced upon her, not chosen. So long as she breathed, she'd never submit to such a life again. "What makes you think Walt's a traitor? Just cause the gang's had a few bad runs don't mean nothing."

"He's a copper. Clint found proof this morning."

Terror grappled with logic. Ma Frances must not truly suspect her, or Lu would be dead by now. "I can't believe it. Walt's too smart to be a copper. Are you sure Clint ain't just being jealous?" His obsession with her was well-known and might cast doubt over his claim. "What so-called proof did he find?"

Ma Frances grabbed a stack of papers off the table and shook them in the air. "Pages and pages of notes detailing our little outfit. He even had a source who'd been supplying him information and agreed to testify against us."

Lu's knees wobbled, and she grabbed the chair's back for support. Ma Frances must know the truth. How could she not with that information? All her talk was nothing more than a cat toying with a mouse until positioned for the final blow, and Lu was good and cornered.

"When I find out who's squealing on us, they'll be as dead as Walt."

Lu blinked. "You don't know who it is?"

"The blasted man disguised their identity."

Giddiness bubbled through her veins, rejuvenating her strength. She was safe. Tonight she, Oscar, and Walt could—

"Wait. Walt's dead?"

"Of course he is—or will be soon enough. I can't let the man ruin everything." She hiked a thumb over her shoulder toward the table. "Gave him pokeberry pie and a good dose of laudanum to knock him out until the effects start. I want that man to suffer for the trouble he's given our family."

"You can't kill him."

"Says who? That high-and-mighty pastor? He don't watch out for our family. I do. When Irvine demanded you for his wife, it's me who bought you from the madam. Me who let you sit on your pregnant backside while the rest of us scraped by. Me who didn't sell you to Molly when Irvine died. You owe *me* your loyalty, not some pastor."

"But if Walt's a copper, won't others come looking for him? We'll have to skip town." At least not all hope was lost. She and Oscar would disappear in the chaos of running.

"We ain't ever skipping town again. Irvine's buried here and I ain't leaving him. Cyrus and Clint will make Walt's death look like an accident." Ma Frances tossed the papers into the fire. "I've taken care of the evidence. You're going to take care of his brother."

"I can't kill Eli!"

"Everyone has a job in this family. You sayin' you ain't part of this family? Because if not, we can do without the money you steal." Ma Frances reached into her pocket where she always kept a derringer at the ready.

An ache spread through Lu's white-knuckled grip. There had to be a way to delay or disappear before adding to her list of unforgivable sins. "It's too late to try anything tonight. He'll suspect and overpower me." The gun glinted halfway out of the pocket. "But if I bring him pie in the morning, he'll just take it as flirting."

Ma Frances stilled and seemed to consider Lu's words. After a moment, the gun returned to its home. "Fine, but go before the shop opens. He'll get sick while working and die with a crowd of witnesses around him. No one can pin it on us if we ain't there when it happens."

Lu nodded, though her head pulsed. "Where's Oscar?"

With any luck, they could shinny out the garret window after everyone was asleep and take Walt's horse. He certainly wasn't going to need it anymore.

"He's camping with Priscill. I didn't want him sneaking bites of poisoned pie behind my back."

Perfect. "Should I change places with Priscill and free her up?"

"Nonsense. You have a job to do. Fail and I'll sell you to Molly or see you buried next to Irvine. Do you understand?"

"Yes, ma'am."

"Good. Now give me tonight's earnings and get upstairs. I can't have Clint coming in and getting distracted by you."

Lu dropped the smallest purse into Ma Frances's outstretched hand and then trudged upstairs. How had everything turned upside down? Wasn't God supposed to save her? Mary Newcomb said He wanted to, and Lu had almost believed He would when Walt offered her a deal. But now?

She stopped at the top of the stairs and peered out the garret window at the endless starry sky. What a fool she'd been. If she hung one sin on each of those stars, she'd run out of stars before sins. God didn't want her to be counted among His saints. Her sins were too many, too unforgivable. And tomorrow she'd be forced to hang another in the sky. She pinched the bridge of her nose and the sticky residue of poisoned pie stuck to it.

Pie. That was the answer to her dilemma.

Walt Kinder's body might have arrived dragged by the stirrup of his horse's saddle, but it wasn't a fall that killed him. Andrew pulled Eli's patchwork quilt over Walt's bruised face, but it did little to dampen the stench of vomit and diarrhea. Given the purplish stomach contents still clinging to the man's clothes and lack of other lethal injuries, Andrew suspected poisoning was to blame. No one deserved to suffer such a death. Certainly not a man who sought to bring justice to a town ruled by villains. May Walt's soul rest with God now.

Leaving behind the quilt-covered body on Eli's parlor couch, Andrew walked down the hall and entered the kitchen.

Josiah looked up from his position next to Eli at the table. "Find anything useful?"

"If he had anything on him identifying the informant, it's gone now." Along with the actual informant. Whether they double-crossed Walt, were dead too, or were in hiding, they never showed for last night's meeting. "The gang must have discovered Walt was a marshal. It looks like they beat him before they killed him."

Eli's head hung between his hands, and his brittle voice cracked. "What am I gonna tell his wife and kids?"

"That he loved them." Josiah pushed a glass of water toward the man, but Eli ignored it, still sobbing.

Andrew shifted uncomfortably. The man had every right to grieve, but they didn't have the luxury of time. On the chance that the informant was alive and in danger, they needed to identify who it was. "Did Walt give any clue to who he worked with?"

Eli ran an arm under his nose as he took a moment to answer. "No. I was lucky to know he was a marshal. He never trusted me with anything. Used to joke that three can keep a secret if two are dead, and he'd hate to have to kill me."

Smart man. Too bad that left them with no direction to turn except southwest. Although Eli had every right to bury his brother, staying in Landkreis any longer than necessary risked his life. "We'll take care of all the funeral arrangements, but you need to leave town now."

"I can't leave. The tack shop's my livelihood, and I'm too old to start over elsewhere."

"Would you rather start over elsewhere or be murdered here?"

Josiah skewered Andrew with a silent reprimand. "Listen, Mr. Kinder. Once we root out the Thorne gang, Landkreis will be safe for you to live in again. Why don't you go to Walt's family and comfort them? We'll stay behind and mind the shop."

"We're not here to run a business, Joe."

"It's the perfect cover. You're an itinerant nostrum vendor and I'm an investor looking for a job." He threw his arms out wide. "Looks like I found one, and it comes with lodging."

Eli nodded. "It doesn't take much to run the place. Lots of folks come here just to chew the fat. I'll give you half the shop's profits if you help me leave town and run the place while I'm gone."

By the way Josiah rubbed his hands together, the decision was made whether Andrew agreed with the idea or not. Fine. Private living quarters worked better for their needs anyway. "Pack light and be ready to go in ten minutes."

Eli scuttled out of the kitchen and down the narrow hall to his bedroom.

"What's the plan?" Joe leaned back and stretched his legs out like he owned the place.

"I'll escort Eli to Evansville and put him on a train to wherever Walt's family lives. You start mingling with the people in town and winning them over."

A knock sounded at the apartment door.

"I've got Eli." Josiah joined him in the bedroom.

Andrew took position beside the front door, ready for a gunfight. "Who's there?"

"Only the best thing that ever happened to you." The raised female voice was familiar. "Open up, sugar."

The lilt and use of a pet name confirmed the speaker's identity. Lu Thorne. A beautiful decoy to get the door opened and allow access to any number of gang members. He strained to listen for groans on the steps to the shop below. Anything to signal more than she stood on the landing. Nothing. "I'm not dressed yet."

"All the better. I brought pie for breakfast and an offer you can't refuse."

Given her behavior last night, that offer could lead to the bedroom, or, given that she was a Thorne, it could lead to the grave. Neither appealed.

After an extended silence, she added. "Please, Eli. I sent you a note that we needed to meet. It's important."

A meeting with Eli? Andrew glanced back at the closed bedroom door. Was Eli playing him and Josiah for fools? Better to twist this situation to his advantage and find out. To uncover valuable information, nothing worked better than knocking a criminal off their balance.

He opened the door and yanked Lu inside.

She stumbled against him in a flurry of red and black, her focus on keeping ahold of the plate in her hand. "My, you're an eager one this morning." Plate secure in her grip, she looked up. Her eyes widened and all pretense of a smile dropped. "You."

"Lu."

She lurched away with the pie a shield between them. "What are you doing here?"

"I'd ask the same of you if it weren't obvious."

Sizzling fury burned him before it simmered into an alluring, saucy grin and a distracting shake of her bare shoulders. Lu was a confidence woman to the end, but she'd met her match in him. Andrew locked his eyes on her blue-gray ones instead of letting them wander to where she dictated.

"It ain't polite to treat a lady so poorly."

"My apologies, I didn't think you qualified as one."

Pie smashed into his face and the glass plate clattered to the floor. The warm sticky mass dropped in chunks at his feet. The barb of his words hit him belatedly and shredded his conscience. He deserved every bit of her reaction. Lu's shoulder clipped his as she scooped globs of berries from his eyes and flicked them to the floor. He fumbled with a handkerchief to wipe the rest away, and then followed her into the parlor.

Lu gawked at the blanket-covered body. "Is that . . . Did you . . ." Her face swiveled toward him, and the terror there suggested she believed him a cat and she a canary. "Did you kill Eli?"

"No." He could pull the covers back to prove his claim, but he wouldn't subject even her to the gruesome scene. "He skipped town as soon as we found his murdered brother being dragged behind a horse."

Her relieved sigh reached him from across the room.

"Eli said the Thornes would kill him next. Am I to assume that's why you are here?"

Her fists perched on her hips and her head tilted in challenge. "I said I needed to meet with Eli."

"And why was that?"

"That's none of your concern. Why are you here if Eli's gone?"

"He sold us the business and left Walt's arrangements to us."

"Sold? So he ain't coming back?"

"No."

A grin the length of the Mississippi stretched her lips. "I'm sorry to hear it. I would've enjoyed sharing one last piece of pie with him."

At the mention of pie, warning bells clanged in Andrew's mind. Between the purple color of Walt's vomit and the purple stain on Andrew's handkerchief, sharing "one last piece" suggested poison would've reunited the two brothers if Lu'd gotten her way. Poison that likely seeped into Andrew's system as they stood here talking.

"Eli's gone, and it's time you left." He gripped her arm, ready to drag her out if necessary.

The point of her elbow rammed into his gut. "I can walk myself out, thank you." At the door, she pivoted toward him. "You can tell Pretty Boy I look forward to the next time I see him."

"He's learned his lesson. You'll not be picking his pocket again."

"Too bad you ain't as quick a learner." She held up his wallet for a split second before dashing out the door and down the stairs.

Confound that woman! At least he kept only a few bills inside. All the rest of his money remained securely tucked elsewhere. Andrew locked the door and hastened to the kitchen's sink. By the time he finished scrubbing his face raw, Josiah and Eli waited at the table with Eli's bag on the floor.

"I swear, I didn't get any note." Eli raised his hands and shook his head.

"Relax. She was here to kill you."

Josiah massaged his forehead. "Your lack of tact never fails to astound me." After a moment, he dropped his hand. "The store is probably being watched. We'll have to hide Eli here until tonight and then smuggle him out."

"Agreed. In the meantime, you see to Walt's burial arrangements. I'll stay with Eli and search the premises for Walt's notes."

Lu might not know him as her brother-in-law, but that didn't mean one of the other Thornes wouldn't recognize him as he walked around Landkreis. Andrew couldn't put the case at risk by proceeding without first conferring with Captain Abbott in Evansville regarding his coincidental connection.

The Thornes had to face justice. One way or another, he'd see to it.

CHAPTER 3

How MANY LAYERS OF COLD cream would it take to stop looking like a raccoon wearing face paint? Lu frowned at her exhausted reflection as she dabbed a third, thicker layer over the puffy dark circles under her eyes. Ma Frances was not going to be pleased with her appearance. Although did it really matter? The men she swindled rarely looked above her chest, and if they did, it was only to steal a kiss. As long as Ma Frances didn't discover Lu's lack of sleep was due to baking a safe-to-eat elderberry pie at Mary Newcomb's house in the middle of the night, she'd be fine.

At least until Ma Frances learned Eli wasn't dead.

If only the coward had stuck around long enough to fake his own death. She couldn't even *pretend* that she'd killed him, because Doc and Pretty Boy knew Eli had fled. Punishment might not come in the form of death or being sold, but Lu would suffer. There was no doubt of that.

The soft leather of Doc's wallet brushed against Lu's skin as she retrieved the cold cream lid, and an unexpected giggle bubbled out. Oh, the flicker of frustration on Doc's purple-tinged face when he discovered she'd outwitted him! It was the perfect retaliation for his foul treatment of her. Between that laugh-inducing image and the knowledge Eli was safe, Lu would be able to endure any punishment Ma Frances exacted.

The bedroom door flew open and Oscar bounded into the room. "MawMaw says it's time to get up."

His gaze swung from the empty bed to where she sat at the dressing table. Joy at seeing her resulted in a giddy smile. As he skipped on lanky legs to her, his shaggy, dark hair flopped against the big ears that stuck out from his square face. Oscar looked just like his daddy, the only Thorne with a quarter pinch of goodness in him.

He climbed into her lap. "I wanna go fishin'. Can we? Please. Please. Pleeeeeeease."

Her heart squeezed. How she wanted to say yes, but since Lu had allowed Pastor Newcomb's church talk to influence her, Ma Frances had forbidden her from taking lone outings with Oscar. "Not today."

His lip stuck out in an adorable pout, and she rubbed noses with him until he giggled.

"How was camping with Aunt Priscill?"

He shrugged. "She wouldn't let me do nothin' fun. Made me stay in the tent the whole time and didn't take me explorin' or nothin'. She said monsters would get us if we did. I weren't afraid, but she made me stay and protect her."

"That was very brave of you." Although she didn't appreciate Priscill putting the thought of monsters into her baby's head. Nightmares came easy enough to the poor boy.

"I *was* brave." Oscar's chest puffed out. "I want to go fishin' for my reward."

Bless him. Rewards were as necessary to him as air. Deny him and he turned blue. Only one redirection worked every time. "How about we go to the barn and check on Tabby instead?"

"Yay!" He jumped up and down. "I'm gonna get a puppy!"

"That's not what I said."

"I'm gonna name it Jack, like the story."

It was no use arguing. In his eyes, those soon-to-be born puppies were already his. "Give Mommy a minute, and then we can ask Maw-Maw if we can go."

Oscar wiggle-danced. "Yay!"

His antics reignited the embers of her determination. They would escape the Thorne family. She just needed to keep Ma Frances happy until she had a new plan, and that meant presenting herself as a new lamb instead of a raccoon wearing cosmetics.

She examined her image in the mirror. Age had been kind to her, but at thirty-five, a new lamb she was not. A quick dusting of face powder disguised the appearance of wrinkles and the addition of a bit of red to her lips and blue to her eyelids ensured distraction. To complete the facade, she pinned a false fringe to her forehead and fluffed it. She might not be a fresh lamb, but at least she wasn't a raccoon anymore either. With her modest skirt and blouse in place, it was time to beg permission for an outing from Ma Frances like a child.

Oscar hopped down each step and words tumbled from his mouth like a rockslide. "Jack this" and "Jack that" until finally he reached the bottom step in the kitchen.

He ran to Ma Frances kneading dough at the table. "We're gonna see Tabby. Wanna come, too?"

Ma Frances stopped and frowned at Lu. "You're doing what?" The threat behind that tone could intimidate a bear. The woman ran her family like a prison warden. Any perceived offense required swift and cruel punishment.

Lu folded her hands and dipped her chin. "I told him we had to ask you for permission first."

Satisfaction at Lu's submission curled Ma Frances's lips before she spoke to Oscar. "Of course we can go. We have work to do anyway."

Not that Lu agreed with making counterfeit coins, but at least it didn't involve men, and Oscar could be nearby. Ma Frances finished kneading the dough, flipped it into a bowl, and covered it with a towel.

As soon as Ma Frances gave Oscar the nod of permission, he pulled Lu toward the door, his grandmother plodding behind them. "Come on! Jack's waitin' for me!"

Slowing his pace was easier than slowing his chatter. As they skirted the browning cornfield, Oscar spouted grand plans of his one-day adventures with his new puppy—despite Ma Frances's constant correction that the mutt would live in the dilapidated wood and stone barn. According to Oscar, he and Jack were going to plant beans to find giants and then steal their treasures. Oscar broke from her hold when they reached the end of the field and sprinted toward the barn's side door.

Though he'd always followed the secret knock instructions taught to him, a tremor ran through Lu. What if Clint or Cyrus didn't hear him knock and turned on the unexpected intruder? She rushed forward and cut in front of Oscar. As the door opened, Cyrus glanced toward them, his hands on the bricks he stacked—not a gun. Towers of pressed hay bales edged the open space, but there was no lethal threat.

Oscar shot past her, too eager about the pregnant mutt to care about gunfire. Tabby greeted him with a whole-body wag. When he dropped to get eye level with her bulging belly, she twisted to bathe his face with kisses.

"Hurry up, Jack! I wanna play with you."

Oh, her sweet boy. One day, he would have a normal childhood with puppies and friends. No unspoken threats would jeopardize his innocent actions. She watched him for a moment before tucking the dream away.

With a sigh, she joined Cyrus on the other side of the barn. "Want me to stack those?"

He arched a brow. "Trying to get back on everyone's good side?"

"Just trying to do my part. Unless you want me to work with the molds again."

Last week's attempt to help produce a new batch of coins ended in disaster. Instead of making money, she'd broken their best coin mold and three others as well. Although, in her defense, she hadn't broken them all on purpose. Smashing the one mold over Grossman's head when he'd pawed at her absolutely was, but his falling onto the table and breaking the others was not.

Cyrus dropped the brick onto a pile, rose from the ground, and wiped the grime onto his pants. "Make the wall two deep and six tall, then fill the cracks with mud. I've already got the space for the hearth built out."

Lu claimed his spot and set to work.

Ma Frances circled the structure and frowned. "Why are you building another smelt?"

"That stupid mutt's claimed the other one as a birthing den. You can't go near the blasted thing without her growling and biting at you."

"You could just shoot the dog."

He arched a brow. "And upset Oscar?"

She changed the subject as if unwilling to admit she despised the dog more than she wanted Oscar's happiness. "Did you get Walt to reveal who squealed?"

The brick fell from Lu's grasp and smashed her fingers when she fumbled to catch it.

Cyrus snorted. "Man did nothing but retch and groan up to the last."

"Call a meeting with the boys. See what information you can scare up." Ma Frances drove her boot heel into a clod of dirt and ground it into a fine dust. "I want to know who'd dare defy me."

Lu swallowed and stacked another brick onto the growing circle. No one in Cyrus's group should know anything about her involvement, but in this small town, there were no guarantees. Rumors passed like currency—most of it false, but with just enough truth mixed in to fool those not wise enough to examine closer. One whisper and Ma Frances would act with unrelenting force.

"Speaking of traitors, Lu—" Ma Frances wheeled toward her.

Lu sucked in a breath and prayed her face remained impassive.

"—is Eli taken care of?"

"Well, he's gone."

Always the smartest brother, Cyrus measured Lu's words with a calculating squint. "Gone but not dead?"

Ma Frances didn't need confirmation and raised her hand for a back-fisted strike. "You stupid girl!"

Lu dove behind the smelt and shielded her head with her arms. "It ain't my fault he found Walt's body and took off before I got to him."

"I always knew that man was a coward." Cyrus spat, and the wet glob splattered on her arm and cheek. "Don't fret, Ma. He ain't going to the police. He knows we'd hunt him down."

Ma Frances kicked Lu's back. "He better not, or you'll be taking Eli's punishment."

Once she pivoted and strode to the plank atop two sawhorses a dozen feet away, Lu sat up.

At the makeshift table, Ma examined the last run of coins. "What are your plans for the train robbery now that we know we've been ratted on?"

Cyrus joined her and swiped the remaining coins from the surface. "Shouldn't risk it."

"Where are we going to get the gold to make more?" Ma Frances stared at the empty, ceramic crucible. "Oscar's birthday is coming up, and I've already got a half-dozen presents picked out in the Montgomery Ward catalogue."

"Not to worry. You can still spoil Oscar and even build that addition you want. My inside man told me about another train coming through in a few weeks that will give us more than enough gold. We can live high and easy for the rest of the year."

"I always knew you were my favorite." Ma Frances patted his cheek before surveying the largely empty barn. "It's time we expanded operations. I hear banknotes are more profitable. If that haul's as good as you say, we'll have enough to invest in a press. It'd sure beat having to start up a fire, and it'd be a lot less risky too."

Cyrus crossed his arms and bore a hole into the floor with his fierce scowl of concentration. Of the Thorne brothers, he was the one who sought to please Ma Frances the most. If she wanted someone dead, he took care of it. If she wanted to try a scheme, he made it work. Wherever they went, he did his best to make life easy for her. But even Lu knew taking on making paper money was far more complicated than coins and harder to pass without getting caught.

"I don't know, Ma. Printing money ain't as easy as making coins."

She patted his arm with that knowing smile. "You'll figure it out."

His Adam's apple bobbed as he gave a nod. "Once we get past the train robbery, I'll give it some thought. Right now, we need to focus on getting coin production back up and running. Priscill's making the new molds." He glared in Lu's direction.

"Catch me, Uncle Cyrus!"

They twisted to find Oscar standing atop a nearby stack of wobbly hay bales, arms stretched out and knees poised to jump. Lu's heart clogged her throat as she struggled to her feet. Oscar vaulted forward, and Cyrus lunged for him. He caught Oscar inches from the ground and swooped him into the air.

After a round of giggles from Oscar, Cyrus set him down. "What have I told you about climbing on the bales?"

Oscar's face fell. "Don't do it."

"You can't have a puppy if you break your neck before they come."

His chin lifted and his eyes widened. "You promise I can have one?"

Cyrus rose to his feet and ruffled Oscar's hair. "Sure, Runt, whatever MawMaw says."

Oscar whooped before running back to Tabby, who'd reclaimed her spot at the smelt-turned-den.

"Land sakes, that child is going to be the death of me." Ma Frances fanned her face.

Cyrus took her elbow and guided her to a tree-stump seat. "He's fine, Ma. No worse than the rest of us boys were. All it will take is a broken bone or two to learn his lesson."

"As long as it ain't a broken neck." Lu swallowed as she watched Oscar lay down next to Tabby and stroke her back.

"Just finish the smelting furnace. Clint and I'll be back later to test it out." He faced Ma Frances. "Are you okay if I leave you alone with her?"

"I'm not a fragile old lady, Cyrus. If she gets out of line, I can handle it. Besides, Oscar and I'll leave soon. She'll stay and finish the smelt and all will be fine."

Lu turned back to stacking bricks and clenched her jaw. Submission and silence had gotten her this far in life. If she wanted another chance at tomorrow, she had to choose her rebellions carefully.

CHAPTER 4

THE SUN SANK LOW BEHIND the trees edging the small corral at the back of Kinder Tack and Feed, making the trees cast long shadows beneath a pink and golden sky. Andrew slid out of his saddle and winced as his feet hit the ground. Every muscle, bone, and joint screamed at him in rebellion after the abuse of nearly one hundred miles in four days. He grimaced as he eased his bowlegged stance straight. Twisting relieved some of the stiffness in his back, and he surveyed the row of more than a dozen houses and businesses that stretched along the main road. Praise God he was finally back. With Landkreis being set in the center of half a dozen private coal mines and acres of woods and farmland, traveling anywhere was an ordeal. Escorting Eli forty-eight miles to Evansville had made for torture of the highest degree.

Andrew's ears still rang with the man's incessant vomiting of words. All he asked was how Eli had come to live in Landkreis. In response, Eli spent the entirety of their journey detailing every sorry event of his life, from ingrown toenails to the onset of his rheumatism. By the time they'd reached Evansville in the late afternoon of the second day, Andrew seriously considered the merits of removing his shoe and stuffing Eli's mouth with a dirty sock. No wonder Walt hadn't shared any information with the man.

The tack store's back door opened, and Josiah stepped out with a rifle in hand. After making eye contact, he lowered the barrel. "You're back sooner than I expected."

Andrew unlatched the corral gate and led Morgan, his horse, to where Josiah's and Walt's horses munched hay in a feeding trough. "I shipped the package on the first available train and returned directly." If hidden ears overheard the conversation, no one would suspect the true nature of his trip.

"What about meeting with Abbott?" Josiah entered the corral and set the rifle down within easy reach while he helped to unburden Morgan of his travel gear.

Andrew frowned at the cocked Springfield. Trouble must have visited while he was gone for Josiah to be so openly vigilant. He glanced around, but other than the raccoon eating scraps atop a trash pile, nothing moved in the areas behind the buildings or the woods and empty fields beyond. Whatever trouble lurked, Josiah would give the full details when they were inside.

Andrew loosened the straps holding his pack behind the saddle. "Abbott left for Indianapolis before I arrived. I mailed a letter voicing my regrets at missing him and extended an invitation for him to visit at his earliest convenience."

With brows bunched, Josiah pulled the saddle off, set it aside, and grabbed a sponge from a bucket to wipe down the sweat and trail dust. "Why would Abbott need to come out here?"

Perspiration beaded his back like condensation on a glass. He could no longer delay the revelation. "Because the Thorne gang consists of my former family."

Josiah froze. "Former family?"

"Richard, Frances, Cyrus, Clint, and Irvine Thorne were my father, mother, and brothers until I was arrested and then adopted by the Darlingtons."

Silence stretched as Josiah snapped his mouth shut and scrutinized Andrew. Like a judge, Josiah visibly reviewed their acquaintance, evaluated the hard-line actions Andrew had taken over his career, and rendered a verdict. If a fair man who'd worked with Andrew on multiple cases viewed Andrew with such disgust, there was no hope for a better response from his superiors. All Andrew's striving to earn the department's esteem burnt to unrecognizable ashes under the flame of his past.

Morgan shifted and Josiah snorted. "You and Cosgrove are really a pair, you know that?"

Andrew dug his nails into his palms. Of all the insults that could be lobbed at him, none struck as more undeserved. Cincinnati operative Broderick Cosgrove compromised February's counterfeiting case through lies and the concealing of evidence, all to protect a woman's reputation. One whose complete innocence Andrew still wasn't convinced of.

"Broderick Cosgrove and I are not the same. He blatantly lied to protect Theresa"—the most annoying and impulsive woman Andrew'd ever met—"from being investigated, even after we knew her grandfather was involved."

Josiah tossed the sponge into the bucket and folded his arms. "I suppose the lie of omission to save your own hide is better?"

"I've held nothing back from Captain Abbott. The letter I sent details every aspect of my relation to the Thornes and my life after leaving them. I'm not moving forward with this case under false pretenses."

"Then I need to know your story too."

It was a fair request. The Cosgrove debacle would've not been quite the scandal it was if Broderick had been open about his connection with Theresa Plane. Andrew wasn't so bullheaded he couldn't learn from Broderick's mistake. He rubbed down Morgan and gave Josiah the abbreviated version of his history.

"The Thornes have a long legacy of intimidation and theft. My brothers and I were raised to continue that legacy in various ways. My specialty was picking pockets." Lu flashed to his mind. He hadn't been as good as her, but he'd been close. "When I was twelve, Pa planned a robbery of the First National Bank of City of Kansas. Mistakes were made, and I got arrested. The Thornes abandoned me. I was given a second chance through the firm guidance of Chief Speers and the adoption by my arresting officer David Darlington and his wife. I'm an operative today because of the man they raised me to be."

Josiah nodded but said nothing as they finished brushing Morgan down and checking his hooves. The silence beat Andrew like a meat tenderizer. Had what he said been enough to convince Josiah to trust him?

After the horses were secured for the night, they returned to the store's storage room where Josiah confronted Andrew with crossed arms. "Have you considered *how* you're going to move forward with the case? What if the Thornes recognize you?"

What little remained of Andrew's confidence rallied. The questions didn't guarantee Josiah's trust, but at least the man was willing to work with him. "I've been working through that problem for the last thirty-six hours. If they recognize me, I'll proceed based on their response. If they don't, we'll stick to the plan." Sell Grandma Darlington's home remedy and weasel his way into the gang.

"You won't have to wait long. They'll seek us out soon." Josiah exited the storage room into the main store.

Andrew gawked at the wrecked storefront. Where a large window should've given clear view of Main Street, boards nailed to the window frame blocked the way. Overturned shelves and barrels battled for space on the floor with the dispersed goods they once held. Piles of glass shards glimmered in the kerosene light.

"What happened?"

Josiah set one of the rocking chairs to rights. "Clint happened. He heard Eli turned the reins of the store over to us and came by to offer his protection. Of course, we need to make up for Eli's missed payments as well as cover this month's."

It sounded like something Clint would do. At the age of six, he'd pummeled boys twice his age who didn't give him their lunches. "You told him no."

"He warned this was a dangerous town not to have protection in, but he'd give me a couple of days to reconsider. In the middle of the night, I woke up to this." Josiah fisted a hand. "His thugs might have done worse if I hadn't come down and gotten a couple of shots off."

"You're lucky they didn't shoot back."

"They were only here to prove a point. They scattered like chickens after the first blast."

"Did you see any of their faces?"

"No. It was too dark, but there were four of them. Clint came by this afternoon and acted surprised. Said he'd be at the saloon all night if I decided I wanted to make a payment. According to him, second attempts can get deadly."

Andrew raked a hand through his hair. He couldn't wait until he received directions from Captain Abbott to confront the problem. Though he'd much rather collapse in bed after the last four days, it would be best to meet this problem head-on. Once he knew Clint's reaction to him, he'd know how to proceed. He grabbed the bag holding bottles of "Doc Andrew's Miracle Remedy" from behind the counter and picked his way across the littered floor to the front door.

Josiah followed. "What's the plan?"

"You stay here and clean up the storefront. It's what will be expected. I'll confront Clint and negotiate terms."

"You need me around to corroborate your story should Captain Abbott question your loyalty to the case."

As much as he didn't want an audience for his first meeting with a Thorne, he wouldn't risk his reputation as a trustworthy operative more than revealing his history already had. He nodded but didn't break stride as he hit the boardwalk. Any slow to his step and the doubts surrounding his plan might take hold.

They crossed the alley between the buildings to the boisterous entrance of Horace's Saloon.

More than two dozen patrons crowded the tables and counter. Competing shouts arose from a tight circle of men waving money in the back corner.

Andrew approached the bar and Horace met him there. "Coffee."

Horace shook his head. "That last batch oughta taught you to go for the stiffer stuff."

"From what I recall, there isn't anything stiffer than what you served me on Monday."

"Got me there." Horace poured mugs for Josiah and Andrew. "What's brought you back? I know it ain't the coffee, and whiskey don't seem to appeal neither."

"Can't sell my medicine if I don't meet the people. What better place than here?"

"Tonight's a good night for that. Might even sell a few bottles. Clint's takin' on challengers, and ain't no one walkin' away without somethin' hurtin'. So far tonight he's broken one arm and sent four home with their tails between their legs."

"Sounds almost as painful as drinking this sludge." Josiah tilted his mug and made a face before pushing it away.

Horace's laugh shook his whole body. "Same pot from this mornin'. Ain't too many folks who come in here wantin' coffee. If you promise to buy the whole pot, I'll make some fresh."

"Deal."

Andrew stood. "I'm going to check out the arm wrestling. Watch my bag."

He wandered over to the half circle of men blocking his view of the arm wrestlers. Clint *would* be the brother he met first. Only ten months apart in age, they could've been best friends. Instead, they'd grown up enemies—Clint always intent on asserting his dominance as the older brother, and Andrew determined to prove he wasn't a runt. If Clint recognized him, his first response might be to repay Andrew the broken nose the younger Thorne had given him the day before the failed bank robbery. Whatever Clint's response, Andrew needed to be ready. He pushed his way to the front of the observers.

Two shirtless men leaned against the table with elbows propped on the surface and fists grappling for dominance. Veins bulged and their muscles quivered under the pressure. Though both could be considered bulls of men, the taller man lacked the cruelty in his face necessary to be Clint. One look at the shorter man's unnaturally crooked nose and mottled face under thick mutton chops confirmed his identity. Clint mirrored their raging and drunken father in every way.

The opponent's arm slammed against the table.

A fit of coughing interrupted Clint's victory cry as a cacophony of cheers and groans surrounded him and money changed hands. After he regained his breath, he straightened. "That's twice tonight I've beat you. Care to make it a third?"

The other man shook out his hand. "Nah, I give."

"Any others want to take advantage of a sick man?" Clint spread his arms.

A few men hemmed and hawed, but no one stepped forward.

It was speak now or lose his courage. Andrew folded his arms and widened his stance. "I'd like a word with you, Sheriff."

Clint angled toward him and sized him up. Arrogance defined his features, but there was no hint of recognition. "Looks like we have a volunteer. Place your bets, boys."

"I'm not interested in wrestling."

"Afraid of losing?"

"It doesn't seem right to rob the man who's supposed to protect Joe's and my store."

Clint's guffaw turned into a cough. He took a swig of his drink and then smirked. "So you're the doc. Shame what happened, but I did warn your friend Landkreis is a dangerous place."

"I want to negotiate protection fees."

"You wanna negotiate, you gotta wrestle." Clint resumed his position at the table and nodded to the open spot across from him.

If Andrew wanted to worm his way into the Thorne gang, he'd have to do it Clint's way. Andrew removed his coat and tossed it over the back of a chair. It'd been a while since he'd arm wrestled, but he'd still be able to make Clint work hard for his money. Andrew leaned in, hip close to the table, and planted his elbow on the surface. Clint gripped his hand, and a referee stepped in to hold their fists in place.

"I hope you brought some of that miracle medicine your pal tried to sell me. You'll need it when I'm finished with you." Clint wheezed and then gave a short cough.

"Sounds like you're the one who needs it."

The referee counted down and then released their hands. "Go!"

Andrew locked his wrist and leaned in. Every muscle in his body constricted in an effort to push against the upright hold. Clint smirked and then pulled toward himself. In one swift movement, he twisted his hand over Andrew's and slammed it to the table. Needles of pain shot up Andrew's arm, and he flexed his fingers to work them out. So much for making Clint struggle for his win. Andrew wouldn't underestimate the brute's ability again.

"I can see why people pay for your services. Just exactly how much is it going to cost me?"

Clint gathered his winnings from the table and pocketed them. "That's enough for now, boys. I've got business to tend." He threw an arm around Andrew's shoulder and directed him toward the bar counter. "Six dollars a week, unless you got something better to offer."

The man must be insane. As a Secret Service operative, that amount required a full day's wages. How did farmers and coal miners manage such a staggering amount?

Horace refused to look at either man as he set a mug of beer in front of Clint without being asked. He retreated to the other end of the bar, tail tucked firmly between his legs. Even those sitting nearby scooted further from Clint as if afraid they might incur his fury if they accidentally bumped into the man. In more than twenty years, nothing had changed. Men might be willing to bet on him, but none dared cross him.

Clint quaffed the contents and then slammed the mug on the counter. "So, what's your offer? Here, I get all I want in free drinks."

Andrew only had one product with which he could bargain. He glanced at where his bag sat on the counter unprotected. Where was Josiah? A quick glance around confirmed his distraction by a pretty face in the corner of the room. So much for him being around to corroborate Andrew's story. He turned back to Clint. "I propose a partnership. Ten percent of the profit from my remedies."

"A nostrum that people will try once and be done with? I don't think so."

"For personal use, then? It works." Even for a cover he wouldn't sell a lie. Grandma Darlington's folk recipe had been passed down for generations and cured minor ailments from ague to catarrh without fail. Andrew retrieved a sample bottle from his bag. "Two teaspoons of this, twice daily for a week and you'll be breaking arms again in no time."

"I can do that now. Care to see?"

The door behind them opened. Clint's attention snagged on the newcomer and a lecherous hunger contorted his mouth. Andrew twisted in his seat to find Lu in a red dress so tight and revealing it left no room for imagination.

"Three dollars and a bottle of your stuff for this week only. I'll be by tomorrow for the money." Clint snatched the bottle from the counter and then swaggered toward Lu. "Come to tease me again, have you? Or have you learned your lesson?"

Lu flinched as Clint's finger grazed her cheek and drew Andrew's notice to the discoloration beneath her powder. The revolting cur. Abuse was far too common in her line of work, but it didn't make it right. Thief or not, she deserved better.

Defiance carved sharp lines around her stormy eyes. "Go home to Priscill, Clint. I'm working."

His hand slithered to her waist. "We could work together."

"Ma Frances'd have our hides."

"I know you want me."

"Go. *Home*. Clint."

She stared him down with daring bravado. Too bad Clint didn't take the hint.

With surprising speed, Clint stole a kiss and dodged before her slap could make contact. "If you get lonely tonight, you know where to find me."

He left, and Lu closed her eyes. For a moment, compassion for the woman squeezed from the dry places of Andrew's soul. Then her eyes popped open and the grin of a seductress replaced the tense grimace of before. All of Andrew's sympathy fled in the face of her sultry allure. May God pity the man who fell for that temptress's trap.

Lu sashayed to the counter and leaned next to him. "I see Pretty Boy's already found himself another girl. Don't worry, his pockets are safe with her. I'm the only pickpocket in town. Speaking of which . . ." She extracted his stolen wallet from her pocket and slapped it against his chest with a wink. "Refill it for me, sugar, won't you? I'm saving up for a new dress."

So this was to be her game with him then. He'd have to sharpen his own pickpocket skills to combat her attempts. "If the dress goes to your ankles and covers everything to your neck, I'll pay for it myself."

"Like 'em pious, do you? Sorry 'bout your luck. Ain't a church in the country that wouldn't burn if I walked through their door. But since you're so eager to help me, I've got a better idea." She pounded the counter. "Gentlemen!" The room quieted. "Doc here just agreed to buy a round for everyone. Drink up. Nothing's off the table."

She smirked as men stampeded to the counter, shouting orders for the high-priced stuff.

"You've been planning that for days, haven't you?"

"Spur of the moment, actually." She patted his cheek. "Thanks, sugar. I'll have that dress in no time now." She sauntered off and joined the men at the counter, enjoying a free-for-all of picking pockets.

"Horace, don't fill a single glass." The bartender looked from him to Lu. Whatever she said was lost to the noise. When Horace looked back at him, he shrugged and started pouring drinks.

If Captain Abbott didn't question Andrew's character after the revelation, he would once he received Andrew's expense report. It might be best to swallow the loss as his own. Infiltrating the Thorne family was going to require playing their game, and it was going to cost him more than money.

CHAPTER 5

THAT INFURIATING MAN WAS EVERYWHERE. Lu ducked into Grossman's General Store to avoid another run-in with Doc, and the overhead cowbell clanged loud enough for the entire town to hear. Skunk tails! Sliding to the side of the door, she peeked out the window. Dark, annoyed eyes connected with hers, and Doc redirected his steps toward her.

What did it take to make the man avoid her? It wasn't as if he had any interest in her. If he had, at least one of her usual methods would've worked on him by now. She fingered the worn leather wallet in her pocket and frowned. Of course, if she stopped stealing his wallet, he would have no cause to seek her out.

She blew out a frustrated breath. She really had no excuse for her behavior. He didn't visit Molly's, he had no family the funds needed returned to, and neither did he thirst for the devil's water Horace served. In the ten days since he arrived in town, she'd not seen him take even so much as a sniff of liquor. The sweet satisfaction of success wasn't enough to warrant theft. She had plenty of targets whose monetary losses served to help others.

But that didn't mean she couldn't retaliate for the way he spoke to her.

She stepped over to the wood stove. With the morning already hot enough to make pigs sweat, Grossman hadn't bothered to light it. She opened the stove door, and the acrid smell of ashes puffed into the air while gray powder spilled onto the floor. Perfect. It hadn't been cleaned out for days. She tossed Doc's wallet in and slammed the door shut as he entered the store.

Doc stopped midway to her and appraised her appearance with open disgust. "I hope that's not the dress you bought with all the money you stole. It looks like a circus tent that's been dragged through the mud."

The man had no concept of when to keep his mouth shut. It didn't matter that she knew the orange material did horrible things to her skin tone and was so large it hid every curve of her body. Her purpose was to deter Clint, not have Doc hurl insults at her. "What? Not pious enough for you?"

He harrumphed. "I want my wallet back."

"And I wanted to find money in it instead of a lousy piece of paper."

"Did you even read the note?"

"Why bother? It wasn't money and I don't want any more admirers." He didn't need to know she couldn't read it even if she wanted to.

Doc snorted. "You're not my type."

"And what would your type be? Oh, let me guess." She trailed a finger around his shoulders and chest as she circled him. "Deaf, so she's not turned away by your words. Mute, so she won't talk back. Oh, and she must be covered from head to toe like one of those church women I saw at the mission. What are they called again?"

"Nuns do not marry."

"Pity. One of those would suit you perfectly."

"Where's my wallet, Lu?"

She leaned against the stove and shrugged. "I doubt it's worth dirtying your hands to get."

His glance swung from her to the ashes on the floor, to the stove, and back again. "Was that really necessary?"

"For you? Always."

He stomped to the stove and yanked the door open. Ashes spilled onto his shoes and ragged pants as he pulled the coated wallet out. "I'm offering you a trade. You introduce me to the people of this town, and I'll pay you a dime for each bottle of my remedy sold."

"A dime! I'll make more by stealing from you."

"Not if I don't have the money to steal. No one in this town will deal with me."

"And you think I can change that?" No one dealt with a Thorne unless drunk or coerced. There wasn't a woman in Indiana aside from Mary who'd share the same boardwalk as Lu. If anything, she'd manage to deter what little business Doc might obtain on his own. "Get some pointers from Pretty Boy. I'm sure he can get anyone to eat out of his hand. Now if you'll excuse me, I have some shopping to do."

She strode to the corner holding fabric bolts and forced her attention on the meager selection. Oscar was growing like a weed, and while pants that ended at his calves might be fine for summer, winter would require that she sew a new wardrobe. Especially if they escaped and had to live on the run for a while. Without housing, there would be no relief from the cold and the elements.

At long last, the cowbell clanged. She glanced over her shoulder to where the patches on the back of Doc's raggedy coat were visible through the door's window. A new suit would go a long way to making him more appealing. Perhaps Mary could drop Doc a hint that he might sell more if he didn't always look like a vagabond in a bad mood. Lu shook her head at the thought even as she watched him disappear from view. Doc's appeal should be of no concern to her. If only it weren't so fun to banter with the infuriating man.

"Clint won't take kindly to you flirting with the doc."

Of course Grossman had seen her with Doc. Lu faced him with a placating smile as he snarled at her from behind the counter like a gangly, half-starved wolf with perpetually bared teeth. The last thing she needed was for Clint's best friend to share and embellish every detail of the short exchange. Clint's growing delusion of her secret love for him was reaching unmanageable levels. Someday soon, Ma Frances's staying hand would no longer be enough. If Clint were drunk when he heard whatever story Grossman spun, he'd let his anger override fear of Ma Frances. Another sleepless night with her dagger near at hand loomed in her future.

"Flirting is part of my job, and Clint knows it. Telling him will only upset him, and you're too smart to do that. You'd be just as likely to end up with a fist in your face as I would." Lu selected a bolt of sturdy fabric for Oscar and then dropped it on the counter. "Cyrus needs a bottle of OK Bourbon and a box of cigars from the back." Maybe bringing home a little something to smooth things over with Clint would be wise. If both brothers were sated, she'd be under less scrutiny while she made getaway plans. "And grab me a half pound of Clint's favorite candy while you're at it." With horehound perpetually in his mouth, he'd be unable to succeed at kissing her.

Grossman disappeared into the back room but didn't stop talking. "I heard a rumor you and Walt were getting close. Even planned on running away together."

He let the sentence hang, and Lu's heart bucked. "Where'd you hear a fool notion like that?"

"Clint."

"And you believed him? Clint gets jealous if I look at a rock."

"He said he found your bag packed upstairs." Grossman set the items on the counter, his mouth probably salivating at the thought of catching her.

It was a good thing she had an honest answer, or she might not have been able to maintain her facade of annoyed disbelief. "Of course my bag is packed. I've Oscar to worry about. With all the times we've had to up and run in the middle of the night, I've learned to be prepared."

"You expect me to believe that?"

She planted a fist on her hip and speared Grossman with the fiercest replica of Ma Frances's glare she could manage. "Let's get one thing straight. There is only one man I would run away with, and he's dead and buried right here in town. I ain't leaving Irvine behind unless I have to."

"Whatever you say. Just know Clint's keeping an extra close eye on you."

"The man can't help but keep his eyes on me. Ain't nothing new.

Now tally up my items so I can be on my way. I got a long list of things to accomplish for Ma Frances today."

After finishing business with Grossman, Lu scurried out of the store. Clint was always a problem, but never more so than when he believed he held something over her. If he suspected she was the traitor, he'd use every ounce of leverage to manipulate her. She couldn't let him figure out how close to the truth he really was. If she wanted to escape with Oscar, she'd need to tread with more caution than ever before. Their lives depended on it.

CHAPTER 6

ANDREW STOPPED HIS HORSE IN front of the ash and wooden remains of a church at the boundary between country and town and surveyed the area. No one was about, and with the curtains drawn against the afternoon sun on this side of the nearby parsonage, it was unlikely the pastor or his wife would take notice of his presence. Finally he could take a respite from his duties.

The raw skin of his inner thighs welcomed the relief from pressure as he dismounted. He hadn't ridden this much since he left the Western District six years ago. At least then his riding had yielded results. Now, not even free samples of his medicine earned him any civility from the homes he visited. One look at him and the door slammed. The only person he'd managed to form a relationship with was Lu—if one could call her constant stealing of his wallet a relationship.

Andrew hobbled around the perimeter of the remains of the church to work out the stiffness in his legs and the frustration over his case. Walt hadn't kept any of his case notes in the building with Eli, and his original reports sent by the US Marshals sunk with the *Belmont* ferry last week when a tornado hit it. Andrew still had no idea who the informant could be, and while the Thorne gang was at the center of the case, they certainly weren't the only ones involved. Instead of having a case prepared to the point of a medium rare steak, he was stuck still searching for the cow.

On his second pass by the church, Andrew stopped at the partial steeple. Like a beacon of hope, it rose in defiance from the rubble and pointed its spire heavenward to the God who knew and saw all. Andrew might be stumped and frustrated, but God was not.

God, You are sovereign and faithful. You brought me here knowing the Thornes were at the center of it all. Show me what to do because I'm at a loss.

His stomach grumbled, and he almost laughed. Nothing helped his mind to work through a problem like cooking a complex meal. Grandma Darlington hadn't held to the idea the kitchen was a woman's domain, and she'd seen to it he could cook anything. Andrew grabbed Morgan's reins and led him toward the tack shop.

As he passed the parsonage's gated fence, Mary Newcomb approached from the side of the house. "Wait here, Doc Andrew. I've got a welcome-to-town gift for you."

Illness rendered it impossible for Andrew to determine the age of the pastor's wife. Rail-thin, with sallow cheeks and pale skin, she appeared more walking corpse than living being. While she disappeared into the house, he pulled three full-sized bottles from his bag. Grandma Darlington's remedy probably wouldn't cure her ailment, but it might help her quality of life to improve.

When she returned with gray material in hand, he held the bottles out. "Here, you look like you need these."

She blinked as if not quite sure she'd heard him right. When he repeated himself, she shook her head and tucked the bottles into her apron pocket. "Most people wouldn't dare mention how awful I look, but thank you for your generosity."

Andrew flinched. Tact had never been a natural skill, but now he wished he paid a little more care—at least where Mrs. Newcomb was concerned. "My apologies. I didn't think . . ."

She waved her empty hand. "It's quite all right. Illness has long been a companion of mine, though it's one I'd love to be rid of."

"May I ask what ails you?"

"Words like cancer, chlorosis, scurvy, and anemia have all been tossed around, but no two doctors agree. After much prayer and debate, we've decided to stop searching for an answer. I'll serve next to Ephraim as long as the Good Lord allows."

"I'm sorry."

"Don't be. We each bear our crosses for His glory. I'll receive a perfect body in eternity. It just may be sooner than I expected, and who am I to argue with that?"

"Well, I hope that my remedy will relieve some of your symptoms."

"Thank you. Now for my gift to you." She extended a folded stack of clothes. "I noticed your suit was nearing the end of its life when you came by the other day, and I thought you might benefit from one of our recent donations."

"My suit is fine. Save that for someone who really needs it."

Mrs. Newcomb stepped forward and thrust the stack at his chest, so he had to maneuver to catch it before the pieces hit the ground. "Trust me, you need it. Especially if you want to sell your medicine at the church picnic on Sunday."

"Church picnic?"

"Yes. Joe accepted the invitation on your behalf. You're to be our honored guests. Go on ahead and take it home. It should fit perfectly."

"And how would you know my measurements?"

A mischievous spark glinted in her eyes. "I have a friend with a keen eye for taking a man's measurements. You might need to make a few minor adjustments, but you'll come across far more professional in this. I won't take no for an answer."

He eyed the wool fabric. It would be a bit warm for summer weather, but he'd oblige her. She and her husband were the only people to show him and Josiah any sort of hospitality since their arrival. "Thank you."

"Good. Now, go home and try that suit on. If any adjustments need to be made, come back tomorrow. If not, I'll see you at Horace's—where we hold Sunday services now—at ten, and a picnic lunch at the Kohlman farm following." Inside, someone called for Mary. "Oops, I forgot about the stew on the stove again." She dashed back into the house.

The woman was odd and—he looked back at his suit—persistent.

He'd wear the suit on Sunday, but he wouldn't ruin it by wearing it every day. After stowing it inside his saddlebag, he led Morgan toward the tack shop. The picnic was a step in the right direction. An introduction from the pastor's wife guaranteed a friendlier reception and could lead to the right connections. Even troublemakers attended church on occasion.

Two buildings down, a door banged. Lu stalked out of Horace's with fists clenched and body stiff. That woman certainly was a troublemaker, though he had no interest in becoming more acquainted with her than necessary.

Clint tottered behind, caught Lu around the middle, and flipped her toward him. She arched back and clawed at his arms, but he held firm.

"Let me go, Clint!"

In broad daylight, his mouth claimed her neck. Only a cur would ignore her distress and move on.

Andrew stormed forward. "Let her go."

"This ain't your business." Clint's continued amorous pursuits and slurred speech impeded his words.

"I say it is."

Clint pulled back and squinted at him through bleary eyes. "She's fine. Ain't you, Lu?" He shook her.

Her nostrils flared, but she looked away. "Go on. I don't need your help."

The woman might be an excellent pickpocket, but she was a terrible liar. "Let her go or I'll force you to."

"That so?" Clint shoved Lu away and his hand flew to his holstered gun.

The mollycoddler likely couldn't hit a hole in a ladder as unsteady as he was, but even fools got lucky. Andrew folded his arms over his chest to disguise his reach for his shoulder holster.

Lu jumped between them and covered each of their weapon hands. "Don't!" Though her grip was firm, a tremor revealed she knew the weight of the risk she took. "Clint, listen." Her drawl dripped thick and sweet. "He's new in town and don't know no better. Go home afore Ma Frances finds out you been dallying with me."

Clint's murderous scowl shifted to Lu. "Ma don't need to know nothin'."

"And she won't if you leave now."

He spat at her feet and then sneered at Andrew. "This ain't over."

Of that, Andrew was certain.

Clint staggered off, gun in hand. Lu remained a barrier until he disappeared into Molly's. She spun toward Andrew. "What kind of idiot are you?"

"I'm not the one who jumped into a gunfight." He released his grip on the revolver and nodded to where her hand still effectively held his.

She jerked back and fisted her hands at her side. "It wouldn't have come to that if you'd minded your own business."

"When I come upon a man harming a woman, I make it my business."

"Then do us both a favor and don't. He woulda come to his senses soon enough. I was just giving him time." She swiped a loose hair out of her face, drawing his notice to the green bruise.

"And how long did it take for him to come to his senses after doing that?" Andrew gestured to her cheek.

Lu lifted her chin and stared him down with more gumption than most criminals he'd cornered over his career. "Not as long as Clint'll hold a grudge against you. You and Pretty Boy best get outta town fast. Once he sobers, he'll be lookin' to teach y'all a lesson."

"That's our problem, not yours."

"You tried to save me. I'm just returning the favor. If you value your life, you'll leave." When he didn't respond, she shook her head and wheeled toward Grossman's.

She only made it a few steps before a dark-haired boy burst from the nearby tree line. "Mommy!"

He vaulted at Lu, and she flung out her arms to catch him. When they stumbled backward, Andrew steadied them, too surprised to move away. Although she wore her usual eveningwear, the hard demeanor edging even her most seductive attempts was gone. Soft warmth radiated as she cradled the boy, even as confusion at his sudden appearance wrinkled her brow. The woman so resembled Mother Darlington in her love and regard he couldn't reconcile what he knew of Lu to what he saw now.

Scrawny arms and legs wrapped around her as the boy hung back to look at her. "Guess what! Guess what!"

Lu glanced at Andrew and drew the boy closer. After a few waddled steps away, she surveyed the empty street and then returned her attention to the exuberant child. "Where's Aunt Priscill?"

His face screwed up, and he looked back at the trees before shrugging. "Lost. Tabby had her puppies and I get to have one. Right, Uncle Cyrus?" The boy's gaze swung to Andrew with expectation. "You promised I could."

Lu blinked. "Honey, that's not Uncle Cyrus."

"But he looks like Uncle Cyrus."

The words grew fingers and strangled Andrew. He'd gambled and lost. In the twelve days since confronting Clint, he'd not been recognized once by his brother, but a boy whom he'd never met called him out in less than a minute. Like the fall of a standing domino, the others would quickly follow.

Lu faced Andrew, and her incredulous smile dropped into the parted lips of doubt. Her eyes darted from one prominent Thorne facial feature to another until her eyes widened, and she mumbled, "It can't be possible." Then louder, "Who are you?"

Claiming the family tie could help him or hurt him, but he didn't yet have enough information to make that call. "Depends on who you talk to, but most just call me Doc."

"That's not what—"

"Oscar!" A woman burst through the treeline huffing and puffing, saving him from further scrutiny. She reached Lu and leaned forward on bended knees, trying to catch her breath. "Oscar, you scamp. Maw-Maw will have my hide if she finds out you ran off."

The boy perked up. "Do I get candy to be quiet?"

"Oscar," Lu's tone held warning. "We don't make people give us things to hide a mistake."

"But—"

"No arguing, young man. Now, I need to finish speaking with Doc Andrew." She threw Andrew a grimace before addressing her son again. "If you're good for Aunt Priscill while in Mr. Grossman's, we'll see if we can convince MawMaw . . ."

Lu's voice faded as Andrew retreated into the tack shop. He needed more time and information before he made his decision. Lu suspected his hand, but he'd yet to play his cards. How he played them now would determine how the rest of the case proceeded.

CHAPTER 7

OSCAR'S COMMENT ABOUT DOC ANDREW consumed Lu's thoughts for three days. Was it possible? Could he be the missing brother? Lu studied the whittled dog on the kitchen mantel as if she could divine the truth from it. Ma Frances said it had belonged to Andrew Thorne before he disappeared, but the crudely shaped toy gave no hint of the former owner's appearance. However, Oscar's confusion held merit. If Doc grew shaggy hair, shaved the mutton chops and mustache, and somehow thinned out his face, he and Cyrus could be twins.

City of Kansas, Missouri, where Andrew had disappeared, was a world away from Landkreis, Indiana, but the Thornes were a transient lot. Already they'd lived in Landkreis longer than anywhere before. It made sense that Doc would follow their pattern. He also picked pockets. With all the times Ma Frances compared Lu's skill to Andrew's, the evidence mounted in favor of Doc being the missing Thorne. But if it *was* him, why hide his identity?

"Watch it jump, Mommy!"

Lu twisted toward Oscar just in time to see his toy horse soar through the air and crash onto a plate. Shards exploded in all directions.

"Uh-oh." The little stinker ran upstairs.

"Oscar Irvine Thorne, you come back here and clean up this mess!"

"Quit yelling at that angel," Ma Frances said from her place at the stove.

"Oscar knows the rules. He should face the consequences."

"I know someone else who should learn that lesson. Or need I remind you about the church?"

Lu dipped her head to avoid Ma Frances's accusing stare, but she couldn't evade the guilt. She should've just stolen the money from the offering plate like she always did. It was the only reason Ma Frances hadn't objected to her frequent visits. Instead, she'd allowed Pastor Newcomb's message to fill her with foolish boldness. She'd returned home empty-handed, declaring that she'd steal no more. That had ended in flames.

"As I recall, you didn't want to accept those consequences either, but"—Ma Frances set the spoon on the counter and cupped Lu's cheek, her crinkled smile and tender touch contrasting with the heartless monster inside—"I want you to know, I've forgiven your insolence. We're family, and I'll do anything to protect that."

So the beast had finally retreated into the shadows and allowed the sweet facade of a loving mother to take over. Lu wasn't fooled. "Does that mean I can take Oscar out on my own again?"

"Of course not." She returned to the pot and poked at the dumplings. "Oscar's young and gullible. I'll not have you filling his head with all those church lies of a merciful, loving God." Ma Frances placed the lid on the pot and crossed her arms. "I've read their Bible. It's full of war, rape, pillaging, and laws that no one could live up to. Do you know what it says they should do to women like you who sell themselves?" At Lu's silence, she scoffed. "Of course you don't. They only share delusions of hope, love, and forgiveness. Well, their Bible says women like you should be dragged into the street and stoned to death. Tell me. What kind of loving, merciful God commands murder? Until you reject their lies, I can't allow you to be alone with Oscar."

Pastor Newcomb never read anything like that when Lu sneaked into services, and he seemed like the kind of man who did what the Bible said. He'd never dragged her out and hurled rocks at her, not even when he caught her stealing half the offering plate. Ma Frances could be lying, but the Bible was a big book, and so far she'd only heard Pastor Newcomb read a very small part. Could she just not have heard it yet?

"Dinner's about ready. Go toss the plate and ring the bell. I'll get Oscar." Ma Frances didn't wait to be obeyed, instead walking to the base of the stairs and calling up in a deep voice, "Snouk but, Snouk ben, I smell the smell of earthly men." She stomped up the steps, pretending to be the giant from the book of old nursery tales she read to Oscar each night.

Lu watched for a moment before carrying the shards outside to the trash heap. How could so much love reside in the same beast that murdered men without a pinch of remorse? Irvine insisted Ma Frances used to be gentle and sweet. Her crushing fist of protection hadn't closed around the family until Richard Thorne forced them to leave Andrew behind. Now she did whatever it took to keep them together and under her control—whether it be murdering outside forces or inflicting illness on her own children to keep them in line.

A horse's snort drew Lu's attention as it walked along the path toward town. Doc shifted uncomfortably in the saddle while Pretty Boy's rich laugh spread across the fields. Doc wore the new suit, so they must be returning from the church picnic. Lu smiled despite her general annoyance with the man. Irvine's best suit looked better on Doc than it had on her husband.

She tugged on the bell rope by the porch and his head swiveled toward the noise. As soon as he spotted her, he looked away and fiddled with his bag. His continued avoidance of her since Oscar's mistake only solidified her conviction. That man was Andrew Thorne. Pretty Boy gave a hearty wave and then slapped Doc on the back while nodding toward her. Doc refused to look and prodded his horse faster.

Her mind whirled with increasing speed. Whatever his reason for hiding his identity, she could use it to her advantage. Introducing Doc to Ma Frances as Andrew Thorne would result in household chaos. For a brief window of time, she and Oscar would be forgotten, creating the perfect opportunity for escape. She'd need to prepare though. Without quick access to money, a horse, and supplies, they wouldn't make it far enough before Ma Frances realized their disappearance.

She'd need to control when the introductions occurred to ensure all was prepared and she and Oscar were together.

Clint would be an obstacle. He already suspected her and dogged her every step. If he learned she was about to run, he'd do anything to stop her. In his eyes, she was his from the first time he'd laid hands on her in Colorado. The fact Irvine had outsmarted Clint by convincing Ma Frances to purchase Lu as his wife only served to make Clint want her more, and Ma Frances's forcing Clint to marry Priscill in order to stop the fighting hadn't changed anything either. Since Irvine's death nine months ago, Clint's obsession had only grown. She and Oscar needed to get away before Clint got what he'd always wanted, and Doc Andrew was her ticket.

"Ain't enough you have Clint pantin' after you, you gotta have the doc, too?" Priscill knocked against her with the edge of the laundry basket.

Lu retrieved a dropped shirt. "You know I don't cotton to Clint, and Doc sure as fire don't cotton to me."

"What? Clint ain't good enough for you?"

Lu couldn't win with the woman. "He's yours, not mine. Irvine being gone don't change a thing. I'd think you'd be happy that I don't want your man."

"I'd be happier if he didn't want you."

On that, they could agree. Lu pushed the door open and allowed Priscill to pass. "How'd the new gold eagles turn out?"

"Terrible. I'll have to make a new mold and try again. Even Oscar can tell the difference between a real and a fake."

As long as Lu didn't have to be the one to make it. She sat next to Oscar, who already had a heaping spoonful of cobbler on his plate. "Dessert is for after dinner."

"But MawMaw said I could have it."

She switched her empty plate for his dessert-filled one. "And you will *after* dinner."

Ma Frances walked by, switched their plates back, and took her seat at the head of the table with a don't-you-dare look pointed at Lu.

Oscar took a messy bite and smiled in triumph. Lu bit her tongue as she heaped chicken and dumplings onto each of their plates. She'd start preparations today so she could make the introductions as soon as possible.

Clint and Cyrus stomped in together, yapping like a pair of dogs after a rabbit. They took their seats—Cyrus next to Lu, and Clint as far from her as possible thanks to the deft maneuvers of his wife. Priscill smiled in victory.

By all means. Lu wouldn't argue.

"I'm tellin' you, Doc's medicine really worked." Clint scooped cobbler onto his plate.

"And I'm telling you, you've got rocks for brains." Cyrus ripped a hunk of bread from the loaf. "Ain't nothing but a bit of watered-down whiskey like the last one that came through."

Ma Frances cleared her throat loud enough to be heard the next county over.

Clint shot from his seat and kissed her on the cheek before diving right back into arguing. "I was sicker than a dog eatin' its own vomit three days ago. Only two doses later, I feel better than before I got sick. I'm tellin' you, we oughta beat the recipe out of him and turn a profit on it ourselves."

"You've been coughing for two weeks. It was bound to go away, eventually."

"Cyrus . . ." Ma Frances's tone signaled a warning.

Lu kicked his leg. No one fared well at the dinner table when Ma Frances felt slighted. Cyrus glared at her a moment before she indicated his mother with the tilt of her head.

"Sorry, Ma." He jumped up to kiss her. "Clint's got it in his fool head to start counterfeiting medicine. Apparently people all over town were flocking to Doc at the church meeting to get some of his miracle drug."

Ma Frances tented her fingers for a moment as Clint and Cyrus waited in expectation. They'd make their own decision behind her back if she didn't agree with them, but it was a risk they didn't often attempt. "If we can't print money, making medicine might work. See what you can find out."

"Good." Clint's lips twisted into a mockery of a smile. "I been wantin' to teach him a lesson."

If Clint got ahold of Doc, Lu's fragile plan might shatter. "I'll get the recipe out of him."

"I just bet you'd like to get it out of him." Priscill's tone implied innuendo and far too much glee. The witch knew exactly what she was doing. "He's done turned your head, and Irvine ain't even in the grave a year."

A storm rolled over Ma Frances's face and jealousy flickered like a wicked display of lightning over Clint's.

"Maybe I should send him a pie." Ma Frances narrowed her eyes. "I believe I saw some pokeberries growing at the edge of the field."

"I want some berries." This came from Oscar with a mouth ringed in cobbler.

A rare, sharp denial snapped from Ma Frances.

His bottom lip stuck out, and tears welled in his eyes. "But don't you love me?"

Ma Frances patted his hand. "Of course I do. Those berries aren't good yet. I'll make you a different pie tomorrow. Now eat your dumplings, and I'll give you another scoop of cobbler." Once Oscar was quietly distracted by his food again, she rebuked Lu. "Didn't you learn anything?"

"I have no interest in the man, believe me. I'd like to see him suffer after he caught me picking his friend—"

"You got caught?" Disbelief rounded the table, though the words came from Priscill. "Oh, do tell."

Of course, the woman would devour any opportunity to gloat in Lu's failure. It didn't matter. Lu wasn't about to let another man die because of her. If they needed a distraction, she would provide one. "He got lucky catching me. I still robbed his friend blind while they watched."

Cyrus leaned back, arms folded. "Let Lu get the recipe. Stealing's her specialty. We need to focus on hitting that train later this week. After that, Clint can beat it out of him if needed."

Thankfully by then Ma Frances would know Doc's true identity and would protect him. However, the train robbery plans left Lu with less than a week to get everything together and hidden—a more involved feat now that Walt was gone—but having Clint and Cyrus five hours away lessened the risk of their interference when she and Oscar fled. The whole thing would be tricky, but doable. Convincing Doc to join them for dinner might be harder, though. He wasn't swayed by her normal tricks, but she *would* get him here. She couldn't lose her second chance at escape.

When she went outside to feed the chickens after dinner, Clint pinned her against the side of the house. "You best not be gettin' any ideas with that doctor like you did Walt."

"I don't know what you're talking about. Walt was just a mark like any other man. So's Doc."

"Don't lie to me. I know you used him to make me jealous. There'll be no givin' Doc what you been denyin' me." His hand snared her neck and squeezed. "Understand?"

Lu clawed at his hold but failed to loosen his grip. Lightheadedness surged and the edges of her vision darkened.

"Clint!" Ma Frances called from the front veranda. "You better not be fooling around."

He released her, and she slumped against the wall on shaky legs.

"Remember, you were mine first, and you're mine still."

He stalked off, and Lu sank to the ground.

One week. This time, she could not fail.

Chapter 8

The pungent aroma of fresh picked herbs rose up from the crate in the bed of the borrowed wagon as Andrew pulled into town. News about Doc Andrew's Miracle Remedy had spread like chicken pox after Mrs. Newcomb's well-placed testimonial at the church picnic. Within three days, he'd run out of stock and had to spend the afternoon collecting herbs and buying supplies in Stendal. Not that he minded. Doors were finally opening and rumors of who ran with the Thorne gang were reaching them. As long as Lu didn't say anything, he might make it out of this case without revealing his relation after all.

Andrew stopped next to the tack shop, and Clint slunk from the shadows like a wolf from the brush. Given the fact that he didn't pounce, it must be another attempt to coax Andrew into a territorial fight over Lu rather than a confrontation after a realization they were brothers.

"Sheriff." Andrew hopped from his seat and tied the horse to the hitching post.

"Just the person I wanted to see." Clint blocked Andrew's attempt to collect his crate of supplies and frowned at the drying herbs. "Plantin' a garden?"

"More like weeding one. Nothing but scrap to add to the burn pile later."

Clint squinted at the plants again but shrugged. It was unlikely the man knew the difference between a dandelion and a cactus, let alone the medicinal qualities of the herbs contained within. "Rumor has it your drug is causin' a stir in town."

Andrew folded his arms. "If you mean that it's healing minor ailments, then yes."

"The weak-minded are fooled by anythin'. I bet it's nothin' more than a bit of watered-down whiskey."

"Sounds like you should know. How's your cough?"

Red mottled Clint's face. He'd hit the mark. The question was, what did the man hope to gain by denying its potency?

"I was gettin' better anyway. Your remedy had nothin' to do with it."

"If you want to renegotiate your protection terms for more bottles, that can be arranged."

"I want to know what's in that stuff."

"Trade secret. If that's all, I have work to do." Andrew edged Clint out of the way and grabbed his supplies.

"I ain't finished with you." Clint upended the crate, scattering its contents across the dirt. "Stay away from Lu. No matter what she tries on you, she's mine."

"And here I thought you were married to Priscill."

"Marriage ain't nothing but a piece of paper. I keep what's mine, and Lu's always been mine."

He wasn't about to delve into those waters unarmed. Lu was no man's woman without her consent, no matter what Clint said. Andrew grabbed the crate from the ground, leaving half the herbs he'd collected scattered around. He'd never kneel before Clint. Andrew entered the tack shop and let the door cut off any further comments. For several heartbeats, he waited for Clint to follow, but the bell behind him remained silent. Praise God.

A quick scan of the open space revealed that Josiah had finally finished calming the chaos Clint's thugs had left behind. Neat stacks and rows of inventory filled the shelves along the back wall. Labeled barrels were arranged about the room. Polished saddles hung over a newly built rail, while bags of feed and seed were stacked in the center of the floor. He'd even set up two rockers around a table with a checkerboard, where two customers now sat chewing the fat while Josiah worked on a tangle of rope at the counter.

Andrew nodded at the visitors but continued his walk past. He should join the conversation, but he didn't have it in him. Since the picnic, conversation and interaction with Landkreis residents had been nonstop. He needed a break from people and time alone to work through the bits of detail he'd uncovered so far. Although he couldn't make more medicine, having run out of the ingredients for Grandma Darlington's complex recipe, Mrs. Kohlman had given them a nice cut of beef yesterday. A braised roast with vegetables ought to occupy his hands while his mind analyzed information.

"Need anything before I take over the kitchen?"

"Nah, meals keep getting dropped off for the two newest bachelors in town." Josiah rubbed his hands together, evidently enjoying the attention. "Even Lu dropped off a pot of stew. I checked. She didn't steal anything from me this time."

The men at the checkerboard laughed as Andrew climbed the stairs toward the private living quarters. Josiah should've turned Lu and her food away. Who knew what she'd used as a base for the stew. Mud and horse manure wouldn't surprise him. Whatever the stew was, it was going in the trash. He shifted the key in his hand to unlock the apartment door, but the handle gave. Andrew frowned. They never left the door unlocked. Any identifying information was hidden, but that didn't mean it couldn't be uncovered by a skillful snoop. He set the crate down on the top step and drew his revolver.

The door opened on silent hinges, and he strained for sound of the intruder but didn't hear anything. He stepped over the squeaky board and eased into the hallway. Shuffling came from the kitchen, but nothing indicated the person had heard his entrance. He crept down the hall, peeking in the vacant parlor on the right and the undisturbed bedrooms on the left as he passed. At the kitchen entrance, he pivoted around the corner with weapon raised.

The hideous circus dress greeted him, though its wearer had her back to him. Lu must have come to confirm what Oscar had unwittingly revealed. Ready or not, it was time to determine where he stood as a former Thorne. He holstered his gun. The only weapon she carried was her beauty, and he was immune to its effects. She seemed oblivious to his presence as she continued to rifle through a stack of papers. One must have caught her eye, for she paused to examine it.

"Is there something I can help you with?"

She startled and spun around. One hand pressed to her chest while the other hid whatever paper she held in a pocket. So they were going to play this game again. He folded his arms and leaned against the doorframe, waiting for her answer.

Lu floundered for a moment before waving to a pot on the table. "I brought you and Pretty Boy some supper."

"Why?"

"I'd like to call a truce."

Was it a ploy because she suspected he was her brother-in-law? "Why the change of heart? I thought you enjoyed stealing my wallet."

A reluctant smile spread across her face. "I do, far more than I should. It's nice to have a challenge in town." She stepped toward him like she planned another attempt—or a distraction from her true purposes.

He pulled his wallet from his coat and tossed it onto a nearby chair. "What do you really want, Lu? I know it's not the two dollars in my wallet."

She retrieved it and held it out it like a peace offering. "I wanted to invite you to dinner at Ma Frances's."

If he were to venture a guess, Lu hadn't shared her suspicions with the family and wanted Frances Thorne to be the one to recognize her son. If he met Frances Thorne again, it would be when it benefited his case and no sooner. He ignored the wallet. "I'm not interested. And you can return that paper you put in your pocket now."

"Why, I never." She flung the wallet to the floor. "Here I was being neighborly, and you wound me with accusations instead of behaving gentlemanlike."

"I'm no more a gentleman than you are a lady. Now hand me that paper."

"Fine. You caught me." She gave a dramatic sigh before handing him the wrinkled sheet. "I just can't help myself." She sashayed to the window, where she looked out and toyed with the open curtain.

Andrew squinted at her. Something was off. She hadn't given up the sheet willingly, but neither had she really fought it. What was she up to? He strode across the room and stood behind her. Clint glared at them from the alley. So she'd been signaling to him. What was it they were after? He looked at the list in his hand.

"What do you want with Joe's inventory sheet?"

"Is that what that is?" She gave a sardonic grin. "And here I thought it was the recipe for your magic medicine."

Now Clint's presence and line of questioning made sense, but not her choice of paper to steal. "It would be some medicine if it required halters, stirrup irons, and lead rope." He studied her as he spoke. Her relaxed stance and smug smile indicated she was confident. This list wasn't all she had. "Give me everything you stole."

"I didn't steal anything."

"Pull out all your pockets, or I'll be forced to frisk you myself."

One side of her mouth curled. "Would you like to?"

"No, but I'm sure I could get Clint to."

Her playful facade disintegrated. "You wouldn't dare."

No, he wouldn't, but he could make her doubt that. He took a step closer and leaned over her. "Try me."

He held her gaze until she huffed and began pulling out the insides of half a dozen pockets. Seven more sheets of paper. All lists of no value. She couldn't have really expected these revealed his recipe. "What did you want with all of these?"

She shrugged, drawing circles on the counter while she stared out the window at Clint. "Doing what I was told—looking for anything that might hint at your recipe."

So her visit truly had nothing to do with his identity. Good. He could continue pursuing information as an outsider, which held more appeal than pretending to be happy about finding his family. At least she hadn't stumbled upon his and Josiah's credentials while snooping.

"I've never written it down. It's all up here." He tapped his temple. "So you might as well leave."

"But those lists—"

"Are Joe's way of getting this store organized and nothing to do with my business."

Panic flickered in her eyes, growing to a steady flame of desperation. "Do you still make it your business to protect a woman from harm?"

"You're in no danger from me."

"No, but I am from Clint. If I don't bring him something, he'll believe I'm holding out on him. A happy drunk Clint like you saw on the street is nothing compared to a mad one." She pulled down the collar of her dress to reveal what appeared to be finger marks on her throat.

The cur. Andrew clenched his jaw but refused to respond. The woman was a good confidence artist, identifying and twisting a man's convictions until they worked against him. This must be how Josiah felt every time a woman wanted him to propose. There was little choice. He couldn't send her into the wrath of that monster, but he wouldn't share the recipe.

In full view of Clint, Lu cupped Andrew's face with an intimate tenderness that sent buzzing tingles into his lips. The woman was a siren. Andrew recoiled from her touch lest he become her next victim.

"Please." The begging tone froze him as her hands fell to his chest. "I need him to believe I convinced you to give it to me. Write something down, anything that I could take to him. I don't care if it's mint and whiskey."

The request was reasonable, but he still hated her winning. "Do you know how infuriating you are?"

Her tight lines melted into warm regard. "Thank you."

He stepped to the table, feeling every bit the captivated sailor, and grabbed a notepad. "Who will be taking it?" If she said Clint, he'd write something that would have the man beginning a love affair with the outhouse.

"He plans to sell it."

Of course he did. Andrew thought for a moment. A mixture of chamomile, honey, mint, black pepper, and willow bark ought to do the trick. It wouldn't be dangerous to anyone, but neither would it provide relief like the real remedy. "Take it, but no more coming up here." He pulled the paper back when she reached for it. "I need your word."

She laughed. "And you would believe it?"

"Probably not."

"Good, then I won't bother to lie." She snatched the paper from his hand and then planted a kiss on his cheek. "Good evening, Doc. And don't forget. Friday at four. I owe you a thank-you dinner."

That was one appointment he would happily miss.

CHAPTER 9

WITH CLINT SATISFIED WITH THE recipe and distracted by preparations for the train robbery, Lu spent the next two days free of his watchful eye. A mile south of Oscar's favorite fishing spot, Lu stuffed the bag of necessities into a hollowed-out log. Thanks to the leftover money from Pretty Boy's wallet, she and Oscar could buy two train tickets in Evansville to wherever they wanted.

She smiled as she wandered back home. Tonight, she would put her plan into action. Clint and Cyrus were already gone for the train robbery in Boonville with other members of the Thorne gang, and Priscill was in Stendal with a friend for the night. Once Ma Frances was distracted by Doc, she and Oscar would bolt.

At the edge of the open field, Lu spotted Oscar stretched out in the sun, enjoying an afternoon nap. She scanned the unoccupied expanse leading up to the house. Oscar must have snuck out to see the puppies again. If Ma Frances caught them together unsupervised, her plans would be jeopardized. Best to wake him and send him on ahead.

When she reached him, a frisson of unease traveled down her spine. What was all that purple stuff on his fingers and mouth? A pile of empty stems lay not far from his reach, one with a berry still attached. She sucked in a breath as she dropped to her knees next to him. *Please don't be . . .* She squished the familiar berry between her fingers and looked beyond Oscar to the tall weed. Clusters of ripe purple berries hung at perfect eye level with Oscar.

Pokeberry.

The breath leached from her lungs. Her gaze dropped back to her baby. His chest rose and fell without struggle, and though his face was flushed, it showed no discomfort.

Yet.

Time was critical. She had to get those berries out of his little body. "Oscar, honey, wake up."

He grumbled and peeked one eye open. When he recognized her, glee split his face. "Mommy!" He sprang to his feet like a belly full of poison was of no concern.

"How many of those berries did you eat?"

He threw his arms wide. "A whole bunch! But I saved one for you!" He examined the ground for the lone berry whose juice now stained her fingers.

God help them. Her baby may be full of life now, but that could all change within an hour.

She swooped him into her arms and took off at a stumbling run. Oscar giggled like it was a game. She was out of breath by the time she stormed up the veranda steps and burst through the kitchen door.

Ma Frances's hand flew to her chest. "Land sakes, child! What on earth?"

"Ipecac!" Lu panted, trying to form the word.

"Why's your face wet, Mommy?" Oscar wiped her cheeks. "Why are you sad?"

Lu ignored his question. "He found pokeberries. Ate a ton of 'em."

A deathly pallor fell across Ma Frances's face. "We don't have any."

"Upstairs, in my jewelry box. I keep some there." Thank goodness she planned ahead for Ma Frances's food poisoning punishments.

If the woman wondered why Lu kept a bottle there, she didn't ask. She bounded up the steps with the energy of a woman half her age.

Lu set Oscar on the tabletop. "Stay right there." She whirled and grabbed a spoon.

"What's wrong?" Oscar's voice trembled.

Her panic was upsetting him. If she were going to get him to take the medicine, she'd have to be calm. With her back to him, she drew in slow, shaky breaths and wiped away her tears. When she felt composed enough to confront him, she squatted until they were eye level. "Those berries are bad. They make people very sick, and we want to make sure you don't get sick."

"They didn't taste bad."

Ma Frances pounded down the stairs, the bottle clutched to her chest.

Lu cupped Oscar's face before he could turn and see it. "Honey, I need you to be a very brave boy. And when you're better, you can have that puppy."

Sunlight beamed from his face. "I can have Jack? Here?"

After last month's experiences with castor oil, she could only hope bribing him to take this bitter emetic would work. "Yes, but only if you take some medicine."

All his sunshine turned into a violent storm as he wrenched away screaming. "No! No medicine!"

Ma Frances dodged a flailing fist and pierced Lu with her eyes. "Why do you have ipecac hidden upstairs?"

Oscar's fist made contact with Lu's temple. Ma Frances would have to wait for answers. Lu pinned him to her body. He thrashed and fought no matter what she said or how she tried to soothe him. They made it to the wingback chair in the parlor, but not before his head busted her lip and banged her nose. Tears flowed freely from both their eyes as Ma Frances forced his jaw open and poured in the medicine. He spit it out twice before they managed a full dose down him.

He screamed and cried as he clawed at his tongue. "I hate it!"

"I know, baby. I know." Lu rocked as she held him tight, tears flowing unchecked. If only it would work. If only it would be enough. *God, please let it be enough. For his sake, not mine. He's just a baby. He doesn't deserve this.*

Soon, he started gagging. Ma Frances held the largest bowl they owned as Lu helplessly cradled his body while he retched over and over. Dry heaves followed, mixed with more wails and tears. When at last it subsided, he curled into a ball against her and cried until he fell asleep. She didn't move. Just stared at the nearly full bowl until Ma Frances disappeared with it.

He'd ingested enough to kill a fully grown man. It would be hours before they knew if giving him ipecac had been enough. For all she knew, these could be the very last moments of her motherhood. She curled around him and sobbed. There was no point in life without him.

Little more than an hour passed before the first cramp struck. Oscar writhed in her arms, screaming and moaning in turn. The poison was in his system and Lu was powerless to stop it. Why, oh why, hadn't she scoured the grounds after Ma Frances threatened making a pie for Doc? She should've known Oscar would go looking for the berries when he didn't get to eat them the other day.

"Owie!"

"We need more medicine." Ma Frances wrung her hands as she paced.

"More ipecac wouldn't do anything even if we had it." Her voice was hoarse as she continued to stroke Oscar's back.

"What about Doc Andrew's remedy?"

Trying to get Oscar to take anything would be another battle, but any possibility of saving him was worth it. "Clint said Grossman's started carrying it. Try there."

"You'll be faster. You go."

Lu gritted her teeth against responding. How could she be expected to leave her baby behind?

He cried out again. "Mommy, help me."

Ma Frances wrapped her arms around Oscar and ripped him away from Lu. She stumbled a step then sat on the couch. Without looking at Lu, she wiped the sweaty curls from his face. "Mommy's going to get you help. Right. Now."

If that woman stole her last moments with her son, Lu couldn't be held accountable for what she might do. She kissed Oscar and choked on her words. "I'll be right back."

Lu raced to Grossman's, only to be met with apology. "Sold the last bottle a while ago, but I think I saw Doc Andrew head toward the tack shop."

A wave a nausea rolled over her as she hastened out of the store. Dealing with Doc was the last thing she wanted in her current state. There was nothing left in her to put up a false front, let alone attempt a confidence game, and he was too perceptive to ignore her signs of distress. If the man asked the wrong question, she'd lose her composure and waste precious time.

The bell jingled overhead as she entered the tack shop. Other than light from the setting sun, the room was dark and empty. Doc's medicine bag sat atop the counter. She released a quivering breath. If she were quick, he'd never know she'd been here.

Andrew held the stairwell door open and listened. He swore he'd heard the store's bell jingle. "Did you lock the front door?"

Josiah shook his head. "I thought you did."

It was still early enough in the evening to be a late customer. Andrew shook his head as he descended the stairs with a lamp. It could also be a mother come to flatter. All the mothers of single young ladies had decided that Josiah was a perfect prospect for their daughters. It really was a miracle the man hadn't been wrangled into marriage vows yet.

Andrew also couldn't rule out that the culprit could be Clint. He paused at the base of the stairs and spied around the corner in case the man had decided to make trouble.

Lu bent over his opened bag.

Of course it'd be her. Clint must have realized the recipe a fake and sent her back. What lies would she concoct this time? A death threat? Maybe she'd show him more bruises. He hoped not for her sake, but he wouldn't put it past her to create the look with paint in order to gain his sympathy.

"Looking for something?"

Her head snapped up as her hand clasped a bottle. Red puffy eyes met his, and she sniffed, though she tried to pull off a confident stance. The woman was good. She looked like she'd been crying for hours. Well, he wasn't going to be manipulated again. If she wanted that recipe, she was going to have to figure it out on her own.

"How much?" Her voice croaked.

"You can't pay me enough for the recipe."

Her nostrils flared. "For the bottle. I don't have time for foolishness."

He blinked. She wanted to pay? Either this was a new strategy or something really did have her upset. "Who do you need it for?"

"Oscar." Her face crumpled and the most awful keening came out.

He'd only heard that sound once—when Father Darlington delivered the news to their neighbor that her husband had been killed in the line of duty. It was not a sound that could be fabricated, but a pure guttural grief so deep it could be expressed in no other way. The boy must be really sick for her to be so undone. Andrew rounded the counter and floundered with what to do. Should he hold her and comfort her? Offer to get her a drink? He settled for shoving a handkerchief in her face and patting her on the shoulder.

At his touch, she seemed to pull herself together. "Please. He's eaten pokeberries."

No wonder she was distraught. He experienced pokeberry poisoning as a boy and barely lived to tell the tale. "Have you tried ipecac syrup?"

Fresh tears rolled down her cheeks as she nodded. "It wasn't enough."

Though there was precious little Grandma Darlington's medicine could do, Andrew snagged his bag off the counter and clasped her elbow. He called to Josiah that he was leaving and then led Lu through the door. "Tell me everything you know."

In between unsteady steps and quaking breaths, he gathered enough information to know the situation was dire. The medicine might dull the pain of Oscar's symptoms, but there was no guarantee of recovery. Only God could provide that. As they reached the house, Lu rushed through the door ahead of him and knelt at the feet of another woman who cradled the child.

Andrew froze. After twenty-four years, she was finally before him—grayer and rounder now, but still the same villainous witch that he'd once willingly claimed as Mother. Even the fierce glower that Pa claimed could scare off death hadn't changed, though it didn't appear to scare Lu. She was too busy extracting Oscar from Frances Thorne's arms to be cowed by the silent threat. And neither would Andrew be cowed. Frances Thorne was not his mother anymore.

"Give Lu her son so I can help him."

Frances skewered him with her eyes but passed Oscar to Lu, who immediately clutched him. Andrew knelt beside them and did his best to examine the boy around the desperate hold of his mother. Stomach cramps and dry heaves were Oscar's main complaints, though the smell emanating from his trousers indicated other symptoms were developing. Andrew observed his breathing closely between heaves. He panted for breath, but not like he was suffocating. A good sign, but it could all change without warning.

"Get him cleaned up and into a night shirt. It should make accidents easier to address. Then we'll try to get some water in him. If he manages to keep it down, we'll give him the medicine."

Lu and Frances disappeared with Oscar into a bedroom off the parlor while Andrew found the kitchen and prepared a diluted dose. The boy's sobs cut through the plastered walls and hollowed out any ability to remain unaffected. It didn't matter that Oscar was the son of a criminal, a member of a villainous family deserving of unrelenting justice. He was still a child designed by God. If the boy survived, which Andrew fervently prayed he would, Andrew would follow in his own adoptive father's footsteps. Once the Thorne family was arrested, he'd take Oscar under his care and give him a new life free of crime. After all, the boy was his nephew, and he had a responsibility to uphold.

A concerning amount of time passed before Lu exited the room with Oscar in her arms, the excess of a man's shirt hanging from his limp body. "There can't be anything left in him."

Frances trudged from the bedroom with her face averted from

the bedpan she carried. The content's putrid odor left no question of which end they'd originated from.

Andrew reeled away before he gagged. "Let's see if he can keep some water down."

Once Lu and Oscar were settled on the couch, Andrew helped her force him to drink. Oscar fought back but was too weak to succeed. Though he heaved most of the water, they persisted in keeping him hydrated. Eventually, the heaving subsided, and they risked giving him the medicine. By God's grace, it stayed down, and Oscar drifted off to sleep in his mother's arms.

"Do you think he'll be okay now?" Fragile hope underlined Lu's tone and her vulnerable eyes begged him to say yes.

Though painful, raw truth was better than hope proved wrong. "He could still end up struggling to breathe. If that happens . . ."

Her eyes squeezed shut, but she remained a solid, albeit exhausted, fortress for her son.

"Rest. I'll watch for signs of distress." He dragged the wingback chair close enough to observe the rise and fall of Oscar's back.

"Thank you." She shifted on the couch until the armrest pillowed her head and Oscar lay on her chest.

Frances dragged her chair closer but said nothing as her gaze flitted between him, Lu, and Oscar.

Andrew rarely openly displayed his faith, but he laid a hand on Oscar's back and prayed silently over him and Lu. For the first time in his career, he grieved over the pain doing his job would cause others. Lu might be a criminal, but her love for Oscar was genuine and selfless. It would devastate them when justice eventually ripped them apart, and well did he know the anguish separation from family caused.

For hours they waited and watched Oscar. Occasionally, Andrew studied Lu as she stared at the ceiling. At each shudder of Oscar's body, she flinched and sought the cause. Finding nothing, she would return to staring at the ceiling. Eventually, her eyes drooped, then closed, and her arms slackened. Andrew continued his vigil, praying off and on as the night crawled toward morning.

CHAPTER 10

A DOOR SLAMMED SOMEWHERE.

Andrew's eyes flew open and his hand reached for his weapon before he remembered where he was. Except for a low burning lamp on a side table, the parlor remained dark. He blinked the grit from his eyes and skimmed the room. Lu and Oscar lay on the couch, but Frances's chair was empty.

When and where had she gone?

Kerosene light flickered to life on the kitchen side of the open fireplace. Given the graying dawn outside the window, Frances must have decided to make breakfast. He released his grip on the revolver and ran a hand over his face. He should never have allowed himself to sleep. Shaking his head to clear the mental cobwebs, he leaned forward to study Oscar. The boy had shifted into the space between Lu and the back of the couch, a small hand reaching out to touch the bottom of her cheek. He appeared to breathe easily, with no lingering signs of pain. Andrew's gaze slid unbidden to Lu's relaxed face. Even in her sleep, she seemed to feel that her son would be fine.

Thank you, God. Andrew sunk back into his seat, wearier than he'd felt in a lifetime. Who knew watching the struggle of a child who wasn't even his own could wring so much out of him? He'd need a long nap and a complex dinner preparation before he could fully shake off the events of last night. He closed his eyes for a moment before pushing to his feet. His presence was no longer needed, and Josiah would no doubt have much to say on his staying the night in his former family's house. Perhaps it hadn't been the wisest idea, but he'd spare no detail in his report. If he were lucky, his help with Oscar might earn him a place with the Thornes, despite his run-ins with Clint. After one more look at Oscar curled up in his mother's protective hold, Andrew turned away.

The kitchen door creaked open. When she spotted him by the front door, she barged toward him. "You can't leave."

"Oscar will be fine, and it's time I returned to the shop." He reached for the handle, but talons dug into his arm and dragged him back with surprising force.

"Don't you know who I am? It's me, Andrew. Your mother."

Revulsion tore through his veins and obliterated every plan he'd prepared for this moment. Only Elise Darlington deserved the title Mother, and he'd not pretend otherwise. Even for the sake of this case. "You are not my mother."

"But I am! Oh Andrew, my darling, my baby." She trapped him in her lung-compressing clutch.

He pried himself free and opened the door. "Good day."

She fell to her knees and wrapped around his legs like a toddler with more stopping power. He teetered against the wall as she bawled. "No! I won't lose you again."

"You didn't lose me. You left me."

"I didn't want to. It was your father. I've done nothing but search for you since he died."

God help him. For there was no way he could get through this moment on his own. He might have forgiven Frances Thorne with the Darlingtons' help, but it had been in word only. Every feeling of betrayal, anger, and torment he'd endured as an abandoned twelve-year-old resurfaced with unwieldy power. He wanted to make this woman, this whole family, pay for their crimes. The only way to do that was to arrest them.

He took a steadying breath and glanced over at the couch to remind himself what was at stake. But the couch was empty. "Where are Oscar and Lu?"

Frances shot to her feet, rage overtaking the hysteria. She looked from him to the open kitchen door and back to him again. "We are family, and *no one* is leaving."

Lu stifled Oscar's confused cries as she sprinted to the cover of the woods. She didn't have long before Ma Frances realized they were missing. Her reaction to Doc had been more dramatic than expected. Thank heavens for that. Had the woman not shrieked and screamed, Lu might have slept through the whole exchange and missed her chance. Fortunately, she'd fallen asleep with her shoes on.

Oscar thudded against her body with each running step. She just had to get past the creek, and then they could slow down.

Before she could reach it, Cyrus and Clint emerged from the shadows with a wagon in tow.

Clint captured her arm, and she stumbled. "Where do you think you're goin'?"

Her mind reeled to find an excuse. "Someone's at the house. He's hurting Ma!"

Cyrus cursed and took off at a run, but Clint held on tight. "Don't lie to me. Who are you runnin' off to meet?"

"No one! We're going for help."

"Away from town?"

She swallowed and tried to find a believable reason, but there wasn't one. "I was so scared, I wasn't thinking."

He hid the wagon full of canvas bags in the bushes. "Let's just go see what's really goin' on."

As he dragged her back to the house, Oscar whimpered against her shoulder. She wanted to whimper right along with him. Soon the family would realize what she was really up to. Her life as a Thorne would be over. A dream turned nightmare. Not even her skill as a pickpocket would save her. If Ma Frances didn't outright shoot her, she'd sell her to Molly. Maybe if she tripped Clint, she and Oscar could still run. She immediately rejected the thought. He'd overtake her with ease.

They reached the veranda, and a shot went off. Clint pulled his gun but didn't release her, then charged inside. They stumbled to a stop at the table's end where Cyrus and Doc wrestled on the floor with guns knocked out of reach. Ma Frances screeched at them to stop, but they continued to roll and throw wild punches. Clint propelled Lu and Oscar toward Ma Frances and joined the fray.

Lu watched in horror as Clint pinned Doc, enabling Cyrus to crash a fist into Doc's face. She should run while she had the chance, but Doc's beating was her fault. What if, like Sheriff Zachary, he died because of her lies?

"Give him to me." Ma Frances lunged for Oscar, which broke Lu free from her frozen state.

Lu careened out of reach, but her foot landed on Clint's leg and rolled out from under her. Oscar's squalls joined the clamor as the pair smacked into Clint and tumbled into swinging arms and kicking feet. Despite the addition of a woman and child, the men rolled over and around them. Elbows, knees, fists, and feet attacked without deference to who they hit. With no other choice to protect Oscar, she released him to Ma Frances. Lu raised her arms to deflect the worst blows as she struggled to roll away and screamed at them to stop.

A shot fired above them, and everyone stilled. Lu's ears rang, and acrid gun smoke mingled with the stench of sweat.

"That's enough." Ma Frances lowered the derringer to point at the floor. "Clint, Cyrus, say hello to your brother, Andrew."

Clint and Cyrus stared at each other before gawking at the man they'd been beating to death only a moment ago. Doc rose to his feet, huffing and with a busted lip and swelling left eye. With all three of them together, there was no denying Doc Andrew's bloodline. He was a Thorne through and through.

And she'd lost her only chance to escape them all.

Oscar wriggled from Ma Frances's arms and ran to Lu, sobbing. What were they going to do now?

Doc glared at both men before kneeling in front of her and Oscar. "Are you all right?"

His genuine concern did a strange flip to her stomach. Oscar, however, wailed.

Ma Frances reached for him, but he buried his face into Lu's neck. "Oscar, come to MawMaw, now."

Oscar's grip became a chokehold.

"This has been too much for him. The boy needs his mother." Doc assisted Lu to her feet while supporting Oscar. "Is there a quiet room we can go to? The last thing we need is for him to relapse."

Lu didn't miss the use of we, and her stomach knotted. Was he protecting her or claiming a spot as first in line to punish her?

Ma Frances leveled a furious scowl at everyone in the room. "Boys, clean this mess up. Lu. Upstairs."

"I'll ensure they get situated." Doc's firm support provided surprising comfort as he guided them to the stairs.

"He's connin' you, Ma." Clint blocked their way. "This ain't Andrew. Lettin' him alone with Lu and Oscar ain't safe."

Wolves would retreat at Doc's ferocious expression. "They're safer with me than with you."

"I want proof you're Andrew." Cyrus joined Clint, solidifying the barrier.

One hand released its hold on her arm and hoisted the left side of his shirt. Lu craned her neck to see a straight, narrow scar stretching from his side to his front. "Pa hit me with the hot poker, even though it was you who stole the last of his whiskey. And you"—he faced Clint— "and Irvine were too spineless to speak up."

Clint charged at them, but Doc twisted to block the attack from reaching her and Oscar.

Cyrus shoved Clint toward the parlor door. "Let's go. We'll deal with him later."

After they'd left, Ma Frances smiled at Doc. "I knew it was you." She turned a glower on Lu. "Now upstairs."

Lu's gelatinous legs refused to cooperate, but with Doc supporting her, she reached her windowless bedroom. She collapsed onto the bed and cradled Oscar. Hiccups and panting breaths shook his little body. Her poor baby didn't deserve all he'd been through in the last twenty-four hours. She'd failed him as a mother, and now he would likely be raised without her by the whole Thorne lot.

Someone lit a lamp and turned up the wick.

Doc rested his hands on her shoulders, holding her steady and encircling Oscar like a barrier to the chaos outside. His serious eyes evaluated hers before kneeling. "Oscar, do you remember me?"

Oscar nodded against her chest but didn't speak.

"Are you having any trouble breathing?" A shake of the head. "Do you feel sick to your stomach?" A shrug. "Do you feel like you can drink something?" A nod. Doc seemed to breathe a sigh of relief and turned toward Ma Frances, who stood by the door. "Can you make him some chamomile tea and bring it up with a slice of bread?"

"Of course." Ma Frances closed the door behind her and a key ground in the lock.

"No!" Doc released his steadying hold and sprang for the door.

He tried the knob, but it only revealed what Lu already knew. Ma Frances was taking no chances of Lu or Doc disappearing. Truth be told, it didn't matter. She didn't have the strength to stand, let alone make a run for it. Doc slammed a fist against the wall. At least Ma Frances kept him here because she wanted him. Lu closed her eyes and swallowed. Ma Frances already made it clear they could do without Lu's income. And keeping Lu around for Oscar's happiness wouldn't hold weight any longer. Ma's image of a happy, controlled family wouldn't tolerate Lu's rebellion.

Doc's hand pressed against her shoulder. "Lie down before you and Oscar fall over."

Why not? There was nothing left to lose. She eased Oscar into a comfortable position and then lay next to him. He snuggled against her, grasping her bodice in his tight little fist. Doc tucked the covers around them and released a breath as he straightened.

"This was not how I planned for this to go." He pilfered the chair by her dressing table but froze when his battered face reflected in the glass. After snatching the washcloth from her water basin, he dabbed at the blood seeping from the split above his eye. "Why did you run?"

The last person she could trust with the truth was a Thorne. "The way Ma Frances carried on, I thought you were hurting her. I ran for help."

A spark of disgust flashed in his mirrored reflection. "I'd never hurt a woman, even *that* woman." Despite his words, the burning coals he then directed at the locked door declared otherwise.

"Then why'd you hide your identity from the family?"

His head dipped so that she could no longer see his face and was silent for several heartbeats. "Because I wasn't sure how I'd be received." Before she could probe further, he tossed the rag in the water and dragged the chair over to her bedside. "How's Oscar?"

Her whole body sighed in relief. Her sweet baby lay tired and upset, but alive, and she had Doc to thank for that. "I think he's going to be okay."

"I agree. Get some sleep. I need to think, and I do that best in silence."

She didn't speak again, but neither did she sleep. The Thorne before her had a rough kindness that reminded her of Irvine. Granted, that kindness was hidden behind manners similar to their dog Tabby— cranky and aggressive, but with a definite protective side. Might there be more to the man than she initially thought? It wasn't likely she'd have an opportunity to find out. Her time here was at an end and her next destination either Molly's or the grave. Lu tucked her chin against Oscar's head. If she actually believed God would listen to prayers from someone like her, she'd be tempted to beg for His intervention now.

Although wasn't Oscar, alive and nestled beside her, proof that maybe He did answer?

God. She shifted. How was one supposed to address a god? Probably not laying down in bed or simply as God. Men of authority always wanted to be recognized as such. Would God prefer King? Emperor? President? Maybe Your Honor would suffice. She almost scoffed out loud. Who was she fooling? It wouldn't matter what or how she said it. He wasn't likely to pay attention, anyway.

But if by some chance You do, Your Honor, would You find some way to keep Oscar and me together? Maybe help us escape?

She knew better than to expect any sort of sign, so she gathered Oscar closer to her side.

Though the silence between Doc and her stretched, the threatening mutters of Cyrus and Clint rose through the grate above the parlor and into the room. By Ma Frances's design, there wasn't a room in the house where someone could have a private conversation without the chance of being overheard. Clint and Cyrus knew that and probably hoped to scare Doc senseless. A hope without merit by the cranky determination in Doc's scowl. Eventually, the key scraped in the lock again.

Doc surged to his feet and broadened his stance, forcing Lu to sit up in order to see around him. Priscill must have returned, for she entered with a smug smile. Ma Frances followed with an elaborate breakfast tray.

"You needn't have locked us in." Doc delivered his words with measured intensity.

"I couldn't have you running off now that you're here. I've decades to make up, beginning with your favorite breakfast. Eggs, biscuits, jam, and bacon."

Likely all poisoned to teach him a lesson on how much he needed his mother.

"All we needed was tea and bread for Oscar."

"I knew he'd be asleep before I got back. Now, have a seat. We've much to discuss."

"I'm not interested."

"Please, Andrew, my dearest. Indulge your dear mother's whim. If when we're finished, you still want to leave, I'll let you go."

Doc hesitated but sat.

The woman was a conniving witch and Doc a fool.

Ma Frances laid the tray on his lap and stepped back with the satisfaction of victory. Lu couldn't let him fall prey to her schemes. She subtly touched his leg, and when their eyes linked, she shook her head. *Please understand me.* His brows bunched in question, but he scooped a generous portion of eggs onto his fork and lifted. Heaven help her survive Ma Frances's wrath.

Lu thrust the tray off his lap, sending everything crashing to the floor and disturbing Oscar. "It's poisoned."

"You ungrateful brat. He would've been fine."

"Not before getting as sick as Oscar."

She and Ma Frances locked glares in a silent wrestling match.

"See, Ma." Priscill slithered into view. "It's like I told you. She cares for the doc, and he already keeps Clint away from her. Oscar needs a father, and well—" The snake's tongue flicked over her lips. "I think it's the perfect solution to everyone's problems."

Ma Frances scrutinized Lu, Andrew, and Oscar with fading skepticism. "They do make a handsome family. All right. Send Cyrus and Clint for the preacher."

The words crushed the breath from Lu's chest. She couldn't be tied to another Thorne. Not again. Yet what choice did she have? Rebel and endure slavery at the brothel? And what about Oscar? Her sweet baby nuzzled against her and her heart lurched. She'd sacrifice anything to protect him, and she couldn't protect him if sold to Molly. She'd survived one marriage. She'd do it again. There was no other choice.

Chapter 11

"Absolutely not! I won't marry her." Andrew bolted from his chair.

Who were they to think they could dictate whom he married? Any protection on his part came out of a duty to God, not affection for the pickpocket who lived to annoy him.

Frances waved away his objection. "Of course you will. I'm your mother and I know what's best for you."

"You better go tell Cyrus and Clint." Priscill handed Frances the key as she opened the door. "I'll stay here and get Lu ready."

Andrew dove after Frances in time to have the door bounce off his arm.

Frances scratched at his hold. "Let this door shut."

"I'm not marrying her." He shouldered past her. At the top step a familiar click skittered his pulse. With hands raised, he rotated slowly on his heel.

Ma Frances directed a Remington Double Derringer at him. "I'm going to give you a little mercy, since you've forgotten the way things work. Now get back in there."

"You wouldn't shoot your son."

"Not to kill. But tending to your wounds would keep you here and Lu busy. Actually, that sounds like a good idea." The barrel lowered to his legs.

He jumped aside as the derringer went off. She reset the hammer, and he hurtled back into the room. The woman had lost her mind!

The door slammed behind him and for the second time in one day, he was held prisoner by his own family. How had he so thoroughly lost control of the situation? Lu stared his direction as she hugged Oscar to her chest, though by the glazed appearance of her eyes, he doubted she saw him.

At the end of the bed, Priscill removed one of Lu's saloon dresses from a trunk, unconcerned he'd almost been shot. "What do you think of your bride wearing this?"

"I'm not marrying her." Andrew pushed from the floor. Picking locks had been Clint's specialty, not his, but he would not be forced into unholy matrimony.

"Say what you will now, but you'll change your tune by the end of the day. Lu, which dress would you prefer?"

"It doesn't matter." Resignation weighed her voice.

"Of course it does. It's a day for celebration. You'll be free of Clint, and Ma won't sell you to Molly."

The madam down the street? Andrew regarded Lu with fresh eyes. Though she rocked Oscar, the movement appeared self-comforting. Her usually vibrant complexion had grayed worse than Mary's, and despondency wafted from her in waves. Considering Frances had attempted to shoot him, it shouldn't surprise him Lu had been threatened with such a heartless notion. Nevertheless, the realization churned his stomach like rancid meat. No wonder she'd run. Once he escaped, he'd ensure she didn't end up at Molly's.

"You should be thanking me." Priscill tossed the dress aside and continued rummaging. "I saved your sorry hide."

Andrew crouched by the lock and examined it. With the right tools, it shouldn't be too hard. Hairpins might do. He rifled through Lu's dressing table drawer until he found the two best candidates.

"This is the one! I haven't seen you wear it since mine and Clint's wedding. Seems fitting for you to wear it now."

Andrew didn't bother to look and set to work angling the pins into the keyhole. It only took a moment to catch one of the tumblers, but with the next movement, he lost it. Frustration mounted as time after time he caught all the tumblers, only to lose them before he could secure them in place. Finally, the latch clicked, and Andrew released a long breath. He opened the door as Frances crested the top stair.

"Pastor Newcomb and his wife have arrived. Why don't you lead the way, son?" Though the question suggested he could say no, the appearance of her derringer insisted he didn't.

Andrew chewed the inside of his cheek as he stared her down.

"It'd be a shame for you to bleed during your wedding." Her thumb flicked the hammer.

Fine. Downstairs put him closer to the exit.

In the parlor, Pastor Newcomb stood with Mary clinging to his arm, held up at Clint's gunpoint. Bald with broad shoulders, the pastor stood with the calm and confidence of a man unafraid. The same could not be said of Mary Newcomb. Even from ten feet away, Andrew saw her tremble and the weakness that had her leaning into her husband.

Andrew ignored Cyrus and extended his hand. "Pastor Newcomb, my apologies for meeting under such circumstances."

The pastor regarded Frances, and he grimaced. "It appears we share similar circumstances."

The stairs creaked behind them and Lu appeared beside him, holding Oscar on one hip.

"Mrs. Thorne"—Pastor Newcomb nodded toward Lu—"it is good to see you again."

Lu huffed. "I didn't think men of God were supposed to lie."

A wry smile tilted the man's mouth. "Perhaps it's not the way I would've chosen, but it doesn't change my sentiment. What can I do for you?"

Frances moved around them. "You can marry them, that's what."

Creases amassed on his forehead. "Is that what you wish?"

Andrew and Lu spoke simultaneously.

"No."

"Yes."

Andrew's gaze shot to Lu's stiff profile. The woman couldn't be serious.

Pastor Newcomb folded his hands and addressed Frances. "I won't unite two unwilling souls."

Frances redirected her aim toward the pastor. "You will, or you'll be meeting your God today."

Though his wife gasped, he stood taller and lifted his chin. "I know where I'll be going. The question is, do you? Strait is the gate, and narrow is the way, which leadeth unto life, and few there be that find it."

Never before had Andrew witnessed someone stand with such confidence and peace in the face of death where a choice existed. Anyone else would've immediately opened their book of ceremonies. Choosing to die when told to deny Christ Andrew could understand, but not marriage. "I'll marry her."

Frances smiled and lowered her derringer. Until the pastor spoke again.

"Marriage is not something to be taken lightly or threatened into. No matter the circumstance of its beginning, marriage is a sacred covenant between God, one man, and one woman. A tangible reflection of Christ's love for us. If you choose to make this vow, you are accepting the full weight of the obligations and consequences of the role of husband."

Andrew shifted under the weight of Pastor Newcomb's words. He did believe marriage to be a sacred covenant, but to make that covenant with Lu? He observed her from the corner of his eye. The woman was a harlot and a thief. She probably wouldn't stay faithful for even a week. God might have called Hosea to such an arrangement, but surely God wouldn't hold Andrew to the same vow—especially given the circumstances. Marrying Lu would destroy his reputation. Confirm him unchanged from his youth. He'd be removed from the Secret Service. But to refuse condemned others' lives. Duty as an operative demanded he do whatever necessary to protect Pastor Newcomb, Mary, Oscar, and Lu. Saying yes to a temporary, paper marriage would save them, and when the case ended, even God wouldn't hold an annulment against him.

Certain of his decision, he nodded. "I understand."

Pastor Newcomb assessed Andrew for several heartbeats. "Then let us proceed."

Mary sagged in relief before mouthing, "Thank you."

The ceremony moved quickly.

"This is your last chance to change your mind, son. Do you take this woman to be your lawfully wedded wife?"

Andrew surveyed each of the four victims his vow would protect. Mary who leaned heavily on the strength of her husband, a man unlike any other Andrew had met. Oscar, who sucked his thumb as he watched Andrew with wary eyes from his mother's shoulder. And then there was Lu. His soon-to-be temporary wife. Though she stood now as if she were carved by stone—back rigid, shoulders stiff, and gaze fixed—her vulnerability revealed upstairs and in the tack shop proved her need for rescue as much as the others. *It is only a paper marriage. It will be annulled in the end. Just say it and get on with the case.*

"I do."

The book of ceremonies closed with a clap. "I'll need you both to come to the house to sign the certificate, but it's official in the eyes of God and man."

Priscill and Frances squealed, while the rest exchanged strained congratulations.

Clint shook Andrew's hand with bruising strength. "Don't think you've won."

Frances clasped her hands beneath her chin. "Finally, all my family's together. Nothing'll ever tear us apart again."

Ma Frances accompanied the Newcombs, Lu, Oscar, and Doc to the parsonage where the papers to make the marriage legally binding awaited. In Pastor Newcomb's office, Lu stared at the line where Pastor Newcomb indicated she should sign her name. She and Irvine had just made their marks, neither of them able to read or write, but Doc had neat penmanship. Next to his, whatever she put would show

how right her only teacher had been when he said Lu was all beauty and no brains. Still, she didn't want him to think of her any less than he already did. She was bound to him. Owned by him. Oscar shifted against her shoulder and she drew a deep breath. She'd made the most of life with Irvine, and she'd do it again with Doc. She picked up the pen but couldn't quite figure out how to hold it. She dropped it twice, using Oscar's interference as an excuse. Finally, she scribbled something she hoped resembled her name.

As soon as the pen hit the pastor's desk, she turned and blocked Doc's view. "I guess that's it then, Doc. We're married."

"Andrew." He cleared his throat. "Call me Andrew, not Doc."

"What? The lie rub you wrong when it comes from your wife?"

Something undecipherable flickered across his face. "You could say that."

Ma Frances stood outside the office door, rubbing her hands together. "Well, it's done. Time to go home and get Andrew situated upstairs."

His face twisted like he'd stepped in cow pie. "The tack shop is my home."

"Not anymore. You'll live upstairs with Lu and Oscar like Irvine did. Families should stay together."

"My family *will* live together. Above the tack shop."

Rocks for brains must run in the family. He should know by now that what Ma Frances wanted, she got. One way or another.

"Not if you're injured." Ma Frances tapped her pocket.

"It will be just as easy to maneuver the shop stairs as yours."

For pity's sake, Lu was going to have to get this mule-headed man to see reason. As much as she hated to, she'd have to intervene the only way she knew how. "Ma Frances, will you take Oscar home and tuck him in bed? Andrew and I'll be home shortly."

The woman eyed her with suspicion. Lu drew closer and dropped her voice. "I'll convince Andrew his needs'll be best met at home. I just need the space and privacy to do so."

A feline smile smoothed the hard lines. "Of course. I'll take Oscar and see to it his bed and toys are moved to the other room. I'll even have Priscill put fresh linens on for you."

Oscar objected, but Lu passed him into Ma Frances's waiting arms. "I'll be home soon, baby. I promise."

Satisfied, Ma Frances disappeared out the door with Oscar.

Pastor Newcomb stepped forward. "I'm sure there are many things you two need to discuss, but I'd like to have a word with you first, Mr. Thorne. Alone, if possible."

Andrew jumped at the opportunity like a frog out of a boiling pot and shut the office door nearly on her toes before she'd formed a reasonable protest. She blinked at the oak panel then veered toward the kitchen. It wasn't as if she *wanted* to seduce her husband into the marriage bed. She'd be content if the man never found her desirable, but she knew better than to expect such luck.

In the kitchen, Mary gestured to a vacant chair. "Perhaps a strong cup of coffee's the best way to conclude this morning."

Lu slumped onto the chair and rested her head on the table while Mary prepared their coffee. Had she really found Oscar full of pokeberries only yesterday afternoon? It felt like an entire lifetime had transpired since then. And now she was married to a Thorne. Again. She banged her head against the table as if that might dislodge the memory and free her from its reality.

The chair across from Lu creaked. "So Doc Andrew is the missing Thorne. The poor man. What a trial it must've been to raise himself."

Lu gaped at the only friend she could claim. "I wouldn't have too much pity for him. He's still a Thorne, through and through."

"I don't know. He seems to be a decent man, despite that tactless mouth of his. He keeps me stocked in his medicine for no cost." She flicked her hand to where three large bottles sat next to the sink. "And you said it yourself. He stepped in to protect you from Clint. He can't be all bad. If you had to marry a Thorne, at least it's that one."

She couldn't deny it. He'd already proven himself a superior Thorne, but that was like marrying a skunk instead of a rattlesnake. And it didn't change her need to escape or the complications of attempting to while married. Ma Frances was bound to keep a closer eye on them, and Clint wasn't likely to restrain his jealousy. She shivered despite the growing warmth in the kitchen from the stove.

"What am I supposed to do?" Lu dropped her voice. "You know I want to get Oscar away from these people. Now we're stuck again."

"I'm not so sure about that. What if God brought Doc Andrew into your life to help? He didn't cow beneath Ma Frances."

"All that proves is I married an idiot. Between Ma Frances and Clint, he doesn't stand a chance."

"I have a feeling he can take care of himself."

"Sure. Take care of getting himself killed."

Mary smirked. "Well, wouldn't that solve at least one of your problems?"

The joke failed to soothe Lu's nerves. "Maybe, but only one." She glanced over her shoulder to ensure they remained alone and then leaned in. "Clint caught me trying to escape with Oscar when Ma Frances was distracted with Andrew."

The levity dropped from Mary's face. "Does Ma Frances know?"

"I'm sure once the chaos of this morning settles, she'll either figure it out or Clint'll tell her. Either way, I'm in trouble. Neither one of them will allow me out of their sight again, and I wouldn't be surprised if I'm sick with food poisoning by nightfall."

"Can't you just not eat what she makes?"

"No one tells Ma Frances no."

"Doc Andrew did." Mary rose to retrieve the percolated coffee. "Maybe by staying in the tack shop, you'll have a chance to persuade him to take you and Oscar far away. His loyalty to them can't be as strong as Irvine's was."

A perfect solution if it would work, but she didn't hold out much hope. Andrew might not have grown up with his family, but he certainly hadn't left town when he realized the Thornes were here. What else could that mean but that on some level, he wanted a restored relationship with his family? She'd be no more successful at getting him to leave them behind than she had Irvine, and Irvine had said he loved her. Andrew didn't even like her.

"You know I can't allow him to defy Ma Frances and live in that tack shop. She'll burn the place down to prove her point like she did the church. Doc and Pretty Boy could end up injured, or worse. I'll have to coax him back to the house."

"And how do you plan to do that? He seems plenty determined."

"I have my ways." Dread pooled in her stomach like acid.

Her plan to seduce Andrew shouldn't bother her. She enticed men almost daily. But in truth, she always knew it would never lead anywhere. She retrieved whatever money she needed to steal and then sauntered away before things escalated out of her control. With Andrew, it would be different. She couldn't walk away.

"I still think you can convince him to leave with you and Oscar. A man will do a lot for the woman he loves."

"The only reason he married me was because he had a derringer to his back. He doesn't love me any more than I love Clint."

"Maybe not yet, but give it time. I think there's a fair chance of love for the both of you, if what I've seen of his character stands true."

The only thing love was good for was pulling the wool over the other person's eyes and getting them to do what you wanted. She might be able to get Andrew to fancy himself in love with her, but she'd not be so foolish. Pa had been bad enough, proclaiming that selling her to the madam in Colorado was an act of love and protection. Then Irvine said he loved her—as long as she did what he wanted. Lu was done with so-called love.

"Mary, Doc's a confidence man. He makes sure you only see what he wants you to see. Now that he's been reunited with his family, you'll learn what I already know. A Thorne can't be trusted. If Oscar and I are to escape, we'll have to do it on our own. I just have to placate Andrew and the family until I can figure out how."

CHAPTER 12

PASTOR NEWCOMB GESTURED FOR ANDREW to sit in one of the wooden chairs and collected the signed marriage certificate before settling behind his desk. "Thank you for the private audience, Mr. Thorne."

"It's still Andrew, or Doc if you prefer, but not Mr. Thorne."

He nodded. "From our previous conversations, I had the impression that you are a man of faith. Is this true?"

"I am."

"Then as Lu's husband, you should know she is not yet a believer, though there are signs she is wrestling with the concept."

Her lack of faith wasn't surprising. Over the course of his career, he'd learned that while some criminals claimed to have devout lives, most lived without regard to or with outright anger toward their Creator.

"It'll be your duty to guide her and be an example of Christ. I'm afraid she hasn't had many in her life. The congregation has been less than understanding of her need for compassion. Mary and I are the only ones who've made an effort to befriend her."

Andrew chafed under the pastor's admonition. To his shame, Lu wasn't likely to view his actions up to the current moment as a good Christian example either. Gentleness, compassion, and mercy were areas he'd long struggled to cultivate, and God's gentle reprimand to do better pierced to his marrow. Though his faith may lack words, he'd take special care to ensure his actions spoke volumes. "I appreciate the warning. I'll endeavor to point her toward Christ. However, there are complications that may impede my attempts."

A skeptical brow lifted. "Such as?"

Andrew hesitated, opening the door and stepping back to check the hall. Lu and Mary's voices carried from the kitchen and didn't indicate they moved toward the office. He shut and locked the door before crossing to the window. No one traveled the road into town, and the fallow fields of the Thorne farm gave a clear view of Frances entering the house with Oscar.

He returned to his seat before speaking. "I need your word that you'll not share what I say with anyone, not even your wife."

"Anything said in this room is between you, me, and God."

He took a risk in telling Pastor Newcomb, but the man had proven his character by standing up to Frances, and frankly, Andrew needed all the help he could get. "I'm an undercover operative for the Secret Service."

Pastor Newcomb blinked. "So you're not really Andrew Thorne?"

"Yes and no. I'm Andrew Darlington, formerly Andrew Thorne." He briefly explained how he arrived in his current situation—including Walt's death and the missing informant. "It's my job to discover all who are involved and arrest them."

"I see." He tented his fingers. "And how will Lu and Oscar play into all this?"

"Lu will be arrested with the rest of the Thornes, and I'll take charge of Oscar's care. As for our marriage, as long as you don't file the paperwork, it never happened."

"You made a vow before God. You cannot toss it aside as if it were nothing."

"Given the circumstances, I'm sure God doesn't hold me accountable."

The chair creaked as Pastor Newcomb leaned back. "Do you believe God is sovereign?"

"Of course."

"Do you think God was surprised by the circumstances of this marriage?"

Andrew didn't like the direction the pastor was going. "His knowing doesn't equate with approval. God called me to be a Secret Service operative, and I can't remain one if I'm married to a criminal."

"We know that all things work together for good to them that love God, to them who are called according to *His* purpose." Pastor Newcomb arched a brow. "Regardless of what you were called to do before, your purpose now is to be a husband to Lu until death do you part."

"My purpose is to arrest the Thorne gang, and your assistance would be appreciated."

"I'll be happy to assist, but I *will* file the paperwork with the correct names. What happens to your marriage after the arrests is between you, God, and Lu. However, I challenge you to treat Lu now as if she's the wife of your dreams and not the criminal of your nightmares."

A snort escaped before Andrew squelched it. The wife of his dreams was everything Lu was not. Modest, moral, faithful, kind, and generous. "I'll think about it. Right now, I need information about the Thornes' arrival, what's happened since, and with whom Walt kept company."

Pastor Newcomb didn't have much to offer that Andrew hadn't already heard. The Thornes had shown up in Landkreis, gotten the lay of the bankless land, and then robbed the Stendal hotel. When Lu and Irvine fled, Irvine was shot and killed by Sheriff Zachary, who was executed in turn by Clint. It hadn't taken long for them to establish their reign, as others in search of ways to make easy money conspired with them. As for Walt, the man had been affable, and no one stuck out as receiving his special attention. Whoever the informant had been, they'd been careful to keep their relationship with Walt unnoticeable.

When Andrew and Pastor Newcomb concluded their meeting, they found Lu kneading bread in the kitchen alone.

"Mary needed to lie down. I told her I'd set the bread to rise and then leave."

Pastor Newcomb nodded. "Thank you. If you'll excuse me, I should check on her."

She didn't acknowledge his comment and concentrated on the dough with an intensity the task didn't require.

Andrew tugged at his cuff. What was he supposed to say to her? His supposed wife. He had to make it seem real for the benefit of his case, but he couldn't bring himself to accept it as a long-term arrangement. Lawmen didn't marry criminals, and she'd attempted to kill Eli, picked pockets without remorse, and flirted with any man in sight. Their marriage would prove to everyone he hadn't really changed. In their eyes, he'd be the same selfish, unprincipled lowlife criminal as before.

Lu dropped the dough into a bowl and covered it with a towel. Keeping her back to him, she washed up in the sink. "Ma Frances will expect us home soon."

At least he knew how to respond to this. "Home is above the tack shop." He needed the privacy from the other Thornes and the ability to control his surroundings. Besides, Josiah would know how to handle Lu, though it would chafe to ask for his advice.

"Are you sure that's the best idea? I've been up there." She turned toward him and dried her hands on a towel before removing her apron. "The apartment won't hold all four of us."

He hadn't considered sleeping arrangements, but he refused to give Frances the illusion of control over his decisions. "I'll sleep on the couch or share a room with Joe." Sharing a bed with her was unthinkable.

"I don't think Pretty Boy will cotton to us staying with him. Besides, do you really want him flirting with me? He don't seem the type to mind I'm married."

Josiah probably would flirt. The man seemed incapable of anything else around a pretty woman, and Lu was that. Andrew had been too preoccupied with the circumstances of their marriage to notice her attire earlier, but the tasteful, simple design surprised him. Every inch of her was covered, from the deep green skirt that nearly swept the floor to the modest white blouse with a high-necked collar. She could easily pass for a penitent congregant on her way to Sunday service.

Something akin to satisfaction flickered in her eyes, and a confident smirk stole across her face. With a saunter that dispossessed the dress of its modesty, she transformed into a licentious siren.

"You know, at Ma Frances's we'll not only have more room, but more privacy."

As soon as she was within reach, she began unbuttoning his vest.

Did the woman have no discretion? Andrew forced her hands away. "This is neither the time nor place."

"I agree. Our bedroom at Ma Frances's would be much more comfortable." Her hands found their way back to his chest.

By God's grace alone, his tone remained flat instead of revealing the increasing speed of his pulse. "Home is the tack shop."

Annoyance flickered across her face, followed by determination. She pressed the length of her body against his and wrapped her arms around his neck. Many a sailor must have drowned by her skill, but he would not be one of them. He backstepped. She followed, step by step until she'd trapped him against the wall. Her mouth traced his neck with kisses, and he gulped for air. This was a game to her. Nothing more.

Warm breath puffed against his skin and her lips teased his earlobe. "Believe me, you don't want to share a home with Pretty Boy."

His chest pounded and demanded he respond. God help him. He wasn't as immune to her advances as he believed. He had to stop this before he lost his control. He thrust her back a step. "That's enough, Lu."

Victory sparked in her eyes. "Come home to Ma Frances's. Our bed is waiting."

He choked and coughed. There would be no sharing a bed with her. Ever. No matter how she enticed him. This was purely a manipulation tactic. It was time to get to the truth of the matter and prove her lack of power over him. "Why is it so important to go to Frances's? I know you don't want me any more than I want you."

She reeled back as if struck. "You don't want me?"

"Of course not. Why is it so important to go to Frances's?"

Her mouth gaped, then snapped closed. She whirled around and wrenched the door open. Cool air swept through the room as she kept her back to him. "If we don't, she'll burn the tack shop down and someone will get hurt. Do whatever you like, but I'm going back to Ma's."

The door slammed in the wake of her exit.

Andrew stared, shaken by his base response to her advances and her sharp turn of emotions. Pretending to be Lu's husband was going to be harder than he imagined. Heaven help him. Not only would he have to inform Josiah he'd ended up married, but he was going to have to ask for his advice on how to proceed.

As Andrew approached the tack shop, Josiah appeared on the boardwalk with a man whose patched and oversized work clothes failed to disguise his military bearing. Andrew's steps faltered. Of all the days for Captain Abbott to arrive.

"How the deuce did you end up married?" Josiah blurted before Andrew reached them.

So much for breaking the news himself. "Word travels fast."

"Like lightning." Josiah's dry tone lacked humor. "Cyrus just left after threatening to burn the place down if I don't ensure you return to Ma Frances's house by nightfall."

"Take this conversation inside." Captain Abbott's command came with a nod toward the wagon rolling down the street.

Josiah led the way into the tack shop, and Andrew locked the door behind them. Not trusting the windows to be enough protection from eavesdroppers, they proceeded to the upstairs parlor where Captain Abbott stationed himself beside the wingback chair like an executioner waiting to get to business. Andrew half expected him to launch into an immediate interrogation or dismissal, but he remained in silent condemnation.

"I'll spare you the small talk, sir. I may be a former member of the

Thorne gang, but I hold no loyalty to them. If anything, I am more determined than ever to see each member arrested."

"Even your *wife?*" Captain Abbott gritted.

"I have no affection for Lu." Even if the woman had garnered sympathy from him. "Frances Thorne recognized me as her son and determined the best way to keep me from leaving was to tie me to the family through Irvine's widow. When I opposed her, she threatened to kill the pastor and his wife. I had no choice but to marry Lu."

Captain Abbott pinched the bridge of his nose. "First the Cosgrove fiasco in February, and now this. You two are going to have the Secret Service digging into operatives' lives more than the criminals we investigate." After a moment of massaging his forehead, he gestured for Andrew to take a seat on the couch while he claimed the wingback. "I've long trusted your word and methods, Darlington. I'm going to give you the benefit of the doubt, but I want the full of it, from beginning to end. No omissions just because they cast you in a poor light."

Andrew spared no detail in the retelling, emphasizing the change the Darlingtons cultivated in his life, from his complete rejection of crime to his tireless pursuit of justice. Josiah jumped in to verify Andrew's story when he reached their acquaintance and shared casework. Once he reached the end, Captain Abbott leaned on his knees and rubbed his knuckles like a one-man jury in deliberation.

As the minutes ticked by, Andrew's muscles coiled tighter. His entire career hinged on Captain Abbott's verdict.

Eventually, Captain Abbott spoke. "The way I see it, you're inextricably tied to this case. Not even Chief Brooks can deny that. Your link to the family is as good as any informant we could rope in, especially since the one Walt used is missing. Besides, if we pulled you out, it would compromise the case and force us to start over. Do you think you can maintain your cover?"

Though he wanted to slump in relief, he remained seated at rigid attention. "Absolutely. They'd never suspect a Thorne would become a lawman. Frances rules the family, and she's thrilled to have her long-lost son home. Even if Cyrus and Clint object, I'm going to get pulled into the family dealings."

"What about Lu?" Josiah straightened away from the corner he'd been leaning against. "You'll be living with her, and she's a beautiful woman with no reserve. I doubt even you can withstand her advances for long."

Her attempt to lure him back to Frances's left *him* questioning his ability to stand on neutral ground until the case was over. He could take precautions—sleep on the floor and limit their time together—but creating the illusion of marriage would be tricky. He'd never been a hand with women, and taking the pastor's advice of treating Lu like the wife of his dreams was ridiculous.

Discomfort niggled his conscience. *God, I'll be a Christian example to her, but You called me to be an operative, not her husband.*

Captain Abbott cut into his thoughts. "There'll be no taking liberties with the woman. You're strictly there to gather information and evidence. I'll arrange for annulment papers to be filed the moment this case is concluded. It'll be difficult enough to use you as a reliable witness when the trials come around. I want nothing to happen that will jeopardize the evidence you collect."

"Intimacy shouldn't be a problem. I've already upset her."

"You? I never would've guessed." Josiah crooked a wry smile. "What did you say this time?"

"I rejected her advances."

"Good." Captain Abbott straightened. "Knowing your personality, it won't take long for her to give up on that front."

Josiah coughed to cover a laugh, and Andrew bit his tongue. He well knew he wasn't an easy man to live with, but he hoped he held at least some appeal.

Captain Abbott continued. "How do you plan to move forward?"

"Given Cyrus's warning, it appears I'll be relocating to the Thornes. I'll ingratiate myself with Frances and win Lu's affections enough to get her talking to me."

"You couldn't win a puppy's affections. How do you expect to pull that off?"

Andrew hated to admit any truth lived in that insult, but he couldn't deny it. He needed help wherever women were involved. "Considering I have the Charmer as a partner, he can counsel me."

"This should be interesting." Captain Abbott leaned back, arms knotted over his chest.

"I'd say be yourself, but we both know how that would go." Josiah fell pensive for a moment, then added. "A woman like Lu will be immune to compliments about her appearance or appeal. Gifts might endear you to her. Acts of service, maybe. You cook. Cook her a meal. Just be sure to clean up after yourself." Josiah chuckled. "Shauna loved it when I made a meal, but always got madder than a hornet when she found the kitchen in shambles."

"Which fiancée was she?"

Josiah's smile dropped. "The first." He rushed on, leaving no room for further questions. "If you want to follow through with this farce, you'll have to be careful. Tangling with a woman's emotions is a dangerous thing. When this is over, you might not like where it leaves you."

Andrew would deal with the repercussions tomorrow. Today he had a wife to make a truce with and a family to arrest.

CHAPTER 13

A FLYING PLATE CRASHED AGAINST the wall near Lu's head and sent shards bouncing back at her.

"You miserable little chit. Where is he?" Ma Frances lobbed another her way.

"I don't know." Lu dodged, but the plate hit her arm with throbbing force. She should've known better than to walk through the door without Andrew.

"You good-for-nothing failure! You had one job."

One impossible job. The man was as stubborn as Ma Frances and as repulsed by her as she was by Clint. Lu ducked behind a chair as another piece of dinnerware met its fate. Of course, Priscill provided no help, instead standing at the parlor door watching with all the amusement of Oscar playing with Tabby. The woman deserved to be a Thorne.

"He's not normal. I did everything I could—" Lu risked a peek and almost kissed a teacup.

"Lies!" Veins bulged from the woman's face and her gray hair frizzed out in wild directions. Lightning bolts would soon fly from her fingers with all the friction generated from her temper. She grabbed another plate from the shrinking stack and hurled it Lu's direction.

It was a good thing her aim failed more than it succeeded. If Lu didn't get out of the kitchen soon, there'd be no cups and plates left. What would Ma Frances use then? Knives? Getting nicked by a plate was one thing, but a blade to the head or face? Lu hunched behind the line of chairs and scooted closer to the veranda door.

More ceramic shards rained down on her.

"I can't help he doesn't want me." She scooted another chair closer toward freedom.

"Everyone wants you. You just want to make Ma suffer."

Priscill. Curse the woman! She purposely sought to stir Ma Frances's wrath. A double crash. One plate grazed the top of Lu's head before spiraling into the bedroom behind her. The other crashed onto the floor ahead of her.

"You should thank me for gifting you to my favorite son—"

Lu made a blind lunge for the door and crashed into legs. She looked a long way up to Clint's mottled face, but he glowered at Ma Frances, not her.

"Clint. You're home." Priscill's footsteps crushed glass as she approached. She stepped around Lu and tried to kiss Clint.

He pushed her aside and fully entered the kitchen. "What's going on here?"

"Nothing to concern you." Priscill waved aside the mess of the room. "Lu couldn't get Andrew to come back home with her."

Clint squinted at Lu. "Couldn't or wouldn't?"

"You know Lu. Always making trouble. I'm sure she didn't even really try."

Clint's mouth curled into a satisfied grin. Whatever was going on in that man's head, Lu didn't like it.

Ma Frances stalked around Clint and jerked Lu to her feet. "You're his wife. Figure out what he wants and bring Andrew back here. I don't care what it takes."

The stairs creaked, and Oscar appeared sniffling and dragging the stuffed puppy Lu had sewed him. "Mommy."

Dodging Ma Frances's grasp, Lu reached Oscar before he hit the last step. She swooped him into her arms and hurried upstairs. Thankfully, no one followed. "Tell me what's wrong, baby."

Oscar's muffled cries soaked her shoulder with tears and snot, but anything was better than enduring Ma Frances's temper and Clint's lecherous smile. She kicked the door shut behind her as she carried Oscar inside her room, but the stupid thing bounced open again. After settling on the bed with Oscar cradled in her lap, he sniffed and sniveled his way through an explanation of some undecipherable nightmare.

What she wouldn't give to be able to protect her son from the nightmare they lived. It'd been foolish of her to think that she could manipulate Andrew the same way she did every man. He wasn't Irvine or Clint, and even Cyrus showed more interest in her than Andrew ever had. She should've known it was useless. He saw through the facade to her real worth—or lack of it. Had from the very first moment he refused to lay eyes on her. Her eyes drifted to the dressing table filled with products Ma Frances insisted she needed. Her only worth came from those tonics. Yet even she was not foolish enough to believe beauty would last forever. Eventually, she'd turn into a shriveled old hag, and then any use to the Thorne family would be extinguished.

Soft snores and a relaxed body indicated Oscar won the battle against his nightmares. If only she could do the same. Escape was the only way, and Andrew the key. There had to be some way to manipulate that man to serve her needs. Jealousy? Likely not. But the man did have a soft spot for a woman in trouble.

"I'm glad to hear you didn't give Andrew your best. I know you're really savin' that for me." Clint's voice jolted her from her thoughts. He closed the door and approached with the swagger of a man drunk on obsession and delusions.

Skunk tails! She should've prioritized securing the door. "You best leave before Ma Frances realizes you're up here."

"No worries there. She left to find Andrew. We have the whole house to ourselves."

Lu stiffened. "Where's Priscill?"

"Outside tossin' trash, and Cyrus is finishing up hidin' last night's loot. Set Brat on the floor so we can take advantage of everyone's absence."

"Get out."

"Is that any way to treat the man who holds your secret in his hand?"

"I don't have any secrets."

"Not even your plan to run off with Walt or your runnin' with Oscar this mornin'?"

Her throat tightened around the words and threatened to cut them off. "Walt was just a mark. And I was going for help this morning."

"I don't think Ma will see it that way, but if you give me what I want, she'll never know." His finger traced down her cheek to the top button of her blouse. "What do you say?"

Keeping Oscar on her lap would keep Clint from achieving his purposes, but it wouldn't keep him from trying. She eased her hand under her pillow and grasped the hilt of the dagger kept there for such a time as this.

He reached for Oscar. "I'll take him."

The door bounced open. "Clint Russel Thorne, you get downstairs right now."

He snapped straight and put a step of distance between them. "I wasn't doing nothin', Ma, I swear."

At the woman's glare and pointed finger, the man cowed like a whipped puppy and backed out of the room with hands raised.

As soon as he was out of sight, she turned on Lu. "I won't tolerate you tussling with Clint. Andrew's downstairs, and I expect you to see to it he never wants to leave again. Change into something better than that potato sack and be downstairs in five minutes." She pivoted on her heel and slammed the door.

Oscar whimpered, and Lu rocked him as her mind suffocated under the growing pile of troubles. If Clint caught her alone again, he wouldn't bother toying with her. He'd go straight to taking what he wanted. Survival depended upon her ability to make Andrew want to love and protect her.

It was well past the five minutes before Oscar relaxed back into a deep sleep. She whipped out her red saloon gown, fixed her hair so it drew attention low, and painted a smattering of red on her lips. Not even Molly could pull off the full turnaround in such a short time. Andrew better appreciate her attempts, for both their sakes.

She jogged halfway down the stairs and slowed near the bottom. Confident, calm, mysterious. The triple threat. No, that was what worked on other men. Manipulating Andrew would require a different technique. The man seemed to like rescuing her, and she could play a needy damsel all he wanted.

She entered the kitchen, where Priscill was sweeping up the shards. Andrew stood with his profile to her while Ma Frances blocked his exit to the veranda and prattled endlessly. By his disgusted expression, the experience was as pleasing as eating a cockroach.

The *mmm-mmm* of a man savoring food came from Clint. "I didn't realize you were bringin' dessert to the table."

He leaned back on two chair legs and feasted upon her appearance. Shivers zinged down her back, and it took everything within her not to retreat.

"Shut your piehole, Clint. She's my wife and you won't talk to her like that."

Lu's attention snapped to Andrew. Had he just spoken up for her?

Clint smirked. "I got more right than you. I know how sweet—"

Priscill jabbed the broom into his chair leg, and Clint toppled. Over the top of his head, Priscill stabbed Lu with eye-daggers before dropping to give false apologies. Clint cursed and slapped away her fawning. The pair deserved each other.

"Quit rolling on the floor and go get Cyrus like I told you." Ma Frances kicked Clint in the side. "Dinner's ready."

When Clint moved too slowly for her liking, Ma Frances wrenched the broom from Priscill's hands and swatted him with the bristles embedded with shards. He hustled out the door.

"Going out?" Andrew's question came from near Lu's elbow.

She forced down the dread in her throat and adopted a seductive mask before facing him. Her saucy grin almost faltered at the revulsion clearly displayed on his face. She should've ignored Ma Frances's directive and came down in her skirt and blouse. At least when she'd worn that, he'd shown a modicum of interest. Instead of helping her cause, her faithful red dress had crushed it.

"Of course she's not. This is all for you." Ma Frances turned a bright smile on him. "Ain't she enticing?"

"No."

"Come now, Andrew. Look at her. She's exactly the kind of woman all Thorne men desire."

He jerked his gaze toward Ma Frances. "Not me. I don't want a harlot and a thief."

The verbal slap destroyed all pretense of a mask and Lu plowed over Ma Frances's indignation. "Well, I don't want a husband, period. Especially not you."

Andrew's face snapped her direction. Instead of anger, unexplainable regret pinched his features. "I didn't—"

Ma Frances interrupted whatever he was about to say. "You most certainly do. Oscar needs a father, and you need someone who can keep you under thumb."

Too tired to hold back her frustration, Lu turned on the woman. "What? Afraid your thumb isn't big enough to control me?"

Ma Frances's hand raised, and Lu braced for impact. Andrew's hand shot out. A puff of air hit her face, but nothing else. She glanced from Ma Frances's open hand, stayed by Andrew's grip around the wrist, to the seething anger Ma Frances's eyes directed toward Andrew. The man did not cow or release his hold but met her fury with unshakable courage. For a moment, the image of Jack tackling the giant head-on sprung to Lu's mind. A ridiculous notion, but she couldn't deny the admiration that blossomed from the idea.

"If you want me to stay here, then there are going to be rules. Otherwise, I take Lu and Oscar with me to an undisclosed location." Andrew released Ma Frances's wrist and pulled Lu closer to him. "First, no hitting my wife. Any discipline comes from me alone."

The momentary lift of hope dropped from her stomach and hit the floor. Ma Frances was strong enough to pack a wallop, but nothing in comparison to the strength of the Thorne men.

"Second, Oscar is my son now, and what I say goes. Third, I want the key to our room. No one will lock me in or invade my privacy. Understood?"

If Andrew believed Ma Frances's silent stare meant agreement, he was about to learn a lesson no rebellious Thorne ever forgot. Ma Frances stood rooted to the spot, face flushed and nostrils flaring. Lu held her breath as the seconds ticked. A slow sneer chiseled into Ma Frances's stony face.

"Fine, Son." She pulled the room key from a pocket and handed it to him. "But I have a few rules of my own. You're part of this family, and you're gonna act like it. I'm your mother and you'll respect me as such." An emphatic nod accompanied a don't-you-cross-me-again glare. "We have dinner together every day at four o'clock sharp. Be here. If you have a scheme, you hatch it with the family. Your brothers need something, you help. Anything you earn or steal comes to me. We are a family, and no one gets left behind again."

Contempt flashed across his face, but he gave a curt nod.

"Good. Now have a seat. I made something special to celebrate your homecoming and marriage."

"Should I wake Oscar?" Lu eyed the counter where the pestle and mortar were pulled out for use.

"No. Let the poor boy sleep. I'll make him something else when he's ready."

Ma Frances's answer confirmed Lu's suspicions. "Something else" meant Ma Frances had poisoned dinner just enough to teach Andrew how much he needed her and to punish everyone else for their earlier misbehavior. With no ipecac left in the house, there would be no lessening the effects this time. By morning, the entire household would be miserable and Ma Frances in her glory.

Lu sat next to Andrew at the table and whispered, "Eat as little as possible. I'll take care of the rest."

If Ma Frances caught her filching food off Andrew's plate and stuffing it in her pockets, she'd suffer more than food poisoning, but until he learned to fend for himself, she'd spare him some suffering. When he frowned, she risked one more whisper. "Trust me."

CHAPTER 14

TRUSTING ANY THORNE WAS NOT a mistake Andrew would make, but Lu's tightened features as Frances set an extra-large serving of gravy-laden fried pork chop and mashed potatoes in front of her made him reconsider. Frances had already attempted to poison him at breakfast. A second attempt made sense. What he didn't understand was Lu's motivation for warning him.

"I'll be watching to make sure you eat every bite, Lu. I made it especially the way you like."

Lu's false smile trembled at the edges. "Thank you."

"Priscill, go ring the bell and tell those boys to hurry up."

Frances served him an equal portion, and when she returned to the stove, Lu transferred Andrew's pork chop to her plate. Lu then scooped his potatoes and gravy onto the napkin hidden on her lap beneath the table little by little. When heavy steps approached from the parlor, she snatched his fork, stirred the remains around his plate, and then flicked a spattering of gravy at his face and shirt. Clint, Cyrus, and Priscill entered the room, and she shoved the fork back into his hand.

With theatrics worthy of a stage, Lu inspected Andrew. "You can't wait for the rest of us before shoveling food down your gullet?"

"Do you want more? I've got plenty." Frances set smaller servings in front of Clint, Cyrus, and Priscill as they took their seats across from him and Lu.

117

By the uneasy glances they spared their plates, they all knew what awaited them.

"No, thank you."

Andrew studied the remaining scraps on his plate. The pinkish color of the normally white gravy suggested Frances's favorite method of poisoning hadn't changed since his childhood. He twisted to examine the counter next to the sink where Frances had been working. A mortar and pestle sat at the edge with a few kidney beans scattered around the surface. While powdered raw kidney beans weren't fatal, ingesting them would make for a miserable evening.

He glanced from his empty plate to Lu's full one. The quantity sitting in front of her was sure to make her sick for days. She obviously knew the consequences, so why spare him? Thornes did what was best for themselves, not others.

"Just look at us!" Frances sat at the head of the table and clasped her hands beneath her chin like a euphoric toddler with candy. "I never thought this day would come. It's just like old times."

Andrew eyed the bare spot before her and the heaping plates of poison in front of everyone else. *Definitely like old times.* "Aren't you going to eat?"

"I nibbled as I cooked. Besides, we're out of plates and I'd rather my children eat their fill." She scanned the table of untouched food. "So eat up. Now. Before it gets cold."

Each reluctantly retrieved their cutlery and poked at the gravy-doused meat like cats testing water.

"I didn't get to tell you, we ran into trouble at the train station last night." Even twenty-four years later, Andrew recognized Cyrus's distraction strategies.

"What sort of trouble?"

"Killing Walt wasn't enough to silence the snitch." Andrew's attention jerked away from Lu's stealthy attempts to remove food from her plate. "Two train agents were waiting for us inside the train car when we went to offload the bank's money."

"Those could've been the regular guards," Priscill said.

"I thought so too, 'til I heard one of them say they weren't expecting so many of us. We still got about half the loot, but reinforcements arrived and we had to hightail it out of there."

A storm cloud of fury washed away all remains of Frances's joy. "When I find out who's interfering with our operations, I'm gonna make them suffer worse than Walt."

"Speakin' of Walt"—Clint pushed his untouched plate away and leaned toward Andrew—"how do you know him?"

Andrew bobbed a shoulder, unaffected by the intimidation attempt. He had anticipated the question and already worked out his answer with Josiah. "I don't know him. Joe saw Eli's ad in the Evansville newspaper looking for a buyer, and I came along to sell my remedy."

"So you didn't know he was a US Marshal?"

"Had I known there was a marshal in town, I wouldn't have set foot in the county. I've got enough warrants out for my arrest to make me worth hauling in."

Clint's lips twitched, like the thought of hauling Andrew in was appealing enough to risk Frances's wrath.

Frances patted Andrew's hand. "No need to fear. I took care of him, and Eli won't pose a threat even though Lu failed to kill him."

At Frances's pointed look, Lu diverted the fork holding food from her handkerchief to her mouth. "I can't help the man was gone before I could feed him that pie."

Her confession of attempted murder curdled his stomach worse than any raw kidney bean could. "Sounds like it's a good thing I didn't eat it instead."

Lu dropped her gaze and picked at another small bite. "God's mercy to be sure."

Frances harrumphed. "None of that God stuff here. We got lucky, that's all." She shifted conversation to Cyrus. "Did we get enough money to start counterfeiting banknotes?"

Maybe this case wouldn't last long after all. With them actively seeking a new venue of income, they'd likely be easier to catch.

Cyrus laid his napkin over the full plate. "Not if you want to build that addition and get Oscar all those gifts too."

"We'll wait on the addition. The more I think about it, the more I want to expand into banknotes. The profit margin's bigger, and we won't be dependent on access to gold."

"We don't have the contacts or know-how to do it."

"My mind's set, so make it happen. We can't risk robbing more trains or the Boonville Bank to keep the smelts going, not until we figure out who's snitching on us."

Andrew couldn't have contrived a better opportunity to bring in more operatives, and Broderick Cosgrove's experiences made him perfect for the job. "I have a friend who prints money." All heads swiveled toward Andrew. "I'll see if he'd be interested in moving his operations here."

Frances rubbed her hands together in anticipation. "Good. Now to dispatch that snitch before we get set up. Have you noticed anyone hanging around the tack shop or anything left behind that doesn't belong to Eli or Walt?"

"Nothing I've noticed." Not that he'd share. He was as interested in finding the informant as them, albeit for different purposes. "I'll head back to the shop after dinner and see what I can find."

"Not tonight, you won't. You have a wife to get acquainted with."

"I have a lifetime for that. I'd think finding a snitch would be more important."

"It can wait one night. You're staying here, and that's final."

Lu's nails dug into his thigh.

"Understood."

The grip on his leg disappeared, and Lu returned to her subterfuge.

"Lu!" Frances shot from her seat. "What are you doing?"

Something heavy and warm plunked into his pocket, and it squished when he adjusted his coat. A glimpse at Lu's empty lap confirmed that a napkin full of mashed potatoes was the culprit.

"I'm eating."

"Don't lie to me." Frances marched over, heaved Lu to standing, and scanned the surrounding area. "Where are you hiding all that food?"

"I ate it."

"Then where's your napkin?"

By the accelerating burn of Frances's temper, Lu was about to be struck despite their agreement. Andrew took his napkin from his lap and tossed it beneath Lu's chair. "Looks like it fell to the floor." He retrieved and then held it up.

Seeds of doubt sprouted across her face. "Fine, but you two are switching spots."

He shifted to Lu's vacated seat and Lu took his.

Frances replaced Lu's almost empty plate with one dripping in gravy. "Eat. Every. Bite."

Lu's complexion acquired the color of rotten meat as she shoveled forkfuls into her mouth, wincing with every swallow. Frances's sneer grew as the number of Lu's remaining bites shrank.

Andrew balled his fists beneath the table. Frances's treatment of Lu was intolerable. As a Christian, he should have compassion for the broken woman who gave birth to him, but all he felt was hatred for who she was and what she did. *God, help me to see her through Your eyes and to forgive her as You command. Because I can't do it. She doesn't deserve it.*

Cyrus interrupted his silent prayer. "My contact at the Boonville Train Depot is looking into how the train agents found out about our plans. We'll have information soon, and then you can do whatever you want with the snitch."

Lu's fork clattered on the plate. "Excuse me." She sprang from the table, hand over mouth, and sprinted upstairs.

"Excellent, Cyrus. Keep me informed." Frances addressed Andrew. "You ought to go check on Lu. Maybe bring her some of your remedy. It appears she's sick." A satisfied smirk curled her lips. "I hope it's not contagious."

Andrew collected the single satchel that held his belongings and marched upstairs. The woman's statement made it clear she had every intention of his becoming ill by morning. Frustration and anger roiled through him. The woman was loathsome, and sending her to jail was the only thing that could mollify him. When he breached the stairs, Lu beckoned him into what appeared to be a child's room at the end of the garret. Late afternoon light from the windows illuminated her sickly pallor. He might have no love for her, but it gut-punched him to see her in such a state all because she'd protected him.

"Unless you'd like to relive Oscar's illness, you'll want to sleep in here tonight."

While it provided the perfect excuse, he couldn't allow her to suffer alone. "I can take care of you as well as I did him."

"I prefer to suffer in private. But thank you for saving Oscar." Her gaze wandered to the other room. "I don't know what I would've done if I'd lost him."

"His living is God's grace alone. I had nothing to do with it."

"Then I'm glad He at least cares for Oscar."

Her words served as a reminder that Lu lacked the assurance of Christ's love in her life, and it was his temporary duty to point her to it. "God cares for you too, you know."

"Trust me. He doesn't want me any more than you do."

Andrew scrubbed a hand down his face. How was he supposed to respond to that? He *didn't* want her, but God did, and being that godly example to Lu meant laying his own opinions aside and viewing her through God's eyes. He dropped his hand and regarded the sick, vulnerable woman before him—his bride. Like the church was called the bride of Christ. Perhaps the pastor's statement about treating Lu like the woman of his dreams was more about reflecting God's love than actually accepting their marriage as permanent. Not that applying that principle was any easier. It still risked his reputation. His calling as an operative. He released a frustrated breath. Why couldn't Josiah have been the one to marry Lu instead?

"Give me time, Lu. I may not have wanted this marriage, but that doesn't mean I don't want it to work now that we're stuck. What I don't want is for you to seduce me. If you need something, tell me. I'll do my best to provide it. If I'm being hardheaded, convince me with reason."

Her face screwed up like he'd spoken a different language. Given that she'd married Irvine and lived with the Thornes, what he suggested probably was a foreign concept.

A high-pitched gurgle fomented in her stomach and she winced. "I think it's best we part ways now."

"Allow me to take care of you."

"No. I'll be fine. It's not my first, nor will it be my last, time. For you either. I hope you're a good actor. Ma Frances will expect you to be as sick as me and in need of care come morning. Let her fawn over you, and tell her how glad you are she's here to take care of you. And for heaven's sake, don't eat or drink anything she gives you. It will only extend your illness." Her stomach gurgled again, and she scooted past him in a hurry. "Good night."

Andrew watched her dash into the room and slam the door. A few moments later, the sound of retching cut through the thin walls. Lord help him. Less that twelve hours into this mess and already his responsibilities as a temporary Christian husband muddled his responsibilities as an operative. No matter what that stubborn woman said, she needed to be cared for as much as Oscar had. Andrew procured a pillow and blanket from Oscar's bed and set up camp outside Lu's door. If she needed anything, he'd be right there to get it.

CHAPTER 15

THREE NIGHTS PASSED BEFORE LU could leave the bed without running for the privy or getting violently ill at even the whiff of food. Of course, it didn't help that Ma Frances watched her eat every meal to ensure she suffered the longest of everyone in the house. If it hadn't been for Andrew sneaking her untainted bread and water, she'd probably be too weak to stand now. Lu opened the garret window to air out the sick smell of the upstairs and stared at the Newcombs' house and the church ruins next door.

Mary suggested a man would do a lot for the woman he loved—even leave the Thornes behind. Was it more possible than Lu thought? After Andrew's surprisingly gentle care of her, a fluttering hope developed—one that Lu wasn't sure what to do with. Should she cling to it or release it to the brutal winds of reality? Could he love her and provide freedom for her and Oscar? He clearly said he didn't want her usual attraction ploys to be used on him, and she'd respect that. Strangely enough, part of her actually wanted Andrew to like her for something other than her physical desirability. Not that she had much else to work with. She had no education to speak of. None of her domestic skills were above average, and her manners lacked refinement—but then again, so did his.

She fingered the skirt of her dress and grinned wryly. Never again would she be able to think of it as anything but a mud-dragged circus tent. He seemed to appreciate the green ensemble from the morning they married. Once she finished chores, maybe she'd slip into that and find a way to sequester Andrew away. Until she knew him better, she wouldn't begin to know how to convince him to leave.

The door behind her creaked, and she turned around the same moment Oscar launched into her legs. She toppled, and he bounced onto her middle, reawakening her nausea.

"I'm Jack the Giant Killer!"

"Better be careful, Jack. Where there's one giant, there's likely another." Andrew stepped from Oscar's room.

Oscar jumped to his feet, raising a pretend sword, and charged toward him. Andrew sidestepped, then caught Oscar around the waist and tossed him into the air. Oscar's squealing laughter wrung the breath from Lu. Not since Irvine died had that laugh been heard. And Andrew's face! Years of life shed from it, rendering him just as handsome as Pretty Boy.

"Do it again!"

Andrew obliged another four times before setting him on the ground. "Remember our deal. Go play by yourself for a few minutes so your mother and I can talk."

Oscar disappeared into his room.

She struggled to shake her tongue free of the shock they'd put her in. "Your deal?"

Andrew shrugged sheepishly. "I told him I'd let him ride on my shoulders all the way to the tack shop."

"Ma Frances is letting you leave with him?" The woman must have really been taken by Andrew's return.

"What does she have to do with anything? Oscar's my responsibility, not hers."

Bless that fool. The man might be educated, but he obviously wasn't very bright. "Haven't you learned anything? Ma Frances's word is law. She ain't gonna let you wander off with Oscar alone, not when you've already proven you're willing to defy her. You may be her long-lost child, but she'll choose Oscar over any of us every time."

He was quiet for several breaths. "You obviously know a great deal more about Frances than I. Help me get reestablished with the Thornes, and I'll see to it you have as many respectable dresses as you want."

And there was that brutal wind of reality. If Andrew wanted to be reestablished with the family, it wasn't likely he'd be willing to leave. "All I want is protection from Clint."

"You have it."

He spoke the words with the conviction of an unbreakable promise—which was ridiculous. No one kept promises. But it did give her pause. How far could she push? Conscious someone might hear what she said through the grate, she drew closer and dropped her voice. "What if that meant taking Oscar and I away from here? Running away to live on our own, without Ma Frances or Clint."

His suddenly shrewd eyes made her regret the question. "Do you want to leave? I know you ran before."

Why must the daft man speak so loudly? She turned her back on him to shut the window. If she didn't get control of her mask, he'd know the truth and use it against her. "Of course not. The Thornes are the only family I've got. I'd do anything for them. And I wasn't running away, I was running for help. Remember?" His reflection bounced back at her in the windowpane, doubt on full display.

"There is no need to fear Clint here. I'll protect you and Oscar."

"I'm not afraid." To prove it, she presented him with her sauciest grin.

"Good, because I need to stay close to the Thornes, and for now, that means we stay here."

Why had she even bothered to hope that this marriage would be any different? When forced to choose, loyalty to the Thorne family would always win over her. She'd known it all along, but the confirmation of it brought a surprising burn to her eyes. She lifted her chin and blinked several times to keep the tears from falling.

Andrew cleared his throat. "I'm going to the tack shop to search for clues of the snitch. Finding an answer will help me curry favor with Clint and Cyrus."

The change of subject washed her with relief. "Good luck currying favor with those two, but it might be worth a try."

Aside from formulating escape plans during her illness, she'd pondered the possibility of another informant. She certainly hadn't warned the station master of the impending robbery, but Walt never mentioned anyone other than her as a source of information. If she discovered the identity of the other informant, she could determine if she had an ally or an enemy. They could be just as intent on getting her in a hangman's noose as she was intent on fleeing with Oscar before the Thornes corrupted his innocent spirit. "Let me talk to Ma Frances. I'll convince her to allow the three of us to go. I spent a lot of time at the tack shop apartment. I'll know if something isn't Eli's or Walt's."

"I'd rather not hear about your exploits with other men." His flat tone held an edge of censure, but what else could she expect? He thought her a harlot and a thief. Of course he'd think her familiar with the tack shop for all the wrong reasons.

"Give me thirty minutes to get Ma Frances to agree, and then we can start our snitch search."

On the way to the tack shop, Lu trailed behind Andrew, who carried Oscar on his shoulders, and Cyrus. Thanks to three days of a fully recovered and overly exuberant Oscar, Ma Frances was more than happy for Andrew to take Oscar out from underfoot—with stipulations. Much to Lu's chagrin, Cyrus joined them on their outing.

"Uncle Andrew! Stop that!" Oscar squealed again as Andrew did a hop-step and jostled Oscar in a playful manner.

Lu smiled despite herself. How could this dour man with the verbal gentleness of a charging bull be so free and joyful with Oscar? Never would she have pegged him as the type to tolerate children, let alone enjoy them. Though, in all fairness, Clint was the only Thorne who hated children. Another reason to be glad Clint wasn't the one escorting them, even if Cyrus was grumpier than a spooked porcupine because he'd been woken up before noon. She glanced toward the sky. Was this a grace from Him or just coincidence?

Oscar filled the silence of the unanswered question with his usual conversations about giants, Tabby, and Jack the puppy. When they reached the tack shop, Andrew swung Oscar to the ground and opened the door.

Oscar bolted straight for an empty rocking chair and began stacking checker pieces into a tower. "Uncle Cyrus, play with me!"

Cyrus muttered but took the seat opposite. "You do the searching. I'll keep Runt entertained."

The way he tilted the seat back, it was more likely he'd let Oscar have the run of the store while he napped.

To her disappointment, Pretty Boy exited the storage room with a humorless man dressed in patched farmer's clothes. In a sweeping glance, they took in the room and its occupants. By Pretty Boy's expression, he wasn't happy with the invasion.

Lu stopped Oscar's vigorous rocking and prayed he wouldn't cause trouble for Andrew's friend. "Remember my rules. No climbing or jumping. Don't leave the store. Better yet, don't leave this chair."

"What do I get?"

Lu chewed on the inside of her cheek. How would she ever break him of expecting rewards just for doing what he was supposed to? Ma Frances saw no problem with it, but Lu didn't like the entitled attitude it was forming in him. If she didn't start correcting it soon, he'd be as demanding as Clint in no time.

Andrew joined her and pinned Oscar with a look that'd make Ma Frances proud. "You'll get the satisfaction of doing the right thing. If you don't do what you're told, Joe here will set you to work mucking the horse stalls."

Oscar's nose bunched. "What's mucking?"

"You'll be scooping out the horses' poop, Runt. Best stay in that chair and let me close my eyes." Cyrus did just that and was snoring within seconds.

Oscar pouted, but soon became distracted by stacking the pieces and battling the towers. Lu had no doubt once he bored with that, the allure of mucking stalls would tempt him into doing the job with a hefty side of troublemaking. Adventure and muck went hand in hand.

"What can I help you with?" Pretty Boy stood behind the counter like a businessman rather than a friend. Had his realization Andrew was a Thorne damaged their relationship? After all, Clint and his friends had tossed the store last month.

"I apologize for not checking in. Frances's cooking made everyone sick." Andrew wandered toward the counter. "They revealed some disturbing news, though. Walt Kinder was a US Marshal, and his snitch is still on the loose."

Pretty Boy's gaze swung to her and then Cyrus before returning to Andrew. "Do they know who?"

"No, but identifying the person has become a priority. Lu thinks there might be evidence upstairs."

Pretty Boy's stance eased. "You're welcome to search, though you aren't likely to find anything."

"Are you going to make introductions?" The man who hadn't stopped scowling at Lu since he entered the room finally spoke.

Andrew straightened like the man held the same power over him as Ma Frances did over the rest of the family. "Captain, I'd like you to meet some of my family. That's my brother Cyrus in the rocker, my nephew Oscar knocking down towers, and this is Lu."

"Your wife." Given the way he hurled the words, Pretty Boy had probably informed him of her assumed profession.

Maybe he'd like to learn her real profession. She advanced and jabbed him in the chest while her other hand made quick work of finding his pocket. "I'd watch what sort of tone you take with me, *Captain*. It sounded like you meant that as an insult."

Pretty Boy hurried around the counter, wrested her arm, and guided her away. "Don't pay him any mind. He's just miffed that Doc married you and not his daughter."

Lu stumbled. Andrew'd been planning on marrying someone else?

That meant the likelihood of him ever loving her enough to run away equaled nil.

At her glance his way, Andrew shook his head. "His daughter is twelve. That was never going to happen."

Captain's menacing glower declared otherwise.

"And I'd appreciate it if you didn't steal from my friends." Andrew pulled the wallet from the hand hidden behind her back and returned it to Captain.

The man reared back, and she envisioned steam puffing from his ears like an engine at full tilt. At any moment his control might derail. She edged closer to Pretty Boy, glad he stood as a barrier between them.

"Is there any chance you'll be running into Broderick soon?" Andrew continued. "I've got an opportunity for him. The Thornes want to expand into banknotes."

To her relief, Captain redirected his attention and the steam sputtered out. "I have business with him in a few days. If you give me the details, I wouldn't be surprised if he arrived within a fortnight."

"Good. We'll go upstairs, and I can fill you in while Lu looks for evidence of a snitch. Joe, do you mind staying down here and keeping an eye on that rascal?"

Pretty Boy released her arm. "Which one?"

She whispered, "Cyrus might be some trouble when he's awake, but Oscar—Oscar'll open every crate, barrel, and bag if you don't keep your eye on him."

"Sounds like your typical boy to me. I'll keep a vigilant watch."

Andrew and Captain were on the top stair before she caught up, abruptly ending their whispered conversation.

Once inside the apartment, Andrew turned to Lu. "You search in the parlor, and I'll start in the kitchen."

For being a man who wanted to win the favor of his family by finding the snitch, he certainly didn't seem too concerned with an actual search. Already, he was talking through breakfast options with Captain. Men and their stomachs. Although, did she really want him to be the one to find evidence of an informant if there were any to be had? Her key out of this miserable family may very well be the snitch everyone sought.

As soon as Andrew and Captain disappeared into the kitchen, Lu snuck into Walt's old bedroom. With Eli's penchant for gossip, Walt wouldn't hide anything where Eli might stumble upon it. She left the door cracked so she could hear if Andrew or Captain approached and took stock of the room. It'd probably surprise Andrew to know she'd never actually been inside either of the bedrooms. After marrying Irvine, her so-called exploits had been limited to illusions of fantasy to get men to do what she wanted.

Whoever slept here obviously didn't care about making their bed before starting the day. The quilt and sheet were kicked to the foot of the narrow bed, and the pillow lay on the floor. Stacks of notes scattered the surface of the nightstand, barely leaving room for the kerosene lamp or empty glass pushed to the back. A quick perusal indicated they were probably more of Pretty Boy's lists—useless to her and unlikely to have any connection to Walt. Anything Walt left behind would be long gone or hidden. She opened the nightstand drawer and rummaged through. Shaving soap, razor, comb, pomade, paper, pen, and, crammed into the back corner, a small cedar box.

Lu pulled it out and flipped open the hinged lid. Two wedding bands lay on black velvet, and attached to the lid was the photo of a grinning woman and a much younger Pretty Boy. So the flirt once had a wife. Interesting. Perhaps she left him after catching him one too many times with another woman. Love was a fleeting thing, after all.

She picked up the smaller band, and the old ache spread across her chest. She and Irvine had matching bands once—until he decided melting the two-dollar bands to gild one more counterfeit double eagle was more valuable than the visible reminder of their marriage. What would it be like to walk around again with the announcement that she belonged to someone who'd protect her? After setting the box aside, she pushed the smaller ring onto her finger. A little snug for her liking, but not bad. Would Andrew buy rings and publicly claim her as his? Or would he be like Irvine and claim her only when it suited him?

Best not to think about it. She tried to yank the ring off, but it refused to move over the bulge of her finger. Even wetting it with her mouth didn't get the stupid thing to come off. Oh, for pity's sake! She'd have to sneak into the kitchen and use soap to slide it off after she finished her search.

She returned the box to its corner and closed the drawer. The rest of the sparse room held only a few pegs for clothes and a commode cabinet against the wall. Her nose wrinkled. If Walt had hidden information there, it would stay hidden. Nothing hung on the walls, so she checked for loose floorboards. Nothing.

"Who was your snitch, Walt?" She planted her hands on her hips and blew out a breath as she peered at the tin-plated ceiling.

Eli had always seemed a bit eccentric, but putting costly details in this squalor of a place proved it. The least he could've done was install all the decorative pieces in the same direction instead of leaving one cock-eyed and in complete opposition to the others. She eyed the odd piece with chipped edges. Had someone pried it free?

"Walt, you're brilliant."

Lu dragged the commode beneath the piece and climbed on top. Her palms barely reached the ceiling, but with a pop to her toes, she shifted the tile. A dusting of plaster rained down. A few more attempts and the tile came completely free and fell on her head, along with an odd-sized wallet that thudded to the floor. She left the wallet there for a moment and checked for any other paperwork or hidden items in the ceiling. Satisfied that nothing else remained, she wiggled the tile back into place and climbed down. After returning the commode and wiping up the dust, she retrieved the wallet from the floor. Except it couldn't be a wallet.

The black rectangle resembled a small, thin book and weighed more than Pretty Boy's wallet had that first night. She flipped open the cover to find a typed document fixed to one side and a silver five-pointed star pinned on the other. Over the years she'd seen plenty of lawmen wearing something similar, though none anywhere as nice. Even Walt's had been nothing more than a circular piece of tin with triangles cut out to look like a star in the middle. This was different, and certainly didn't belong to him.

She touched the two giant letters stamped in the center of the star. She struggled to pull from the decades-old reading lessons she'd failed, but it was no use. She couldn't recognize the letters, nor the words curving above and below them. Whoever this star belonged to had to be important. Maybe even the key to still escaping the family without having to risk jail time herself.

Pulling her skirt waist loose, she tucked the book into the only pocket inaccessible from the outside—her safety measure for hiding anything she wanted kept away from prying paws. After one last careful check of the room, she tiptoed out and shut the door behind her. Andrew peeked his head into the hall, and she scrambled to look behind the only painting.

"Come eat. I've made breakfast." He disappeared into the kitchen again.

A fragrant and enticing aroma greeted her when she breathed. Her stomach growled in response, anxious for anything not poisoned by Ma Frances's hand.

When she entered the kitchen, he set a bowl of oatmeal and a steaming mug on the table. "I didn't think you'd want eggs and the like yet. The tea should help settle any queasiness you still feel."

Had he really made her a breakfast with consideration to her needs? She glanced at Captain's egg- and ham-laden plate. It would've been easier for Andrew to give her the same instead of laboring over oatmeal.

The captain laid his fork down and stood. He made no disguise of his disgust as he pushed in his chair.

She waved her spoon at his untouched meal. "Aren't you going to eat?"

"I've lost my appetite." He exited without another comment, and the door banged in his wake a few moments later.

"He's a pleasant fellow." She scooped a bite of oatmeal and sniffed it cautiously. She'd yet to meet a male Thorne who could cook anything other than hard eggs and warmed beans. The oatmeal didn't smell burnt, but the oats could be undercooked. Still, anything was better than Ma Frances's poisoned food. She spooned a bite into her mouth, surprised to find the texture perfect and the taste sweet.

Andrew claimed Captain's seat. "If he's pleasant, then you must think me charming."

Lu choked on her bite and then pounded her chest. Was that a joke coming from *him*? His ghost of a smile suggested it was, and it only made her choke all the more. He shot from his chair and walloped her on the back. Oatmeal spewed from her mouth, but at least she could breathe again.

He passed her a napkin but frowned when he noticed the hand still pressed against her chest. "Where'd you get that ring?"

Lu rammed her hand into her lap. She'd forgotten she wore it, and embarrassment flooded her cheeks. "I found it in a drawer and thought I'd try it on."

"Which drawer?" He held out his hand like he expected her to hand the ring over.

"It's kind of . . . stuck."

"Give me your hand." When she obliged, he yanked at the band.

"Ow!"

"Sorry." He started twisting and pulling only slightly more gently than the tugging. She gripped the chair with her other hand as he continued to pry. "Where'd you find it?"

"In the nightstand in Walt's room, with Pretty Boy's stuff."

"It's Joe's?" His frowned deepened as he gave another hard tug. At her yelp, he released a frustrated sigh. "Come to the sink. We'll soap it up."

She followed him, and he wet a bar before scrubbing it over her finger above and below the ring. With the next tug, it flew off and rolled along the floor.

He retrieved it and jammed it into his pocket. "I'll get you a ring. You don't have to steal one."

She huffed and rotated her back to him, washing the soap from her hand. There was no way she'd allow him to see how much a ring actually meant to her, and she didn't want one given out of obligation. "I don't want a ring from you. I was merely curious. Do you know what wearing a ring would do to my ability to pick pockets? It's best if those I swindle don't realize we're married."

"Everyone in town already knows we're married, and I don't see a ring diminishing their interest."

Well, that was promising. She swiveled to brace her forearms on the sink and sent him a playful smile. "Are you jealous?"

His gaze swept the length of her like she'd intended but then locked back on her face. "A man doesn't have to be jealous to not want other men touching his wife."

"Too bad. I rather liked the idea of you being jealous." He opened his mouth, but she pressed on. No need to hear any false words from him. "I didn't find any evidence of the snitch, so we'll just have to keep our eyes and ears open. Who knows? Maybe Cyrus's contact at the station will have information." Though she desperately hoped he wouldn't, at least not enough for Cyrus to beat her to the other snitch.

"We can only hope. Finish your breakfast. I'm going to put this ring back and do my own search."

Lu watched him walk out, leaving her lost in a myriad of emotions. It was going to be harder to dislike the man than she'd thought. She took another bite of oatmeal and sighed. Especially if he cooked for her often.

CHAPTER 16

NEVER DID ANDREW EXPECT TO feel a kinship with Hosea from the Bible. Yet here he sat, forced to watch from a corner saloon table as his faithless wife flirted and catered to every man with a coin purse. Men who *knew* she was married to Andrew but gave no objections as she caressed their faces, planted kisses, and whispered who knew what seductions into their ears. It might be a sham marriage, but *they* didn't know that. The beginnings of jealousy nipped at Andrew like a dog he couldn't shake. God saw past His jealousy to Israel's eventual redemption, but Andrew was not God. The experience of a faithless wife destroyed all of his willingness to submit to his temporary role. How was he supposed to treat Lu as the wife of his dreams when she refused to behave like one?

"It's a good thing your marriage isn't real. I don't know that I could stand to watch my wife sit on another man's lap." Josiah's eyes followed Lu as she flounced toward Bill.

An ache spread through Andrew's clenched jaw as Bill leaned in for a kiss. Andrew turned his back on the scene lest he stomp over and knock out a few of Bill's teeth before dragging Lu from the saloon. Whether or not she was purposefully trying to make him jealous, she'd achieved it.

He topped off his cold coffee with some from the fresh pot Horace brought to the table and changed the subject. He could only stomach so much tonight. "Did you find out anything from the station master in Boonville?"

Josiah nodded. "The informant is a woman, but he couldn't give much more of a description than that. She wore several layers of veils, seemed to disguise her voice, and wore a dress so baggy that it left little room for identification."

"What about height?"

"She wore an extra tall hat and heeled boots, so he couldn't say exactly. However, with those on, she stood about eye level with him, and he's five seven."

"So likely taller than the average woman."

An informant who was both female and knowledgeable about the gang's movements significantly reduced the circle of possibilities. Andrew's gaze drifted to where Lu leaned against the counter, flaunting her chest as she filched another coin purse. She did have an overly large dress and was taller than most the women around. Add in that she'd mentioned wanting to leave the family and that stacked enough pennies to buy some doubt. Not much, though. After all, she'd attempted to murder Eli, stolen without remorse, and had no qualms with exhibiting her blatant disregard for their marriage vows. She seemed as criminal as the rest of them. But he wasn't foolish enough to completely dismiss the prospect that she was the informant.

"See if you can find any evidence that Lu and Walt were more than casual acquaintances."

Josiah choked on his coffee. "Her? You don't think . . ."

"I don't, but I won't rule it out either. Anyway, Frances forced Cyrus to invite me to the weekly game of cards with some of the other gang members later tonight. I'll get their wives' names, and we can start branching out from there."

"Trouble's coming." Josiah dropped his voice and tilted his head toward Clint, who'd appeared by the door.

When Clint spotted Andrew and Josiah, he stalked over, hooked Josiah's chair with his foot, and dragged it about-face. "You're behind on your protection fees, Joe. You don't get off free just on account of bein' Andrew's friend."

"Wouldn't dream of it." Josiah tossed a few bills on the table.

"Good. Now get lost." He swiped the money as Josiah wandered to the bar, far enough to give the illusion of obedience but close enough to help if needed.

Clint claimed Josiah's abandoned chair and thunked an arm on the table. "Just 'cause Ma told you to join us tonight don't mean you're welcome. Find somethin' else to do."

"Like what? Since the town learned I'm a Thorne, no one will buy my medicine."

Clint huffed. "Force them."

"That's not my way. Besides, Frances told you to bring me into the family business. Are you going to defy her?"

"We already got a snitch wreckin' our plans. We don't need someone else helpin' them."

"I'm not wrecking anyone's plans. I'm the one who's bringing in what we need to expand into banknotes."

"You've done nothin' but wreck our family since you been born. It's your fault that bank robbery went wrong. Your fault that Ma lost her mind. We can't even take a leak without her knowin' when, where, and why, while you been livin' free and easy."

"I wouldn't call my life free or easy."

"It's better than what we live with."

He'd had enough of Clint obstructing his admittance to the family business. Andrew planted his hands wide on the table and leaned forward. "I'm back, Clint, and there's nothing you can do to change it. Just tell me what I need to do for you to accept me."

Clint twisted his entire body Lu's direction, his smile vulgar. "Trade me your wife for mine."

Anger ramped Andrew's pulse into a thunderous stampede, and he white-knuckled the edge of the table to keep from launching himself at the blackguard. Clint didn't care about Andrew's presence in the family after all. He just wanted to manipulate the situation to gain Lu.

"Lu won't dare defy Ma, but I know I'm the one she really wants. Convince Ma of the trade and you'll not have troubles from me." Clint eyed him side-on. "It's not like you want her. You haven't even shared a bed once, while I've been makin' frequent visits."

That was an outright lie. Andrew'd slept in front of her door every night since they married, and Lu's whereabouts never went unaccounted for.

Footsteps approached, and Lu came into his periphery. "What's going on over here? Shouldn't you be breaking arms by now, Clint?"

"Just closing a business deal." Clint stood and winked as he walked past. "I'll see you tonight, sweetheart."

Lu whirled toward Andrew and seethed through gritted teeth. "You sold me to him?" He started to deny it, but she sliced the air. "I'm not your pawn to sacrifice. Nor am I a woman who sells herself to men, no matter what you might think of me."

His own anger erupted. "That's hard to believe, considering you allow men to put their hands all over you just for a bit of coin in your pocket."

"I don't have a choice."

"You always have a choice."

She scoffed. "Men's hands or Ma Frances's wrath. That's some choice. At least with picking pockets I can help others."

"You mean help yourself."

Her fists clenched and for a moment, it seemed like she might slug him. Instead, she released a protracted exhale. When she spoke, pained disappointment strained her voice. "So much for being the best of the Thornes. Good night, Andrew." Lu spun around and marched out the door.

Andrew growled as he scrubbed a hand over his face. Why did everything with this woman have to be so difficult? Of course, if he'd held his tongue inside his head instead of allowing his temper to get the best of him, it might have gone better. The only thing he should've said was the truth about the deal with Clint. There wasn't one, and there never would be.

Father, forgive me, and help me make this right. I don't want to be a Hosea to her, but I submit to your authority. Teach me to show her Your love and help me to want to, because I confess I don't at the moment.

"You can't let her stomp out of here." Josiah hauled him from the chair. "Go make amends before that woman builds a wall so tall you'll never get over it. We need her to talk to you."

Leave it to God to give him a physical push to pursue Lu. Andrew snagged his hat from the table. His displeasure at being married to the woman hadn't changed, but he'd do his duty and assure Lu of his protection.

Upon his exit, a flash of red disappeared down the alley between Grossman's and the tack shop. He blinked. Where was Lu going? As she veered away from the direction of the Thorne farm, Andrew followed, keeping to the cover of the shadows and far enough back to prevent detection. Although, given the way she stomped and muttered to herself, he needn't have bothered. She wasn't paying attention to anything beyond her angry rampage. Branches and weeds snapped underfoot, and birds scattered. Even a raccoon who'd started coming down a tree scuttled back to the top in the wake of her tirade. Only when she reached a log cabin in a clearing did she stop and look around.

Andrew ducked behind a tree. *Please, God. Don't let her be making a house call.*

He better drag her home before she offered her services to whoever waited inside. An invisible hand stayed him as Lu darted to the cover of a wagon. There, she again checked her surroundings before sprinting to the nearby rain barrel. She lifted the lid and removed a jar from inside. After unscrewing the top, she added the contents of a coin purse to the loose change already there, then returned the jar to its hiding place.

For more than an hour, Andrew followed as variations of the same scene repeated itself. Some of the locations he recognized as the homes of men who frequented Horace's. More often than not, the houses wove a tale of struggling and neglected families. What had Lu said— at least with picking pockets she could help someone? Who was this woman? She certainly wasn't what he thought.

Somewhere near Stendal, Lu stopped at the edge of an unfamiliar property and stood ramrod straight, her heavy breaths audible over the rustling leaves. Darkness had long taken over, but light from the cabin window cast her strained face in a soft glow. After a determined nod, she pulled out another coin purse and poured its contents into her palm. She tucked a couple of coins into her pocket, dashed to the porch, dropped the purse in a corner, and wheeled around. Before she made it three steps into the yard, the door swung open and a woman stepped out with a gun leveled at Lu.

Andrew's heart jumped from his chest to his throat, and he drew his revolver. He wouldn't kill the woman, but he wasn't about to let Lu get shot either.

"I told you to stop bringing that blood money. You can't buy your way out of murder."

Lu stepped into his line of fire with hands raised, blocking any ability to make a safe shot. "You know you need it to pay off Clint and to buy food for you and your daughter."

"What I need is my husband!"

"I know, but I can't bring him back."

"Take your blood money and get off my property before I shoot." The woman stepped farther out and kicked the coin purse off the porch. Her finger slid to the trigger.

Andrew swallowed. This wasn't mere intimidation. If he didn't shoot the woman, Lu could end up dead.

"Please, Widow Zachary—"

Before Andrew could aim, the Widow Zachary fired, and an explosion of dirt blasted near Lu's feet. Andrew shot at the porch steps. Like he'd hoped, Widow Zachary raced into the house and slammed the door. He sprinted to Lu, grabbed her still-raised hand, and hauled her into the woods. The sliding of a window echoed behind them. A shot pinged into a nearby tree, followed by a second. Andrew dragged Lu into a run. It was unlikely Widow Zachary would follow. Which was good, because Andrew had questions. Lots of them.

CHAPTER 17

ONCE THEY RAN NEARLY A mile and Andrew felt sure Widow Zachary wasn't foolish enough to chase, he released his grip on Lu. "What were you thinking?"

Lu gawked at him from her bent over position with hands on her knees and a slight sway to her stance.

"Sit down before you fall over."

She panted as her gaze flicked between him and the deer trail that led away. By the time she'd taken two steps, he had her in hand again. "Enough running in the dark. It's dangerous, and I want answers. That woman almost took your feet off."

Moonlight peeked through an opening in the branches above and illuminated Lu's panicked eyes following his gun as he spoke with his hand. He blew out a breath and holstered the weapon. "I'm not going to hurt you, but I want answers. Why did you bring money to the woman whose husband killed Irvine?"

Lu wrapped her arms around her middle and sunk to the ground against the tree's base. "Please, you can't tell Ma Frances."

Terror shook her like the leaves overhead, and well it should. Frances might kill her should she find out Lu was giving away money. What he didn't understand is why she took the risk.

"Why do you do it?" He crouched so he could evaluate the truth of her answer.

"It doesn't matter, just please don't tell her. I'll do anything. I'll . . ."

She swallowed and dropped her gaze to the ground. "I'll even go to Clint without a fight."

The thought of what she offered turned his stomach as surely as it must hers. Something wasn't right about the situation. Why would she place giving away money above her own safety? Images of the bruises she'd already borne from Clint flickered across his mind and boiled his blood. She deserved better.

"You're not going to him. Ever. You are *my* wife." The declaration that she was his wife hit with a different flavor than before. Not nearly as abhorrent, though not exactly welcomed either. He pushed aside the unnerving feeling and lifted her chin so their eyes met. "Protecting you and Oscar is part of my job, and I take that very seriously. Haven't you noticed I sleep outside your door each night?"

"I thought that was to make sure I stay in."

"I do it to ensure Clint stays out."

Even in the shadows, the crinkle of her brow and pursed lips were clear. She sat silent for a full minute before her thoughts spilled out on a whisper. "I don't understand you. You're not like them, but you pretend to be."

He was beginning to believe the same of her. Could everything he knew about Lu be part of a facade? "Did you really try to poison Eli?"

"No. I made another pie and planned to have him fake his death." She averted her eyes like the information was something to be ashamed of.

Andrew stared at the enigma before him. He'd always believed himself a good judge of character, but the illumination of Lu's true self intrigued and unsettled him. Though the time for the card game drew near, he needed to take time to explore who this woman really was. He shifted to sit flat on the ground, cringing at the way his legs tingled from crouching too long.

"What about the money you left for those other families?"

"If I have to steal, I'm going to at least do some good where I can. I know what it is to suffer because a man wants drink more than his family."

"Irvine?"

"And my father." A derisive laugh followed. "He loved me so much he sold me to a madam for a keg of beer."

Implacable anger scorched the cool evening. And he'd thought Frances a monster. "How old were you?"

"Nine."

His arms trembled with the need to bash the man's face. If her father still lived, Andrew prayed he not only regretted his part in the debauchery of his child but also suffered like he was on the receiving end of one hundred lashes from a cat-o'-nine-tails.

Lu shifted to her knees, desperation carving her features and edging her voice. "Irvine's the only man I've been with since Ma Frances bought me. I'm not what you think I am. Not anymore."

"What do you mean Frances bought you?"

Lu's head dropped and tears choked her. "I was Irvine's favorite girl, and he refused to leave Colorado without me, even though the marshal actively sought him and his family. Ma Frances caved under his demands and bought me so he'd leave."

No wonder Lu assumed the worst. She'd been bought, sold, and passed around as if she were nothing more than an object. A burden to be discarded.

The fist of conviction slammed into his gut and nearly doubled him over. He wasn't any better than Clint, Irvine, Frances, or even Lu's father. His vow to love and cherish her had been a lie before it ever left his lips. Just like them, he'd viewed Lu as something to be discarded as soon as the case ended. His career and reputation had been worth more to him than her life. Would he have even said yes to the marriage if only Lu's life had been at risk, instead of the pastor's and his wife's? The vile truth rose to expose the rancid places of his own heart.

God forgive me.

He was as broken a man as Lu was a woman. How could he have allowed his hatred for the Thornes to blind him to the wife God had appointed for him? He studied the woman on bent knees, stripped of all self-worth and garbed in a robe of shame forced upon her by others.

She waited in broken submission for him to cast stones at her, to end her life by one word to Frances. But he could not. For the first time, he was seeing her, *truly* seeing her, through the eyes of Jesus. And what he saw shattered his stony resolve.

Lu was a woman in need of love, compassion, and protection . . . from a husband. Him. He closed his eyes and pinched the bridge of his nose. He didn't want it, couldn't claim he even liked it, but if God chose to change his heart toward Lu, he would no longer fight it. Unwilling to immediately consider what that meant for his reputation and his career, he dropped his hand and cleared his throat.

For now, he needed to guide the topic back to case-pertinent information. "Why did you bring money to Widow Zachary? Her husband killed Irvine."

Her voice came out low and quiet. "I can't let what happened to me happen to her and Emma."

Her heart was in the right place, but she was going about it all wrong. Committing these crimes did not make up for the sins of others, nor was it her job to try to do so. He clasped her shoulders. "You can't save them, Lu."

"Someone has to, and I'm the only one able to steal the money they need."

"Stealing doesn't make their situation better. You aren't their savior. That's God's job. He'll provide for their needs."

Her face hardened. "He didn't provide for mine. You see how I turned out. A harlot and a thief, just like you said."

One of these days he was going to learn to weigh the cost of his words before spending them. "You just told me you've been with no one but Irvine since Colorado, and now that you're married to me, you don't have to steal ever again. Seems to me like God is providing."

She huffed. "But He could've stopped it all from ever happening. What kind of loving God allows a father to sell his daughter or a husband to beat his wife?"

Andrew scrubbed his jaw. God desired men to set a spiritual example for their households, and yet Andrew had no explanation. He'd never been called to make a defense of God before. He didn't even have an answer that was satisfactory to himself.

"I don't know what to tell you, Lu. God created a perfect world and then man ruined it by choosing his way above God's way. The same is still happening now. Could God have stopped it? Yes, but He didn't. I don't know why. Answers aren't promised to us. What I do know is that God is not like your father, Irvine, Clint, or even me. God has always loved you and will always love you." When she opened her mouth to object, he shook his head. "No matter what you've been through, God has been right by your side, grieving every sin committed *to* you and *by* you. Sometimes the sound of His love is drowned out by the evil in this world, but it doesn't mean He isn't speaking words of love and hope to you. It just means you have to listen harder to hear it."

She shook her head. "He has a strange way of showing love."

"Stranger than you know." He well remembered how foolish and strange God's love sounded the first time Father Darlington explained it to him. What God sent His Son to be hated, reviled, and crucified by the very people he came to save? It didn't make sense, but Andrew knew it to be true, believed it with every fiber of his being. He still failed often, but he was a changed and better man since acknowledging his need for and surrendering his life to Christ. The peace he had now soothed the past hurts, even as he still struggled to come to terms with them.

He shifted and took her hand in his, but she snatched it away with wide eyes. Not that he could blame her. Until this moment, he hadn't wanted her touch either. Instead, he opted to speak as gently as possible. "Lu, I know it's hard to believe given your experiences, but God really does care about you, those families, and even the Zacharys. You have to stop picking pockets and delivering money. Helping them through stealing isn't the right way to go about it. I'm sure with the Newcombs' help we can find another way."

"You're a Thorne. Why would it matter to you if I steal?"

"Because I want better for you." He took a deep breath, well aware that the words to follow required the complete surrender of all his plans. "I want better for us. My hope is that we can build an honest future together."

Her brow furrowed as she seemed to contemplate his words. "But you want acceptance into the family, and you're going to help them counterfeit banknotes. How is that honest?"

If only he could trust her with the truth. Although his view of her had shifted, her tie to the family and Frances's control over her made revealing his secret an impossibility. "I've spent twenty-four years wondering what happened to my family, and how it would be if we ever crossed paths again. I need to explore those answers."

She sighed, disappointment evident in her expression. "I'll agree to work with Mary, but I can't stop picking pockets. If I spend an entire evening away but come home with nothing, Ma Frances will find creative ways to punish me."

"I'll provide you with the money she requires. She'll never suspect it."

The rustle of leaves and chirp of crickets filled the silence between them. He felt they stood on a precipice. Her entire life could change if she'd come alongside him and allow him to help her. Like his father, he extended his hand, offering Lu the chance at a new life. And as he himself once had, Lu stared at that offering with a mixture of longing and fear.

"You better be getting to your card game. You wouldn't want to miss out on your chance to be a real part of the family." She rose from the ground and shook out her skirts.

The wind of defeat blew through him for a moment, yet hope anchored him in place. Hosea wasn't just a story in the Bible to him anymore. It was personal. Lu might be running back to her old life like Gomer, but God wasn't going to leave her there. Andrew felt the calling as surely as Hosea must have. He was to pursue Lu and be the illustration of God's love to her. A lifelong illustration.

"I want you to stay at the Newcombs' house tonight so there's no chance of Clint catching you alone."

"Clint'll be with you at the card table. I'll be fine."

"When I show up, he'll take that as my agreement to his proposal and might leave. I need you to be safe."

"But Oscar—"

"Will be fine with Frances for one night. I'll go with you to tuck him in bed and then escort you to the Newcombs'."

Her mouth spread into a grim line, but she directed her steps toward Landkreis.

Andrew didn't love Lu as Father Darlington loved Mother Elise, but love was a choice, not a feeling. He would choose to love Lu as best he could, though his decision meant a future of hardship. It wasn't likely the Secret Service would allow him to continue on as an operative if he refused the annulment, and experience told him the community at large would shun him and Lu after her release from prison. Even so, with God's grace and mercy, their marriage would survive his duty as an operative to arrest her, and affection would eventually grow. They would have a future of shared love, trust, and faith. He couldn't imagine it, but he would hope for it. After all, wasn't hope the anticipation of something not yet seen?

Chapter 18

Light filtered through the window as Lu fluffed the sheets of her borrowed bed before tucking the corners back into place. It had taken hours to fall asleep after Andrew left her at the Newcombs' last night. Everything he'd said in the intimate shadows of the woods had rolled through her mind, twisting up her emotions as much as the sheets around her. After tossing the pillow to the head of the bed, Lu spread the coverlet over the remade sheets. If only she could smooth out the wrinkles of her confusion as easily as the material beneath her hands.

What was she supposed to make of the man who had the most amazing talent for being an inconsiderate jerk, yet somehow proved also to be sweet, caring, protective, and—most surprising of all—a man of faith? When God ripped Andrew from Ma Frances, she blamed and despised Him. Yet Andrew, who had truly lost everything and everyone, defended God. Declared Him loving in spite of His lack of intervention. Granted, she would consider being ripped away from the Thornes a mercy, but still, Andrew must have endured much suffering. Yet he seemed to trust God, and he wanted an honest future with her. A future which didn't include her picking pockets, even if it helped others. But he was unwilling to walk away from the Thornes. It didn't make sense. Honesty and being a criminal didn't go together. All the yets, buts, and stills swirled in her head in a confusing tornado of arguments for and against opening her heart to the man. Who was he really? And was God really what Andrew, Mary, and Pastor New-comb claimed Him to be?

Lu stepped away from the now wrinkle-free bed and held her middle. *Your Honor, Andrew said I just have to listen to hear Your love and hope. Well, I'm listening. If you really love me, if You really care what happens to me, prove it to me. Make Andrew the man he seems to be and not the one he shows the Thornes. Take me, Oscar, and Andrew away from this. Give the three of us a new, honest life, where no one will ever discover my secret. If You do that, I'll believe that You are who they say You are.*

This was no small thing she asked of God. Opening herself up to the possibility of loving anyone was dangerous, but none more dangerous than Andrew. She'd seen his relief at discovering she hadn't attempted to poison Eli. How quickly would he abandon her if he discovered she *had* killed a man? And not any man, but Irvine?

Someone knocked on the door.

Lu jumped as though whoever it was could hear her thoughts.

Mary popped her head into the room. "I was beginning to think you'd died. It's past noon."

Lu expelled a breath and forced a smile. Considering that most nights she went to bed long after midnight, noon was a fairly common start for her. "Thank you for allowing me to sleep."

"Come on downstairs. I've got a plate waiting for you, and I'm dying to know what happened last night to have Doc Andrew insisting all the doors and windows be locked after he left."

Lu followed Mary downstairs. "He's overly worried about Clint trying to take liberties."

"Considering Clint's many near successes, he has good reason to be concerned."

Mary led them past Pastor Newcomb's closed office door and into the kitchen. A half-empty serving dish with shepherd's pie sat next to a place setting and coffeepot. Once Lu took a seat, Mary blessed the meal and served them both.

"Andrew was quite insistent we keep you here until he can escort you home." Her eyebrows waggled and her voice took on a singsong tone. "I think he cares for you."

"Nonsense. He just knows Clint's temper. Andrew refused Clint's deal of exchanging me for acceptance into the family."

"How does that contradict my statement?" Mary shifted her chair closer and clasped Lu's free hand. "I realize you don't welcome this marriage and loving another Thorne wasn't in your plans, but I think you should open your mind to the possibility that this is God's way of caring for you."

Lu chewed slowly as she considered sharing Andrew's words from last night and how closely they resembled Mary's now. Mary could be a hopeless romantic if allowed to run with her fantasies, but she was also a practical woman with a wisdom Lu trusted and depended on. "He did say he hoped to build an honest future together."

"See! God's working things out for your good and His glory."

"But Andrew won't leave his family, and he's helping them to expand into counterfeit banknotes. How is that building an honest future? At least when I pick pockets I use most of the money to help others." She bit her lips together. She hadn't meant for that last bit to tumble out.

"So you *are* the one depositing money on doorsteps. I admit, I had my suspicions."

"I can't stand what those men are doing to their families."

"Two wrongs don't make a right, Lu. You can't fix their problems by committing a crime." Why did Mary have to sound so much like Andrew? She wasn't supposed to take his side. "There are consequences, even if they don't happen immediately. Running away with Oscar and Andrew to a new location won't free you from them."

"I'm well aware that I'll never be free of my past."

"I didn't say that. Christ wipes away the guilt of our past the moment we admit our need for forgiveness and accept Him as our Savior. Remember Ephraim's sermon on David and Bathsheba? Not only did David take another man's wife, he killed the man to cover up his sin. David was a murderer, and yet God still granted him forgiveness when he sought it."

Lu's throat constricted, making it hard to breathe. Did Mary choose the example of a murderer because she suspected that Lu was the real cause of Irvine's death?

Mary continued. "However, that didn't remove the consequences for disregarding God's law, and those consequences didn't just affect him. It was his sin, but the consequences destroyed the life of his innocent son."

Mary's words echoed Andrew's, and Lu saw the evidence of her own life. One man made a decision, and it had destroyed an innocent life—hers. "But my stealing and returning the money doesn't affect anyone else. It helps, not hurts."

"What about Oscar? You could be home each night, cuddling him and caring for him instead of leaving him to the influence of Frances Thorne. He hears about and sees your participation. He learns it's okay without you ever having to say a word to him."

A knock sounded at the front door.

Mary squeezed Lu's hand. "Just give it some thought while I go see who's here."

Lu picked at her food. Mary did have a point, though it hurt to admit. She was no better an example to Oscar than any of the other Thornes. If she and Mary came up with a plan to help the families and Lu stopped picking pockets, then her actions could match her words to Oscar. But how to show him without alerting the rest of the family?

"Where is she? I heard she's here."

Lu stiffened at Priscill's shrill voice in the foyer. What was she doing here?

Priscill bounded into the room and toward Lu like a coon dog treeing its prey. Before Lu could fully rise, Priscill knocked her backward. Her back slammed into the table's edge, and she landed sideways in her chair.

"Clint's my husband, not yours!"

"And you can keep him. What's this about?" Lu winced as she straightened from the table and faced off with Priscill. The woman never fought fair, and Lu would not be caught at a disadvantage again.

"Don't you play coy with me. I know you slept with him last night. The whole town knows."

"I didn't go anywhere near your husband last night. I was here the whole time. You can ask Mary."

"Ha! Like a pastor would allow a harlot to sleep under his roof." Fury as hot as smelted gold poured from Priscill's eyes. "The whole saloon heard Clint's deal with Andrew and saw him follow you out. And then neither one of you came home last night."

Clint followed her? But she hadn't seen him. Then again, she hadn't seen Andrew until she was suddenly running behind him through the woods. What had Clint witnessed? One problem at a time. "You saw me yourself when I came to tuck Oscar in."

"And then left for the night."

"I came here."

Pastor Newcomb entered the room with Mary hovering at his side. "That's correct. Lu arrived around ten last night and didn't rise from bed until recently." He approached cautiously, as if determining what sort of threat Priscill posed to their safety.

Priscill's fists clenched, but she made no move of attack. "How do you know she didn't sneak out and then come back?"

For pity's sake. The woman was being completely unreasonable. "Why would I even do that?"

"To hide your affair from Ma. But your days of skulking off with Clint are over. I've had enough of this humiliation. If you don't quit fooling around with him, I'll make you suffer and ensure Ma gives her approval of it."

Lu had no doubt the woman would hold true to her word, and given Ma Frances's predisposition to condemn Lu, something worse than food poisoning would follow.

"You've made yourself abundantly clear. You may leave now." Pastor Newcomb opened the kitchen door.

Andrew stood outside, stiff as wash left hanging out in winter. His fists clenched around a bouquet of various flowering weeds and a small paper bag. "What's going on here?"

Priscill stalked to him and swatted the bouquet from his hands. As she ground the daisy heads into the dirt, she matched his scowl. "I refuse your and Clint's deal. I'll never be your woman and Lu'll never be his. You just remember that." She disappeared around the corner.

Andrew grumbled as he retrieved the ruined flowers from the ground. "I take it Priscill heard the rumor going around?"

All the strength left Lu's legs and she slumped into her chair. If there was a rumor going around, Priscill wouldn't have to bring Ma Frances's wrath down on Lu's head. The rumor would do that all on its own. Flattened and dirt-covered flowers appeared in her face.

"Here, I brought these for you." Andrew's gruff voice sounded more like that of a petulant child than a man with romantic intentions.

Mary laughed and immediately covered it with a cough. Pastor Newcomb gave what could only be called a grunted reprimand before pushing Mary toward the door. "We'll give you some privacy." They disappeared out of the kitchen, and the office door clicked shut.

Frown lines grooved the edges of Andrew's mouth as he dropped the paper bag into Lu's lap. "I didn't know what you liked, so I had Grossman put in a little of everything."

Lu laid the flowers aside and a smile crawled up her face as she peered into the bag of assorted candies. Since joining the Thornes, the only time she had candy was when she snuck it from Oscar. She wouldn't withhold it from her son, but having some to call her own tickled her more than she'd ever anticipated something so simple could. "Thank you, but why bring me flowers and candy?"

Panic and confusion seized his expression. "Because you're my wife and I thought you'd like them?"

Andrew had proved considerate on the practical front from the beginning of their strange relationship, but never romantic. Something was wrong with his gesture. Irvine only brought gifts when he'd drank too much. That and when he wanted her to show him gratitude. "Have you been drinking?"

She sniffed, but no scent of alcohol tainted the air.

"No, I haven't." Andrew folded his arms and grunted. "I told Joe his idea was stupid. I wanted to bring you something sensible, like a fresh set of clothes, but he said women preferred flowers and candy."

Now that was the Andrew she expected. She picked up the stem of a crushed black-eyed Susan and twirled it in her fingers. If he wasn't apologizing for being drunk, there was only one other option. She tried to smother the apprehension growing in the pit of her stomach. Even if he was the best Thorne ever born, she wasn't ready to consummate their marriage.

"Clothes would've been fine and welcomed, but candy and flowers don't hurt." She broke off a piece of peppermint stick and plopped it in her mouth, hoping it would settle her stomach. "What I don't understand is why you felt the need to soften me up with gifts."

Andrew tugged the collar of his shirt, and his eyes didn't quite meet hers. "I've decided if we're going to make this marriage work, we need to go about it the right way."

The soothing peppermint turned poisonous in her stomach. Though she anticipated his next answer, she asked the question anyway. "What do you mean?"

He coughed and a flush crept up his neck. "I'd like to court you properly."

Lu blinked. "You'd like to what?" The man must have gone daft in the head. No one courted someone they were married to, and no one in their right mind would court her. Married or not.

Looking more uncomfortable than a caterpillar in a bird's nest, Andrew pulled up a chair next to her and leaned forward. "I want to get to know you, the real you—not the one you portray to the rest of the world."

"You mean you don't want . . ." Her mind stumbled over the words like she were an innocent instead of the practiced professional she'd once been. When she awkwardly gestured to her body, his eyes nearly bulged from his face.

"No!" He cleared his throat. "We'll wait until later. Much later." The more he spoke, the redder his face grew. "After another conversation where we *both* agree we're ready."

Such sweet, blessed innocence. She could kiss the man simply because he didn't want to kiss her. In fact . . .

She popped out of her seat and pecked his cheek. "Thank you, that's the best gift anyone has ever given me."

"Surely you've gotten candy and flowers before."

She sat back down, lighter than she'd felt in her life. "Yes, but no one's given me a choice about bedding down before."

For a moment, his mouth hung open, then his usual scowl anchored into place. "I'm sorry."

"For what?"

"That being given the choice is seen as a gift. I hate how that common decency has been denied you."

Unsure of how to respond, she rummaged through the bag until she found one of the cinnamon hearts she'd seen earlier, then extended the bag toward Andrew. "What's your favorite kind?"

"Sour drops." He plucked out a piece and popped it into his mouth.

"That's Oscar's favorite."

He gave a half smile. "I know. I bought some extra for us to share. Ready to go see him? I'm sure he's driving Frances crazy by now."

Lu rose and accepted his arm when he came around the table. It might actually be fun to get acquainted with this man, to be treated like the lady she'd dreamed of being. Maybe soon Andrew would change his mind and take them away. Then God will have finally given her all she dreamed, and she would know without a doubt He loved her.

CHAPTER 19

MORNING LIGHT FILTERED THROUGH THE garret window as Andrew blinked the sleep from his eyes and rolled to his side on the pallet in front of Lu's door. Stiffness in his arms and legs protested the movement, turning into knots as he tried to stretch them out. He was getting far too old to sleep on the floor every night, even if Lu had scrounged up every extra blanket in the house to cushion him. Sitting up, he rolled his shoulders and stretched his neck from side to side before standing and placing his ear against the thin door. Oscar's snore rumbled an even rhythm. He tested the doorknob. Locked, which meant the bolt he'd installed to lock from the inside remained in place. Good. The safety measure wouldn't stop a determined Clint, but he'd make enough noise to alert Andrew.

Andrew rolled up his pallet and carried it to Oscar's toy room to store. A wide spread of tin soldiers and wooden horses waged battle on his bare feet and almost sent him crashing to the floor. Andrew kicked aside the toys with a grumble. He'd told Oscar to put them away last night. Now he'd have to follow through with a consequence—something he didn't want to deal with before coffee. He jammed the pallet under Oscar's unused bed and collected the toys to put on a shelf out of Oscar's reach until a chore to earn them back could be determined.

Having fatherhood foisted upon him was a challenge, but one he surprisingly enjoyed—despite the constant test to his patience. Oscar was exuberant, curious, quick-minded, and determined to prove himself a man. All wonderful qualities, but Andrew knew the danger of them as well. If he didn't remove him from Thorne influence soon, Oscar might choose to prove himself in ways that would forever brand him to the world as a criminal. No matter how well hidden, the blight of a criminal record rose again and again to threaten hopeful futures. Andrew left the toy room and checked Lu's door once more. Satisfied, he headed downstairs.

A full week of courting Lu had strengthened his conviction that God meant for this marriage to be a permanent situation. Their frank personalities suited each other well, and while he knew Lu held back, they were growing increasingly more comfortable with one another. With time and nurturing, a deep and lasting love could develop. That was, if the requirement of arresting her at the end of the case didn't destroy their tentative partnership. The familiar knot of anxiety constricted his stomach. Even if they did survive, he still had his position as a Secret Service operative to contend with. He couldn't lose his job. He'd worked ten years to establish his reputation and had aspirations of rising to the top of the department within the next five. Losing his position would prove to all the naysayers that they were right. He was nothing but a third-class citizen unworthy of the second chance he'd been given.

He forced himself to stop midway down the stairs and pray for the dozenth time for God to guide him through this. Worrying about the future served no purpose. His biggest concern right now was finding the informant and ending this case before Clint's plans succeeded. Although Andrew and Pastor Newcomb had soundly squashed the rumor, it hadn't stopped Clint from attempting to catch Lu alone and make it true. Several times already, Clint had manipulated Andrew's need to be a part of gang activities so that Lu remained vulnerable to attack. Praise God for Priscill's jealousy, Frances's need for control, and Josiah's willingness to step in when neither woman could serve as protection. If Andrew didn't discover who the informant was soon, Clint might finally succeed.

Andrew stepped into the empty kitchen where a half-prepared breakfast lay abandoned on the stove.

Frances's voice carried from the front door. "May I help you?"

Someone must have knocked before he came down. Andrew crouched to peer through the backless fireplace to the front door where Broderick Cosgrove stood, hat in hand, with another operative next to him. Finally. Reinforcements had arrived. "Let them in, Frances."

He joined them in the parlor, and a short blur of Union blue launched at him from between the two men. What the devil was Theresa Cosgrove doing here?

"Drew!" Theresa threw her arms around him like he was a beloved brother and grinned like the she-devil she was. "What do you mean by going and getting married without inviting the rest of us?" She claimed his arm and steered him to the sitting area. "The poor thing must've been duped to say yes."

Could the woman not shut up? She was worse than he remembered.

"Where is your darling wife? I simply *must* meet her and pass on my condolences."

"Who are you?" Frances clawed at Theresa's shoulder and hauled her away from Andrew.

Finally free, Andrew scrambled to put a chair between them and glared at Broderick. What had possessed him to bring his *wife* here? She was going to ruin everything.

Broderick gave a resigned shake of the head and joined him at the chair. "She's been planning that this whole trip. She's still not forgiven you for keeping her in that flooded building."

"I'm Theresa, and this is my husband Broderick Smith, and that's his partner Hayden." She gestured toward each man and smiled broadly at Frances. "We're like family to Drew."

"He already has a family." Frances snapped.

"Oh, sure, but we're more than family. Right, Drew?" She winked at him.

"She's like the annoying little sister I never wanted." Whatever game she played, Andrew wouldn't contradict it—yet.

"Don't be so sour. I brought my tools so we can set up shop here in town."

She couldn't mean what he thought. "What sort of tools?"

Theresa glanced at Frances. "Do you really trust me to say it in front of her?"

Not really. "Yes."

"My engraving tools, of course."

Frances perked like a cat offered catnip. "Engraving tools? What do you engrave?"

"Banknotes, of course." She waved as if it were nothing. "You didn't think fake medicine was the only thing Drew dabbled in, did you?"

"So these are the friends you spoke of." Andrew could almost hear Frances purr with pleasure.

"They are, although I didn't expect *you* to come." He pinned Theresa with a glower.

Annoyingly, she appeared unaffected by his barbs. "Where's the fun in me staying behind? Besides, you need me to make your new plates. We sold the last batch before Broderick learned about your new setup, so unfortunately, I'll have to start fresh."

What was this woman doing to his case? "You've said enough. I think it best we discuss business elsewhere."

"Nonsense, Andrew. We're all going into business together. They should stay." Frances claimed Theresa's arm. "I was just starting breakfast. Why don't you come help and tell me all about your process of printing money."

"I'd be delighted." Theresa flashed a triumphant grin and waved at them before disappearing into the kitchen.

Andrew ignored the other operative for the moment and wheeled on Broderick. "What have you done by bringing her here?"

Broderick rubbed his neck and dropped his voice. "It's part of Captain Abbott's plan. He thought bringing a woman to earn the confidence of your wife might benefit the case. It doesn't hurt that Theresa is knowledgeable about engraving and printing."

"And so you let her run her mouth and possibly upset everything?"

"In fairness, everything she said was agreed upon by us and Captain Abbott, but I'd hoped to rope you into the plan before she dove in headfirst."

The other operative stepped forward and extended his hand. "Hayden Orton from the Philadelphia District. We should head to the tack shop. Josiah's waiting, and there is much to discuss without prying ears present."

Hayden's serious demeanor was something this case needed to drive it to a quick end. With Theresa's presence, Andrew desired its conclusion even more than before. "We'll have to wait until after breakfast. Frances Thorne is very particular about the family eating together."

Theresa's annoying laugh carried to the parlor from the kitchen.

Andrew hated not being briefed on the plan before diving in, but he wouldn't risk the possibility of Theresa messing up his case if he wasn't present. "I think it best if we adjourn to the kitchen for now and play up our past partnership. I'll follow your lead."

Something slapped against Lu's face, startling her awake. Oscar's arm lay across her face and his leg stretched over her stomach. Bless the child's ever-loving soul. Now she was awake and needed to use the privy. This was why she preferred him to sleep in his own bed. She carefully eased out from beneath his sprawled-out form, holding her breath until she was sure he remained asleep.

Good. She'd be able to crawl back into bed and sleep more before another day of false pretenses demanded her sharp vigilance. Between Oscar's wriggling and Andrew's snoring, sleep had been hard to come by. Heaven help her when it came time for them to share a room. Even through the door, the man snored loud enough to be heard over the cotton stuffed in her ears. Irvine had been a snorer too, but nothing compared to the sleep-inhibiting roar Andrew managed.

After Lu relieved herself in the room's chamber pot, she glanced at the crack under the door. By the way light reflected off the floor, Andrew must be up for the day. Bed called for her to return, but the yearning to steal a few minutes alone with him called louder. Yes, she enjoyed the new routine of his reading *Jack the Giant Killer* each night while she cuddled with Oscar in bed, but it left little time for them to talk alone like they had in the woods and at Mary's. Clint was never far behind when Andrew walked her to the saloon for a night of pretending to pick pockets, and Ma Frances monopolized any time he spent in the house. Maybe if she were quick and quiet, she could get dressed without waking Oscar and request a morning walk with Andrew.

Fumbling in the dark, she found the new shirtwaist and skirt Andrew bought her and did her best to look presentable. As she cracked the door, the hinges squealed.

"Mommy?"

Tamping down the disappointment, she returned to the bedside. "Good morning, baby. Ready for a new day?"

"Yes!" He hopped to his feet and jumped on the bed. "Uncle Cyrus is taking me to see Jack!"

"Stop bouncing on the bed before you hurt yourself."

"Catch me!"

Before she could properly adjust her stance, he launched at her. She caught him but stumbled back. Her foot caught the edge of the chamber pot and it flipped toward her as she thudded to the ground. Liquid splashed over her skirts and spilled onto the floor.

Oh, for pity's sake.

"Sorry, Mommy." Oscar crawled off her lap.

Lu sat for a moment, trying to get control of her frustration before she lost her temper with Oscar. Instead of a morning walk with Andrew, she'd need to do laundry.

After helping Oscar dress before he rushed downstairs, Lu sopped up the remaining mess with her soiled clothes. She was tempted to freshen up, put on the green ensemble Andrew preferred, and just shove the mess into the corner to be dealt with later. However, Oscar's nights of soiling the bed were not so far removed for her to forget how much she would regret that when the heat of the day arrived. After switching into a simple, if wrinkled, work dress, she collected her dirty clothes and the chamber pot. What a way to start her day.

At the bottom of the stairs, Lu froze. Ma Frances sat at the head of the table with the family on one side of her and three strangers seated on the other. Having Andrew see her carrying her own soiled clothes and chamber pot was embarrassing enough, but strangers?

Andrew rose from his chair nearest the stairs with a frown firmly in place. "I didn't expect you up so soon. Are you unwell? You look terrible."

That man and his mouth.

Priscill smirked. "By the look and smell of things, I'd say Lu wet the bed. I think we still have some of Oscar's nappies if you need one."

"That's enough, Priscill." Andrew's sharp tone silenced further comments. With an unreadable face, he extracted the chamber pot from her hand. "Oscar, take care of this. Then wash up so you can have breakfast." Once Oscar took off with the ceramic pot outside, Andrew reached for the clothing in her arms.

"No!" She clutched them closer. Heaven help her, that man would not touch her dirty laundry. Heat flooded her face as she strode to the door and tossed the pile into a corner of the veranda. As Oscar jogged back toward the house, she pointed to the same corner. "Just leave it there."

Without looking anyone in the eye, she returned inside and scrubbed her hands at the sink.

Andrew came behind her and then rotated her toward him once she'd finished. "Are you all right?"

Of course she wasn't all right. She was mortified! Couldn't he have given her some warning they had guests? "I'm tired. Maybe if you didn't sound like a train in your sleep, I would've rested better." She immediately regretted the barb. A sharp tongue would never endear her to the man.

Feminine laughter from the table drowned out Ma Frances's reprimand. A petite brunette sat between the two strange men, failing to hide her smile—and laugh—behind a napkin.

The man to the woman's right shook his head. "Please forgive my wife. She's forgotten her manners."

"Come now, Broderick. You have to admit that was funny." The woman rose from the table and extended her hand. "I'm Theresa, a friend of Drew's. I've come to offer my condolences on marrying this insufferable man."

Lu looked from the extended hand to Andrew's dour expression. Whoever this Theresa was, it was clear Andrew was not fond of her. Lu wasn't sure if she should be pleased with or concerned by that information. She accepted the woman's handshake, but then stepped close to Andrew's side. She owed Andrew a defense after insulting him in front of his friends. "While I would say his snoring is insufferable, the man himself is not."

Priscill scoffed while Clint mumbled something indecipherable next to her. Cyrus's knife scraped against his plate, loud and shrill. Though quieter in expressing their opinions, Andrew's friends exchanged quizzical glances as if surprised by her praise.

Andrew wrapped an arm around her waist and gave a gentle squeeze. The gesture was startling, yet it didn't send the same sense of dread through her as when it came from other men. His arm quickly dropped, and he moved away. To her shame, she missed his closeness. How was it that she could so quickly enjoy his touch after being repulsed by the idea of it little more than a week ago? Perhaps it was because she was beginning to see he was a man of his word. If he said they would wait, then the touches were meant as nothing more than genuine support and encouragement.

"Lu, I'd like you to meet Hayden, Broderick, and Theresa." Andrew gestured to each individual. "They've come to help with the printing."

Dread twisted her stomach. She'd mentally pushed aside the confusing duplicity the determination to win his family's approval brought to his character. She wanted to believe him, to believe they had the chance at an honest future, but if he got tangled up with the Thornes and the other informant turned them in, that future would be ruined. She needed to figure out who that other informant was since trying to identify the lawman without being able to read his credentials was too risky. At least if the family discovered her nosing about for the informant, she'd be praised—not killed.

Theresa elbowed Lu. "What do you say we let everyone else talk business, and you show me what this little town has to offer? I absolutely cannot wait to get to know you."

Lu glanced at Andrew, who gave her no indication of if she should accept or not. "But I have laundry I need to do."

"That's fine. I'll help you. Believe me, after traveling with these two for three days"—she tossed a thumb over her shoulder—"I am willing to do anything for some girl time."

"Not before breakfast." Andrew carried two plates to the table and set one in his spot. "Sit. Eat."

Oscar clambered into the chair. "I love flapjacks."

"And you'll eat flapjacks on the stairs with me. Your mother gets the chair."

"Not unless you want more food on you and the floor than in his mouth." Lu stepped away from Theresa and picked up the fork and knife sitting next to the plate. "Just let me cut his food into bites, and then I'll sit next to you on the stairs to eat."

"You can have my chair." Broderick stood. "I've finished."

Lu hoped her disappointment didn't show. The space on the stairs meant they would've had to sit close enough for their legs to brush. Of course, given her disastrous morning, she probably would've dumped the plate all over herself instead of balancing it on her lap.

When she went to sit, Clint plunked his muddy boots in the way and eyed her appearance. "Shoulda worn the red dress, Lu. It makes a better impression."

"She looks perfect in what she's wearing." Andrew set her plate in the vacated spot and shunted Clint's feet off the chair. "Keep your feet to yourself and off my wife."

They stared each other down until Ma Frances cleared her throat. "Boys."

Andrew wiped the mud away and then withdrew to lean against the sink next to Broderick. Lu and Theresa reclaimed their seats, and the conversation returned to what must have been the topic before she had interrupted.

"I'll see if Grossman can put an order in for the equipment we need or if I'll have to go to Stendal." Cyrus tapped his finger for a moment. "Whoever we order through, it's going to have to come by ferry to Newburgh and then on the train to Boonville."

"That's perfect. Put my order in for—" Ma Frances nodded toward Oscar, "and everything should arrive by the end of next month."

"While we wait, I'd like to get a feel for the area," Hayden said. "We need to know who we can trust."

Though Ma Frances prodded Clint to participate in the conversation about the people who helped with various aspects of their operations, he just stared at Lu in hostile silence. Andrew must have noticed, because he moved to stand behind her and rested his hand on her shoulder. While his touch provided a measure of comfort, the raging jealousy in Clint's eyes twisted her insides until she could no longer eat.

"I'm done! Can we see Jack now?" Oscar shoved his plate away and stood in his chair.

"Sorry, Runt. We'll have to go another time," Cyrus replied.

When Oscar pouted, Theresa turned in her seat to face him. "Who's Jack?"

"My puppy!" He jumped and Andrew grabbed him before he toppled the chair.

"How wonderful! Do you think I can see him? I love puppies. Your mommy and I can take you."

Lu's gaze shot to Andrew's. He knew as well as she that the outing opened up the opportunity for Clint to follow. "I'm sorry, but I really need to do laundry."

"It can wait." Ma Frances waved a hand dismissively. "We've got plans to make, and Oscar will only be underfoot if he stays here. Go on now."

Andrew set Oscar down and clasped Lu's hand. "I need to speak with Lu first."

No one objected as Andrew led Lu upstairs and closed the bedroom door.

"I'll ensure Clint doesn't follow, but just in case . . ."

Andrew knelt and pulled a derringer from a strap hidden on his ankle. "This should be easy enough for you to wield. Have you ever shot a gun before?"

She backed away, bile rising in her throat. Never again would she touch one of those horrifying things. "I don't do guns."

"They're not hard to use. Point, pull the hammer back, and squeeze the trigger."

A fact she knew all too well.

He must have realized her distress, for he returned the weapon to its holster and immediately grasped either side of her shoulders. "I forbid you to faint."

As if his forbidding it would change anything. "I'm not the fainting type." Still, her legs wobbled, and it was a relief to be guided to the bed. "Let's just say my last experience with a gun didn't end well." She ducked her head from his scrutiny lest he suspect her meaning.

"Using a weapon can have serious consequences, but nothing else will give Clint pause."

"If you haven't noticed, he's not exactly slow to use his own. I'd never have a chance."

He turned pensive at her words, and after a moment, he retrieved the dagger she kept under the mattress edge.

"How did you know that was there?"

"I make it a point to know all the dangers that might befall me in my sleep." He gave a half smile as he wrapped the blade with a handkerchief from his pocket. "The only reason I left it was because I was more afraid of Clint finding you alone without it than of you trying to wield it against me."

"Oh."

He handed her the dagger. "Keep this in your pocket. The handkerchief should protect from accidental cutting, but if you thrust it forward, it will pierce through. Mind you, it's only a precaution. If he appears, I won't be far behind."

"Can't you go with us?"

"If I didn't have Broderick and Hayden to contend with, yes, but their presence complicates things. Frances won't allow Clint to follow you, so I feel you'll be safe. That being said, don't linger. Let Oscar see his puppy, and then go to the tack shop. Joe'll serve as protection until I can get to you."

Of course he'd choose to stay and make plans with the others rather than go with her. Rejoining his family was still the priority. She was merely a pleasant diversion. How had she allowed herself to become dependent on him so quickly? Frustrated with herself, she took a deep breath and gripped the hilt of the dagger in her pocket. She could take care of herself. Just like she always had.

CHAPTER 20

LU GLANCED OVER HER SHOULDER as she, Theresa, and Oscar reached the edge of the cornfield. Andrew still stood in the doorway, half in the house and half on the veranda, watching their progress toward the barn. Though he obviously spoke to someone inside, his eyes stayed fastened on her. His concern and commitment to seeing her and Oscar make it safely to the barn mollified some of her displeasure at his choosing to stay behind. Whether or not he was wrong, the man felt he was making the best decision.

Once the curve of the cornfield cut them off from view, Theresa slipped her arm through Lu's like they were old friends. "Do you really find Andrew tolerable? I simply can't imagine it. All my experiences paint that man as arrogant, tactless, and completely infuriating."

"Oh, he's all that to be sure, but he's also steady, protective, and . . ." Lu tried to find a word that would fit Andrew. After a moment, she shrugged. "I don't know. There's just something different about him that draws me in."

"You poor thing. The quality of men you've been afforded must be very poor indeed if you find him appealing."

She wasn't wrong, but Lu was growing increasingly certain she could meet all the world's men and none would measure up to Andrew Thorne.

"I suppose in such a small town as this, you really don't have much choice. I've never seen so much empty land before. What is it you even do for fun in a place like this?"

"You've never been to a small town?"

"Not unless you call Cincinnati small. Until I married Broderick, I'd never traveled outside of it."

To be fair, Landkreis was small, even by Lu's standards. With only two hundred people spread out over miles, everyone in town knew she picked pockets. They were just too scared of Clint and Cyrus to do anything about it. If it weren't for the regular flow of people passing through on the main road from Boonville to Petersburg, there wouldn't be enough pockets to pick to keep Ma Frances happy. "Unless you have a taste for liquor or cards, there's not much in the way of entertainment. Sometimes I'll take Oscar fishing or swimming at Cup Creek or one of the ponds."

Theresa visibly shuddered. "No thanks. Water and I do not get along."

Oscar reached the barn ahead of them, knocked the code, and then burst inside. Tabby's excited yaps greeted them as they entered.

"Oh! Look how little they are!" Theresa released Lu's arm and joined Oscar with the puppies. "Which one's Jack?"

"This one!" Oscar picked up the noisiest and reddest of the three-week-old puppies.

Theresa swooped in to correct his hold, explaining how it was important not to hurt the puppy. Lu joined them on the ground near the former smelt and chose her favorite. Dark soulful eyes stared back at her from the black and tan face of the puppy who was content to just be held and loved. She cuddled him close and watched the other puppies paw and nip at each other in unstable attacks until they tired and formed a sleepy dog pile next to Tabby. Laying her puppy on top of the pile, Lu instructed Oscar to do the same.

"But I'm not done playing!"

Lu rose and brushed the dirt from her skirts, even though neither Theresa nor Oscar returned their animals to the ground. "Jack is tired and Uncle Andrew wants us to meet him at the tack shop." When he pouted, Lu removed Jack from his hold. "I bet Joe will need some help with the horses again." Like she'd suspected, mucking the stalls had been more entertainment than punishment to him.

Oscar patted Jack's head. "Sleep tight, Jack. I'm gonna go ride a horse."

That wasn't what she meant, but she'd fight that battle once they were under Joe's protective eye. Already they'd stayed longer than was safe. Oscar led the way out and darted through the tree line to the tack shop stable while Theresa and Lu followed at a slower pace. Theresa bubbled almost as much as Oscar did over the puppies, and Lu softened toward the woman. She was exactly the type of person who'd annoy Andrew but who was easy for Lu to befriend.

When Lu and Theresa passed the corner of the barn, the peace of the morning fled.

Clint pushed from the wall. "Took you long enough."

She urged Theresa to a faster pace.

He blocked their path. "I suggest you take off, Mrs. Smith. Lu and I have some business."

"Go home, Clint, before you get hurt." Lu shifted her hand to the pocket with the dagger and moisture slicked her palm.

His eyes darted toward the movement.

She hesitated a fraction too long.

Clint captured her wrist and wrenched it with painful force. "That's no way to treat your future husband."

Though she maintained her hold on the hilt, Clint's strength squelched any ability to direct a stab toward him.

"Let her go! She's already married." Anger sizzled in Theresa's tone, but the only effect it had was drawing his attention.

"Not for much longer. Take off before I decide to arrest you."

Theresa's brow arched, and the foolhardy woman adopted a confrontational stance. "Either release her or suffer the consequences."

Clint's lips curled. "I can snap a twig like you in half."

Theresa stared at him a moment, then with an unexpected launch forward, she kneed Clint in the groin. As he bent forward, she plucked a hatpin free and jabbed it into the hand holding Lu's wrist. His grip released and was replaced by Theresa's. As he bent over and howled in pain, Theresa herded Lu back toward the house.

"But Oscar!"

To Lu's relief, Andrew, Broderick, and Hayden appeared in the same moment. All three drew weapons and pulled the women behind them to form a protective barrier. Despite her resolve to not be dependent on Andrew, Lu huddled close to his back and absorbed the comfort of his nearness and strength.

"Go back to the house, Clint. Lu's *my* wife. Yours is back there."

Clint spewed curses but moved in a wide arc around them. Andrew shifted, keeping himself between Clint and Lu until the man disappeared around the cornfield bend.

"Let's not linger." Andrew curved his arm around Lu's back and urged her toward the tack shop. "Are you all right?"

"We're fine. Theresa kneed him and then stuck him with a hatpin." Pride lit the woman's face even as her husband grimaced.

Andrew frowned at Lu as they walked. "What good is a weapon if you don't use it? I had you carry your dagger for a reason."

"I wasn't quick enough. Clint stopped me."

Andrew ran a hand down his face. "We have to find a way to keep you safe. I can't be around all the time."

"I think I did a fine job of protecting us." Theresa beamed. "If Broderick would give me a gun—"

"No." All three men responded at once.

Theresa stuck out her lip in an exaggerated pout before smiling. "It was worth a try. Broderick and I are going to stay with the Newcombs. I'm sure Mary wouldn't mind if Lu and I spent the majority of our time there."

"That's not a bad idea." Andrew's tone indicated he was surprised Theresa came up with a logical solution. "But we'll need more than that to ensure your safety."

They passed through the tree line, and Joe approached with a rifle in hand and a confused Oscar trailing behind. "I thought I heard trouble."

"You did." Andrew holstered his gun. "Close up shop. We're heading to the Newcombs'. We need to make plans with Pastor Newcomb while the ladies visit."

"Shouldn't Theresa and I be included in the planning?"

"No. You need to keep Oscar entertained, and I don't want him to hear anything that might scare him. I'll share any necessary details."

How could she argue against shielding Oscar from the threat of his uncle? Though she didn't like being left out, Lu nodded, and then all of her energy shifted to calming the temper tantrum that followed the moment Oscar realized he would not be riding a horse or mucking stalls. By the time they were nearly to the house, he'd resorted to displaying his anger through stomping and quiet huffing. Pastor Newcomb greeted them and ushered the men into the parlor, sending the women and Oscar to join Mary in the kitchen.

When the parlor door shut, Theresa leaned over and whispered, "They're not the only ones capable of making plans. Tell me everything you know about the Thornes." A mischievous gleam filled her eyes, and Lu responded with a smile.

Another woman with an independent mind and without any loyalty to the Thornes might prove a good ally. Of course, Theresa was the wife of Andrew's counterfeiting friend and would still be worried by news of an informant sneaking around. Lu would have to be careful about what she shared and be sure to play up her criminal activities. The less they suspected she could be an informant, the safer she'd be.

The fall breeze on the tack shop boardwalk did little to cool Andrew's heated face as he watched an unescorted Lu and Theresa exit Grossman's. Five days. That's all it took for them to discard the agreed-upon plan and place themselves into dangerous situations. Didn't they understand Grossman would have no qualms about forcing Lu upstairs to his living quarters for a private rendezvous with Clint? It's why Andrew expressly forbade Lu from going to Grossman's without him or one of the other operatives.

He stalked toward them and met them at the alley entrance between the buildings. "What were you doing going in there alone?"

Lu glanced at Theresa. "There are two of us."

"Theresa does not count as protection."

"She seemed to do a fine job of it at the barn." Lu stabbed an eyebrow skyward before handing her purchases to Theresa. "Will you please hide Oscar's presents at Mary's? Andrew and I need to talk."

Theresa accepted the box but squinted at Andrew like a wary mother bear protecting a cub. "Are you certain you should be alone with him?"

"Of all the men in the world, I fear Andrew the least."

Grateful as he was that Lu trusted him, at the moment he wished she would listen to him.

Once Theresa left, Lu tugged him into the alley and cinched her arms over her chest. "I can't live under your restrictions. Half the time I need to go somewhere you and your friends are off with Cyrus and the others, or you're holed up in the tack shop gossiping worse than old ladies at a quilting bee. I need the freedom to come and go as I please."

"Then I'll assign someone to stay with you at all times."

"Oh, for pity's sake, Andrew. I don't need a nursemaid."

"But Clint is a threat."

"Yes, and he's always been a threat. I've lived the last ten years trying my best to avoid that man, but I never stopped living my life in order to do it. If you're going to assign someone to protect me, assign yourself. For a man who wants to court me, you haven't spent any time alone with me since your friends arrived. Even our walks to the saloon always include someone else."

Guilt gnawed at him, but the choice had been purposeful. With all the discussions he and the other operatives had about the case, he couldn't risk Lu discovering his true identity. Their future depended on his being able to arrest the Thornes quickly and keep Lu's participation in crime to a minimum. If only Theresa weren't actually doing an exceptional job of earning Lu's trust and then sharing the information with the other operatives. He dragged a hand down his face. The list of crimes Lu revealed in conversation stacked against her. A good portion of them Andrew could mitigate through his knowledge of what she did with the stolen money, but the other things—stealing chickens, helping with the smelting, participating in the robbery that had killed Irvine—he couldn't work around. And if the other operatives discovered his growing affection and plans to stay married, his negotiating powers on her behalf would be diminished.

He glanced toward the tack shop, where Hayden observed them from the side window. Andrew maneuvered them out of view. "I want to be with you, but things have grown complicated. Give me until the printing press is operational and I have my family's full trust."

Lu stared into the distance, chewing on her response like a piece of hardtack. Eventually, she shook her head and spoke. "I like you, Andrew, but there are parts of you I hate. Like the fact it's always going to be money, family, or something else above Oscar and me."

This woman. If only he could share the true purpose behind his distance, make her understand he did place her and Oscar above all else. He just was having a hard time balancing protecting her, courting her, and pursuing this case.

Her hand hesitantly reached for his and hovered close enough to scatter his thoughts. Tingles of anticipation threaded up his arms until, finally, her fingers interwove with his. "Please, Andrew. I know earning your place in this family is important to you, but can you at least include me in that endeavor instead of pushing me off on someone else?"

He stared at their entwined hands, the simple touch more intimate than he ever imagined holding hands could be. While she hadn't rebuffed his occasional light touches, this was the first contact she'd initiated since the peck on the cheek when he declared they'd wait until ready. It was as if she'd granted him a small piece of herself. But was it simply a tactic to get him to do what she wanted? He lifted his gaze. Instead of the confident smirk of a seductress, genuine vulnerability pleaded with him. She really did want him, and it made no sense. "I don't understand why you want to be with me."

"Sometimes I wonder that myself." Her eyes danced with laughter and something more. Something deeper. Not quite love, but the hope of it. She continued, rubbing circles on his palm with her thumb. "But then I remember all you've shown me of yourself in the rare private moments we've had together. I want more of that. More of you."

On an impulse, he lifted their clasped hands and kissed hers. "You really know how to sway a man to your desire, don't you?"

Her smile faltered. "I had hoped it was yours too."

"It is, more than you know."

Was it possible to have her with him while he worked the case? Tonight's meeting would be the biggest yet, with some of the players from farther out joining them for the first time. He could argue for Theresa's presence based on the fact she was the supposed engraver, and then Lu's presence would be natural.

"I'll walk you to Mary's." Without releasing her hand, he led her down the street and waited until the fallow fields were the only thing to hear them talk. "There's a meeting tonight in Stendal where we'll be planning the printing operations with the group at large. Cyrus is hoping to get some of the others to buy into the cost of operations. If Broderick will allow Theresa to come, then you would be able to join us as well."

"Will I get to ride double-up with you?"

Her hopeful countenance made him wish he could say yes, but Morgan was a temperamental beast, and being in such close contact with her would be a distraction. "Riding double with me is different from riding with Oscar. You'd have the pommel constantly poking you, and I'd have the hard part of my saddle running right across my tailbone."

"I could always sit behind the saddle and hold on to you."

"I don't like the chances of you accidentally sliding off. Morgan is a good horse, but he's grouchy and doesn't like his rules upset."

"Sounds like the horse matches his master." After a brief chuckle, her tone sobered. "But I understand. I've been tossed from a horse once and prefer not to repeat the experience. Do you promise to ride next to us?"

He squeezed her arm. "I do."

The look she gave him declared him a hero. "I've never met a man

I could trust until you, even if you're a bit grouchy." She nudged him with her shoulder.

"I hear grouches make the best husbands."

She laughed. "Only if his wife is exceptionally long-suffering."

He stopped at the Newcombs' gate and shifted so they faced one another. "Then I'll count myself lucky. Not only are you beautiful, but you're also the most long-suffering woman I've ever met. Look at how you've put up with me so far." Though he shouldn't press his luck, he caressed her cheek.

She tilted her head into his touch and smiled. "I think Pretty Boy may be rubbing off on you."

"Maybe, or maybe you're bringing out a side of me I didn't know existed."

"Just don't lose the grouchy side in the process. You wouldn't be you without your mouth getting in the way."

He'd like his mouth to get in the way in a very different manner, but she was far from ready for such things. Instead, he lifted her hand and kissed it like he'd seen Josiah do whenever trying to charm the sense out of a woman. It was only fair since she was charming the sense right out of him. "Stay safe, and I'll see you tonight."

"I look forward to it."

He watched her sashay to the front door and cast him a flirtatious smile over her shoulder before slipping inside. For a man who prided himself on his sensible head, he found that Lu was making him awful foolhardy. Part of him looked forward to a quick conclusion of the case, while the other feared what would happen to this newly developing relationship between them when the case ended. He stared at the closed door far longer than he should and prayed God would see them through the approaching catastrophic storm. Only by God's grace and mercy was it possible, and only by His will could it happen. Andrew just had to cling to hope. *Please, let it be so, Lord.*

CHAPTER 21

WHY DID PRISCILL HAVE TO insist on coming? The iron armrest bit into Lu's hip and ribs as Priscill wiggled on the wagon bench and encroached on Lu's ever-shrinking space. Riding double with a pommel bruising her front and Andrew's arms wrapped around her back sounded more and more appealing. At least then she'd be close to him and have a chance at private conversation. Instead, thanks to the manure-caked wagon bed, she, Priscill, and Theresa squeezed onto the front bench.

Priscill wiggled again.

Lu stiffened her elbow against the attack. "How much further?"

"We'd already be there had you ridden horses." Clint groused from his mount on the other side of the wagon.

"You know there weren't enough." Lu flashed him a smile. "Maybe if you rode double we could make it there faster?"

Andrew guided his horse closer to her side of the wagon, disapproval stamped in the grooves of his mouth.

Clint, however, reveled in the suggestion. "Need a ride?"

"No, but Priscill does."

Using the armrest to propel herself, Lu rammed against Priscill. Though Priscill yelped and almost toppled into the space between wagon and the horse's rear, Clint made no move to aid her. Instead, he cantered forward to catch up with the others. After regaining her balance, Priscill jammed herself back into the narrow space and wriggled with more force than Oscar with poison ivy on his backside. The iron armrest banged into Lu's bruised hip with painful repetition.

"That's it. I'm walking." Lu pulled the reins from Theresa's grip and stopped their progress.

"You can't walk." Andrew blocked her exit from the wagon. "It's dark out, and we're almost late for our own meeting. We should be there in ten minutes if you'll just hold out."

"I'm bruised all the way up and down my side. If I go any longer, either I won't be able to walk or I'll be guilty of forcing Priscill to get acquainted with the horse's hooves."

"Not if I beat you to it." Priscill pushed Lu from behind.

Lu fell across Andrew's lap, and he fumbled to grab her as she slid headfirst over the side. The wagon pulled away, catching her feet and knocking them into the horse's face. The animal skittered sideways, and Lu plummeted the rest of the way. At the last second, her fall slowed, and she hit the ground with a dull thud. To Morgan's credit, he stayed still and didn't trample her, although Lu was sure Priscill wished he would. She rolled away lest he change his mind and lay trying to catch her breath and assess what hurt the most.

Andrew's feet hit the ground, and a moment later he was by her side. "That was the stupidest thing I've ever seen anyone do."

Admittedly, she'd seen stupider, but she was too sore to think of an example at the moment. When she shifted to sit up, he commanded her to be still. A quick succession of questions about her symptoms followed, most of which she didn't have time to answer before he barreled on to the next. Once satisfied she didn't have a concussion or broken bones, he helped her to her feet.

"What happened?" Pretty Boy must have ridden back after the commotion of her fall.

Hayden sat atop his horse next to Pretty Boy. "Does she need a doctor?"

"Maybe one for her head," Andrew mumbled, then more loudly, "There are less dramatic ways to ride double."

"All I wanted to do was walk."

The three men looked at her like she was out of her mind, but they weren't the ones being forced to become one with the iron armrest. She should've known coming with Andrew was foolish. It wasn't like they had any more privacy than sitting at home at the dinner table. What had she thought would happen? Andrew would ride alongside the wagon, talking away while Theresa and Priscill faded silently into the background? She was too old for such naivety.

Andrew ran a hand over his face before addressing Hayden and Pretty Boy. "Go on ahead and arrive at the meeting with the others. Lu and I won't be far behind."

They rode back, leaving Lu to face a disgruntled Andrew. "I'm sorry. This isn't how I planned for things to go tonight."

"I should hope you wouldn't plan to pick fights with Priscill or dive over the tops of horses."

If Lu could shrink to the size of an ant, she'd crawl off and hide. Instead of encouraging attraction, she'd only fostered annoyance and dissatisfaction.

"Let's go before we're any later."

As the rest of the group disappeared up the road, Lu tried her best to be cooperative and compliant. Unfortunately, Morgan did not have the same aspirations. The horse shied away from her each time she approached. Even when Andrew held the bridle firm in hand, the animal sidestepped her every attempt to mount. Apparently, the horse was as unforgiving as its master. Her kick to the face would not soon be forgotten.

"Just ride ahead without me. I'll walk the last bit by myself."

Andrew blew out a frustrated breath. "We walk together or we ride together. Those are the two options, and since Morgan won't allow us to ride, we walk."

She stayed on Andrew's left and gave the horse a wide berth. Though they finally had the alone time she'd craved, the tension between them was too high for speaking. Her inability to tolerate Priscill's childishness had led to her behaving no better. Now Andrew suffered the consequences of her actions. The walk took more than double the time it would've taken to ride, and by the time they made it to Stuart's in Stendal, no one remained outside.

Though Andrew said nothing, his irritation at their tardiness was palpable.

"Here," Lu reached for the reins. "I'll take Morgan into the barn so you can join the others."

"Not with the way he feels about you. You'd never manage him. Wait here. I'll be back."

As Andrew took the horse into the barn, Lu waited by the door.

The tittering laugh of a girl and the tenor tone of a man's voice came from around the corner. With everyone in the meeting, no one should be lingering near the barn. She peeked around the corner to find Emma Zachary kissing the newest and youngest recruit to the Thorne gang, Günter Zimmerman. What was a Zachary doing here, let alone kissing a gang member? Didn't Emma have any idea what sort of trouble she was courting?

Lu didn't know what Widow Zachary would do if she found out her seventeen-year-old was in a relationship with one of the Thorne gang members, but she knew well enough what the Thornes would do to Emma. She shivered, though she couldn't blame it on the cool evening.

Emma leaned back from Günter, breaking the kiss. "Now go on in and find out who all came and don't let on what you're doing. Once we have names we can turn them over to the Boonville police and they can tell the marshals."

Lu sucked in a breath. Was Emma the other informant? There was no doubt that Widow Zachary sought justice for the death of her husband, but would she stoop to involving her daughter? Or was Emma acting on her own?

Günter rushed to the house, and Emma disappeared into the tree line.

Lu bit her lip. Too bad Lu couldn't approach the Zacharys herself. They'd never view her as an ally, and she wasn't naive enough to have even the faintest hope that they would share the identity of their police contact.

Andrew exited the barn and annoyance dripped from his tone. "What's wrong now?"

She focused on relaxing the tension she felt in her face and forced a small smile. "Nothing. Let's go inside before we're any later."

Doubt squinted his eyes as he regarded her a moment longer, but he led the way into the farmhouse without further questions. Cyrus stood on a box in the middle of the main room talking about the benefits of buying into the newest venture. Nearly twenty members from two counties crowded the room, all of whom Lu had met at some point over the last few months. Half the lot were gentlemen with honest professions—a doctor, a few merchants, hard-working farmers struggling to provide for their families, and an owner of a failing coal mine. The other half ranged from down-on-their-luck gamblers to men of Clint's ilk. All were after easy money and willing to work with the Thornes to get it.

Pretty Boy grumbled as Lu and Andrew edged into an empty space next to him. "About time you showed up. Cyrus already laid out the plans for how the printing operations will work."

"It's my fault. I kicked Morgan's face during my fall and he wouldn't let me on. We had to walk."

Sympathy replaced his scowl. "Theresa's over there, and Priscill's in the kitchen."

"I'll be keeping an eye on you. Don't leave the room without me," Andrew whispered into her ear before releasing her.

It was a comfort to know that even when angry, he still cared for her safety. Lu picked her way to Theresa, taking the longer route to avoid Clint and those most likely to take liberties. By the dark looks Broderick gave any man who stepped too close to Theresa, he'd already intervened on Theresa's behalf at least once.

When Lu reached her, Theresa latched onto Lu's arm. "Don't you dare leave me with that miserable woman ever again."

They lapsed into silence as Cyrus continued to lay out the benefits of investing in banknotes. Lu sought Günter with her eyes. The boy stood in the corner, studying each face in the crowded room as if committing them to memory. How could Lu support Günter's endeavors to turn in the Thornes while protecting Andrew and herself from the consequences? And should she do something to warn the Smiths? Theresa was a criminal in her own right, but she was kind, adventurous, and quickly becoming a friend she trusted like Mary. Shouldn't Lu do something to help them elude punishment? Her stomach twisted. It had been so easy to know what to do when it was just her and Oscar. Collect information and turn it over in exchange for a new life. The more her world expanded to include others, the harder it was to think only of her and Oscar's futures.

"I heard there's a snitch. How you gonna protect our interest in the deal?" One man asked. Others echoed the concern with cries of their own.

"After tonight, it won't matter. We know who it is, and the snitch's days are numbered." Cyrus slowly circled the room in an attempt to sweat out the snitch.

When he stopped before Lu, she maintained her well-practiced mask by sheer force of will. Günter's fear was not so well masked. Cyrus lingered uncomfortably long, and the poor boy started to sway. If she didn't divert attention, he was going to make his guilt obvious to everyone here.

Lu stepped forward. "One of you's in a tiff with your wife, and she's taken it upon herself to go to the police."

Cyrus swung his stormy gaze toward her the moment she spoke.

"So if you don't go blabbering to your wives, our operations are safe. If you do, then the consequences fall on both your heads."

The more she spoke, the more ferocious it became, but at least her distraction worked. Günter breathed easier and stood straighter again. At home, Andrew would protect her from physical harm, and if he couldn't, she'd bear it as best she could. At least Günter's youthful foolishness wouldn't get him and Emma killed.

CHAPTER 22

WHETHER OR NOT LU'S OUTBURST at the meeting last week was a part of a larger plan to ensure she got more time with him, she'd achieved it. The woman managed to upset every member of the Thorne household to the point that Andrew feared leaving her at home, even if Theresa was there. Thankfully, the illusion of his contribution to the printing operations allowed him a little leniency from Frances, and Oscar had been allowed to tag along with them unsupervised the last three days.

Today's visit to the barn served as a cover to meet with Broderick while Theresa kept Lu and Oscar occupied with the puppies. As much as Theresa annoyed him, her knowledge of animal care proved a useful distraction to a puppy-obsessed little boy. Andrew made the obligatory knock before entering the barn and checking the surroundings. The smelt was cold, and the room empty save the dogs. Once allowed, Oscar ran straight for the puppies.

Lu followed at a snail's speed, that pensive expression on her face again. Something was wrong and had been since the moment he walked out of the barn before last week's meeting. Andrew was as certain of it as he was of waking each morning with a new knot in his back. Normally, when they visited the puppies, she was as captivated and enamored by their antics as Oscar. Today, he wouldn't be surprised if she suddenly looked around and asked how they got to the barn.

When her foot snagged a rough patch of ground, he caught her elbow and prevented her from falling. "What's got your head on the moon?"

"Hmm?" She blinked owlishly at him before shaking off the cobwebs of her thoughts. "Oh, nothing."

"I've never known anyone to think so deeply about nothing."

Oscar giggled as he held Jack aloft and the puppy licked his face.

A soft smile bloomed across her lips. "Theresa says Jack should be weaned and able to be brought home by Oscar's birthday."

"That's good, but not what you were thinking about."

"You're not easily distracted, and I find that annoying."

"Then consider yourself annoyed. We've time to talk before the others arrive." He led her to a low stack of hay where they had a clear view of Oscar and a modicum of privacy from anyone entering the barn. She leaned against him when they sat. "What's been on your mind so heavily these past few days?"

"The snitch."

Apparently, it was a topic heavy on everyone's minds. Hayden, Josiah, and Broderick had run information on each of the new members who'd shown at the meeting into the ground. While they'd collected plenty of names and evidence, nothing had developed with regard to the informant. If they could identify who it was, then their case would be stronger and the trials much more likely to bring about the severest punishments possible.

After an extended silence, he asked, "Are you going to elaborate?"

She gave him a sideways glance. "No."

"Two minds are better than one, especially when one of them is mine."

"I have such a humble husband." Her eyes sparkled with laughter and a playful smile teased her kissable lips.

He forced his eyes away and settled for brushing loose hair from her cheek. "What's bothering you about the snitch?"

She nibbled her lower lip as she stared at him, silent as she decided whether to speak. "Do you promise not to be angry with me?"

"I won't make a promise I'm not sure I can keep." When she looked away, he cupped her cheek and brought her gaze back. "I can, however, promise to listen with patience and not react in haste."

"Fair enough." She sighed. "I don't think Walt was the only under-cover lawman in town."

All moisture fled his mouth. "What makes you say that?"

"Whoever the snitch is, they must have a police contact somewhere. According to Priscill, the Holman brothers were arrested two days ago during a side heist they'd planned at the meeting."

An unrelated but unfortunate incident for his case. Josiah already checked into the matter. The Holman brothers had planned poorly, choosing to attack a mail wagon guarded by a plainclothes officer.

"It's not safe for us to stay here no matter what Ma Frances and the others say." Desperation colored her features, making her look ragged and beaten down. "I want to leave, Andrew. I know staying with your family is important, but it's not worth the risk. What if we're arrested? What will happen to Oscar? To us? If we leave now on our own before anything happens, we can do it the right way and take everything we need. We can have that honest life you talk about."

Her pleading made him ache. Of course she would be afraid of arrest. Maybe he could soften the blow, prepare her for the inevitable. "Oscar will be fine. I can't imagine that you will be in jail for very long. Your crimes are considered petty. Your stay would be a few months to a year at the most."

She recoiled from him and jumped to her feet as if he were a rat. "You can't be serious. What about you? You said there are plenty of warrants for your arrest."

"I'm not worried. I'll be fine no matter what happens."

"I thought you cared about us." Her breathless words and a soul-deep pain radiating from her eyes revealed the magnitude of his blunder.

Though the barn door creaked open, he kept his focus on Lu. It was too late to backtrack. If she could only see this as an act of love instead of harm. "I do care, very deeply, but there comes a time when everyone must face the consequences of their actions."

"And their words. You needn't worry about Oscar and me. We'll be fine without you."

Her piercing arrow found its mark as she barreled over to Oscar. Lu *would* be fine without him, but Andrew didn't want a without. He wanted to prepare her for the storm ahead so they could weather it *together*. He massaged his temples. Why did saying the right things have to be so difficult?

The dogs yipped and Theresa, gushing over how big the puppies had grown, joined Lu and Oscar.

Broderick rounded the haystack and offered Andrew a hand up. "Lovers' quarrel?"

"It's nothing." Andrew led the way to the other side of the barn. "Discover anything on the informant?"

"Nothing, and there's no evidence the Thornes actually know who the informant is either."

"I know we don't need the informant's testimony to have a solid case, but I'd feel more comfortable if we did."

"I've spoken with the Stendal police in case the informant tries to make contact. If they come forward before the arrests and agree to testify, the offer Walt made will stand. Otherwise, they'll serve the full sentence. That bit of information should stir them to action."

Oscar squealed from the other side of the room, drawing Andrew's attention. He joyfully pointed to one of the puppies who was rolling and playing with its siblings. Lu sat next to Oscar, nuzzling a black and tan puppy against her face as if it could wipe away the sadness. Her reaction now was only a taste of the hurt and anger she would feel toward him when his role in her arrest became evident. He couldn't change that, but he could prepare to provide her with an image of hope.

Though it chafed to ask, Andrew turned back to Broderick. "Do you think Theresa would make some sketches for me?"

"She'd love to, for the sheer satisfaction of you needing something from her. But I'm sure she'll only do it if you're the one to ask. Why? What do you have in mind?"

"Sketches of Oscar and Lu." He didn't dare ask for one of the three of them, though he wanted it. "It might make the separation easier."

Broderick's perceptive eyes studied Andrew, and Andrew tried to remain stoic and unreadable. An almost imperceptible curl to one side of his mouth followed a small nod. "I'll see to it that Theresa makes several copies."

"Thank you." Andrew cleared his throat. "Where are we with the arrest plans?"

"Isaacs is on his way to Petersburg to make arrangements with the Pike County police, and Orton is heading south to Boonville to do the same with the Warrick County police. From there, we'll coordinate with the US Marshals for two arresting parties. By the time the printing press arrives, we'll be ready."

Andrew's gaze drifted back to Lu. The Secret Service was ready to make arrests, but was he? His relationship with his wife stood on shifting sand, and he had a feeling that when the storm blew through, there would be nothing left from which to rebuild. "How long?"

"The shipment is anticipated to arrive on the sixteenth. We'll strike three days later, when everyone comes together for the first printing."

Ten days to strengthen the foundation of his marriage. It was going to take a miracle.

CHAPTER 23

Lu HID IN THE COPSE of trees across from Mary's until Broderick and Theresa wandered arm in arm down the country road. If they followed the same pattern of most evenings, Lu would have almost an hour alone with Mary. As much as Lu liked Theresa, there were some things that could not be discussed in front of her. Once they were out of sight, Lu jogged to the front door and rapped.

Pastor Newcomb opened it and glanced around as if looking for her escort. Finding none, he ushered her inside with concern etched in deep grooves on his face. "What's wrong? Why are you alone?"

"I need to talk to Mary. Privately."

Some of the tension eased from his shoulders, but the weariness remained. "Today's not been a good day. She's hardly moved from the parlor couch."

Though Lu desperately needed to talk to her friend, she wouldn't risk making her illness worse. "If you think I shouldn't—"

"She'd tan my hide if I turned you away, but just be mindful of her needs. I'll be in the office if either of you requires anything." The way he lumbered down the hall indicated the weight of a felled tree lay across his shoulders. Never had Lu seen a man love and care for his wife so deeply, though she'd thought maybe Andrew could get there as well. Until today.

Once Pastor Newcomb disappeared, Lu peered through the door to the darkened parlor.

Mary lay with a book splayed over her chest. She peeked one eye open. "Quit standing there like a stranger and come in." She waved to a nearby chair. "Sorry if I don't get up. The world won't stop spinning when I move."

"Is there anything I can do?"

"Just shut the door, turn up the light, and tell me what's troubling you."

Lu did as bidden and pulled a chair closer. "I'm in a mess, Mary, and I don't know what to do."

"Starting from the beginning usually helps."

It would, if she knew where the beginning was. Her troubles with Andrew, the Thornes, informants, lawmen, Clint, Priscill, Oscar, and even Irvine were such a tangled mess that all she'd managed to do was further confuse herself. For almost a week, she'd turned over the problem of Emma and Günter. When she'd finally decided on a plan, Andrew flatly rejected it. Rejected her. How could Andrew say he cared for them when he didn't oppose their going to jail?

"Emma Zachary and Günter Zimmerman are the snitches. If anyone in the Thorne family finds out, they'll kill them. But if the Thornes don't find out, it's only a matter of time before the police arrest us."

"So you don't know what to do?"

"I did until Andrew turned down my plan. I figured if we ran away before the arrests, we could start our new life. The rest of the Thornes would be arrested, and everyone would get what they deserved."

"Running away won't solve your problem. There would always be warrants for your arrest threatening the peace of your new life."

"But we can't have a new life together if we're in jail and Oscar in an orphanage. I don't understand him, Mary." Every time she thought she'd finally figured him out, he said or did something to confuse her. This time was the worst, and most painful, of all.

"Andrew doesn't seem the type of man to make rash decisions. I am sure he's already given this quite a bit of thought and has an explanation for why he thinks staying is best."

"Only some line about there comes a time for each man to face his consequences."

"Perhaps it has to do with all the private meetings he and Ephraim have been having lately. It sounds as if he's trying to become the man God called him to be. It takes a brave soul to look an ugly consequence in the face and not run from it or lie to get out of it. He must have made his peace with his past and is willing to do whatever God calls him to do, even if that's going to jail for a time."

"But what if it's more than jail?" Her throat constricted as if a hangman's noose already tightened around it in preparation for the floor to drop out from beneath her. "What if the consequence of my—his—crime is death?"

Mary regarded Lu with the love of a mother consoling her child. "If Andrew has placed his hope in Christ, he knows that death here on earth isn't the end of life but the beginning of it. I am sure there are people, like you and Oscar, whom he doesn't want to leave behind. But he also knows there is no grief or sorrow in heaven, and that, Lord willing, you and Oscar will join him one day and never be separated from him again. He's trusting that no matter the outcome of his being arrested, God will take care of you both in his stead."

The picture Mary painted was beautiful. It was the story of a hero, but that didn't make it her story. Andrew was a much better man than she was a woman. "God doesn't want me in heaven. I need to make up for my past and become a better person first, and I can't do that from jail."

"Oh, sweet friend," Mary brushed a tear from Lu's cheek. "Putting your hope in running away, in starting a new life, and even in becoming a better person will never be enough to heal the brokenness inside you. Only Jesus can do that. And He will if you ask."

"But Mary, you don't understand. I . . . ." The words clogged in her throat. Once she said it, there would be no going back. Her darkest secret would be out and her future in the hands of another. Lu squeezed her eyes shut, unable to bear the look on Mary's face once she discovered the true monster Lu was. "I killed Irvine."

For several pounding beats of Lu's heart, Mary said nothing. Then the couch creaked and the sound of feet hitting the floor made Lu open her eyes. Mary sat, pale and clutching the couch's arm, regarding Lu not with horror, but with the purest compassion Lu had ever seen come from another human. "Tell me what happened, not because I need to hear it or because it will absolve you of wrongdoing, but because it will heal you."

"How can telling you heal me?"

"Peace and fear cannot reside together. You either have one or the other. Never both at the same time. Confession opens your heart to hope, and hope brings peace beyond understanding." Mary grasped Lu's hand, and though weak, squeezed it. "You can trust me."

Though the chair hardly had space for it, Lu brought her knees to her chin and wrapped her arms around them. For months, she'd silently relived the nightmare. Giving it a voice couldn't be that much worse. "Clint's always claimed me as his because he was the first Thorne to . . . visit me. When Irvine convinced Ma Frances to buy me for him, Clint declared he'd been robbed. He and Irvine fought all the time, but the night before the hotel robbery, Clint went further than ever before and threatened to kill Irvine and Oscar. Irvine didn't take the threat seriously and refused to run away from his family, so while everyone slept, I snuck from our campsite to the sheriff's house and warned him about the robbery. I figured that when the robbery failed and the others were arrested, Irvine would finally run away with Oscar and me."

She should've known better than to believe such a plan would work. "The next morning, I drugged Irvine so he wouldn't go. Only I was afraid of giving him too much and it didn't work. He was woozy but refused to stay behind. I followed, begging him the whole way not to go. We were almost at the hotel when I had to confess what I'd told the sheriff or risk him getting arrested with the others."

That part of the story had been easy to tell. It was what came next that tightened the invisible noose around her neck until she could no longer speak. No matter how many times she opened her mouth, the words would not come. Only tears.

Mary staggered to kneel by Lu's side. She remained there, a silent pillar of strength and support despite her weakened body.

At long last, the words escaped in a whisper. "He turned on me. Said he wished he'd never married me." His hatred for her had been so sudden and vehement it had struck her dumb. "He pulled his gun and said Oscar didn't need a mother like me."

In that moment, something had snapped in her. Instead of running or awaiting her death, she'd attacked. Grabbed for the gun. Heard the hammer click back. Felt the barrel push against her chest. Then, with a strength she hadn't known she possessed, she'd twisted Irvine's hand away.

"The gun went off in our hands. He fell to the ground, dead. The sheriff showed up seconds later, and when Clint followed, I didn't contradict his assumption that the sheriff had been the one to kill Irvine. They're both dead because of me."

There was a heavy sigh, and then Mary shifted back to the couch. "Look at me, Lu." She waited in silence until Lu summoned the nerve to obey. "As far as the sheriff goes, Clint alone is responsible for his death. And you might have killed Irvine, but it was an accident. Even if it wasn't, nothing is too big for God to forgive.

"And when He forgives, He no longer holds it against you. Don't get me wrong. Forgiveness doesn't mean you escape the consequences here on earth, but it does help you to face them, because you're not doing so alone.

"He stays with you forever. Right here, and here." Mary touched the spot over Lu's heart and her temple. "I know it's frightening to trust someone with what you've done wrong, but He'll take it. Not just a little bit. He'll take all of it. You don't have to carry it anymore."

Lu stared at Mary, longing for it to be that simple. Could she really hand over her guilt and be given a new life like Mary said? She didn't quite understand what all it meant, but she wanted it—the love, the forgiveness, the hope that Jesus offered. "But how do I give it to Him?"

"Talk to Him like you're talking to me. There are no magic words. God listens and knows your heart."

Lu swallowed as nervousness thrummed in her body. Where should she look? What should she say? Did she close her eyes and bow her head like she'd seen in church? Or should she lift her face and hands toward the ceiling as she had sometimes seen Pastor Newcomb do? She cleared her throat a few times before allowing her gaze to bounce around the room as she talked. Tears pooled in her eyes and ran down her throat as her anguished confession and the desire to be forgiven poured from her soul. Oh, how she wanted to change! But lacked the power to do so. She needed help. She needed Jesus. Lu spoke until sobs choked out her words and cut off her prayer. Mary enfolded Lu in her arms and rubbed circles on Lu's back until the tears dried up.

Lu pulled away and looked at Mary's wet face. "Did I do it right? Was it good enough?"

"Whenever you give Jesus yourself and your guilt, He makes it good enough."

Her next breath came freer than she could ever remember. Though her past had not changed, something else had. Something inside her. There was a peace that she couldn't quite explain. Though she knew consequences might still come, the fear of them didn't have quite the same grip they did as before. Undeniable hope for a future with Andrew and Oscar filled her, even if their future together didn't come until much later.

"Take this." Mary handed her the worn leather book that had lain across her chest earlier. "Keep it and read it."

As Lu held the Bible in her hand, tears pricked her eyes again. "But I can't."

"Yes, you can. Ephraim will happily buy me a new one."

"No, Mary, I can't *read*."

"Then it's a good thing God provided you with a husband who can."

She spoke as if that were the easiest answer in the world. "But Andrew doesn't know, and I don't want him to."

"You're married, Lu. He's going to find out eventually. Take this to him, tell him what you've done, and I promise you, Andrew will read to you without shaming you. He's a good man who has a heart for the Lord."

She couldn't deny Andrew was a good man—better than she deserved—but that didn't stop the cold sweat from breaking out on her back at the thought of telling him. She rather enjoyed his fond looks of admiration. To lose them because of her deficiencies would crush her. It was probably best to wait until the evidence of her crying faded, and she'd had time to come up with a reasonable excuse for why she'd broken the rules and gone off by herself again.

Lu resettled Mary on the couch and covered her with a blanket. The chill of night had crept into the room without notice, but now that she felt it, Lu couldn't ignore it. "Are the windows open?"

"Just the one behind the couch." Mary waved in the direction of the still curtains. "Ephraim opened it to help with the nausea, but you can close it now."

Dread pooled in her stomach even as reason argued that no one passing by could've heard her confession. She choked back her fear, squeezed behind the couch, and pushed aside the curtains. Alcohol stench strong enough to be straight from the bottle punched her in the face. The Newcombs were teetotalers, not even keeping it in the house for medicinal purposes. Bile burned in her throat as Lu stuck her head out the window. On the ground, a bottle of Clint's favorite brand of whiskey lay on its side.

God, please, no!

She searched the creeping shadows of late evening, but there was no evidence he'd stuck around. Lu clutched her throat and reeled back. If he'd heard anything of what she confessed tonight, his power over her would be complete.

CHAPTER 24

CLINT WAS PASSED OUT IN his bed when Lu arrived back home, but that hadn't helped her to sleep. All night long she tossed and turned, trying to anticipate when and how Clint would use his power over her. She should tell Andrew, but that meant confessing everything to him, and if she wasn't willing to share with the man that she couldn't read, she certainly wasn't going to tell him she'd accidentally killed his brother.

She waited until Andrew had left for the morning to get dressed. She didn't want to leave Landkreis without him, but if she and Oscar didn't leave before Clint awoke, there would be no future for them. First, she'd gather some food to take with her, then wake Oscar and leave under the guise of seeing the puppies. If they were lucky, they'd be able to take a horse from the corral without notice.

When Lu stepped into the kitchen, Priscill turned from where she stood at the counter stirring biscuit dough. "'Bout time you got up. I was afraid you'd miss all the fun." Villainous excitement sparked in her eyes. "Cyrus knows who the informants are and is gathering a posse to go kill 'em."

Lu froze in her reach for the remains of yesterday's bread loaf. Surely this wasn't happening. "Who?"

"Emma Zachary and Günter Zimmerman. For good measure, we're going to shoot the widow too."

The world wavered beneath her feet, and she gripped the counter.

No. This couldn't be happening. Not now. If she didn't leave before Clint woke, she'd lose her chance, but she couldn't leave Emma, Günter, and Widow Zachary to die. She squeezed her eyes shut. Why did doing the right thing have to mean sacrificing her only window of escape?

She blew out a slow breath. It didn't matter. She'd not be responsible for more deaths when it was in her power to stop them. "I'll saddle the horses so we can join them on the hunt."

Priscill smirked. "You go do that. We'll be ready when you get back."

The summons to Pastor Newcomb's office was curious, if not a bit unsettling. While the man had been made responsible for mailing and retrieving all communication with Captain Abbott, Andrew had the sense that whatever Pastor Newcomb wanted to talk about had to do with Lu. Ever since her short disappearance and then red-faced return last night, she'd been . . . quiet. At first, he'd attributed it to their disagreement, but the way she'd watched him as he tucked Oscar in told him it was something different. Almost like she wanted to tell him something and was either too afraid or didn't know how. When he'd asked her directly, she'd deflected and then pretended to fall asleep.

Theresa rose from the rocker on the Newcombs' porch, a book in hand. "Is Lu awake?"

"No. She doesn't usually get up for another hour or so."

"I think she knows something." Theresa's brows furrowed. "Yesterday, she warned me that Broderick and I should leave town as soon as possible so we don't end up arrested."

"The Holman brothers' arrest has her spooked. That's all."

"It's more than that, I think. I'm going to watch for her and see if I can get her to talk."

Andrew nodded and entered the house, but Theresa's suspicions rolled around in his head until they became his own. Was it possible

Lu was the snitch? She had access to information, had defied the family in other ways, and wanted to leave. The possibility had merit, but he'd need something more than circumstantial evidence before confronting her.

Pastor Newcomb called him back into the office. With dark circles under his eyes and a pallor closer to his wife's usual shade, the poor pastor looked exhausted.

"Thank you for coming. Help yourself to the coffee if there's any left." After closing the door behind Andrew, he dropped to his chair like the weight of the world shoved him into it. "It's been a long night with Mary, but I felt the Lord pressing upon me not to delay this talk."

Apprehension flooded his veins.

Pastor Newcomb continued. "Are you still considering an annulment?"

Some of the tension released. "No."

Although he'd expected the pastor to show relief at his answer, the man's burden only seemed to increase. "Then I fear God has called you to walk a very difficult road. Lu came to Mary last night and . . ." Pastor Newcomb tapped his clasped hands against his lips for a moment before blowing out a long breath. "And all I can say with confessional privilege is that Lu needs your full attention right now—not as someone connected to your case, but as your wife."

"Did she share something about the case?"

"Let the Cosgroves, Hayden, and Joe focus on the Thornes. All else will come in time."

The office door banged opened. "Lu snuck out of the house." Theresa's words flew out in breathless panic. "Clint's following."

Andrew shot to his feet. "What direction?"

"If she kept a straight path, toward the woods behind the cornfield. Maybe toward Stendal?"

Andrew brushed past her and his legs ate up the distance between the Newcomb house and the Thorne woods. Clint catching Lu alone would not end well.

She should've known better than to think Günter wouldn't eventually give himself and Emma away. The boy was too wet behind the ears to keep his composure under pressure. Lu ducked under a branch and cut the straightest path possible toward her hidden supply bag. There should still be enough money to get the Zacharys to Evansville, where they could start a new life. Staying any longer was a risk to their lives. Lu wasn't sure yet how to protect Günter, but she'd find a way. First, she had to convince Widow Zachary to take the money and run— before the woman shot her.

"Where're you going in such a rush?"

Clint was following her? He was supposed to still be asleep. She hopped over a log and veered her path away from her hiding spot and the Zacharys'. She'd never make it to either before Clint caught up, but she couldn't risk him realizing her plan.

"You can stop running now. Ain't no one going to catch us together."

A frightening truth. The only path leading to help was behind her—and through him. Running aimlessly wasn't the answer. She had to be smarter than this. She glanced around, and the pond ahead gave her an idea. Stopping just short of the edge and on the other side of a log, she faced Clint.

He slowed to a panting strut, his predatory eyes gleaming with the thrill of a chase. "I always knew you favored me over Irvine, just didn't realize how much 'til last night. Never woulda thought you had it in you to kill him."

So he had heard. With every fiber of her self-restraint, she forced herself to remain rooted to the spot. Escape depended upon him getting close enough to touch while still being caught unawares. "I don't know what you're talking about."

"You don't have to lie out here. If we work together, we can get Andrew and Priscill outta the way. Make it look like an accident."

"We'll never get away with it."

"Sure we will. Andrew and Priscill will get sick on Ma's cooking and never recover."

As Clint drew closer, continuing to lay out his delusional plan, Lu watched his steps. The moment he started to step over the log, she'd act. Too soon or too late and she wouldn't be able to throw him off-balance. "Don't you think she'd suspect?"

"Not if the rest of us get sick too. We'll just make sure the arsenic doesn't get in our food. It's high time Andrew got what he deserved." His savage eyes flamed with murderous glee. Lu took an involuntary step back.

Mud sucked her boot under, trapping her foot in its unyielding grasp. Before she could yank free, Clint began his step over the log. It was either free herself or enact her plan. She ensnared his arm and yanked with all the strength her body could muster. He hooked his free arm around her waist and dragged her down with him.

Stagnant pond scum splashed over her head and filled her nostrils, mercilessly burning its way down her throat. She tried to lift her head to gasp for breath, but Clint's weight pressed her body deeper into the slimy sediment and prevented her head from breaching the water's surface. His elbow jammed into her gut as he shifted away, forcing the remaining air from her lungs. She thrust her head above water and gasped for breath. Her hand found the muddy bank and she clawed her way toward it. Water weighted her skirts and her feet slipped on the slick, sludgy bottom. Getting free of the pond was as impossible as escaping Clint.

"What'd you do that for? Now Ma'll realize we were together." He grabbed a fistful of her bodice and hauled her forward onto the grassy edge. "I might as well get some enjoyment out of the deal."

Lu drove the heel of her boot into his shin and scrambled on hands and knees to gain distance from him. By the time she struggled to her feet, he was clutching the hem of her skirt.

"Let go of my wife."

Lu whipped toward Andrew's voice. Bless her soul. She'd never been so glad to see a gun drawn and a man laying claim to her.

Clint's hand flew to his waist, but his confident reach turned into a frantic pat. Using his momentary search for his weapon as a distraction, she bolted toward Andrew.

"Go." Andrew remained intent on a frustrated Clint.

Not without him. As soon as Clint found his gun, he'd go straight into a shoot-out. Lu grabbed Andrew's arm and tugged him in the direction of the house. "Come on."

"I'm not putting my back to him."

"I'll guide, you backstep."

Clint spun in a circle and searched the ground while Lu guided Andrew backward toward the house. When Clint didn't find his gun, he dropped to his knees at the bank's edge and splashed around in the murky water with his back to them.

Andrew wheeled around and gripped her hand. "Run."

In two strides, he pulled ahead of her. The splashing behind them stopped, and Lu dared a glance over her shoulder. Something large and gray flew past her face and made a thud as it connected with the back of Andrew's head. He crumpled face-first to the ground.

"Andrew!" She dropped to his side, her hands fluttering, unsure where to land.

With a pained groan, he rolled over and blinked at her with an unfixed gaze.

After another splash, Clint shouted a victory cry. "Looks like we don't need that poison after all." He rose from the pond's edge, weapon in hand.

Andrew fumbled with his gun but with the way his hand shook, the shot was likely to miss.

"Pathetic." Clint took aim.

Lu couldn't—wouldn't—lose Andrew to Clint. She wrenched the gun from Andrew's grasp and shielded his body with her own as she twisted to face Clint. With quavering hands, she lifted the heavy revolver and pulled back the hammer. *God, forgive me.* She squeezed her eyes shut and pulled the trigger.

A double blast echoed in her ears, leaving behind a ringing that competed with her heartbeat for volume. Sulfur filled her nostrils, transporting her back to the last time she'd held a gun. Though her eyes stayed closed, the image of Irvine's confused face before he collapsed at her feet filled her vision. Her grip tightened around the weapon, though all she wanted to do was let it go.

Killing Irvine had been an accident.

This . . . this wasn't.

A sob broke loose. Though someone said her name, she refused to open her eyes. She couldn't do it again. She couldn't see the consequences of her actions.

Andrew's arms came around her waist and pulled her to his chest. His voice rose over the ring in her ears. "Lu, put my gun down."

Swallowing hard, she lowered her head before opening her eyes. With her eyeline reaching no farther than Andrew's feet, she laid it on the ground. He shifted beneath her and then rotated her so that she became tucked against his chest. Never in all her life had she found comfort and safety in a man's arms, but Andrew's strong hold provided that and far more. Her whole body relaxed under his touch and the gentle reassurances murmured in her ear as his head rested atop hers. Slowly, the ringing and thrumming dulled to where Clint's curses overpowered the noise.

Thank you, God.

After gathering her nerve, she faced Clint. He sat on the ground as Theresa bandaged his leg with what appeared to be strips of her petticoat. Broderick stood guard nearby.

Clint's furious glare found her. "You shot at me."

"You're lucky she missed, or you'd have had two holes in you." Broderick stepped out of Theresa's way as she shifted positions.

Theresa paused in her ministrations and looked up. "How do you know it wasn't Lu's bullet that hit him?"

"Because I aimed for his thigh, and that's what I hit. I figured killing him would cause more troubles than it solved."

Feeling steadier, Lu pulled away from Andrew. Blood dripped from his nose and he winced as he moved his head.

"Oh, Andrew!" She clambered off his lap. "You're hurt!"

"I'll be fine. Just help me home."

He wasn't fine, and it only became more evident as they struggled to stand. Even with Lu as his support, he stumbled every other step. Theresa abandoned Clint and supported Andrew's other side. Given that the man didn't argue, he must be far worse than she'd first suspected, and that scared her more than anything.

CHAPTER 25

CHAOS ERUPTED WHEN THEY ENTERED the house. Ma Frances became hysterical, Priscill spewed accusations, Cyrus escaped by going to fetch the doctor, and poor Oscar, overwhelmed by all the commotion, added his own wails. It took hours for the household to settle. Even after the adults had calmed, Oscar remained clingy and afraid. Lu crept into the bedroom with him on her hip, careful not to let too much light into the room from the door. Andrew slept with a bandage wrapped around his head to protect the few stitches he needed from catching and tugging in his sleep. Though no blood remained around his nose, it had taken on a darker shade that spread to his eyes.

She tiptoed to the bed and whispered, "See Oscar, he's sleeping."

Oscar's hands fisted around her shirt. "But not like Pa, right?"

Her throat constricted as she rubbed his back. She'd forgotten that's how they'd described Irvine's death to him. "No, baby, not like Pa." Though Andrew had come closer than she liked to joining Irvine.

"Can I sleep with New Pa?"

"New Pa?"

He nodded against her shoulder. "MawMaw says Uncle Andrew's my new pa."

How was she supposed to react to that? Irvine was his pa, not Andrew, even if she wanted Andrew to become like a father to him. And how would Andrew feel about being called New Pa? He hadn't exactly planned on marrying her, let alone becoming a father. "I don't know that Uncle Andrew wants you to call him that."

"It's fine." Andrew's voice came out gravelly and his eyes were slow to open. "Come on, Giant Killer. Climb in next to me."

Given the fact that Andrew barely moved enough to pat the spot next to him, his head must still pain him. Careful not to jostle Andrew, she lifted Oscar over him to the empty space between the wall and his body.

"Here." Oscar laid his stuffed dog on Andrew's chest. "He'll make you better."

"Thanks." Though Andrew winced as Oscar wiggled and nestled against his body, he didn't complain.

The image they formed held her entire heart. How was it God could love her enough to forgive her and still have enough grace to bring Andrew into her life? Mary said they had an eternal future together, but was it wrong to hope and fight for an earthly one? Walt had made her a deal based on the testimony she was going to give. Maybe if she figured out who his partner was, that person would be willing to expand the deal to include a pardon for Andrew.

She unlocked the trunk at the end of her bed and pulled out the document and badge booklet from her circus-tent dress. Mary already knew her darkest secret. Revealing that she was Walt's informant would be nothing in comparison. Once Mary read the words on the other side of the star-shaped badge, maybe she and Pastor Newcomb could help her find the officer and make arrangements for him and Lu to meet secretly. How Andrew would react once he found out the truth, she wasn't sure, but after today's fiasco with his family, surely he would be closer to accepting their need to leave them behind.

Tucking the items in her pocket, she padded downstairs. Perched at the table's end, Ma Frances waited like a dragon with smoke smoldering from its nostrils.

Lu rubbed her arm. "Andrew needs more medicine. I'll be at Grossman's if you need me."

"You're not going anywhere. Not for a long time."

"But Andrew—"

"I'll see to purchasing any needs he may have later. It's time we address a bigger problem in this house than a lack of medicine. Sit." The single word scraped like the strike of a match before a flame.

Lu dropped into the nearest chair and braced for Ma Frances's wrath.

"I've long ignored Priscill's concerns about an affair between you and Clint, but no more. You've pitted all of my sons against each other since Colorado, and I won't tolerate it any longer. I've already lost one son because of you. I ain't losing any others."

Ma Frances circled and stopped behind Lu. "If Andrew weren't so enamored with you, I'd kill you now." Fingers bit into Lu's shoulders. "You will stay faithful to him and abandon your harlot ways. No more evenings at the saloon and no more sneaking out. You and Clint are never to be in the same room without me present. My son deserves a wife in all manner of the word. No more of this sleeping on the floor nonsense. You will share his bed and tend to his *every* need."

Her grip released, leaving behind an ache that promised bruising come morning. She returned to Lu's front, and her knifelike eyes stabbed through any bravado Lu might've had.

"Any disregard for even one of these rules, and you'll join the likes of Walt. I will have my perfect and happy family, even if that means killing you to achieve it. Am I understood?"

Unable to speak, Lu nodded.

"Good. Return to your room. There's no need to be downstairs again until Andrew's fully recovered. I'll see to dinner after I've returned from Grossman's."

Lu felt Ma Frances's piercing eyes following every step of her climb. Had a door been at the base, she was certain Ma Frances would've locked it. At the garret window, Lu watched Ma Frances leave. She'd never make it to Mary's and back before the woman returned and followed through with her threat.

The stairs creaked and Lu turned.

Priscill stood on the landing with a smug smile. "Now that Ma has laid out her rules for you, I've got some of my own. Well, not so much rules as warnings." She sauntered forward and lowered her voice. "I know you're the snitch. You confirmed it when you left to warn Günter and Emma after I lied about Cyrus going for a posse."

Only by the thinnest of threads did Lu hold on to her composure. "I was going out to meet Clint."

"I might have believed that if I hadn't found this while exploring with Oscar." Priscill returned to the top of the steps, bent down, and tossed a canvas bag onto the floor by Lu's feet. "The next time you pack a bag to run away with a marshal, you shouldn't use one with his name stitched on it."

The feeling of ice water splashed over Lu's body, and she tried not to shiver. "That bag could be anybody's."

"It's filled with your and Oscar's clothes and enough money to disappear for good. Or at least, it *had* money. I spent it."

With that evidence, Priscill could show Ma Frances, and Lu would be murdered. The fact Priscill hadn't didn't bode well. "What do you want?"

Her coy demeanor dropped. "I want you gone."

"I'll gladly leave with Oscar and Andrew the first chance I get."

"No. I want *you* gone. Oscar and Andrew stay."

"Why? You don't need them."

"Oh, but I do." A bark of laughter followed her sneer. "Poor Ma. It will be such a devastation to find Andrew dead, poisoned by the woman she forced him to marry. She might have failed in killing herself the first time she lost Andrew, but I can't imagine she'd fail again. I might even help her along."

The woman was as delusional as Clint. "I'll tell her what you're planning."

"She'll never believe you, especially when I prove you're a snitch." Priscill picked up the bag and held it up with a devilish smile.

"I'll tell Clint and Cyrus. They won't allow you to kill their mother."

"Cyrus might not, but my little plan will endear me to Clint. He's tired of Ma's control over us all. He'll ensure Cyrus doesn't interfere.

Once you and Ma are out of the way, I'll have everything I want. Including a son."

Lu's composure crumbled. It didn't matter what happened to her, but Oscar could not be left to be raised by these monsters. "I'll never leave."

"Don't be foolish. I'm giving you a gift. The chance at a new life, free of this family."

She'd never choose a future without Oscar and Andrew. Priscill had to know that. "Why?"

"Because it's fun to watch you suffer like I've suffered as a second-choice wife and daughter. Choose your suffering well. Andrew dies either way, but if you stay, I'll have no reason to keep Oscar alive. But leave"—her fingers flexed and curled as if taking particular delight in Lu's anguish—"and you get to live the rest of your life wondering what he looks like, what he's become, and if Clint beat him like his Pa beat him. But at least he'll be alive."

Priscill wasn't just delusional; she was evil. There must be something about the Thorne family that sucked people in and corrupted them to the point the devil would be proud. Lu would not allow evil to win. She'd leave and go straight to the Petersburg police. They would be outside the Thorne influence and could act before Priscill killed Andrew, and rescue Oscar too.

"I can see your mind working." Priscill lifted her chin like she was a queen and peered down her nose at Lu. "I've never believed you to be the empty-headed harlot they all think you are. I love Oscar, but he's not my own flesh and blood. If you go to the police, he'll just be another casualty of a crime gone wrong. I imagine it will go a bit like when Irvine died. Only I'll be holding the gun instead of you."

Horror struck her like Cyrus's lead knuckles.

"Don't act so surprised. Clint muttered about it all night in his sleep. It's only a matter of time before they all find out. There's no way you can win." She shook the bag again. "You have one week to disappear. If you even think of telling Andrew, I'll slip him one of Ma's poisons and make it look like you killed him to be with Clint. Then Ma will kill you, and I'll still get everything I want."

"I can't sneak out of here. I'll be dead before I make it off the property."

"That's not my problem. One week, Lu. Don't take advantage of my generosity. This is your only chance to leave and have Oscar live." Priscill slung the bag over her shoulder and disappeared downstairs.

Lu thudded against the wall. How was she going to save her family? There were no right choices, only death and destruction. Her gaze lifted to the wooden beams of the angled ceiling. *God, You promised to be with me. Save us, because I don't know what to do.*

Chapter 26

Pastor Newcomb must have a bit of prophet in him. Since getting hit in the head with a rock three days ago, all Andrew'd been able to do was give Lu his full attention. Well, that and sleep. Although he suspected the amount he slept had more to do with his body relishing the soft mattress instead of a hard floor than it did with avoiding his constant headache.

Andrew peeked an eye open and caught Lu in her usual spot, sitting in the rocker pulled from Oscar's room and staring at the closed Bible in her lap. It was a curious sight given that the Bible appeared well-worn and he was certain that Lu was not the one to have brought it to that state. More curious still was her attempt to hide it every time she realized he was awake. Certainly she wouldn't have stolen a Bible when his was among their things and easy enough to read if she wanted. He'd been too miserable to press for answers before, but now curiosity outweighed his discomfort.

"Where'd you get the Bible from?"

Lu startled and each word hesitated before releasing. "It's Mary's. She gave it to me."

"Why?" Not that it was out of character for a pastor's wife to hand out Bibles, but to give her personal one?

Lu ducked her head. "Because I asked Jesus to forgive me."

"Oh, Lu." It was all he could manage to say, though his soul welled with praises to God. To have a shared faith in marriage was no small gift. One he hadn't even realized he'd already accepted as something he'd never have. He sat up, despite the wave of nausea it brought on, and drew her next to him on the bed.

Wide eyes regarded him with apprehension.

He wanted to embrace her and kiss her breathless, but settled for caressing her cheek as he sunk into the endless fathoms of her blue-gray eyes. "There is nothing better in marriage than when a husband and wife walk in Christ together. God is so good to give us that gift."

She blinked. "You mean it? You're happy?"

"Of course I am. I've always wanted a wife I could share in God's Word with. What do you say?" He collected the Bible from the rocker and extended it toward her. "Would you read from Luke for us?"

She gaped. "Aloud?"

"How else would you read it?"

Red crept up her neck into her face. After a visible swallow, she looked away. "I don't know how to read."

He sat stunned—so long that he wanted to kick himself. He should've known, or at least suspected as much. The inventory lists when she'd been looking for his recipe. Her insistence he be the one to read at night while she cuddled with Oscar. The lack of writing materials in the room. All of it pointed to something more common than not of a woman in her position. He might not be able to change the past, but he could provide an education.

"If you want to learn, I'll teach you."

Her face snapped toward his. "You'll what?"

"I'll teach you. I can't promise to do it well, but my—" He'd almost said mother. Lu didn't know of Mother Elise, but God willing, she would soon. "A dear woman I know will be delighted to step in where I fail. She was a teacher before she married."

"You're not bothered that I'm stupid?"

A spike of anger shot through him, along with the compulsion to punch whoever planted that seed in Lu's head. "You are not stupid, and I'll not tolerate you thinking so." Cupping her cheeks so she couldn't look away, he held her gaze. Doubt trembled there, yet tentative hope hovered on the edges, longing to take hold. "You are the smartest woman I've ever met, and anyone who says different is an idiot. You've been given circumstances no one wants and yet survived. No one could've done better, whether able to read or not."

A tremulous smile chased away any remaining fear etching her face, and she leaned into his touch. "I don't understand why God brought us together, but I am glad He did."

"So am I." He leaned in with every intention of capturing her lips but stopped short at her quick intake of breath. Curse the men who robbed Lu of choice and stole her ability to be unguarded in moments like these. He pulled back, the desire unmet. After situating himself with his back against the head of the bed, he patted the space next to him. "I'll read."

She nibbled her lip before easing next to him. Remembering how Mother Elise pointed to the words as she read to him, he angled the Bible on his lap so Lu could follow along. As he read, Lu snuggled against him with her head on his shoulder following the slide of his finger across the page. This peaceful, sweet moment felt hallowed and created a yearning for a miracle that only Christ could provide. The miracle of a marriage that survived and thrived like the woman beside him.

Progress was slow, as Lu peppered him with questions after every sentence. Verses that had become stale from years of study became fresh and new again as he saw them through Lu's eyes. A hunger for understanding burned in her voice, and her concentration on the page never wavered. By the time they'd reached the midpoint of chapter one, his head throbbed and the words blurred. The disappointment in having to stop was evident in her face, but she smiled at him anyway and pecked him on the cheek.

"Thank you for teaching me."

The heartfelt gratitude and the softness of her words swelled in his heart. Having her near and so open with him made him want her all the nearer. When she moved to get up, he held her tighter. "Stay. Lie with me."

She froze, dread replacing the prior contentment. After a moment, she swallowed. "Of course." Her hands fumbled with the top button of her blouse.

Realization of what she thought he'd meant dawned. Not that the idea wasn't appealing, but he'd never force it. "I just want you next to me while I sleep. My head hurts too much for anything else."

Her evident relief at avoiding intimacy pinched, but the concern and care for him that shone in her eyes soothed the sting.

"Do you need medicine?"

"No. Just you next to me while I rest."

She shifted to lie down next to him, the cover a barrier between them. With one arm around her, his whole body relaxed and sleep came quickly.

Though his snore reached full capacity within minutes, Lu stayed in his one-arm hold and stared at the man she hadn't chosen but would now if given the chance. His often-dour face was smoothed into placid contentment, and the hint of a smile lifted his lips as his arm tightened and then relaxed around her. She'd never wanted to be in a man's arms before, let alone felt this contented to be held. It was all so new and . . . exciting? She smoothed a wild hair on Andrew's muttonchops and sighed.

He'd almost kissed her, and while in the moment it had scared her stiff, she wondered now what it would've felt like. Everything about Andrew was so different than the others. She could almost feel the gentleness he'd bring. Even though the thought of going further sent her heart into a stampede, it couldn't be so bad. Not when love—genuine love, one that reflected God's care for her—was at the foundation.

But this love for him wasn't simple. Andrew frustrated her beyond words with his determination to be accepted by the Thornes. In truth, each time he chose them over her and Oscar, it hurt worse than when Irvine attempted to kill her. She understood the need to be accepted and wanted by family, and if his family was anyone else other than the Thornes, she'd want that for him too. But she knew what he didn't. They were a poisonous and delusional lot. If Andrew stayed with them, he'd change and be lost to their never-ending pursuit of control, wealth, and power. If he didn't die first.

She laid her arm over the rise and fall of his chest and wrestled once again with what to do. Priscill couldn't really expect Lu to abandon Andrew to a death sentence and Oscar to live as a criminal. Even if she *were* willing to abandon them, the moment she disappeared, Priscill would rat her out as the informant to Ma Frances. Leaving or staying would end the same for her. Death. Given the chance to choose her death, she'd prefer one where she rescued Andrew, Oscar, Emma, and Günter. Ma Frances's rules left little room for Lu to maneuver to get help from Mary without alerting Priscill, but all she needed was one hair-width opportunity.

Oscar's voice joined the creaking door. "Mrs. Resa's here."

Pulling from Andrew's hold, she eased from the bed and followed Oscar downstairs.

Theresa stood in the kitchen with sketching supplies in hand. "I needed a break from engraving plates and thought it'd be fun to make some sketches of you and Oscar."

Ma Frances looked up from her and Priscill's work at the counter canning beans. "A sketch sounds like a wonderful idea. You'll do Oscar and me first."

"Then me and Oscar." Priscill leveled a poison-tipped smirk at Lu. "I must have a picture with my favorite child."

Rage coiled inside Lu until her nails bit into her palms. Oscar would *never* be Priscill's anything.

"It's settled then. Lu, return to Andrew. You're not needed here." Ma Frances's dismissal left little room for Lu to argue.

Not so for Theresa. "Actually, you and Priscill are a mess from canning. You'll need to change and freshen up before sitting for me. I simply cannot work with anything less than a pristine model." Theresa flashed an impish smile that made Lu appreciate the woman even more. "Lu and Oscar will be perfect for warming up my skills while we wait."

The shocked and then restrained expressions of frustration from Ma Frances and Priscill almost coaxed a victorious laugh from Lu. As they had mussed hair, wet dresses, and were dripping with sweat, they couldn't argue. Theresa was a bold and brilliant confidence woman.

"We'll be at the barn with the puppies. You can join us when you're ready."

At that, Ma Frances put her foot down. "Lu is forbidden to be so far from Andrew. The parlor will suffice. Priscill and I will be ready in ten minutes."

"Take your time. I have all afternoon to sketch." Theresa nudged Lu's arm, and once the door shut behind them, she whispered, "I'm sorry. After three days locked up with Andrew, I thought you might want a break."

"It's all right. There's no escaping Ma Frances or Priscill. Believe me, I've tried."

Theresa lowered her voice to barely audible. "Do you want to escape? For good, that is."

Lu hesitated. Theresa had no loyalties to the family and trusting her might be their only way out of this mess. Lu glanced toward the open fireplace. On the other side, Priscill's skirts hovered dangerously close to the flames, indicating she listened intently.

After a silent nod to Theresa and then a tip of her head to indicate Priscill's presence, Lu spoke. "Oscar, why don't you grab your horses so we can play while Mrs. Theresa draws."

"That sounds like a wonderful idea." Theresa grinned and directed them to the wingbacks farthest from the fireplace. She flipped to a fresh page in her sketchbook and laid out several pencils on the low table. "It's not like Drew to be laid low for so long. How is he doing?"

Other than the death threat looming over him? Lu lowered onto the edge of the other wingback chair and wished Priscill's skirt would catch fire and give Lu the ability to speak freely. "He has a headache that doesn't go away and is resting a lot, but he's fine enough." At least, she hoped so. Going on the run was never easy on a body, but they didn't have time for a full recovery.

"I'm glad to hear it. Hayden and Joe returned this morning and want to meet with Andrew as soon as possible. Do you think he could meet today?"

Were circumstances different, she'd insist on waiting a few more days, but none of his injuries were life-threatening. Staying here any longer, on the other hand, could be. If they met at Mary's, she could at least give Mary the lawman's documents before running and have her notify him of the danger to Emma and Günter. "I'll help Andrew to the Newcombs' after he's finished resting. It's closer than the tack shop."

"Perfect."

Theresa shifted to inane topics while they waited for Oscar, but Lu's mind, preoccupied with the possible ramifications of encouraging the meeting, couldn't keep up with the conversation. Once they left the house, Priscill would set her plans into motion. It wouldn't be safe for Andrew, Oscar, and Lu to return, but could Andrew handle the physical strain of running now? And what would she have to reveal for him to agree to try?

Chapter 27

Enough was enough. Andrew swung his feet over the bed's edge and stretched. He'd taken advantage of Josiah's and Hayden's absences by luxuriating in bed, but no more. Headache or not, he had work to do—even if spending endless hours with Lu appealed more than closing the case. As much as he hated Broderick's tactics in the Cincinnati investigation, Andrew was beginning to understand them. Loving a woman changed everything.

Especially when that woman was Lu.

Lu stood before him and worried her hands as he prepared to push from the bed. If he staggered, would she try to catch him? He dipped his chin to hide a rogue smile and purposely stumbled forward. With a yelp, she jumped to his side, wrapped an arm around his back, and placed a hand on his chest. Warm tingles radiated from her touch and tempted him to postpone the meeting a few more hours.

"Stubborn man. What am I going to do with you?"

"I'm not stubborn. I wanted you in my arms."

In a smoothness not even Josiah could achieve, Andrew tugged Lu in front of him and drew her against his body. Though her eyes widened at the suddenness of it, she didn't stiffen or pull away. Instead, her arms looped around his neck and her warm breath reached up to tease his lips. She peered at him through flirtatious lashes with those brilliant blue-gray orbs and a saucy smile that made his heart race and challenged his restraint. But until they talked and agreed they were ready for more, he wouldn't steal even a kiss from his wife.

"All you had to do was ask." She pecked his cheek, only further tempting him to have that conversation now. "I'm here for whatever you need."

Annoyance with their situation flared. What he needed was for there to be no secrets between them. No case threatening to destroy this unquenchable hope of something more with this woman. He needed the freedom to love her not as a burden forced upon him, but as a part of him that he didn't want to live without.

He caressed her cheek before pressing a kiss to her forehead. He wanted to do more, oh so much more, but he released her and stepped back before he succumbed to the urge. Walking out the door was the wisest, but hardest, step to take. Depending on what Josiah and Hayden had to say, this may very well be the last moment of total ease between them. No matter how much he wanted to ignore it, the torrential storm of arrests was coming, and neither of them would escape unscathed.

Lu's smile faltered, almost as if she could read his thoughts. "Andrew?"

The hesitancy in her voice made him wonder if she had.

She drew a shaky breath. "Do you trust me?"

"Yes." More than he ever thought possible.

"I need you to do something without asking any questions. Please." She pointed at the floor grate where Frances's voice invaded the room.

The desperation and fear in her tone aroused every fiber of protectiveness in him. He strode to the bed, tossed a pillow over the grate, pulled her to the farthest corner, and leaned in. "What's Frances said now?"

"Not her—Priscill. She's going to kill you. We need to get Oscar, go to Mary's, and then leave Landkreis for good."

"Why me? Of anyone, it's you she'd want to kill, and I won't let that happen."

"She gave me an ultimatum, and in both choices, you die. I can explain everything when we leave, but please, trust me. Once we walk out that door, we can't come back."

"Are you certain the danger's imminent?"

"I am."

He couldn't leave Landkreis yet, but at the very least he could get Lu and Oscar out of Priscill's reach. Once Lu shared Priscill's plan, he should be able to avoid any attempts on his life until the arrests occurred. Hayden, Josiah, and Broderick would provide any support he needed.

Andrew collected his revolver and derringer from the dressing table. "Where's Clint?" Although he was feeling better, he wasn't up to an encounter with the man just yet.

"Probably in bed. He's been milking his misery for all it's worth."

"Good." He crammed extra cartridges into his coat and then retrieved Lu's dagger from the drawer. "Keep this on you at all times."

Lu secured it in the waistband of her skirt. "We just need Oscar."

At his nod, the lines of fear and anxiety smoothed into her familiar saloon mask. Though he hated she'd had to develop the skill, he was glad for it at this moment.

Downstairs, Frances sat at the table with silent tears running down her face as she stared at a piece of paper. Whatever upset her, he hoped it kept her distracted enough to ignore them. He stretched to skip the last two noisy steps, but didn't turn to lift Lu over them in time.

At the creak of the stairs, Frances looked up. "Where do you think you're going? You should be resting."

"Lu's helping me to the tack shop to visit with Joe and Hayden."

"Ain't no need to overtax yourself. They'll come here."

She swiped away her tears and stood, reverently placing the paper—a sketch of her and Oscar—on the mantel next to Andrew's childhood attempt at whittling a dog. Andrew edged Lu toward the door as Frances stood transfixed on the image while her free hand wrapped around the dog. Before they could sneak past, her voice cracked, hoarse with emotion.

"I wish I had a picture of all of us together, especially with Irvine. He would've loved having you back."

Red and puffy eyes turned to meet his. Grief beyond verbal expression cried out to him, mourning her child like any other mother would. The evil part of her that killed without remorse and poisoned her children to keep them under her power had retreated elsewhere. She was exactly the woman Mother Elise had taught him to forgive—broken, hopeless, and in need of a savior. Unexpected compassion rose within him, and the anger and hatred he'd struggled with transformed back into pity. He still didn't approve of her or her actions, but forgiveness wasn't about that. It was about following the command given to forgive as Jesus forgave—without that forgiveness being earned or deserved.

Lu shifted next to him, similar compassion breaking through her mask. "I'm sure Theresa could sketch a picture of the family and include Irvine. I still have the wanted poster of him in the dressing-table drawer."

Frances turned away abruptly. "Don't be ridiculous. Irvine's gone, and that's that. All I can hope for is to keep what I've got left of my family together and happy."

"If you change your mind, I'm sure Theresa would be willing. Has she finished sketching Priscill and Oscar?"

"Oscar couldn't sit still for another drawing, so I sent him and Priscill to the barn with Cyrus. Theresa's still cleaning up in the parlor."

Lu's grip around his arm tightened into a tourniquet.

Andrew redirected the conversation back to leaving the house. "Lu, go tell Theresa to have the men meet us at the barn. Oscar's been begging me to come see Jack. It shouldn't be too taxing a distance."

Frances assessed his appearance and laid a hand to his forehead, as if checking for a fever. "I don't think it's wise."

"I'm fine." Though it pained him, he added, "Ma."

If sunshine and rainbows could burst from a person, Frances would blind the room. "Well, don't push it. I'll make a late dinner with the possums Cyrus caught last night."

It was a good thing he wouldn't be around to eat it. Lu disappeared into the parlor while Frances fluttered around the room, bubbling over the prospect of having all her children at the dinner table again. Once Lu returned, they quit the house.

Andrew waited until they wouldn't be heard before clearing his throat. "Now about this ultimatum . . ."

"Priscill wants to make me suffer while earning Clint's favor. She thinks if it looks like I killed you, Ma Frances will blame me and then kill herself." Lu shuddered. "If I leave by Friday, Priscill will raise Oscar and let Clint beat him. If I stay, I'll have to watch both of you die before I do."

He hadn't given Priscill enough credit. The woman was more out of her mind and dangerous than Frances. "All we have to do is tell Frances."

"It won't work." Lu suddenly looked as skittish as a feral cat, her hands twisting and eyes darting anywhere but his face. "Priscill has information that will discredit anything I say and result in more deaths."

Andrew gauged the distance to the barn door. At their current pace, they'd be there within two minutes. Nowhere enough time to discover the full truth of what was going on, but if Oscar were in imminent danger, that information wouldn't matter.

"You said Priscill wants to raise Oscar?"

"Until it no longer suits her."

"Then for the moment Oscar's safe with her."

Lu's jaw unhitched even as her brows slammed into a how-could-you accusation.

He clasped her shoulders and stopped their walk. Pouring every bit of love he had for her and Oscar into his gaze, he implored her to trust him just as she had asked of him. "At this moment, Priscill suspects nothing of our leaving. She believes her plan is secure and thus will not lay a hand on Oscar and risk Frances's ire. I love Oscar as my own son, and I would charge into the barn and extract him by any means if I thought he were in danger. But if we're going to outwit Priscill, I need to know everything before we take action. Oscar will be safe for the moment. Trust me."

Anguish wrung her face like a washrag, and the sight tore at his soul. For the span of several breaths, she appeared to mumble a prayer. Finally, pained but trusting eyes met his and she nodded.

Lord, don't let me be wrong.

He led her through a dozen rows of golden corn stalks to a large trampled section where a cow had gotten loose and feasted. Gold and green sentinels circled the clearing and shielded them from view. For the moment, they would be safe here.

"What information does Priscill have?"

Lu closed her eyes and bit her lips. From his experience with interrogations, he knew there was a time to give an informant space to think and a time to press in. This was one of those times to press in. He stepped forward and wrapped his arms around her so that she might feel safe and protected.

"Knowledge is power. Take it away from her by telling me so I can help."

"Emma Zachary and Günter Zimmerman are snitches."

He was only mildly surprised by the information. The Zacharys were fiery and resilient, and he'd already suspected Günter, though he hadn't found evidence of it yet.

"I'll ensure they're protected, but I don't understand how Priscill could use that against you. It's not as if you're a snitch."

Her face blanched, and she stiffened in his hold.

Andrew blinked against the pure terror reflected in her eyes. "You're Walt's snitch."

Hadn't he suspected her several times? If this was the information Pastor Newcomb thought was detrimental to their marriage, the man was wrong. While Lu looked to be in anguish, Andrew didn't know whether to whoop, swing her around, or kiss her until she felt the same spark of excitement he did. It was a godsend. Her deal with Walt would stand without him ever having to fight for it.

He must have stood frozen for too long because Lu clutched his shirt sleeves and spoke in a flood of words. "Please, don't hate me. I had to protect Oscar, and now I'm doing what I can to save you too. Walt had a partner. All we have to do is figure out who it is, and then we can make a deal with him." Her hand disappeared into a pocket and reappeared with a Secret Service credentials book. "I can't read this, but you can. Please, Andrew. It's the only way to get our honest future."

He accepted the credentials book, bewildered by her possession of it. She must have found it the same day she'd found Josiah's secret ring box—something he'd yet to confess to Josiah. Andrew flipped open the credentials and scanned the line identifying him as the owner. Wherever Josiah had hidden it obviously hadn't been good enough. "Have you shown this to anyone?"

"Of course not. Ma Frances would've had whoever it is killed. I was going to have Mary read it and help me find him."

How ironic that he'd been looking for Walt's informant and she a Secret Service operative, and they'd been married nearly the entire time. God's sense of humor was almost irksome. More than a month of working together toward the same purpose lost, all because they were trying to keep up appearances and protect their secrets. He shoved the book into a pocket and took Lu's hands. "I'm the Secret Service operative that you've been looking for."

Though he'd expected surprise and joy to brighten her countenance, horror darkened it and she shrunk back from him. He didn't understand. Shouldn't she be as happy as him? All their troubles would soon be over. They had a bright future to look forward to, didn't they?

By the look on her face, he wasn't so sure anymore.

CHAPTER 28

ANDREW HAD TO BE LYING. No Thorne would ever become a lawman, and there was no denying he really was Andrew Thorne. Ma Frances recognized him, and he bore the scar with a story that Cyrus confirmed as truth. Why would he lie to her? Was it so he could hand her over to the rest of the family to earn his place? And now he had the identity of the real officer too. Had she just sentenced another man to die? Bile burned in her throat.

"Lu, talk to me. We're on the same side. We both want the Thornes arrested."

"But you *are* a Thorne."

"By blood alone. I haven't been a Thorne since my arresting officer and his wife adopted and raised me. Like Father Darlington, I'm an officer of the law." His hands squeezed her hands as if that might prove the veracity of his words. "I'm here to arrest the Thornes, not join them."

Denial screamed at her to run, but reason whispered in her ear. Hadn't she struggled with the contradiction of who Andrew was alone with her and who he was the rest of the time? Had what was different about him really just been the heart of a lawman? She scrutinized his dark eyes and every crinkle on his face. Though as dour and stoic as ever, he appeared to speak the truth. He really was a Secret Service operative—whatever that was—intent on arresting his family.

As quickly as relief washed away the fear, realization shattered her hope for the future. All this time with the Thornes, with *her*, had been a ruse. He'd never been afraid of arrest because he knew it wouldn't happen to him. Yet he'd known of and planned hers. It explained everything. Why he'd insisted on not sleeping together. Why he'd never taken the ten minutes needed to buy a wedding ring from Grossman's. Why he'd courted her and then stopped when his friends arrived.

His friends.

She closed her eyes, afraid of what she suspected to be the truth. "Are Hayden, Theresa, Broderick, and Joe operatives too?"

"They are."

Everything she'd ever shared with Theresa to prove herself a criminal would be held against her. With Andrew a part of the family, there would be no need to make a deal with her. She'd be convicted and serve every last day of her sentence—unless Clint or Priscill revealed her part in Irvine's death to make their own deal. Then she'd swing.

Either way, Oscar would be left to live in an orphanage, alone and unloved.

She grabbed a corn stalk to steady her trembling legs, but it bent and she tumbled sideways. Andrew's quick reflexes kept her from falling, but he didn't let go once she stood.

"What will happen to Oscar?"

"We'll raise him together."

Her heart lodged in her chest. "How is that even possible? We aren't even really married."

"But we are. Both in the eyes of God and man. Pastor Newcomb filed the paperwork with my correct name." He brushed the hair from her face and smiled. "Given the deal Walt made with you, there will be no need to worry about you serving jail time like I originally feared. As soon as the trials are over, we can put the past behind us and move forward."

So long as her secret stayed a secret. Nausea heated her face and turned her stomach.

"Oscar will get the schooling he needs, and you, *Mrs. Darlington*," he hugged her close, "will never have to worry about picking pockets again."

Her head spun with the image he painted. From the day she joined this family, she'd dreamed of escaping it, of discarding their name and everything that went with it. She'd wanted to start a brand-new life with a brand-new name.

Mrs. Luella Darlington.

It couldn't be real. The story sounded like one of Oscar's nursery tales, but she wasn't one of those rescued princesses. And Andrew wasn't her prince, no matter how she longed for him to be.

"You're a lawman. You don't want someone like me as your wife. Just give me the same deal as Walt did, and then you can be free of me." Though she tried to break loose of his hold, it tightened around her.

"I don't *want* to be free of you."

"Have you forgotten what I am?"

His hand captured her chin and he regarded her with a zeal that made her knees weak. "You are a woman created by God and broken by the world, but I'm a man just as broken. Let's allow God to bind our brokenness together and make one life. You're a part of me, Lu. For now and always."

The earnestness in his face and the frank words—so very *Andrew*—knocked her speechless. A Thorne turned lawman really did want her as his wife. Mary often said God had a sense of humor, but she wasn't sure what to make of this joke. It was too real to laugh at. Andrew wanted her—*her*, of all people—to bind his life with. Not to be owned by him, but to be a part of him. And she wanted it too. More than she'd ever thought possible.

"Joe must be rubbing off on you. Those are some pretty persuasive words."

"If you need a different kind of persuasion, I can provide that too." The pad of his thumb traced her lips and sent thrilling zings over her skin and down her spine.

"And what sort of persuasion would that be?" Given the way his mouth inched toward hers, she had a pretty good idea of what he had in mind.

"May I show you?" His question came a hair's breadth from her lips, hovering and waiting for her reply.

Instead of words, she leaned forward and let the meeting of their lips do the talking. His body relaxed beneath her touch like a sigh of relief. A slow, tentative kiss followed, giving her ample time to change her mind. Her response was far less reserved. She wanted to leave him with no doubt of her love and desire for him and only him. Surprise froze him for a moment, then he discarded all reserve. Passion for passion, they met, declaring promises that bound them together without a word between them. Love, not lust, poured out, and she drank it up until her love-parched heart overflowed with the joy of it.

"Found you, Mommy!"

Andrew snapped away from the kiss, and the abrupt end left her mind stumbling out of a world with a population of two into a cornfield of confusion.

Oscar. It had been Oscar's voice. Lu thudded her forehead against Andrew's chest in frustration. How could she have forgotten about her son? She turned, and her forced smile faltered. Oscar held Priscill's hand and grinned at Lu in sweet innocence.

Priscill, however, delivered murderous threats with the mere squint of her eyes. "Your friends arrived at the barn expecting to find you inside. Imagine my surprise when I discovered that you and Andrew had snuck off alone."

Oscar wriggled free of Priscill's grip and ran to Lu and Andrew as he called at the top of his lungs, "Mrs. Resa! They're over here!"

Lu pulled him into the protected space between her and Andrew.

Priscill flicked an annoyed frown at Oscar but remained where she stood. "Just what *were* you two doing out here?"

Andrew snorted next to Lu. "I think that pretty obvious, and I don't appreciate the interruption."

"Then perhaps you should return to the house where doors can be locked. Although I'm not sure time alone is in your best interest. I'd hate for you to relapse." Ice frosted her words. "Wouldn't you agree, Lu?"

Lu leaned into Andrew and wrapped both her arms around Oscar. "I would never do anything to jeopardize my family."

"Actions beg to differ. I'd give careful consideration to the choice you're making."

Andrew pushed Lu and Oscar behind him and then squared off with Priscill. "Threatening my family comes with consequences. I'd give careful consideration to the choice *you're* making."

The rustle of corn stalks came from their right. One by one, Andrew's friends emerged, flanking either side of the clearing with similar stances.

Theresa joined Lu's side from behind the wall of men and cast Lu a courageous smile. "There's nothing like a standoff to get the blood flowing, huh?"

Theresa's levity did little to ease the tension. Priscill might be scared off by the numbers, but it wouldn't be long before she acted, now that she knew Lu's choice.

"Is there a problem here, Andrew?" Hayden was the only one without crossed arms and wide stance, but he looked as fierce as any of the others.

"None at all. Priscill was just leaving. Weren't you?"

"It appears so." Her voice rose louder. "I hope you're happy with your decision, Lu. There's no going back on it now."

If Priscill were a man, Andrew would grab her by the shirt front and punch her so hard she'd smile with a few less teeth. They should arrest her here and now, but any ruckus she made would be heard by Cyrus or Frances. Waiting to make their move until three days after the delivery in Boonville was no longer an option, but he couldn't risk their cover without having made a new plan. For now, all Priscill knew was Lu's status as a snitch, not his identity as a Secret Service operative.

Priscill sneered before slithering into the next row of corn stalks like the snake she was. Hayden trailed behind her without being told she needed to be shadowed. As soon as Priscill revealed Lu was an informant, the Thornes would pursue Lu until death. The tense silence as they waited for Priscill to move beyond earshot lasted all of twenty seconds before Oscar broke free from Lu's grasp.

Coming around Andrew's legs, Oscar tugged on his hand. "Come on, New Pa, you gotta see Jack!" When Andrew didn't move, he pulled with both hands. "Come on! Mrs. Resa said he'll be big enough to live with me soon."

The boy was oblivious to the situation, but Andrew couldn't move them to the barn with Cyrus there. "Not now, I need to talk with my friends."

"But you promised."

"I didn't say we would see him right now, only that we would visit him when I felt better."

"Don't you feel better?"

"No. I feel much worse." And it wasn't a lie. Despite all the rest, his head pounded with a fury, but he wouldn't succumb to the urge to lie down. Not with his family in danger.

Lu slid under his shoulder to support him, though he remained steady on his feet. "Oscar, sweetheart, I need you to be patient. We'll see Jack as soon as we can. Will you be a big boy and help me walk New Pa to . . . ?" Her eyes rounded as she looked at Andrew. "We can't go back home, and the barn won't be safe now either."

"Would someone explain what is going on?" Broderick asked. Theresa joined his side.

Andrew rubbed his throbbing temple. "Lu is the missing informant, and Priscill knows it. Neither Lu nor Oscar is safe to stay here."

"Don't forget she plans to kill you too." Lu shifted to address the whole group. "None of us are safe here."

He pulled from her support and lifted Oscar. The last thing they needed was for him to run off. "How would you like to go on a secret adventure?"

"Can Jack come?"

"I'm afraid not."

"Then I don't wanna go!" He tried to wriggle free, making it difficult to keep ahold of him.

Lu spoke in a soothing tone. "Jack's too little, remember? He can't leave his momma yet. He'll have to join us later."

"But he can come, right?"

Traveling with an untrained puppy at the speeds he hoped to achieve wouldn't be safe or wise, and he couldn't promise to return for the puppy either. "No."

Lu and Theresa pinned him with death glares as Oscar fought and wailed.

"You mean, not right now. Don't you, Andrew?" Lu emphasized her words and gestured to Oscar behind the boy's back.

"I'm not going to lie to him." Oscar's tears might eat at his resolve, but their safety mattered more. How could he make a child understand? "Stop crying and look at me."

Oscar didn't stop, only fought harder and louder. This was one of those times Andrew wished he could shake the child and make him listen, but that would make him no better than Pa or Clint. He was trying to be a hero, not a villain.

Hero. The thought sparked an idea. "Oscar, someone wants to hurt Mommy."

That got the boy's attention. He sniffled and frowned. "What?"

"Giants want to hurt Mommy, and I need your help to protect her until it's safe. If you take Jack, he'll bark and the giants will find you."

"Jack'll be good."

Andrew released a frustrated breath. The boy was five. Logic wasn't going to work. "Jack has a job to do for me here. You're going to protect your mommy, and Jack's going to protect me."

"You're not coming?" Panic edged Lu's voice.

If only he had a free arm to pull her close again. "I need to stay here and ensure everyone is arrested, or else you'll never be safe."

"It's all right, Lu. We'll keep him safe." Josiah's reassurance did little to mollify Lu, but she didn't argue.

Andrew returned his focus to Oscar. "Can I trust you to protect Mommy for me while I'm not here?"

Oscar straightened, puffed out his chest, and gave a serious nod. "I'll protect Mommy real good."

"I'm trusting you, Giant Killer." He set Oscar down. "Listen to Mr. Joe and don't let Mommy out of your sight."

Oscar grabbed Lu's hand. "You stay with me, Mommy. I'm going to keep us safe."

At least that managed one problem. "Joe, I need you to stay with them until arrests are made."

"Where do you want me to hide them?"

It was a good question. They couldn't go anywhere the Thornes would suspect. That meant the Newcomb home was out of the question—and so was anywhere else in town, for that matter. Once the Thornes discovered her missing, they'd likely search everywhere, including Stendal.

Lu huddled against him. "What about Günter and Emma? They won't be safe either."

Putting Lu and Oscar with the Zacharys and Günter wasn't ideal, but it would make it easier for Josiah to protect everyone. "Do you think if warned, they'd have a safe place to hide for a few days?"

"Günter might."

"Good. You'll join him and the Zacharys so Joe can protect all of you until it's safe."

"Are you insane? Widow Zachary would just as soon kill me herself than agree to hide us."

Broderick slapped Josiah on the back. "Just leave it to the Charmer to work his magic. She'll agree and probably be happy about it. If he's not careful, he'll have a widow as his next fiancée."

Lu didn't appear pleased. "Where will you be?"

"I have to convince the family that you and Oscar ran off without me and direct them to behave in a way we can predict. Otherwise they'll leave town before we can gather the support we need to arrest everyone."

"But you can't walk into that family. They aren't going to trust you. Priscill already believes I told you about her threat."

"It shouldn't be too hard to convince them you ran off with me." Josiah shrugged. "Given your history with men—sorry, Lu—it wouldn't be a far stretch of the imagination for them to think you manipulated me. We'll stage a fight between you and Andrew in front of Cyrus at the barn. Andrew'll storm out with Broderick and Theresa, and I'll take Lu for a walk to cool off. We'll meet at the emergency spot."

It was a workable plan, but not foolproof. Andrew wasn't much of an actor, but Frances already favored him over Priscill.

"What's to keep Priscill from telling Ma Frances while we stand here talking? She has physical proof to support her claims. They could even now be heading to the barn to kill me."

It was a fair point. "Hayden will delay them if that's the case, but we need to act quickly."

"But why can't you disappear with us?"

He wished he could, but the best way to protect his family was to do his job. "I'm the only one who can influence Frances's response to your disappearance and create time to alert the county police to the change of plans." He caressed her face, needing to touch her as much as he needed to sway her. "Please, Lu, I need you to work with me. I can't do this without you."

A resigned sigh blew against his hand. "I suppose it shouldn't be too hard to find something to fight over. You're really good at putting your mouth in the way of things." A smirk tilted the corner of her mouth, hinting that she wasn't just talking about his tactless tendencies.

"Maybe, but you're pretty good at it yourself."

Despite the tension, she chuckled. In the next breath, she turned somber and crouched to eye level with Oscar. "We're going to go see Jack for a few minutes, but then it'll be time to protect me. Are you ready?"

Oscar nodded, and Andrew prayed all would go according to plan.

CHAPTER 29

LU GRIPPED OSCAR'S HAND, DOUBTING every detail of this plan as they passed through the corn rows toward the barn. Would they have enough time to enact their theatrics before Ma Frances and Priscill charged into the barn? Ma Frances wouldn't shoot Andrew, but Priscill would, and she'd do her best to make his death appear an accident or Lu's fault. How could Andrew seem so stoic and confident when her whole body screamed they should run for the woods and never look back? What if everything went wrong?

When his hand swung near hers, she caught and clung to the strength there.

He brought her hand to his lips and kissed it. His voice lowered for her ears alone. "Promise me you'll do everything Joe says to stay safe."

The concern in his voice warmed her. Maybe he wasn't as confident as he appeared. "I promise."

He gave a stiff nod and released her hand. They'd almost reached the barn door. "Joe, turn on your charm and start flirting with my wife."

Pretty Boy cut between her and Andrew and jutted out his arm for her to take. "My lady."

"Don't overdo it. I'd hate to have to punch you." Andrew dropped behind them, an underlying growl to his tone.

"How can a man not overdo it when in the presence of such a beautiful woman? Especially when she's proved to be a surprising ally."

"Joe . . ."

Pretty Boy winked at her and then broke away to open the barn door with grand fanfare. Behind her, Broderick started up a conversation with Andrew about printing presses and Theresa's progress on the plates.

Oscar patted her hand. "Don't worry, Mommy. I'll protect you."

Oh, her sweet baby. They just needed to survive a little while longer. Before she passed through the door, she let out a long breath and hoped it carried her silent prayer to listening ears.

Cyrus looked up from his work at the glowing smelt. Sweat glued his shirt to his back, and dark streaks of soot marred his face where he must have brushed the moisture from his eyes. "Good, they found you. I've made enough coin to hold out until we get the press up and running. Priscill's latest mold is the best one yet. It should pass at the bank with little question."

Joe and Theresa lagged a moment behind, but he quickly rejoined Lu. Without a hint of embarrassment, he pulled her against his side and wrapped an arm around her waist like she was his. Despite years of practice, a flicker of surprise and displeasure tightened the muscles in her face. She relaxed them quickly and offered an encouraging smile.

"I suggest removing your hands from Lu." Andrew's furious expression didn't look like an act.

Joe grinned before releasing her. "She looked like she was about to fall."

"New Pa, come see Jack." Oscar grabbed Andrew's hand and guided him to where the puppies rolled and played near their mother.

Andrew followed, casting scowls over his shoulder, while Broderick joined Cyrus inspecting the pile of coins on the makeshift table. Theresa lingered nearby as if unsure of what to do or how to act. That didn't seem to be a problem for Pretty Boy.

"That dress looks beautiful on you, but I think you need some jewelry. I saw a necklace at Grossman's that made me think of you. Tell me what you think." He pulled a beautiful pink cameo necklace from his pocket. An exact match to the one Theresa wore.

A glance at Theresa's bare neck confirmed it. The man really was a sly one to be so quick to plan a way to make it a believable affair. She accepted the necklace and crowed over it like it was a cherished gift.

After returning it to him, she turned and lifted her hair from the back of her neck. "Would you put it on me, sugar?"

Joe brought the necklace around her neck and clasped it. When she released her hair, he came to her front and adjusted where the cameo lay on her chest. Andrew appeared as if he was about to suffer an apoplexy. Perhaps she and Joe were playing the game a little too well.

"You two need to stop." Theresa's voice was too loud to be considered a whisper, but low enough to give the illusion of trying to be secretive. "He's going to catch on sooner or later."

Broderick broke from his conversation. "Let it be, Theresa. Drew knew what kind of woman he married. Come tell Cyrus about your progress on the plates and mind your own business."

Cyrus's gaze cut to Lu and Pretty Boy. She flashed him a nervous smile.

He straightened from his spot on the ground and cracked his knuckles. "I thought Ma warned you about taking up with other men. I don't like to see Ma unhappy."

As Cyrus stood, Lu pushed Joe toward the door. Pretty Boy wasn't going to have to worry about being pretty for long. Cyrus was going to solve Andrew's problem for him.

"I think you misunderstand my relationship with Lu. We're just friends." Joe backed up with raised hands, his face more distressed than a chopping board.

Andrew stepped next to Cyrus in a rare show of solidarity. "It's long past time you consider yourself an enemy. It's time you look for a new opportunity elsewhere."

"This town was getting crowded, anyway." Joe fled the barn faster than any yellow-bellied coward Lu'd ever seen.

The man was either a great actor, or he really did fear for his life.

One peek at Andrew and she understood why. Furious jealousy creased his face so deep, she feared he'd never smile at her again.

Andrew reached for his gun. "I'll go make sure my so-called friend never comes back. Theresa, take my *wife* home."

Lu cringed at the way he said wife, like it was a vile burden rather than a cherished gift. He disappeared out the door without looking back, and she didn't have to pretend to be worried. "Oscar, I think it's best we go."

He obediently rushed to her side. "You need me to protect you?"

"Yes, baby. Always."

"I'm gonna protect Mommy from giants." He beamed up at Cyrus, unaware the biggest immediate threat came from him.

Cyrus squinted at her. "I'll come along to help with any giants you can't handle."

Theresa pushed her way to Lu's other side. "I'll go. I need to work on the plates some more anyway. You and Broderick should stay to discuss plans while you finish making coins."

Somewhere in the distance, two shots fired.

"Sounds to me like Joe won't be a problem no more." Cyrus folded his arms. "Take her home and tell Ma not to let her out of the house. Andrew'll deal with her when he's finished hiding Joe's body."

Lu sagged against Theresa. Cyrus would probably think it was the result of distress, not the relief she felt. They'd gotten away with it.

Theresa led Lu and Oscar out of the barn, through the corn rows, and into the woods. Though Oscar chattered almost nonstop about what he would do to the giants, Lu kept her ears attuned for anything that might indicate they were being followed. They'd almost reached the pond where they were to meet when the sound of horses' hooves pounded through the brush behind them. Lu grabbed the nearest rock, pivoted to keep Oscar behind her, and faced their attacker.

Broderick slowed his horse to a stop next to them. A horse from the Thorne farm followed behind him on a lead. At least now if they pursued, they'd be slowed to a foot pace.

Broderick dismounted and handed Theresa the other horse's lead. "I left Cyrus with the excuse of going to help Andrew hide the body.

Unless Frances or Priscill pull him away, it'll be awhile before he heads to the house. There was a lot of gold melted in his crucible."

The news didn't bring comfort, but it wasn't much further to the meeting spot. They quickened their pace and soon arrived at the pond. Andrew sat on a log with his head in his hands and Joe resting a hand on his shoulder. Hayden stood a few steps away, frowning. Something was wrong.

Lu coaxed Oscar into a race to Andrew. She outstripped Oscar, and Hayden moved out of the way so she could kneel before Andrew. Forest debris clung to his clothes and blood dripped unchecked from his nose and a fresh cut on his cheek. The poor man looked like he'd been in a dogfight and lost.

She retrieved a handkerchief from her pocket and waffled on where to apply it. In the end she decided the cut mostly superficial and gently pressed it against his nose. He jerked away, claimed the handkerchief, and applied it himself. Apparently gentle was not gentle enough.

"What happened?" she asked.

"He fell. Says his vision blacked for a second and his foot hit a root." Joe shrugged. "At least it will play into the story that I beat him before taking off with you."

"His concussion." Lu wanted to cry for having pushed him to this point. It wasn't safe for him to continue. "He needs to rest, not go against the Thornes."

"I'm right here." He lowered the handkerchief and winced. "We stick to the plan."

"I don't see that we have any other choice." Hayden stared at Andrew as if calculating his endurance for what lay ahead. His conclusions didn't appear any more satisfactory than hers, but he didn't change his answer. "Lu and Oscar can't return to the house, and Frances isn't the type to wait until morning to see if she comes back. Priscill hadn't said anything before I left, but she was too smug not to be planning something."

"I agree, but Andrew should rest while we figure out details."

Broderick rubbed a spot on his arm. "Injuries have a way of ruining the best-laid plans."

Theresa joined the circle with Oscar, and Oscar climbed onto Andrew's lap, frightened questions about a giant attacking Andrew flying from his mouth. When Lu bent down to console him, Andrew made one last swipe at his bloodied face and pocketed the ruined handkerchief. His fingers entwined with Lu's and he tugged in silent entreaty. Apparently, he'd already forgiven her part in the barn scene. She curled up close to him on the log and rubbed circles on Oscar's back while the conversation returned to their plans.

Pretty Boy propped a shoulder on the nearest tree, looking for all the world a man at leisure—so long as one didn't notice his deep-set frown. "You can't just walk in and make arrests. It's three against four, even if you plan on Andrew being able to help."

"There are four of us. I'm perfectly capable of fighting." Theresa folded her arms and tapped a foot.

"No. No women." Andrew shook his head then stopped with a wince. "We'd be too distracted with your safety to give the situation the full concentration it needs."

"Then I'll go with Lu to the Zacharys'."

Broderick disagreed. "You'll go with us to confirm Lu and Oscar ran off with Joe, then go straight to the Newcombs'. They'll keep you safe, and if someone follows you, you won't expose Lu's location."

"I hate arguments that make sense."

Lu smiled despite the mounting stress. Theresa was quite the mix of impulsive child and fierce woman. "That brings you back to two—"

"Three," Andrew corrected.

Stubborn man. "All right, three against four. What are you going to do? None of the Stendal police will help."

Andrew caressed the inside of her palm with his thumb for a moment before squeezing and pulling free. "You and Oscar need to get to the Zacharys' before we give the Thornes any more time to act. Joe—"

"You can't expect me to leave you. Not when you're hurt." Lu cupped his face and made him look at her. As sure as her own heartbeat, a headache pounded behind those pained eyes.

His hand covered hers. "I need to do my job, and I can't do that if I'm worried about you. I've had worse than a concussion before."

"Why do men always say they've had worse?" Theresa pulled Lu up by the arm. "Come on. When this is all over, we'll compare notes on what it's like to be married to a Secret Service operative. Until then, you have a son to protect."

If only that didn't mean leaving an injured Andrew behind to do it. How was he going to survive against a group like the Thornes?

Oscar stuck his lip out and crossed his arms. "I'm supposed to protect Mommy."

Theresa tweaked Oscar's nose. "Yes, you are, little man, and it's time to follow Mr. Joe to your secret hiding spot so you can do it right."

Andrew set Oscar on the ground and stood.

Though he tried to hide the wince as he did so, Lu saw it. "Tell me again why we can't just run away?"

"Because if we do, the Thornes will continue to wreck lives and families. Doing the right thing is rarely the easy thing, but I'm not going to back down. Once this is over, you can doctor me all you want."

Pride for this man's selflessness welled within her while simultaneously wringing her heart with anxiety and fear. Andrew's arms encircled her, and she buried her head into his shoulder, clinging to him as if it would be the last time. Given he faced the Thornes, it very well might be.

"I don't want to lose you."

He laid his head alongside hers and spoke for her ears alone. "Nor I you. When this is over, I promise to give you the future you deserve for as many days and nights as God allows."

Lu kissed him on the cheek—though she really wanted to give him something more substantial to encourage him to come back to her—and reluctantly pulled away. "Be safe."

"God willing, I will be. Now go, before any more time is wasted."

When they faced Joe, everyone except a crouching Oscar had their backs to them, talking in hushed voices.

Andrew cleared his throat and waited until they faced him. "Don't leave them for any reason, Joe. If the Zacharys and Günter don't have a place to hide, head straight to Petersburg. We'll convince them to look for you in Boonville."

Joe gave a clipped nod.

Oscar stood up with an armful of rocks. "I'm ready to fight giants like David."

"David?" Lu asked.

"Yeah! He killed a real giant with a rock."

"By God's power." Theresa broke off from the huddle of men and gave a tentative smile. "I told him the story of David and Goliath while sketching him and Frances. I hope you don't mind."

"It's fine." Andrew knelt and squeezed Oscar before ruffling his hair. "You take good care of your Mommy for me, Giant Killer. I'm counting on you."

"I'll take care of them, Andrew. You have my word." Joe shook Andrew's hand, and then, without further goodbyes, he helped her and Oscar onto a horse.

Everything was out of her hands now. All she could do was hold on to the hope that God was with them all. Mary said He promised it, and she would choose to believe it.

"Oscar? Can Mommy have one of your rocks?"

He rummaged through his little collection and handed her a jagged, gray stone. "This one will make a giant cry."

She smiled at his sweet innocence. The rock wasn't likely to be used as a weapon, but it would serve as a reminder until all this was over. It was time to face their giants and trust God whatever the outcome.

CHAPTER 30

HAVING LAID OUT THEIR PLAN, Andrew allowed Hayden and Broderick to assist him to the house. Although his head really did throb and he was pretty sure he'd broken his nose again in the fall, they'd agreed they needed to play up his injuries as much as possible to Frances. If she reacted anything like she had last time, her panic would buy Josiah enough time to get Lu and Oscar to safety. He had his doubts about sending her with the Zacharys and Günter, but it was all he could think of to suggest.

Frances rushed onto the veranda before Theresa reached the door. "Priscill, go for the doctor!"

"No!" Andrew didn't want her out of his sight. "We've a bigger problem."

Broderick relinquished his spot to Frances. "I'll go warn Cyrus that they're gone."

"Gone?" Frances's head snapped up and nearly knocked Andrew's nose. "Who's gone?"

Hayden and Frances maneuvered Andrew into the kitchen and onto a chair while Theresa spoke from behind. "Lu and Joe. They beat Drew and ran off together. I should've followed, but Drew was hurt."

They'd agreed to leave Oscar's name out until they needed Frances to escalate into hysteria.

"That's convenient." Priscill's serpent eyes flicked over his injuries.

"It's not convenient to have my wife cheat on me right before my supposed friend smashes in my nose."

241

"You didn't seem to mind her cheating when it was Clint."

"At the time I didn't believe it." He had anticipated convincing her would be difficult. "But now that she's run off with Joe . . ."

Frances patted a wet cloth against his bloodied face. "I never should've married you to that harlot. You're better off without her."

"You're not going to go after her?" Priscill's posture snapped straight.

"Of course not. She's nothing but trouble. I'd think you'd be happy to not have the competition anymore."

"But she's Walt's snitch!"

Frances huffed without stopping her ministrations. "The only thing she ever shared with Walt was a bed."

"I can prove it." Priscill ran to her bedroom attached to the parlor and returned a minute later with Clint hobbling behind her on a crudely made crutch.

"What's going on? Priscill said somethin' about knowin' who the snitch is."

She shook a canvas military pack with *W. Kinder* stitched on the flap onto the table. An empty wallet, basic camping supplies, toy soldiers, a single dress, and several changes of clothes for a boy Oscar's size dumped out. How Lu fit all that in there was a mystery. Andrew couldn't imagine what she would've done if she'd actually had to carry it while contending with Oscar.

Frances snatched a shirt and soldier from the pile. "I sewed this for Oscar, and Cyrus made this for his last birthday."

"That's why she begged me to leave with her." *Please, buy the story.* "She must've realized you'd found out. When seducing me didn't work, she turned to Joe."

"When I find her . . ." Frances's grip around a soldier whitened her knuckles even as her face reddened and nostrils flared. "Wait. Where's Oscar?"

Before they could answer, Cyrus burst through the open door. "They took the horses."

The room burst into exclamations and curses. When Cyrus learned

Lu wasn't just running off but was also an informant, he grabbed a fire poker and slammed it against the stone fireplace until it became bent and misshapen. Ringing shrilled in Andrew's ears and bright flashes of light passed across his vision. Were not so much riding on this mission, he'd lay down and allow the others to take over.

Hayden's voice rose over the din. "There are four horses at the tack shop, providing Joe didn't set them loose too. We can use them to split up and search."

Clint knocked his crutch against the ground and cursed again. "I can't walk yet, let alone ride."

"You'll stay here in case they try to sneak back for supplies." Vengeance fueled the frenzied flames of Frances's commands. "Priscill, Theresa, and I will search Landkreis on foot. Cyrus, give Priscill and Theresa guns. If anyone finds Lu, shoot her. We need to bring Oscar back home where he belongs."

Cyrus retrieved two revolvers from a wall of shelves. "We gotta keep this quiet, or the others'll find out and pull up stakes. We can't print money if we don't have investors to front the cost of supplies. Buying that press ate up all our capital."

The moment Cyrus handed a gun to Theresa, giddy joy beamed from her face. Thankfully, Broderick was quick to intervene and tucked it into his waistband before she accidentally shot anyone while trying to figure out how to use it.

Theresa pouted. "But if I go with them, I'll need something."

Broderick snatched a butcher knife from the sink and handed it to her. She frowned but made no further argument.

"Where are they most likely to head?" Andrew posed the question, though he'd already determined which direction he wanted to push Cyrus to take.

"Joe found a woman in Petersburg to swindle out of her inheritance while there a few days ago. He'd go to a sure thing before considering anything else." Hayden checked the cylinder of his revolver as he spoke.

Cyrus disagreed like Andrew suspected he would. "Boonville makes more sense. It's the quickest way out of the area. They can catch the train to Newburgh and get on a ferry. We need to beat them to the Boonville station and nab them there."

If Andrew didn't push back at least some, it would seem too easy a win. "She'll know that's the most logical path and avoid it. I say she'll head north and stay a night or two in Petersburg before moving deeper into Indiana."

"Enough arguing. If we don't get moving, she'll use the dark to cover her tracks. Andrew and Broderick, you go to Petersburg." Frances pointed north. "If you don't find her by tomorrow night, come back here. Same for you, Cyrus and Hayden, except you'll go to Boonville. I want Oscar found and Lu's head on a platter. Priscill, you and I will start at Molly's and work our way back. Theresa, see what information the Newcombs can provide. Clint, you be ready for Lu to sneak in when she sees everyone leave."

He nodded, but by the grin on his face, he didn't plan on shooting her. Though Andrew knew Lu would be safe, the urge to slug Clint thrummed stronger than reason.

"We should check at the Zacharys'." Strangling dread tightened his throat at Priscill's words. "Emma Zachary and Günter Zimmerman are working with Lu."

Frances whirled on Priscill. "And how long have you known this?"

Priscill must have realized her folly and shrunk against the wall like a whipped dog. "Just since this morning." A lie, given she'd threatened Lu long before that.

Oscar's tin soldier bounced off the wall above Priscill's head. "I'll deal with your failure later. For now, we check the Zachary place and then burn it down."

Andrew gripped the table's edge. "It'll be dark before you arrive. Let us handle it."

"Hayden and I'll take care of the Zacharys. We'll need to go that direction for Boonville, anyway." Cyrus grabbed a box of strike anywhere matches from next to the oil lamp. "Where's the turpentine?"

"Locked in my bedroom cabinet. If they're not there, burn the place and move on. I want them found tonight."

"Andrew and I will leave from the Newcombs'," Broderick said. "I need to get supplies before we head out."

"And I'll see if I can get anything out of Mary about where Lu and Oscar might run." Theresa examined the butcher knife and tested the edge with her thumb. "I'm not a fan of torture, but it has its purposes."

Andrew had always believed that woman had too much criminal in her. Theresa was enjoying her pretended role far too much to claim innocence.

But Frances seemed satisfied. "Do whatever you need to, but Lu dies."

Without further discussion, everyone split directions. Theresa and Broderick for the Newcombs', and Frances and Priscill toward Molly's. Clint claimed the parlor couch, propping his leg and laying his rifle across his lap. Cyrus went to his bedroom off the kitchen to throw together supplies.

Hayden gestured outside with his head to Andrew and waited to speak until they stood at the veranda corner farthest from Cyrus's window. "Delay Cyrus coming to the shop. I need time to get rid of the horses."

"You delay him. If I leave now, I can take care of the horses, warn Josiah Cyrus is coming, and still beat Cyrus to Boonville."

Something akin to compassion creased his face. "They'll be fine. Theresa and Broderick are probably already on their way to warn Josiah. Your job is to get to Boonville ahead of us and set everything into motion for the raids. Until this is over, Lu and Oscar won't be safe. You have to entrust them to us."

This was a fine corner to be painted into—choose his duty as an operative and win the favor of his colleagues or protect his wife and son and toss any chance at keeping his job into the fire. The choice rankled. Although, if he were honest with himself, the potential for loss of life was slim. Should Cyrus act, he would be largely outnumbered.

Even if Hayden and Josiah weren't enough, Widow Zachary would no doubt be glad to shoot a Thorne.

Andrew tugged at his coat. He didn't really have a choice in the matter. If they didn't coordinate the raids from Petersburg and Boonville to happen all at once, word would get out and the gang members would run. He had to trust his fellow operatives would do their jobs, and they needed to trust he would do his. *Lord, protect Lu and Oscar, because this choice is killing me.*

After Andrew agreed to stick to the plan, Hayden left. Andrew stalled his preparations as long as possible, but even he couldn't stretch out packing an overnight bag for more than fifteen minutes. It must have been enough. By the time he and Cyrus walked to the tack shop, Hayden had turned out the horses, hidden all the saddle gear the store contained, and blamed it all on Josiah. Finding and calming the now skittish horses took twenty minutes, and it took another thirty minutes to find and untangle all the saddle gear. In all, they'd bought Theresa and Broderick an hour.

Lord, please let it be enough. He'd never forgive himself if it wasn't.

CHAPTER 31

JOSIAH ISAACS COULD CONVINCE VINEGAR it was honey with all his charming ways. A good thing too, because Widow Zachary would've blown a hole in Lu's chest if it weren't for his smooth talking. Lu still didn't understand how he did it, but Widow Zachary had invited them in and was even now serving them chicory root coffee.

Lu stared at the dark liquid in her cup. The woman was being too nice. Maybe she thought to offer Lu as a sacrifice when the Thornes arrived. She *had* refused to leave the house no matter how Josiah sweet-talked her. Or maybe she shared a meal with her enemy—the woman responsible for her husband's death—as a cover for revenge. Was chicory root all Widow Zachary had put in Lu's cup? Or had she laced the drink with something poisonous like Ma Frances would've?

"I'm sorry. I don't have any tea or regular coffee. It's too expensive for what little money we have." Widow Zachary was all sweetness and butter toward Josiah, but the moment her gaze landed on Lu, her face curdled.

Poisoned, definitely poisoned. Lu scooted the cup and saucer away. As long as she didn't eat or drink and stayed in Josiah's presence, she should be safe from the woman until Andrew returned for them.

Widow Zachary took a seat across from Lu and arched a brow. "What? Not thirsty?"

"No."

She took Lu's rejected beverage and drank it as she conversed with Josiah.

Okay, so Widow Zachary hadn't tried to poison her. This time. Maybe not poisoning it was her way of thanking Lu for not turning her daughter over to the rest of the Thornes.

"Now this rock is gonna kill him!" Oscar's glee filled the small room.

Lu twisted in her seat. Emma and Günter sat on the floor nearby, playing David and Goliath with Oscar. "No throwing rocks inside the house."

"Here, Oscar. I have the perfect pretend rock." Emma pushed from the floor and grabbed a down feather from a basketful near Lu's feet waiting for use in a pillow. "They're leftover from when Clint came through and killed all our chickens a few days ago."

Widow Zachary scowled as Emma returned to playing with Oscar. "Now we don't even have eggs to fall back on. If it weren't for Günter bringing food, we'd starve."

The glare she directed at Lu billowed the guilt for Sheriff Zachary's death into full flame. Had Lu not betrayed the Thornes, he'd still be alive and able to provide for the needs of his family. And now she'd betrayed them again. Would the Zacharys continue to be a casualty of her mistakes? If only Widow Zachary wouldn't be so stubborn in refusing to leave the house.

Eager to give an outlet to her building anxiety, Lu wandered to the window. Though the sunset fought valiantly to illuminate the colorful treetops, darkness crowded in, determined to beat back the light. In a final blaze of glory, the light succumbed, and darkness snuffed out evidence of a sun. Lu shivered. How long until the Thornes evaded Andrew and rode in to extinguish their existence?

She gripped the rock Oscar gave her and took a deep breath. She couldn't give in to fear and forget the hope promised to her. God was with her, just as He was with Oscar and Andrew. Their futures extended beyond the trouble of today into an eternal tomorrow. No matter what the darkness tried, the sun would rise. Tomorrow would come. Whatever happened tonight, she had to cling to the hope God provided.

"Come away from the window. It isn't safe."

A flicker of light in the shadowed woods caught her attention, and she ignored Josiah's warning. The yellow glow floated and wove between the trees, approaching the house like a specter in the night.

Only, Lu didn't believe in ghosts. "Someone's coming."

Chills skittered down her back as she rushed to Oscar and scooped him into her arms. The Thornes couldn't have been arrested yet. Josiah had warned Widow Zachary they would likely be here a couple of days, barring an attack.

Josiah jolted to his feet. "Everyone hide in the bedroom."

Widow Zachary grabbed the rifle she'd initially greeted them with and took up position at the window.

Lu squelched the urge to haul the woman by the collar, instead carrying Oscar into the bedroom. The house had once been a one-room cabin and the design of the windowless walls and the size of the room showed as much. The bed and trunk took up all but a small walkway. At least if lead went flying, it likely wouldn't pass through the walls. Still, she'd not take any chances with Oscar.

"Crawl under the bed." Lu set Oscar down, but the boy folded his arms and scrunched his face instead of doing as told.

"But I'm 'posed to protect you."

"New Pa told us to listen to Mr. Joe, remember? Under the bed is the best place to hide."

He didn't seem happy about the arrangement but crawled under. Emma and Günter sat in the space between the bed and the wall, leaving nothing but standing room for Lu between the trunk and door. At least those three would be safe.

Lu snuck out to rejoin Josiah and Widow Zachary in the main room. Positioned at the two front windows, they intently watched whoever approached, ignoring her presence.

After several minutes of tense silence, Josiah lowered his revolver. "It's Theresa and the Newcombs. Let them in."

"I said I'd hide Oscar because he's a child, and I only let that wench in," Widow Zachary gestured to Lu, "because you promised to protect my family. I'm not letting more people in."

"Pastor Newcomb has been working with us for weeks. If he's coming here, it's because he has information we need."

Pastor Newcomb knew Andrew was Secret Service? If Mary told Pastor Newcomb about Irvine, did that mean he'd told Andrew? Her stomach vaulted.

Josiah opened the door, and Pastor Newcomb hurried inside with Mary and Theresa. "Cyrus is on his way here to search for you and burn down the house."

Widow Zachary staggered back. "But this is all we have left."

"Then I recommend stuffing what you can in a bag and following us. The reverend of the Lutheran church in Stendal agreed to hide you until we can figure out what to do next."

"This is all your fault." Widow Zachary rounded on Lu. "If you—"

Mary intervened, shoving a bag into the woman's hand and pushing her toward the bedroom. "You don't have time to waste on angry words. Get your most precious belongings together. I'll collect supplies from the kitchen."

It wasn't right, and Lu wouldn't allow this family to lose one more thing because of her or the Thornes. "Not counting Emma and Günter, it's six adults against one Thorne, and it's not even Clint. Can't we just arrest Cyrus now?"

Josiah raked his fingers through his hair. "We can't risk his arrest alerting anyone else to what's going on. They'll scatter before Andrew and Broderick get the raiding parties in Boonville and Petersburg organized."

"No one will know if we hold him prisoner here until after the raids."

He didn't immediately cast aside the idea and tapped his finger on his arm as he thought.

"You wouldn't be the only one responsible for holding him. Widow Zachary and I'll take turns watching him."

If anyone were eager to hold a Thorne prisoner at gunpoint, it would be Widow Zachary. The trick would be not letting her pull the trigger.

Theresa rubbed her hands together. "I'll help too."

Josiah frowned. "Broderick wouldn't want you so close to danger."

"And pretending to hunt for Lu with Frances and Priscill is safer? Broderick won't allow me to carry a gun. What am I supposed to do? Walk around with a butcher knife all the time?"

Lu knew she liked Theresa. The woman was just the right amount of sass and stubbornness. By Josiah's consistent tapping finger and the way he sucked in his cheek, he was on the edge of agreeing Theresa should stay.

It was time to push him off the cliff of indecision. "If Ma Frances suspects Theresa at all, she'll not hesitate to kill her."

Mary stepped to Theresa's other side. "If questioned, we'll insist she left with Broderick."

With three women against him, Pretty Boy didn't have a chance. He threw his hands up in the air. "Fine, but you're not allowed anywhere near the area while we arrest him. I'll not have Broderick come back to find you hurt. In fact, all women go to the back room with Oscar."

Lu agreed. Although it was one man against three—four if one of the other operatives was with Cyrus—Lu knew better than to think a Thorne wouldn't go down fighting.

"This is my home, and I'll not leave it to be defended by someone who doesn't care about it."

Josiah opened his mouth, took one look at Widow Zachary, and sighed. "You cover the farthest back window."

Widow Zachary followed orders, and Lu ushered Theresa and Mary to the crowded back room. It took some rearranging for everyone to fit. Günter, Emma, and Theresa sat on the bed while Lu sat next to Mary on the floor and held Oscar.

Silence lapsed as they all listened for the coming danger. For it would come. There was no doubt about that.

CHAPTER 32

THE MINUTES STRETCHED TO NEARLY an hour. Was Cyrus coming? Or was he only delayed by gathering people to help burn down the house and catch any escapees? She'd concocted a dozen possibilities, most of which ended in death or injury to one or more people. If she didn't stop this playing through scenarios, she'd go mad.

Oscar's heavy sleep-sigh blew against her neck, and she rubbed his back. At least he remained oblivious to the danger. Theresa and Emma whispered together, apparently too bored to be concerned with listening for any noises out front.

"So you were Walt's informant and Andrew's a Secret Service operative?" Mary marveled as she shifted to a more comfortable position. "You're both full of surprises. No wonder God put you two together."

"Does Andrew know . . . Did you tell him about . . ." Lu glanced to the bed and dropped her voice. "Irvine?"

"I expected you would tell him."

Lu puffed out her cheeks. Then their future was safe, so long as he never discovered the truth. She had no doubts that if he ever learned of her crime, he'd turn her over to the authorities. It was the kind of honorable man he was, and she loved him for it. She could almost stomach the notion of suffering the consequences for her crimes, knowing Oscar would be so well loved and cared for. What she couldn't stomach was the certainty that Andrew'd lose all affection for her.

"There's no need for him to know. God's forgiven me." Even if at times she second-guessed whether He could really love and forgive a woman like her.

"At some point, Andrew'll find out. Jesus tells us everything kept secret will be revealed. Wouldn't it be better for him to hear it from you than someone else?"

She'd rather face Clint in a wrestling match than have Andrew discover the truth about Irvine. Wasn't it good enough God knew? "But you told me I'm forgiven."

"Yes, and we also talked about how we must face the consequences, though we've been granted forgiveness."

"But what if I swing? What if Andrew hates me for what I've done?"

"Then you still have the love of your Savior and an eternal hope that cannot be taken away. God is your hope, not Andrew. He was never meant to fill the place of God. Confessing the truth to Andrew shows God that you trust Him with the outcome, instead of thinking you can control it on your own. Trust Him and tell Andrew the truth. The results may surprise you."

The bedroom door cracked open and Pastor Newcomb's tense voice passed through. "Riders coming."

Lu's throat tightened. It was time to see which scenario from her mind played out. "How many?"

"Two, as far as we can see. Stay in here and keep low."

The door closed again.

Following Lu's whispered directions, Emma squished beneath the bed and used a blanket to pull the still sleeping Oscar toward her. Unfortunately, their hiding spot meant no one could sit on the bed without squashing them, leaving four people to stand and take a bullet if it passed through the interior wall. They needed fewer people in here if they were going to lie low, and considering Lu knew the Thornes better than anyone else here, she would do more good out there.

"Put the trunk against the door once I leave. It should keep it from opening and take the brunt of anything coming through."

Theresa stayed her exit with a hand. "But Josiah said to stay here."

"You don't strike me as the type to listen to foolishness."

The corner of her mouth tipped up. "You're right." Then she opened the door wider and stepped past Lu.

Lu should've known she'd take that as an invitation. By the scraping sound that followed their exit, someone must've shifted the trunk into place. All light in the main room had been extinguished, leaving only the nearly full moon to cast an eerie glow into the house. Widow Zachary and Pastor Newcomb knelt next to the open windows, the barrels of their weapons protruding over the sill.

Josiah laid across the floor, rifle leveled and sticking out the cracked front door. "Remember, no shooting. I want him alive and uninjured."

Theresa and Lu knelt below the windowsill on either side of Pastor Newcomb. Though Josiah gave a disapproving grunt, he didn't send them away. Lu desperately wanted to see what was going on, but she was no fool. If Cyrus caught a glimpse of her head, he'd take his one shot. She settled for listening and praying all went well.

"That's close enough," Josiah called.

"I expected you and Lu to be gone by now." The voice wasn't Cyrus's. Maybe Hayden's? She couldn't be sure as the man rarely spoke around her.

"Change of plans. We're staying here."

The creak of a saddle and the jangle of stirrups indicated someone was getting off of their horse. Pastor Newcomb and Josiah remained still, but Widow Zachary adjusted her angle. Cyrus was cagey. If he was on the move, he had a plan. She peeked over the sill, but it wasn't Cyrus on the ground. Instead, Hayden aimed a gun at the house, although he seemed to be subtly shifting his position to be more behind Cyrus while still out of range of a kicking horse.

"You stay in that house and it's a cremation you'll get." Cyrus's smug voice rang clear. "There's only one way out of that cabin. So if you want a proper burial, I'd send Lu and Oscar out."

"You're in no position to negotiate. You're outmanned and outgunned."

"I think you overestimate your position." Cyrus lifted a glass bottle with a piece of cloth hanging out the neck.

Lu sucked in a breath. Homemade fire bombs were his favorite method to cause chaos and destruction. Once he lit the turpentine-soaked cloth, he'd launch the flaming bottle through the window. It was probably why he remained mounted. Being on a horse gave him the height advantage and speed to get away.

"Shoot the bottle!" Lu yelled. "Don't let him light it!"

His free hand made a quick movement, and a flame sizzled to life at the end of a long matchstick.

Widow Zachary fired.

The glass bottle exploded, and for an instant, the surprised look on Cyrus's face was comical. Then a splash of turpentine must have reached the match. Flames ignited in an arc over the horse. Cyrus's arms waved frantically as his clothing and the surrounding ground caught fire. The horse squealed and reared back, dumping Cyrus onto flaming grass and taking off in a frightened run across the road.

Hayden yanked off his coat and smothered the flames spreading across Cyrus's clothes. Josiah jumped to his feet and dashed outside, pulling off his coat as he ran. Pastor Newcomb, Lu, and Theresa followed at his heels. Theresa yelled something about going after the horse and disappeared into the woods. Pastor Newcomb smothered the flames around Cyrus's legs as the man writhed and rolled with piercing screams.

Lu stood frozen in place until Widow Zachary slapped a bucket against her chest. "The water pump's on the side of the house."

Lu followed her and then pumped until water overflowed their buckets. She'd wanted Cyrus arrested, not burned to death! When they returned, all that remained was a burning patch of grass. On the porch, the three men struggled to carry a yowling Cyrus inside. Too late to help, Lu and Widow Zachary dumped the pails over the scorched earth.

When they entered the house, the scent of singed hair and burnt flesh permeated the air. Lu's stomach flipped. Any injury was unpleasant, but burns provided their own special torture. Pastor Newcomb lit a lamp and adjusted the wick until it gave off the most light possible.

Though she'd rather not see the damage, Cyrus's cries of pain compelled her forward.

Cyrus leaned back in the only padded chair, so the damage must be limited to his front. She shifted to peer between Josiah and Hayden and wished she hadn't. Half his hair was singed or missing, exposing bubbling red skin along his scalp. Sections of eaten-away material revealed red, inflamed skin with giant blisters growing by the second. His hands bore the brunt of the damage. Although the burns on his left hand seemed no worse than the others on his body, flecks of white and charred skin peeled away from bright red portions on his right where he'd held the bottle.

"You're under arrest. Anything you say is voluntarily shared and will not reduce charges. Furthermore, any information divulged may be used against you." Josiah pulled iron bracelets from a pocket, but when he regarded Cyrus, he hesitated. Even she could see there was no way to shackle him without rubbing against a burn.

After a moment of deliberation, he knelt and locked Cyrus's ankles to the legs of the chair. All Cyrus needed to do to get free was lift the chair and wiggle the pliable bracelets off the leg, but based on his moaning, getting away was the last thing on his mind and would be for a while.

Mary opened the bedroom door. "Is it safe for us to come out?"

"Yes," Josiah answered.

Obviously, Josiah didn't have children. The image of a burnt and moaning Cyrus would frighten Oscar to no end. Lu opened her mouth to contradict Josiah, but Oscar darted out, racked with sobs, before she could speak. Trying to keep him from seeing Cyrus, she met him behind the chair and embraced him until the shudderings slowed to sniffling.

"Are the giants gone?"

Lu glanced over her shoulder. "Not gone, but we're safe."

"I wouldn't count on it." Cyrus's pained words caught Oscar's attention.

His face scrunched. "Uncle Cyrus?"

Oscar broke away and circled to the front of the chair. His eyes widened as he took in the monstrous appearance of the man he called uncle.

"Hey, Runt."

Lu pulled him away and shielded him from further viewing.

New tears welled in his eyes. "What happened?"

"He played with matches. We need to leave him alone so Joe and Hayden can doctor him."

She carried Oscar toward the bedroom. Cyrus might be too injured to do them physical harm, but that wasn't his specialty. He was a planner and, burns notwithstanding, he would find a way to escape. And once he did, his revenge would be thorough.

CHAPTER 33

THE FIRST HINTS OF MORNING lightened the inky sky into shades of navy, yet Andrew still hadn't reached Boonville. His head swam and his stomach churned. Morgan's every step pounded like the impact of Clint's hurled rock. Twice during the night Andrew had nearly lost his mount and had been forced to rest or risk breaking his neck. Rather than the five hours or less it should've taken to reach Boonville, more than seven had elapsed, with almost an hour left to go. At least Broderick should be in Petersburg by now. As soon as Andrew made it to Boonville, the raids could be coordinated through telegraph.

The sensation of falling sent warnings through Andrew's body, and he pitched himself up to keep himself from tumbling off the saddle. The sudden movement propelled bile into his mouth. Though he didn't want to delay further, he guided Morgan to a copse of trees at the edge of the road, dismounted, and stumbled a few feet away. What little contents his stomach contained—a bite of jerky and a few swigs of water—splattered across the ground. Once his stomach convinced his brain it could give no more, he struggled back to where Morgan munched, then slumped against the tree's base.

With all the stopping he'd done, Cyrus and Hayden should've overtaken him by now, even with the delays the team had built in to gain him ground. Unless something had gone wrong at the Zacharys'. His stomach cramped again. Cyrus was a resourceful brute. He might have tracked Josiah and Lu's escape when he discovered the house empty.

Or if they hadn't had time to run, he might have realized Hayden was a traitor. Were Lu and Oscar in trouble?

He rested his head against the tree and closed his eyes. *Father God, I know protection isn't guaranteed, but would You see fit to keep them safe? I can't do this on my own strength. I need You. Ease the pounding in my head so I can get to Boonville, do what needs done, and then get back to them.*

Andrew ended his prayer but couldn't silence the worry. How could Broderick drag his wife into cases? And he wasn't the only one. It'd become common practice among the married operatives to involve family members. Now that Andrew had a family of his own, the concept sickened him. No investigation was worth the potential loss of his family. What sort of man would he be if he constantly lifted his family as a sacrificial offering to his career? Not one he wanted to become. There were plenty of other investigative careers that he could take that would be safer for his family. And maybe it was time he considered it. Once the Thornes were arrested, he'd think and pray through what was best for his family.

At this moment, he needed the pounding in his head to abate. After a few minutes of rest, he'd be on his way so he could finish this case. With eyes closed and body relaxed, the pain ebbed enough for a brief rest.

Two minutes. No more. Then he'd start riding.

Someone shook him awake.

Andrew opened his eyes to bright morning light, and blinding pain forced him to shut them again. So much for a few minutes of rest. He blinked until his gaze focused on Hayden crouching next to him, clearly concerned. Andrew silently called himself every name he'd ever heard roll off Pa Thorne's tongue as he jolted to full alertness. Not only had Hayden and Cyrus caught up to him, but they'd also found him lallygagging around like an operative who didn't deserve a job.

He glanced around. "Where's Cyrus?"

"He thought he'd set the Zachary cabin on fire but ended up on fire himself. Josiah's holding him while they tend to his wounds and we coordinate the raids."

"Lu? Oscar?"

"Fine when I left. With the way Cyrus's hands are burnt, he won't be giving them any trouble." Hayden gave Andrew a hand up. "Did you fall? I found Morgan wandering up the road."

Andrew wished he could blame a fall for his laziness. "Stopped before it happened."

"Are you certain you're well enough for this? There's no shame in admitting you're not."

The ache in his head had dulled to something tolerable, and the initial dizziness when he stood had already passed. He'd be fine for this next round of duty. "I'll make do."

Hayden nodded, though a hint of skepticism pinched his lips.

They gathered their mounts and made good time to Boonville. The morning sun touched the roofline of the two- and three-story businesses framing the grassy acre of the town square where a nondescript red-bricked courthouse stood at the center. Hayden led them past it to the corner of the next street where a two-story Italianate house served as both the sheriff's personal residence and the Warrick County jail. They tied their horses to the hitching post along the side and walked up the front steps to the door.

After a few knocks, a broad man with brown hair opened the door. "Mr. Orton, I didn't expect to see you back so soon."

"I'm sorry to impose at such an early hour, Sheriff Campbell. Unfortunately, there's been a change of plans."

"Come on in. Marshals Uppencamp and McBeth haven't left yet. I assume their presence is needed?"

Praise God for that mercy. The investigation and raids were supposed to be shared between the US Marshals and Secret Service. Had they moved ahead without the marshals, the bureaucratic finger pointing would've caused a headache worse than Andrew's concussion. At least this way they would have the manpower and arresting power they needed.

At Hayden's assent, Sheriff Campbell gestured down the main hall toward the back of the living quarters. "If you're hungry, my sister is fixing breakfast for the inmates."

Hayden glanced at Andrew. "Breakfast and some headache powder would be appreciated."

Was his discomfort that obvious to everyone? Andrew ran a hand over his face and bumped his sore nose. With a bruised face like his, people probably hurt just looking at him.

Sheriff Campbell disappeared upstairs, while the main hall led them into a surprisingly modern kitchen with a large stove and cooking area. A young woman with riotous curls pulled back in a ribbon worked over a large pot of what smelled to be corn mash. Her high-pitched voice sent a streak of pain across Andrew's forehead as she asked after their needs.

Thankfully, after serving them a plate of food and settling a glass of water and bottle of powder in front of Andrew, she focused on breakfast for the inmates. By the time Sheriff Campbell returned with Uppencamp and McBeth, she'd disappeared through a steel door at the back of the room to help the deputy deliver food to the individual cells.

Once the marshals, Sheriff Campbell, and Hayden sat around the table, Andrew dove into planning. "How soon can your deputies be ready? The Thornes know who the snitches are and are attempting to silence them. Once the Thornes realize they've escaped, it won't be long before the Thornes scatter, along with all the other gang members."

"I can have all five, plus a dozen more I trust to deputize, here within a couple of hours."

Andrew bit back the frustration that hours brought and reminded himself God was in control, even when everything moved frustratingly slow. Sheriff Campbell didn't wait to finish his breakfast, although he insisted the others did, and left with his sister to round up officers.

"Go rest for a while, Darlington. We can't plan anything until everyone's here, and you've already been up all night. We'll wake you after everyone arrives."

As much as he wanted to argue, he couldn't ignore the wisdom in resting. Once everything was ready to set into motion, Andrew had no intention of resting again until Lu and Oscar were safely by his side.

When Hayden woke him, it was past noon and more than a dozen men were squeezed into the parlor and main hall. Hayden explained the situation, location of the various gang members living throughout the two counties, and the revised plan of attack. Marshals McBeth and Uppencamp, along with four Boonville officers, would join Andrew arresting the remaining Thornes. Hayden would lead the rest of the team with Sheriff Campbell throughout the southern region to capture the other members while Broderick led the raid from the north.

In the kitchen, Andrew outlined his strategy. While all that remained at the Thorne house was an injured man and two women, he wasn't going to take any chances. More insanity resided in that house than on Blackwell's Island. They needed to be prepared for anything.

By the time everyone dispersed to grab the necessary equipment and rations for several days of running criminals to the ground, Andrew's head buzzed with all the hum of activity. He stepped onto the porch to escape the noise only to find Miss Campbell talking to a thin man dressed as a porter on the sidewalk below. He almost turned around but stopped when the topic of conversation caught his attention.

"Did someone rob a bank?"

"It's even better than that, Amos." Miss Campbell leaned forward like a girl dangling a bone in front of a dog. "My brother is finally going to nab all those counterfeiters. They even got multiple parties heading up into Pike County."

For the sister of a lawman, the woman had no discretion. The job was far from ready to start. If word about the raids leaked too soon, the gang members to the south would scatter and spread the word. "That's enough, Miss Campbell. Say anything else and you join the inmates rather than serve them."

Amos checked his watch. "I best be getting back to the station, anyway. The next train's due soon. See you at dinner tonight?"

After she nodded, Amos moseyed down the street toward the town square. Miss Campbell ducked her head as she passed him and opened the door. The excitement from inside buzzed worse than a hive of bees. If he stayed too much longer, his headache would reach dizzying levels again. He could not afford the need to lie down.

He caught Miss Campbell's attention. "Would you please tell Mr. Orton I've left for the telegraph office?"

Free of the commotion, Andrew followed the overhead wires toward his destination. He'd telegraph Broderick and let him know all was in order with his team. Then he'd do what he should've done more than a month ago. Contact Mother Elise and Father Darlington.

Andrew tried to think through what he could say with the limited amount of information that could be communicated over the wire. I'M MARRIED. WANT—no, strike that—NEED YOU IN PETERSBURG. YOU HAVE A GRANDSON. It was all so bare-bones and unfeeling. Had he actually written a letter before instead of putting it off, he could've given them all the details. Explained who Lu and Oscar were. How precious they'd become to him. The struggles they faced.

With the coming arrests, they'd need to spend months in Petersburg. It would be helpful to have his father's advice and his mother's presence as they navigated the trials. Most of all, he wanted his true family surrounding him as he faced his past one last time in the courtroom.

When he entered the telegraph office, Amos huffed at the counter like he was out of breath and patted a handkerchief at the sweat on his neck and face. The incoming train's whistle sounded through the window, and Amos flipped his watch open. After slapping it closed, he frowned. "Have they replied yet?"

Replied? The man must have broken into a run the moment he was out of sight to have gotten a message off before Andrew's arrival.

"Patience, Amos," the female operator said. "I just got the message off. They'll need time to get it to Stuart. His farm's at the edge of Stendal."

There was only one Stuart of any kind in Stendal—the one attached to the Thorne gang. Amos must be Cyrus's contact at the train station.

Andrew approached him from behind and blocked his exit. "Is something the matter, Amos?"

The man turned wide eyes on Andrew and began gulping like something was stuck in his throat. "N-n-no, sir." His agitation spread to his fingers, opening and closing the face cover of his pocket watch.

"Miss, I'd like to see what Amos sent over the wire."

"I'm sorry, sir, but telegraph communications are strictly confidential."

Andrew pulled out his credentials and laid them on the counter for her to examine. "I believe it is the policy of your company to cooperate with law enforcement."

Amos tried to edge his way past again, but this time Andrew gripped his arm. The telegraph operator retrieved the transmission instructions and handed it to him.

PHILISTINES KNOW. COMING. ALERT CYRUS. —A.

Andrew gritted his teeth. He'd found Cyrus's contact, all right, but not before he'd ruined their plans. With about five hours' distance between them, the Thornes would abandon their search for Lu and flee before raids could be conducted. Them, and anyone else the messenger decided to tell. What he needed was a message to control their movements.

"Send this to the same person: 'Lu caught. Bringing her to . . .'"— he searched his mind for a believable location—"'Cup Creek Fork.'"

Frances's anger toward Lu should drive her to seek revenge. She'd blindly walk into the trap.

Andrew settled the account and hauled Amos to the jail. With the revelation of Amos's treachery and Andrew's new plan, the marshals agreed on the need for urgency. As soon as the horses could be readied, they'd leave.

CHAPTER 34

ALTHOUGH EMMA RETRIEVED HELP FROM a trusted doctor in Stendal, little could be done for Cyrus's pain or burns. The doctor slathered on oil and limewater liniment, loosely bandaged Cyrus's hands, and administered a heavy dose of morphine. While the Newcombs slept on the floor and Widow Zachary kept the night watch out the window, Lu spent until dawn ensuring that Cyrus's bandages didn't come off and that he remained as comfortable as possible. Too drugged to do anything else, Cyrus lobbed cruel words at her.

"You think turning us in makes you a good person? You'll never be nothing but a—" The words that followed would make the devil's toes curl.

Though she wanted to deny their power, the words rooted in her wounded heart and grew into strangling weeds throughout the night. By the time Theresa relieved her, Cyrus's insults had become relentless.

After one look at Lu, Theresa turned on Cyrus. "Shut your trap or I'll dig my nails into your hands." Satisfied with his glaring silence, she shooed Lu to bed and encouraged her to ignore Cyrus.

If only it were that easy.

For hours, she wrestled her doubts on the hard floor. How could Andrew, let alone God, love her? She was exactly the woman Cyrus described. Dirty. Worthless. Unforgivable.

No one is worthy, but I love and choose you. I have made you new.

265

The thoughts couldn't be her own. Loved, chosen, new? She'd never use those words to describe herself. But they'd come in the silence of her mind. No one had spoken them to her. Or had they? Slow as a sunrise, understanding dawned. Jesus.

Her breathing eased, and while the floor didn't become any more comfortable, hope pruned away the lies. She *was* a new person in Christ. Clean. Loved and forgiven. Not because of anything she'd done, but because of who He was. She may not know much, but that simple truth brought a peace.

As for Andrew's love? The memory of his kiss and the tingle of her lips provided all the evidence she needed to be assured he didn't hold her past against her. Andrew wasn't like Irvine or any of the other men in her life. He knew her, and yet he still wanted her. And for more than just her body.

Thank you for the reminder and for Andrew, God.

She sat up in the dark room and stretched. By the look of the lump on the bed and the soft breathing, someone still slept there. Although she wasn't ready to face Cyrus again, she couldn't spend the day hiding. Oscar needed her, and she needed to be ready for whatever the day might require.

After a quick prayer for Andrew's safety, Lu entered the bright living area. The angle of light through the windows hinted at early afternoon—much later than she'd anticipated. Josiah sat at the front window, rolling a ring between his fingers while Cyrus slept awkwardly in the chair. No one else moved about the room.

"Where is everyone?"

Josiah stashed the ring in his pocket and then rubbed his eyes like he'd stared too long at one spot. "Widow Zachary's lying down, Theresa and Oscar are taking care of Cyrus's horse out back, and I sent Emma and Günter with the Newcombs into Stendal to buy food."

She dropped her voice as she passed Cyrus. "Is that wise? What if Ma Frances sees them?"

"We need food if we're going to last more than today with all these people. Günter insisted he could get them around town without being seen."

Lu couldn't argue with that. "Do you need a break? I can watch for a while."

"No, but I'll never turn down the company of a beautiful woman." He winked at her. "Especially the one who turned Old Pucker Face into a grinning fool."

"Is that what you call Andrew behind his back? That's horrible."

"You have to admit, the man's resting face is a scowl."

"Only because he carries the weight of responsibility on his shoulders. I understand how that feels." Her mind wandered to Irvine. Would Andrew understand if she told him the truth? Their weights of responsibility were different, and hers not easily dismissed.

"Given I'm known for my smile, you must think me careless and irresponsible." To demonstrate this disposition, he crossed his eyes and grinned with his lips over his teeth.

The comical expression made her chuckle, but then she sobered. "You can't fool me, sugar. You're a man who hides his pain behind humor and kindness."

She wouldn't have said that when they first met, but over the course of the last month, she'd seen the signs. The longing in his face when he played with Oscar. The pained but wistful glances at couples. The strictly surface relationships with the women around him. Of course, that could be the result of his job, but by the flicker of surprise, she'd hit the mark.

"You're more perceptive than I gave you credit for."

"Tell me about your wife. I saw her picture in the ring box when I searched your room."

All pretenses of a smile fell then. He withdrew the small ring from his pocket and stroked it with a pained fondness. "Shauna was an Irish lass with a laugh that made raindrops change into rainbows. You've never met anyone with more life and spunk. She was my pot of gold."

"What happened?"

"Died in a train accident eleven months after we married. She's been gone almost ten years now."

So he was a widower. Their love must have been genuine and soul-deep for the ache on his face to still show so strongly. "Has there been no one else?"

"Oh, I've had nearly a dozen fiancées, but none I'd actually marry. I just can't tell a woman no." He smiled then. "Shauna made it so easy to say yes that I never learned to say anything else."

It was sweet, really, the way he stared at the ring like he was looking at his beloved's face. "Do the others know about Shauna?"

"No, or if they do, they've not said anything." He tucked the ring away. "I'd appreciate it if you didn't share about Shauna with Andrew." His tone took on teasing tone. "I can't have my reputation as an incurable bachelor and lady's man ruined."

"Then why tell me at all?"

"I don't know. I thought as a widow yourself you'd understand. Or maybe I'm just too tired to think straight." He rose. "I'm going to make a cup of chicory coffee to hold over until they arrive with the real stuff. Want some?"

She declined, his words about Shauna wringing from her the guilt that so easily arose whenever she thought of Irvine. She didn't understand what it was like to lose someone she so dearly loved. Irvine's death came with the guilt of her culpability, the sorrow of leaving her son without a father, the ache of loneliness, and the anger of rejection. Love wasn't a real feeling between them, leastwise, not the same love Josiah apparently still carried for Shauna. However, if she ever lost Andrew, then she might understand.

Her eyes wandered to the road that passed through Stendal and eventually on to Boonville. Riding alone for five hours with a concussion worried her. Was he even now laying somewhere on the road in a heap? Had Hayden caught up to him? Or had he made it in one piece, and she was worried for nothing? For the hundredth time, she prayed for his safety, protection, and health. When she opened her eyes, Emma and Günter were running full speed toward the house.

"Josiah, something's wrong." Lu opened the door.

They arrived moments later out of breath and with panic evident on their faces.

Lu scanned the road ahead, but the Newcombs didn't follow. "What's happened?"

Emma dropped the bag of food on the floor, her words rushing out between heaving breaths. "The Thornes are coming."

Lu screamed for Theresa and Oscar and then turned to Günter. "Where are the Newcombs?"

"They're still in Stendal, borrowing a *wagen* from Reverend Stein to help travel." Günter's German accent thickened with anxiety.

Theresa and Oscar ran into the room as Widow Zachary emerged from the bedroom, eyes alert and a rifle in her grip. Even Cyrus stared at them through pained but alert eyes.

"How do you know they're coming?" Josiah asked.

"*Mein bruder* helps at the telegraph office attached to *der markt*. While there, a message came from Boonville for Stuart to warn Cyrus, 'The Philistines are coming.'"

Any criminal worth their salt knew Philistines was simply another word for the police, and for everyone in this house—except for Cyrus—police arrival was a good thing.

Emma stared at Lu with a scrunched brow. "The second message said you'd been caught and they were bringing you to the fork in Cup Creek."

"Me?" That made no sense. She glanced to Josiah.

"Andrew must have not intercepted the message until too late and then sent the second as a decoy."

Thank you, God, Andrew's all right.

Josiah knocked his fist on the table. "When Stuart goes to the Thornes' house to find Cyrus and Clint, Frances is going to realize Cyrus never made it to Boonville."

The lightness of relief transformed into a rock of anxiety that crushed her chest.

Cyrus released a throaty cackle. "By the time the coppers arrive, you'll all be dead, and us, long gone."

"Mommy?" Oscar's voice trembled as much as her legs.

Lu scooped him up, unsure what to do. Did they run? Or stay and stand their ground?

Josiah seemed to have no such hesitation. "Theresa, start gathering anything in the house that might be needed for supplies." He turned toward Günter. "Can you take the Zacharys to hide at the old Lutheran church with the Newcombs?"

"*Ja*."

"Good. I'll take Cyrus and the others to Boonville." With a heavy sigh, he confronted Widow Zachary. "Bring anything of sentimental value with you. Once we leave, there's no telling what will happen to the house."

"No! I'm not leaving the house my husband built with his own hands."

"It's this house or your lives, and I'm not giving you the choice. You're leaving in ten minutes with or without your belongings."

Widow Zachary's whole body trembled with growing rage, and before Lu could react, she shoved Lu and Oscar backward. "This is your fault!"

Too top-heavy with Oscar's weight, Lu lost her footing and fell against Cyrus's chair. It tilted, and Lu could've sworn Cyrus threw his weight to make it topple the rest of the way. She twisted to protect Oscar but overcompensated, and he took the brunt of the fall and her weight.

His scream pierced her ear and her heart.

She rolled off him and checked for injury. Other than a bump on his head, he appeared intact. "Oh baby, I'm so sorry."

"How's it feel to have your family hurt?" Widow Zachary sneered.

A cold flash of anger surged through Lu. She might understand Widow Zachary's fury, but no one hurt Oscar. Not even a woman with every right to tear Lu down and blame her for everything wrong in life. Lu sprang to her feet and stood toe-to-toe with Widow Zachary. "Leave my son out of this."

"Ladies!" Josiah's command for attention went ignored.

"I hope they find you and make you suffer like I've suffered." She spat in Lu's face.

Lu wiped the saliva off with a clenched fist. Back when she lived at the brothel in Colorado, territorial fights over the best clients broke out often. Having participated in a few, Lu knew exactly how to get Widow Zachary on the ground and crying for mercy. The temptation to retaliate thrummed in her veins, but she would not give in. Her son needed to see the better woman she was becoming, not who she had been.

Josiah tried to step in between them, but Lu swung an arm out to stop him.

"She's just angry and bitter. We both want what's best for our families." Without breaking eye contact with Widow Zachary, she spoke evenly. "Do you really want to start a fight in front of Emma and prove you're no better than a Thorne?"

"I'm nothing like a Thorne!" She launched at Lu, and they crashed to the floor.

Landing on top, Widow Zachary grabbed fistfuls of Lu's hair and yanked. Lu's neck pinched at a painful angle and each hair needled her scalp. Lu might not truly fight back, but she wasn't about to endure a beating. She thrust an open palm against Widow Zachary's face and twisted her hips to throw her leg against the woman's side. She was unsuccessful in dislodging the enraged woman, but Widow Zachary's surprise at the action released some of the tension on Lu's head.

Lu loosened one of Widow Zachary's hands from her hair. "Get off!"

The now free hand repeatedly slapped Lu while the other continued to jerk her head sideways.

Emma screamed at her mother to stop. Josiah and Günter jumped in to pry Widow Zachary off. As they pulled, she kicked in a last-ditch effort to cause Lu more pain. Her boot heel connected with Lu's raised arm, leaving an immediate, shooting pain behind.

Lu sat up and panted as she surveyed Widow Zachary—unscathed except for the wrinkles and skewed angle of her dress. Nothing compared to what she'd look like if Lu had used the dagger at her waist or the skills she'd honed at the brothel. Her own injuries were minimal. Widow Zachary hadn't even attempted to gouge her eyes out with her nails or claw her face. As far as catfights went, this one had been loud and unexpected, but pitiful on the scale of damage done.

Though Josiah still held her back, Widow Zachary screamed with all the agony of a wounded animal. "I hate you. I hate your whole family. You've taken everything."

Emma consoled her mother with soft reassurances. "You still have me. I'm still here."

Her screams turned to sobs. "I can't lose your father again."

Lu's heart broke for the woman, even though moments ago she'd contemplated the best way to knock her unconscious. It wasn't fair that the evil of this world sought to destroy the Zachary family further. "Is there any way we can protect their home?"

Josiah released the sobbing woman to her daughter. "My job is to protect people, not a house."

"What if we intercept Stuart? Arrest him before he gets word to Ma Frances?" Theresa asked from where she stood, still clutching a knife like she'd intended to come to Lu's rescue.

"Maybe." Josiah's gaze shifted from Widow Zachary to beyond Lu's shoulder. He blinked, and then immediately pulled his weapon. "Where's Cyrus?"

Lu whirled to face the overturned chair. Empty. The legs where his ankles had been shackled were broken off.

Pounding hooves sounded outside. Visible through the open door, Cyrus urged his horse and the one following it to a gallop. A much smaller body sat in front of him, screaming, "Mommy!"

"Oscar!"

She jumped over the broken chair, almost falling herself, and dashed out the front door. The tight tree line quickly concealed anything more than glimpses of the galloping horses and their passengers. They'd never catch up on foot.

Cyrus was going to get away with Oscar.

CHAPTER 35

THOUGH JOSIAH HAD BEEN TORN on what to do, Lu didn't hesitate to pursue Cyrus and Oscar into the woods. Once Cyrus reached Ma Frances with Oscar, the house would fly into escape preparations. After years of fleeing with the family from one location to another, Lu knew the pattern. Ten minutes and then they'd be gone, along with any chance of finding Oscar. Priscill would get everything she wanted.

Lu ran full steam, skirts hiked while dodging downed trees and bramble. Scraggly branches slapped her face and steep, narrow gullies threatened to steal her balance as she jumped over them. In little more than a minute, her chest burned for breath and dizziness begged her to collapse. She stopped and gulped breaths that pushed against the restraints of her corset. How was she ever going to catch up and save her baby? With legs that wobbled beneath her, she forced one step in front of another, praying for something, anything, to slow Cyrus—without it hurting Oscar.

Several minutes passed of nothing but the sound of her heaving breaths and her heart pounding in her ears. Then she heard it. A horse's snort up ahead. Had God answered her prayers, or was Cyrus planning a trap?

Lu approached cautiously, hiding behind the trees until the extra horse Cyrus pulled behind him came into view, alone. It stomped and flicked its ears. Nothing else moved or made a sound in the surrounding area. No visual hints that Cyrus lingered. Lu spoke in low, soothing murmurs until she reached the horse's lead, which was hanging from its halter. At its end, Cyrus's salve-covered bandage clung to the frayed threads. The rope must have fallen from his grip and taken the bandage with it. Part of her hoped that it hurt like fire, but another part of her prayed it hadn't caused him to fall and take Oscar with him.

She surveyed the area and strained to listen in case Oscar lay hurt somewhere close, but nothing indicated that the case. *Thank you, God. Now get me onto this beast.*

The horse had no saddle. Not her favorite way to ride, but more than one family escape had required her and Oscar to ride double bareback. Unfortunately, this time she didn't have Irvine to help her mount without the aid of stirrups. There had to be a stump or log somewhere that would suffice.

Another minute passed before she found a tree—one that had been uprooted in a storm sometime in the far past. Moss and dark spots of rotten wood covered the top of the trunk, and the odor of decaying wood warned against the tree's ability to hold her weight. It would make for a treacherous climb, but if she made it to the large limb sticking out like a partial bridge, she'd be able to walk straight onto the horse's back.

She wrapped the lead around a branch, whispered a prayer for success, and then clawed her way to the top. Now to not fall off and break her neck. Arms out, she balanced her way to the end of the limb, which drooped under her weight and waved dried leaves in the horse's face.

It sidestepped almost out of reach.

"Easy, girl. Steady." Lu inched forward.

The horse watched her with wary eyes but remained still. When she lowered onto the horse's back, it skittered but then relaxed once she managed a proper seat. With one hand clinging to its mane, she freed the lead from the branch.

"Lu!"

She angled to see over her shoulder. Josiah jogged toward her. Having him with her would be a boon when facing the family, but two adults riding bareback on a horse of this size wouldn't work. The horse would be more prone to falling or getting mixed signals and bucking.

Galloping would be out of the question. She could not—would not—slow her progress to Oscar, even for the sake of having help. Josiah would catch up eventually.

She pressed her heels into the horse's flanks. "I have to save Oscar. They'll be gone before we get there otherwise."

He hollered after her as she galloped away, but she ignored his yells of reason. Had he been in her position and his Shauna the one taken, he would've done the same thing.

Working to keep her seat as the horse barreled toward the house took all her focus. She broke through the tree line into the field behind the barn. Against every motherly instinct that demanded she ride straight for the house, she hid the horse behind the barn. If she was spotted by the family, they'd shoot her.

She used the cornfield as cover to get as close to the house as possible. Crouching low, she peeked through where the stalks were at their narrowest. Cyrus's horse stood tied to the porch railing, and all sorts of yelling echoed through the windows. Though she couldn't discern what was being said, she recognized the underlying alarm. Ma Frances must be enraged and panicked over Cyrus's injured state.

Her hysteria played to Lu's favor. The woman wouldn't be thinking straight. Between Cyrus's and Clint's injuries and the horses still missing from the corral, their usual escape plan wouldn't work. Lu just had to beat Ma Frances to the contingency plan she would make and thwart it. Considering Clint's and Cyrus's injuries, the only option would be the wagon, and the weight of four adults and a child would slow their speed to less than a walk. If she sabotaged the wagon, it might provide her an opening to snatch Oscar away.

When Lu stole inside the barn, Tabby and the puppies barked their greeting.

"Shhh!"

They disregarded her command and continued to yap. Jack and a few of the braver pups strayed from their nesting area and chased a dragging portion of her hem. She ignored them and found a rusted hacksaw hanging on a back peg. It would have to do.

Grabbing it from the wall, she turned toward the wagon and crawled underneath. Where would be the best place to weaken it? The axles connecting the wheels were supported by iron and would destroy what few teeth the saw had, but the rectangular wooden beam down the center of the wagon had potential. Parts of it were supported by iron, but the small section of exposed wood in the center could be sawed nearly through. With all the weight of the passengers, the beam should snap. If it worked the way she hoped, the wagon bed would remain intact and everyone would slide to the ground uninjured when the back tilted.

Jack licked her face as she scooted into a better position. Despite her shooing, he stayed by her side. She set the blade against the squared corner of the beam and tried to saw. The teeth bit into the bar like a baby gnawing on a wooden block. The motion dented the beam, but Lu made no true progress. If only her dagger were larger and had teeth to it.

The dogs barked with renewed fervor, and Lu glanced toward the door. Though the wagon blocked half her view, the unmistakable gait of an injured Clint moved in her direction. Lu sucked in a breath. Believing Clint hadn't seen her lying beneath the wagon was as useless as Oscar closing his eyes and pretending that made him invisible during hide-and-seek. Still, she held on to vain hope.

"I knew you'd come back."

Clint hadn't outright shot her, so maybe he still hoped to have her to himself.

She scrambled from beneath the wagon, put it between them, and slapped on a coy smile. "I couldn't leave you behind, sugar. I've worked too hard to make a future for us."

"You shot at me."

"And missed on purpose. I had to convince Andrew and his friends I was on their side. How else was I going to make sure I knew what their plan was so we could escape before it happened?"

He reached the opposite side and paused, as if gauging the truth of her response—or planning his next move. If she was going to survive, she needed to convince him of her attraction, and that meant playing a game she never wanted to return to.

God help me.

Her skills felt rusty after their lack of use since Andrew'd come into her life, but she knew the routine. Convince the mark of her sincerity and her own mind that this was happening to someone else. She drew a deep breath and blew it out slowly, dispelling reality once and for all. Luella was somewhere in the Tennessee mountains gigging frogs with her neighbors, laughing and full of innocence. Lightning Lu was here, doing whatever needed done to survive and save her son.

She played suggestively with the top button of her modest shirt-waist and sent Clint one of her sauciest smiles. "You can't really believe I'd want a man like Andrew when I have you."

The corner of his lips curled in that arrogant way of his. He leaned his injured side against the wagon and reached an arm out toward her. "Quit standin' out of reach and prove it to me."

"I want to, Clint, but Ma Frances threatened to kill me if she ever found us together."

"She's ready to kill you now, sweetheart, and"—faster than she reacted, Clint drew his revolver—"frankly, I'm not convinced she's wrong."

Lu's breath quickened as she fought the rising panic. With a confidence she didn't feel, she sashayed forward. "Ma Frances doesn't care what you want. She just wants to control you. Why do think she gave me to Irvine when she knew I was yours first?"

Clint's lips flattened and his finger flexed near the trigger.

She flinched. Poking at his sore spot was dangerous, but if she convinced him to rebel against Ma Frances, the repercussions might give Josiah and Andrew time to act or her a way to escape with Oscar.

"Think about it. When me being married to Irvine wasn't enough to keep us apart, she forced you to marry that shrew, Priscill."

With a final prayer this would work, she boldly pushed the revolver's barrel aside and placed a hand on his chest. Lu swallowed, trying to clear a path for the vile lie that she needed to wrap around the truth of her last moments with Irvine.

"And after I got rid of Irvine for us, she forced Andrew on me. She can't stand the thought of you being happy. With Andrew gone, there's nothing to keep us apart. Are you really going to let her determine who you belong with?"

The revolver returned to his holster, and he wrapped his arms around her. "Ma doesn't control my life. I do. You play by my rules and we'll—"

"Clint Russel! You get away from that harlot." Ma Frances's voice rang out behind them.

Lu tensed. "If you step away, she'll kill me. We'll never get to be together."

In giving Clint the choice, she released all control she might've had before. Either she'd done a good enough job of convincing him, or she was about to see that forever tomorrow Mary talked about.

Clint lifted his chin but never let loose of her eyes. "There's no way we'll outrun Andrew and his friends in this wagon, Ma. We need another plan, and I've got one." He gripped Lu's arm, drew his weapon, and flipped them both around so that they faced Ma Frances with his gun pressed to Lu's head. "We've got ourselves a disposable hostage."

CHAPTER 36

NO MATTER HOW MUCH HE wanted the horse beneath him to fly, Andrew could not and would not run the borrowed beast to exhaustion. Though he'd granted Morgan a reprieve and left him behind in Boonville, Andrew refused to delay. Taking the US Marshals and four deputies with him, he'd left within thirty minutes of sending the decoy telegraph. Alternating between trotting and walking, the team had covered nearly twenty miles in three and a half hours.

Andrew's headache didn't abate during the journey, but by God's grace and mercy, it never rose above a tolerable pounding, nor had the dizziness he'd anticipated actually developed. He'd kept pace with the others and probably pressed them harder than they would've proceeded on their own. Before they attacked the Thorne farm, Andrew wanted to retrieve Josiah and leave a deputy to watch over Cyrus and the others at the Zachary house. At least, that was his reasoning to the others. In truth, he wanted to see Lu again and verify with his own eyes she was okay before charging forward to arrest his past and give his family a future.

At long last, the Zachary home came into view. His momentary relief coiled into hard knots of tension as they approached. No smoke rose from the stovepipe, though dinner should be cooking, or at the very least a fire going to ward off the cooling evening. No Josiah-shaped shadows hovered on the edge of the windows keeping watch, nor were the curtains drawn to protect against someone from peeking in. Josiah was too thorough for this lapse in security.

Andrew dismounted and led the approach from the front, revolver at the ready. A gust of wind blew from behind and the door waved an unlatched greeting. This was wrong. Fear nipped at him as he toed the door fully open. Nothing inside moved except for a couple of leaves which skidded across the floor with the sudden breeze. Stacked dishes sat next to the sink, but the basic cooking utensils were all missing from their places on the open shelves and walls. All personal belongings appeared to be missing. The room looked oddly ransacked and tidied at the same time.

As two men checked the bedroom, Andrew knelt by the overturned chair and examined the broken legs. Identical scrape and scuff patterns cut into the wood—circular in nature, like shackles. Thunderation! He flung one of the legs against the wall. The evidence screamed trouble, and Josiah's absence confirmed it.

"Nothing's in the bedroom. Not even clothes. It looks like whoever was here packed up and left."

"Then we head straight to the Thornes'." It was the only sure destination. Whatever had happened here, he'd have to trust God with the details for now and get the answers from Josiah later.

They made good time and arrived at the Thorne farm, which had a similar sense of vacancy shrouding the grounds. The barn side door stood wide open. Before he could warn the team about the dogs, Marshal McBeth entered, prompting the dogs to yap loud enough to be heard from the house.

Over the top of their racket, Marshal McBeth's command rang out. "Put the weapon down!"

Andrew passed through the door as Theresa's voice answered.

"Don't shoot! I'm with the Secret Service!" She stood in the midst of the puppies with hands in the air, clutching a butcher knife. By the glare on her face, she was considering throwing it.

Marshal McBeth gave a condescending chuckle. "You don't actually expect me to believe that, do you?"

"Stand down—both of you. What she says is true." Unfortunately.

When McBeth lowered his weapon, Theresa did the same. "What

did you think I was going to do? Throw a knife at a man with a gun? I'm not stupid, you know." She waved her other hand at the open barn loft. "It's Andrew and some officers, Pastor. It's safe to come down."

The man rose from the loft floor, rifle in hand, and nodded at Andrew before climbing down the ladder.

What on earth were they doing here? A quick visual inspection of the barn revealed the main doors open and the wagon missing. A sense of foreboding like a green sky before a tornado swirled within him. "Where are the Thornes?"

"They left two hours ago. Josiah's following and said to tell you they're heading toward Louisville via Huntingburg."

"Why isn't he with Lu and Oscar?"

Theresa fiddled with the sleeve on her dress. "He is. Sort of."

Foreboding spun into a column of dreaded certainty. Disaster had come. "What do you mean?"

"Cyrus got away with Oscar, and Lu went after them. By the time Josiah got to the Thornes, she was tied to the wagon and forced to walk behind. The best he could do was follow. He instructed us to wait for you and pass on the information."

Andrew didn't know whether to retch or explode over the news. For two hours Lu had been at their mercy, walking, maybe even being dragged behind. Leaning into his fears would only paralyze him. Lu needed the righteous anger pulsing through him to propel him to action. It was long past time to end the reign of Thorne abuse. He stalked to the side door.

Behind him, Theresa asked, "What do you want us to do with Stuart?"

He swiveled to look at her, and she stepped aside to reveal the Thorne messenger bound, gagged, and leaning against the wall.

Though curious, he didn't have time to ask why or how *that* had transpired. What mattered is that the man had been caught—hopefully before anyone else had been warned of the coming raids. "One of the deputies will stay behind to guard him until we get back, and for heaven's sake, remove the gag. We're not cruel."

"So it's cruel to gag a man but not to lock a woman in a flooded building?"

He ignored her recurring complaint and retrieved his horse. The deputy would see to it that Stuart was treated properly. Andrew's only concern was reaching Lu and Oscar before the Thornes decided they weren't worth the effort of keeping alive.

Lu's toes caught the shreds of her hem again, and she stumbled to her knees. Before she could summon the strength to stand, the wagon pulled her forward and grated her body over the rocky ground. Rope chewed the flesh of her wrists, and her shoulders screamed though her mouth could not—not with so much dust in her nose, mouth, and throat that she could barely breathe, let alone make a sound. She'd long lost track of how far and for how long they'd traveled. Or even how many times she'd fallen.

Thank God Oscar had cried himself to sleep in the wagon bed and missed the last half dozen. When she'd fallen the first time, he'd screamed, tried to climb to her, and ended up with his first spanking from Ma Frances. The tight quarters and lack of anything other than an open hand had meant it was nothing severe, but the punishment in combination with Ma Frances's threats had been enough to scare him into silent crying. Lu hated to think how he would react if he woke to find her being dragged behind the wagon like a lifeless corpse. Although, in an hour, it wouldn't even matter if he were awake. With the way the sun dipped into the horizon, soon it would be too dark for him to see at all.

Exhaustion was starting to beat out the will to fight, but she couldn't give in. Oscar needed her.

God, give me strength.

At least the horse struggled to haul the weight of its passengers. The ambling pace was easier to fight against.

With great effort, she flipped onto her side. Using what little arm strength she had left, she curled her body around her rope-bound wrists, wiggled her feet free of the hem, and then rolled so that her feet caught the ground. The momentum provided by the wagon tugged her back to a stumbled walk.

"How long until we kill her?" Impatience laced Priscill's tone.

"We need her for negotiations just in case the police catch up. Otherwise, it'll be Louisville—if she even makes it that far." Ma Frances's one-eyed squint indicated she hoped Lu wouldn't.

Lu swallowed, but the dusty air made her cough and almost lose her footing again. She'd never make it the eighty miles to Louisville on foot.

Clint turned the wagon off the main road onto a trickling creek bed. If she fell in this, she might never be able to pull herself back up. Though she tried to pick the safest path, the unpredictable dips, moss-slicked rocks, and mud-sucking puddles made each step hazardous. After several excruciating minutes, Clint stopped at the edge of a large clearing.

"This is as far as we go tonight. My leg can't take another jolt, and Cyrus has been nursing that bottle of laudanum to the point where I'm not sure he's even conscious."

Cyrus mumbled something unintelligible from his semi-sprawled position next to Clint.

"Fine, but no fire. Open a can of beans and eat it cold if you need something." Ma Frances shifted Oscar to the spot Priscill vacated, then slid off the back of the wagon and confronted Lu.

"I promised my family would never be torn apart again. Now Irvine's forever left behind, Andrew might as well be, and Cyrus is out of his mind with pain. Even Clint's got a hole in his leg. And it's all your fault." She thrust Lu to the ground and released her hatred in merciless blows with her feet.

Rocks sliced across Lu's face as she curled into a ball to protect herself.

"That's enough, Ma," Clint said. "Cyrus needs your help. That bandage on his hand came off again."

Ma Frances stomped off, and Priscill made sure to get her own round of kicks in before following.

Clint hoisted Lu to a sitting position by the collar. "Be ready. Once they're asleep, we'll take off."

"It'll help if you untie me." Or at least loosen the ropes enough so she could feel her fingers. Then she might be able to reach and maneuver her dagger while they slept.

"Not until it's time. Can't have you sneakin' off before then."

Ma Francis barked his name.

He levered her head back and forced a kiss before hobbling off to join the rest of the family in setting up sleeping pallets.

Lu waited until he was out of sight before giving a dry spit and wiping her mouth against her shoulder. Kissing a skunk's rear end would be less vile.

"Mommy?" Oscar's tiny whisper came from above.

Her face lifted in time to have one of his tears splash against her forehead. "It's okay, baby. We'll be okay."

He wriggled off the wagon into her lap, and she brought him into the protective circle of her arms. His scared and confused whisper tore at her. "Why are they being mean? What did we do?"

"Oh, honey." She pulled her knees up, wishing for all the world she could protect him from the evil that was his family. Her mind went back to the words Andrew had once shared with her, and she prayed they comforted Oscar. "They are broken people who don't know how to love right, but God loves us. Them too."

She kissed Oscar's head. "We have to hold on to hope that no matter what, God's with us. We'll get through this, one way or another." She just hoped the one way included a long future with Andrew and Oscar here on earth.

Oscar stayed silent for a few minutes, then his little fist tightened on her shirt. "Is New Pa gonna come save us?"

Lu's throat constricted. She wanted to say yes, but she honestly didn't know. Had they vanished so well that he'd never be able to find their trail? "I don't know, baby, but I do know he'll do everything he can to try."

He nodded against her chest and fell quiet. What would they do if Andrew didn't come? Her death was certain, but what would happen to Oscar? She cocooned around him, rocking as she nuzzled her cheek against his mussed hair. *God, please protect him, no matter what happens to me.*

"Oscar," Ma Frances's voice snapped. "Come with me. Now."

Oscar's grip tightened on Lu.

"Come or you'll feel more than a spanking from me."

"I don't care." His defiant tone swelled Lu's heart and broke it all at once.

She couldn't stand for him to be hurt any more by this family. The way he sat with her now, she'd take the brunt of any attack for him. Until Ma Frances beat her senseless.

No, they needed to bide their time. Andrew would come. He had to. "Do what she says, Oscar." In a whisper, she added, "Just for now. New Pa will come soon."

She uncurled, and Oscar crawled off her lap, sniffling. Ma Frances carted him toward the center of the field, and he cried for Lu over Ma Frances's shoulder.

"Be brave, Giant Killer."

CHAPTER 37

WHY COULDN'T LU HAVE KEPT Oscar with her a few minutes more? Andrew understood she didn't want to cause trouble with Ma Frances, but his team was nearly ready. Now, with Oscar in the center of the Thorne camp and flanked by Priscill and Frances, there was no way to attack without Oscar being used as leverage. He signaled to Josiah to have the officers hold position and evaluated their options.

Nearby, Cyrus lay passed out and snoring. He'd be no obstacle for the deputies on this side. Clint was stretching his leg on the opposite side of the clearing, massaging it in between bites of beans. Other than his hobble, he seemed to be in full control of his faculties. Once the rush of a fight kicked in, he'd be a bear to beat, injury or not. Ma Frances and Priscill would be no problem, *if* they didn't have access to Oscar or Lu. Success depended on getting Oscar and Lu out of Thorne reach before attacking.

Andrew joined Josiah further back in the woods. "We'll have to wait until everyone's asleep. You get Lu to safety, and I'll grab Oscar. Once they're out of the way, we make arrests."

Josiah stealthily relayed the information to the others encircling the field, then returned to his spot. "Rest for a while. I'll let you know when it's time."

"Not possible."

"I can tell by looking at your face how much your head hurts. If you black out like yesterday while getting Oscar, we lose the upper hand."

Blast Clint's good aim. Andrew couldn't deny that Josiah was right. His head pounded so hard it was probably visible in his temples. Sleeping was out of the question, but if he wasn't careful, he'd risk the whole mission.

Picking a spot where he could observe Lu unnoticed, he sat and evaluated her condition. Debris littered her loose hair and dirt covered more of her than her clothes, probably hiding a multitude of bruises. The only visible injury from this distance was the red and raw flesh around her wrists. When this was over, she'd need a doctor and careful nursing to avoid infection. If only he could cut her loose and bring her into the safety of his arms now. She wriggled and tested different positions to sleep, but nothing allowed her to lay flat. Eventually, she rested her head against her bound and hanging hands, though by the wince on her face, it pained her.

Time passed slowly while Frances, Clint, and Priscill talked of plans and Cyrus snored. With Lu so still, Andrew's vigilant watch slacked, and his eyes drooped. The next thing he knew, Josiah was waking him with a poke to the ribs.

"It's a good thing all you Thornes snore, or you might have given us away. They blamed it on Cyrus before adding their own rumbles to the chorus."

Thank God for that. Andrew glanced to where Lu sat, wide awake and staring straight at the bushes in front of him. Had she seen him through the narrow space? While he longed to be the one to release her bonds, it had to be Josiah so he could take care of Oscar. If anyone other than Andrew or Lu tried to sneak off with Oscar, he'd scream and alert everyone else.

"Wait until you see my signal."

Josiah nodded and took position near the bushes closest to Lu.

Andrew sent up a quick prayer for success and skirted the clearing to the unimpeded path that led to where Oscar slept inches from Frances. He visually checked each Thorne in the nearly full moonlight. Frances's sides rose and fell in even patterns, a throaty snuffling issuing forth every few seconds. Variations of the same sound in greater volume emanated from Cyrus and Clint. Priscill was the only quiet one in the bunch. He watched her the longest, but she seemed to be asleep as well. He stood above the bush line and waved.

Lu watched the bushes rustle with a mix of anticipation and anxiety. She recognized that snore, and its sudden stop confirmed her suspicions. Andrew was nearby, had woken up, and was coming to save her.

But it was Josiah, not Andrew, who sprinted from the bushes to her side.

"Where's Andrew?" She whispered as he pulled a knife from his pocket and flipped it open.

"Shhh!" He gestured to the field's center before he cut the rope from around her wrists.

She leaned forward to see around the wheel.

Bright moonlight illuminated the clearing, where on the furthest side, Andrew crept past Priscill toward Oscar. She bit her lips together and held her breath as he stooped to lift the sleeping child. Oscar was a heavy sleeper, but the night's events might make him prone to startling. Movement behind Andrew drew Lu's attention. Priscill shifted too much to be asleep, and her arm slipped behind her back, right where she'd stored her gun earlier.

Panic drove Lu to her feet. "Priscill, no!"

In a blink, Priscill's arm swung over her body, gun in hand. Her muzzle flashed and boomed the same moment another shot discharged from the bushes. Andrew, Oscar, and Priscill went down.

Lu screamed and ran toward Andrew and Oscar as men burst into the clearing ahead of her. A cacophony of warnings ensued. Cyrus and Clint staggered to their feet. Ma bolted upright. Then her head swiveled to where Andrew lay draped over Oscar. Her wails rose above the officer's shouts as she threw her body over the top of them.

"No!" Ma Frances's response couldn't mean Andrew was dead. But how could it not? Priscill was too close to miss the shot.

Clint fired at an officer and a scream of pain pierced the air. Cyrus fumbled with his gun as Lu passed him and a wild shot whistled past her ear. More shots followed, and someone bellowed the command not to shoot her.

From behind her, Josiah yelled for her to drop to the ground. But he didn't understand. She *had* to reach Andrew and Oscar. They needed her. She ignored his calls and pressed forward, ducking as low as she could and still be able to run.

An arm snaked around her waist and pulled her to the edge of the clearing. She clawed at Josiah's hands while keeping her eyes pinned on the heap containing her heart and soul.

Oscar's small body wriggled free from beneath Andrew and Ma Frances.

Lu lurched forward and screamed at him, "Crawl to the bushes!"

His eyes found hers and he froze.

"Go!"

He scrambled toward safety with all the speed of a dog chasing a rabbit.

Ma Frances lunged for him, but Andrew's body twisted upward and forward. A relieved sob burst forth from Lu as he pinned the woman to the ground. Oscar disappeared into the bushes as Andrew rolled Ma Frances over and slapped shackles on her wrists.

When this was over, Lu was going to wring his neck for making her think he was dead.

The quiet of panting breaths replaced the noise of moments ago. Pungent gunpowder smoke tainted the air, drifting away like the chaos of the night. The danger of flying lead was gone, but the evidence of the fight lingered all around. One officer knelt by Priscill with a lantern and a grim look to his face, while another doctored an injured officer. Cyrus lay on his back, motionless. The two remaining officers faced her, guns raised.

Lu blinked. Why would they be pointing at her?

The arm around her tightened and dragged her back with an uneven step. Cold shivers shot through her as dark realization broke through her elation at seeing Andrew alive. Josiah hadn't pull her out of the line of fire. Clint had.

"Let her go." Josiah's voice came from behind them. "You can't escape."

"You shoot me, and I shoot her."

Warm metal pressed against her temple, and Lu closed her eyes. Did the revolver have any cartridges left in the cylinder? She'd heard lots of shots and seen Clint shoot off at least one, but that didn't mean he'd used up all his ammunition. Was she really in danger of being shot, or was he only creating the illusion to save himself? The latter seemed more likely, but she wasn't a gambler.

She surrendered any attempt at making a plan on her own and opened her eyes. Her gaze found Andrew's after he passed Ma Frances off to one of the other officers. If she were going to survive this situation, they were going to need to work together.

CHAPTER 38

REMAINING CALM, RESTRAINED, AND LOGICAL while Clint held Lu at gunpoint was a feat possible only by God's power.

"No one is going to shoot you." Andrew held his hands away from his side holster. Clint already had four weapons directed at him. Adding a fifth wouldn't intimidate him into submission.

"Apparently you've got some brains after all." Clint took an uneven step toward the creek bed, dragging Lu back with him. "You might as well accept it. You've lost, Andrew. You can have the rest of the family, but Lu's mine."

"She's never wanted you, Clint. If you try to take her, she'll fight you every step of the way."

Clint's harsh laugh grated. "Then you don't know Lu. She killed Irvine so we could be together. Go ahead, Lu. Tell him."

Another delusion, no doubt.

The officer by Priscill lifted his lamp and illuminated Lu's wide eyes and parted lips. Her chest heaved like she'd run a mile. A moment of doubt flickered through him. It had to be the stress and fear of a gun to her head. He refused to believe anything else. Lu was not a murderer. He sought her gaze to communicate he knew better, but she averted her face, shame marring her expression. The pastor's warning from a few days ago rose to mind with a sharp pang and Andrew's chest caved in. It couldn't be true. This couldn't be what he'd meant.

The hammer clicked. "Tell him."

"I killed Irvine." Her voice croaked.

Next to him, Frances lurched forward and hurled curses. "Shoot her! She doesn't deserve to live."

"No, Ma. I'm finally gettin' what I want. Lu, and my freedom from you." He crossed the creek, working his way toward the road.

Andrew followed, keeping his eyes on Lu even though she refused to look at him. There had to be more to the story Clint wasn't sharing. A defendable reason. He wouldn't believe anything less of her.

"Where do you think you're going to go? You're walking on an injured leg. We'll follow you until you collapse. It's not like Lu can help defend you. She doesn't even have a gun. The only damage she can do is to you."

Lu's gaze snapped to his. He glanced at her waistband and prayed she understood.

Oscar darted out of the bushes with an armful of rocks. "Let my mommy go!" One at a time he pelted them at Clint like he was David fighting Goliath.

"Stop it, brat!" Clint twisted, causing the gun to point up.

Lu yanked her dagger free and stabbed it through the bandaging into Clint's wound. He yowled in pain and released Lu to clutch his leg.

"Lu! Drop!"

She threw herself toward Oscar and knocked him into the bushes.

Without giving Clint time to readjust, Andrew tackled his middle. Clint fell back and swung with the butt of his gun. Andrew deflected it and ground his knee into Clint's wound. Clint roared in agony. Before he could retaliate, Andrew flipped him over and, with Josiah's help, shackled his wrists.

Andrew ignored Clint's unending curses and threats and left him for Josiah and the marshals to deal with. With steps that bordered a run, he rushed to where Lu held an excited Oscar on her lap at the edge of the creek bed and crushed them in a three-person embrace. Though he'd never admit it to the others, his insides shook worse than an earthquake as the reality of almost losing Lu and Oscar set in. Only when Oscar objected did Andrew let go.

"I did good." Oscar's chest puffed out and a grin split his face as he lifted an unused rock. "Mommy's safe."

Though Andrew wanted to scold him for risking his life, Andrew didn't have it in him. Instead, he ruffled Oscar's hair and sat down next to Lu, though she refused to look at him. "Good job, Giant Killer. We're all safe now."

While the marshals contended with the aftermath in the clearing, Oscar retold the story of his bravery in exuberant volume and animated gestures. Andrew struggled to listen as the weight of Irvine's death settled over him. Her role as an informant had meant a light punishment and bright future—even the possibility for him to remain a Secret Service operative if that's what God led him to. But a murder charge could mean a noose end to their marriage vows. He needed answers so he could strategize how best to move forward. Depending on the circumstances, a future may still be theirs. No matter the reason behind her involvement in Irvine's death, he would stand by her, and he wanted her to know that.

All too quickly, Oscar's excitement of being a hero dissolved. A slew of "why" questions tumbled from his mouth. Fear and anxiety turned to tears, and he demanded to sit on both of their laps at the same time, clinging to their hands as if letting go meant one of them would leave him forever. Andrew didn't blame Oscar. If what Lu confessed to was true, his little family was going to have a lot to work through over the coming months, including separation, and Andrew wasn't looking forward to the pain and struggle that would entail.

"Lu, about Irvine . . ."

"Please, not in front of Oscar."

Strained silence stretched between them, and Andrew's headache returned with a vengeance, along with a new stinging throb streaking up his back. He lightly touched it and jerked his hand away at the renewed pain. Tacky wetness stuck to his fingers. A quick sniff of the iron scent confirmed that it was, in fact, blood. Priscill's shot must have grazed him as he dropped to cover Oscar. If it hadn't been for Lu's warning, the bullet might have gone through him instead of skidding across him. He'd probably need one of the deputies to treat and cover it before they journeyed back to Landkreis for the night.

As the deputies loaded the wagon with their prisoners, Josiah trudged over with his hands in his pockets and a marshal at his side. "Is what Clint said true, Lu? Or did you agree so he wouldn't shoot you?"

Josiah was giving her a plausible denial. There would be a courtesy investigation if she said no, but without evidence Lu wouldn't likely be convicted. His breath solidified in his lungs. Their future hinged on her answer. A "no" would almost guarantee the future he wanted for them. At long last, she met his gaze. Regret mingled with peaceful confidence, even as tears pooled in the corners of her eyes. She clasped his free hand and squeezed.

She addressed Josiah. "It's true."

And with those two words, Andrew fell a little more in love with her. She could've lied to save herself and their future. Had the question been posed to her at the beginning of the case, he was sure her answer would've been a denial. Her truthful answer in face of the consequences only proved her to be a new creation in Christ, and the woman he wanted to spend the rest of his life with. Whatever may come, they would work through it together.

Josiah released a heavy sigh. "Then I'm afraid you're going to have to travel to Petersburg with us tonight."

"Petersburg? Tonight?" Andrew surged to his feet, forcing Oscar to shift into Lu's lap with a whimper. "It's too far and there are multiple injuries." Lu's wrists alone needed attention, plus whatever else she'd endured and now hid beneath the facade of calm.

"It's the only place in Pike County with enough jail space to house them all. I'll travel with Lu, but you need to return to Landkreis with Oscar and tie up loose ends there. Take a few days to recover and pack up Lu's and Oscar's belongings while you're at it. I'll take care of things in Petersburg."

"You can't expect me to leave Lu. You know what will happen." Andrew fisted his hands. Without bail money and a place to stay in town, she'd be housed in the same building, maybe even the same cell, as Frances Thorne.

Oscar clung to Lu's neck as she struggled to her feet. Andrew swooped in to aid her but refused to back away once she was steady on her feet. "The Newcombs' residence will suffice for Lu until tomorrow."

"You know we can't do that, Andrew. She has to be treated like the rest."

"But she's not like the rest!"

Lu cupped the side of his face. "It's okay. Just take good care of Oscar for me." Tears glided down her face, and one dripped onto his hand as he reached to wipe them away. "Oscar, baby, I need you to go to New Pa."

"No!" Oscar fought, but Andrew pried him away.

Oscar lunged toward Lu. "But I want to go with you!"

She stepped out of reach and hugged her middle. "Not this time, baby." Her voice turned husky. "I love you. Both of you." Her eyes met Andrew's.

His throat closed, too thick with emotion for him to breathe, let alone speak. He wanted to tell her. To assure her that his love for her was as steady and true as the rising and setting of the sun. But holding a devastated Oscar prevented any sort of silent action to communicate his thoughts.

"This way, ma'am." Marshal McBeth grasped Lu's elbow and led her toward the horses waiting for prisoner transport.

Andrew swallowed and tried to get the words past, but once he'd managed a strangled, "I love you," Oscar's wails and screams overpowered them. His heart wrenched as he turned away from Lu and carried Oscar deeper into the woods. It was hard enough to watch Lu leave as someone who understood what was going on.

Josiah followed, and once Oscar's sobbing quieted, he spoke. "Deputy Schmidt is going to travel with you and Oscar. I'll do what I can for Lu, but a confession of—"

"I know."

"I'm sorry." Josiah clasped his shoulder before joining the party carrying half of Andrew's heart to Petersburg.

CHAPTER 39

THE IRON RAILINGS OF THE narrow cot made sleep impossible as they bit into Lu's hips and shoulders. She wasn't a large woman, but it was uncomfortable. If the men's quarters were in any way comparable, Clint must be miserable. Not that she felt much sympathy for him. They'd all earned their place here.

Once again, she consoled herself with the reality that she was forgiven, and that God was proud of her for owning her consequences. She'd been sorely tempted to take Josiah's provided excuse, but the moment she'd spoken the truth, peace beyond all understanding comforted her. She had a new promised future to look forward to, even if a portion of it was spent in the dank belly of a ramshackle jail.

Lu blew out a long breath and stared at the ceiling marred by crumbling sections and dark, crisscrossed lines. Given the musty smell and yellowing color, this particular cell must have been suffering from water damage for years. Even the spiders had given up on it being a livable habitat, leaving behind their intricate webs to be coated in dust and dangle in the stagnant air.

The entire building was in such a sorry state that Sheriff Shrode apologized as he locked her in the cell. Although the county had plans to begin massive repairs and an expansion next year, it did nothing for her current situation. At least she didn't have to share the six by seven room with anyone. It was bad enough that she could easily hear Ma Frances's occasional screaming from her own accommodations further down the way. Solid walls might separate the rooms, but the iron-bar doors belied the lack of privacy.

Giving up on trying to nap, Lu stood and paced the few steps the narrow space allowed. Though she was grateful for the provision of a chair and cot, their presence ate up much of the tiny space. She shoved the bucket for personal use underneath the bed to create one more step's worth of room. It wasn't much. Three steps to the bars. Pivot. Three steps to the warped shelf attached to the brick wall. She ignored the useless paper and pen she'd been provided and focused on the drawing that Theresa had sent featuring her, Oscar, and Andrew playing with the puppies.

Despondency won out as she once again lifted it from its sacred place. Nine days and not one word from Andrew. Not since he'd learned the truth of her role in Irvine's death. In fact, she'd not heard from anyone but Sheriff Shrode, and that was when he'd delivered the drawing and informed her of the staggering charges being pressed against her. Theft, counterfeiting, murder. Bail wasn't being offered, and her stay would last until the hearing next month. Sheriff Shrode wasn't aware of any deals made with the US Marshal's office but said the courts would provide her a lawyer if she wanted. She requested one but had yet to meet with the man who'd represent her.

Keys jangled and the main door to the cellblock opened. It was too early for the evening meal and only one set of feet echoed down the corridor, so it couldn't be a new prisoner. Lu walked to the bars and Sheriff Shrode stopped at her gate.

"You've got a visitor." He fumbled with the keys and opened the door.

"Is it Andrew Darlington?"

"Nope. A Captain Abbott from the Secret Service. Maybe you'll get that deal after all."

The original deal had only included the theft and counterfeit charges. Maybe after he listened to her explanation of Irvine's death, he'd be willing to consider expanding that deal into absolving something that would otherwise entail a trip to the hangman's noose.

She didn't really hold out much hope for that, but she wasn't above dreaming.

"Wrists."

She held out her hands and stared at the scabbed and discolored skin. Healing from her time behind the wagon was slow going but at least had progressed enough for the iron shackles to no longer be painful.

Once secured, Sheriff Shrode led her to a small room where Andrew's friend Captain sat at a table with a set of papers in front of him. What little hope she had for negotiation dissipated. That man liked her about as much as a worm liked a hook.

"You may leave, Sheriff," Captain Abbott said. "Mrs. Thorne won't cause any trouble."

The use of her former name scraped like a knife against a plate. There would be no mercy from him. The door closed behind them, and Lu waited for Captain Abbott to speak.

"You previously made a deal with the United States Marshal's office to provide a testimony and evidence against the Thorne gang in exchange for two years of probation and safe passage for you and your son to St. Louis. Is this correct?"

"Yes, sir."

He nodded. "After consulting with the United States Marshal's office, the Secret Service has decided to honor that deal, if you agree to one concession. Your marriage to Operative Andrew Darlington was forced upon him and undesired. If you willingly sign this annulment paper . . ."

Annulment? Their marriage undesired? Was that why he hadn't contacted her? "Does Andrew want an annulment?"

"Of course he does. He has his career to think about. Having you as his wife would ruin his reputation and prevent his goal of achieving director of the Secret Service."

Lu clenched her fists beneath the table, making the bracelets scrape against her scabs. This man painted Andrew as a heartless, selfish monster. Andrew would never toss her and Oscar aside for some job.

This felt like a manipulation of power by Captain Abbott, not a true request of Andrew. At least, she refused to believe it was. If learning of her role in Irvine's death had really destroyed the feelings they'd developed over the last month, then Andrew was going to have to ask for the annulment in person.

"The only person I'm willing to make a deal with is Andrew. Come back with him and we'll talk."

"You don't have any negotiating power here. We have all the evidence we need to convict you and your whole family. Not the least of which is your own confession to murder."

"Are you saying that your deal will extend to those charges as well?" If it did, she might have to reconsider, if for no other reason than having a future life with Oscar.

Captain Abbott's chair creaked as he leaned back with folded arms. "Murder is out of our jurisdiction and, frankly, of no concern to us. The courts will decide your fate on that as a separate charge. However, they'll probably take your situation into consideration, especially if they know of your cooperation with us on the other matters."

Just as she suspected. She could still hang, regardless of if she signed it or not. Truly, there was no benefit for her either way. However, if she didn't sign it, Andrew would still legally be her husband. Oscar would have a father to care for him. Andrew would raise him to be an honorable man. One she'd be proud of.

"The deal walks out the door with me, Mrs. Thorne. Will you or won't you sign the papers?"

Mind made up, she stood. "It's Mrs. Darlington, and I will not sign. If Andrew wants an annulment, he can come ask for it himself."

Andrew paced the lawn in front of the Van Nada Boarding House, trying to work through his frustration before going upstairs to his suite of rooms where Oscar waited with the Darlingtons. He supposed he should be grateful the May fire destroyed the three hotels closest to the

Pike County courthouse. The mile-long walk from the jail gave him time to calm down before comforting a distraught Oscar. Although, after seven days in Petersburg and more than triple that number in failed attempts to see Lu, comfort was becoming more difficult to find.

The unexpected and disquieting emotions surrounding the Thorne arrests didn't help his mood either. He wasn't supposed to grieve, but Cyrus's death had brought a finality to the loss of family he'd thought he'd long moved past. And with the grief came a remorse that he hadn't shared the eternity-changing hope of Christ with any of them. They wouldn't have escaped the consequences of their crimes, but his previously unacknowledged ache for reconciliation might have occurred. There was still time to share with Frances and Clint, but access to them had been blocked too.

Andrew rammed a hand through his hair and stopped at the corner where the two-story clapboard house sat.

"Denied entry again?" Mother Elise rose from one of the chairs Miss Van Nada set outside for boarder use.

He should've known she'd be waiting for him. After the way he'd stormed out this morning, she must have realized he was approaching his breaking point. By the small floured handprints on her dark skirts and the whiter-than-normal appearance of her hair, she'd taken Oscar to the kitchen to bake and pray.

Too bad those prayers had gone unanswered again.

"I've spoken to the city marshal, the deputy sheriff, the sheriff, and the mayor, and still no one will allow me to see her. It doesn't matter what my credentials say, they've been told by Captain Abbott I'm not to have access."

"Have you tried talking to him?"

"Of course I have." And met with the same results—categorical denial.

He'd even endured the expense of a forty-word telegram to plead his case. All it bought him were excuses about protecting the case's integrity and not influencing the prisoner. Josiah had promised to attempt to sway Abbott, but even Josiah's charm had a limit. Broderick and Theresa had prayed with Andrew before returning to Cincinnati, but the peace it brought had been eaten away by worry.

"She's in there alone with no one to rally to her aid, and I hate it."

Mother Elise laid a hand against his cheek, her eyes reflecting the same brokenness he felt. "It hurts not to be able to help those we love, but she's not alone any more than you are. Don't lose hope, Andrew. A love worth having is a love worth fighting for, but sometimes the fight is won in stepping back and allowing God to work where we cannot." She squeezed his hand. "We'll make it through this just like we made it through that first year of you living with us. By God's strength. And cookies. Lots of cookies."

He chuckled and claimed her arm for a turn about the neighborhood, which was ablaze in bright fall colors. Praise God that she and Father Darlington had been able to drop everything and come to Petersburg on the I & E train. Mother Elise's excitement over suddenly being a grandmother brought some solace to the dismal situation, but as long as Lu remained in jail, there was a giant hole in his picture of a happy family. At least Oscar had taken to Andrew's parents quickly, even if the trauma of not understanding where his mother was and why he couldn't see her made him more difficult to manage than normal. Andrew wouldn't know what to do if he hadn't had their steady presence and wisdom to help him navigate parenthood without Lu and his decision about the future of his career.

"Has Father heard back from Chief Speers? Will there be a position for me in the City of Kansas Police?"

"Yes, but he warned you'd have to work your way from the bottom up. Chief Speers likes for his men to prove their mettle and earn positions by merit, not by connections. Are you certain this is what you want? You've worked so hard to get where you are."

He might have wrestled with the concept for a few days after Lu's arrest, but once he discovered he'd been cut off from her for the sake of the department's reputation, he'd become certain enough to write his resignation letter. His worth wasn't defined by the fickle opinions of others. God alone defined his worth, and it had taken knowing and loving Lu to learn it. "I'm certain. I can do similar work closer to home and be what my family needs."

"I'm so proud of you, Son. It'll be such a joy having you, Lu, and Oscar nearby. Did I tell you Oscar and your father fell asleep together in the parlor chair? It's the most precious thing I've ever seen."

He listened to her ramble on about their morning with Oscar as they turned back toward the Van Nada Boarding House. While it comforted him to know Oscar was so well loved, he ached for his family to be whole and sharing those moments together.

When they returned, Miss Van Nada announced that Captain Abbott was waiting for Andrew in the parlor. All the calm Andrew had collected during his walk with Mother Elise vanished. After promising to pray, Mother Elise went upstairs, leaving Andrew to face the man who'd blocked all access to Lu.

He entered the parlor and managed a one-word greeting. "Sir."

Captain Abbott launched straight into his reason for coming. "That woman—"

Did he hate Lu so much he couldn't even speak her name?

"—refused to sign the annulment papers, even when I told her she'd lose her deal with the marshals!"

Andrew jolted. "What do you mean she'll lose her deal?"

"We can't have you attached to a murderess and counterfeiter."

"We agreed the deal with Walt would stand no matter who the informant was."

"The contingency was to protect your career. I never dreamt requiring an annulment would cause her to refuse it. The woman even had the gall to tell me her name was Mrs. Darlington, not Thorne."

Good for her. Neither one of them would submit to Captain Abbott's bully tactics. "With all due respect, sir, I don't want an annulment."

Captain Abbott gaped at Andrew as if he'd taken leave of his senses. "The woman murdered a man—your brother."

"A circumstance which no one has investigated yet. Changing the terms of her deal for the self-serving purpose of preserving my career isn't ethical. Had it been anyone else, the terms of the deal wouldn't have been altered."

"Do you know what staying married to her will do to your career?"

"It can't do anything to a career I don't want anymore." Andrew removed his resignation from his inside coat pocket and extended it to Captain Abbott. "Do the right thing, Captain. Offer her the deal without the new terms, then allow me to figure out the rest with my wife."

CHAPTER 40

Lu scrutinized the document in front of her as if she could verify what it said. Could she trust this man who claimed to be a Philadelphia lawyer hired by Josiah to represent her? By his own admission, he was still working with the local court for approval to appear *pro hac vice*. Something he explained as getting special permission to work on her particular case, even though he was from a different state. It didn't make sense to her, but then again, she'd never worked with a lawyer before.

"Are you sure by signing this that I am not agreeing to an annulment?" She looked again at the tall man whose appearance was fastidious and demeanor serious.

"We read through the entire document together. I've omitted nothing. The Secret Service will honor your agreement with Marshal Kinder without the addendum of an annulment. And with what you told me of the circumstances of Irvine's death, it's probable you'll walk out of here as a free woman in a few weeks."

A free, married woman. If Andrew would still have her. Lu picked up the pen and made her mark.

Mr. Byre collected the papers and writing materials into his briefcase. "I'll confirm as much of your story as possible with the locals, hotel proprietor, and Clint. Then I'll meet with you again before the bench trial. Once presented with the details, I feel the judge will agree that you acted in self-defense and dismiss the criminal charges."

She'd never thought the law would take into consideration how and why she shot Irvine. To her, it didn't matter. She'd killed a man. However, if it meant she might have an earthly future with her family, she'd take it. "I still don't understand why Josiah was the one who hired you and not Andrew." It stung to think Josiah thought her more worthy of defending than Andrew did.

"I assure you, it wasn't for lack of want. They had quite the row over who'd pay my costs when I arrived. However, Mr. Isaacs was adamant that he use his family connections to ensure the best chance at a happy future for the both of you. Something about a belated wedding gift?" Mr. Byre snapped the latches on his case and raised an eyebrow.

"Would you please tell him thank you on my behalf?"

"Of course." He straightened. "I know this has been a long and taxing meeting for you, but I've arranged for a twenty-minute visit with Mr. Darlington if you're up to it."

Lu spun toward the door. "He's here?"

"Am I to take your reaction as a willingness to see him?"

"Yes, of course. Please." She stood and straightened out her wrinkled skirts donated by a local church. Not much could be done for her shoulder-length hair. Without having had a brush-through since the arrests, it had knotted to the point it hung a full two inches shorter than normal.

Before she finished preening, Mr. Byre opened the door and gestured to someone outside.

Andrew stepped into the room. His worn derby hat rotated in his hands as he stood before her in a new pressed suit, looking more like the dapper lawyer than her practical wear-it-until-it's-rags husband. A moment of fear seized her. Maybe he wasn't the man she thought he was. What if he'd been so adept at his job that he'd fooled her about even his character? Her perusal stopped at his face, and some of the fear vanished. This man—with a somber face and dark eyes—was still the same man she knew and loved, whether he loved her back or not.

"You have twenty minutes." Mr. Byre exited the room, leaving the door open.

"So much for privacy." Andrew's scowl deepened as he grumbled.

Though she wanted to throw herself into his arms and have the worry and stress of the last weeks melt away, she didn't dare. "Have you come to demand an annulment?"

Andrew's dour face gave no indication of his answer as he set his hat on the table and approached her. She didn't even realize she was biting her lip until his thumb skimmed across it and his expression softened. "No."

She closed her eyes and the weight of fear released with a sigh. "But then why didn't you come sooner?"

"Because my superiors blocked access to you. They were afraid our marriage would jeopardize the case against the Thornes."

"Will it?" Bands tightened around her chest. If any of the Thornes were released, she'd always live in fear of them ruining her new life with Andrew.

"No. The Thornes are so buried in evidence that the fact I love you won't change it."

His words struck her breathless. "You love me?"

"I do." Unabashed affection caressed her face as his gaze roved over it, taking in every detail. His hands found hers, and he kissed them like she was a cherished prize and not a shackled prisoner. "I'm here to stand by your side, no matter what happens, for as long as God allows. You are my Mrs. Darlington, and I'm proud for the world to know it."

Something between a laugh and a sob burst from her. It was exactly what she needed to hear, and somehow it had come from his mouth without any prompting. Or had it?

"Did Joe tell you to say that?"

Pride beamed from his face. "No. That one's all my own, even if it did take me ten days to get the words right." He tucked her against his chest in a one-arm hold and fumbled around in his pocket before withdrawing a simple gold band. "I should've done this a long time ago."

Her heart did a giddy jig. A ring. He'd bought her a ring. She'd thought his words were all she needed, but that gold circle meant just as much, if not more. Words could be hidden and kept between two people like a secret, but a ring read like a headline in a newspaper for all to see. She was his wife, and no one else could have her.

Pinching it between his fingers, he lifted her left hand and slipped it onto her finger. "I love you, Lu Darlington, and I want to spend my entire life with you." The matching band on his finger declared them a pair.

"You don't care that I'm a murderer?"

"You're not a murderer. I heard your explanation to Mr. Byre. It was self-defense, and even if it weren't, you aren't the same woman you were when it happened. I've seen God working in you. If He forgives you, who am I to deny it?"

All her fears were for naught. God truly had given her the kind of man she'd long ago written off as nursery-tale nonsense.

"I want you to see something." He pulled off his ring and tilted it at an angle. "Can you see the letters on the inside?"

She plucked it from his hand and brought it closer to her nose. Four letters, but she only recognized the "E" at the end. "What does it say?"

"Hope. Your ring has it too."

She frowned. Shouldn't a wedding ring be about love? "Why hope?"

"Because we live in the hope that God will see us through this and every struggle of our marriage."

He slipped his ring back on, and taking her face in both hands, leaned in for a long, gentle kiss. The apprehension she'd held onto for more than a week shed like rain off an oilskin jacket. While her bound hands prevented the full response she wanted to give, Lu leaned into Andrew, taking part in a long communication of love that needed no words.

When he pulled away, Lu sighed with contentment. "I love you, Andrew Darlington."

His eyes creased at the corners. "And I love you, Lu Darlington."

"No. Not Lu." That part of her life was finally over. Her tomorrow was finally here, and she wanted to live in it fully. "It's Luella. My real name from before . . ."

Understanding poured from his gaze. He tested the name, and the way it rolled off his tongue, quiet yet full of fervent love, shot a thrill through her.

He smiled as if he too enjoyed the sound of it and nuzzled his face against her neck. "A beautiful name for a beautiful woman."

Something crinkled inside his coat as she snuggled deeper into his hold.

He reluctantly pulled back and retrieved a folded paper from inside his coat. "Oscar would be upset with me if I didn't give this to you."

Embarrassment heated her neck and face at the realization she'd yet to ask after her own son. "How is he?"

Some of the joy seeped from his face as he handed her the paper. "Hurting, scared, confused. I'm doing my best to comfort him, but it's hard."

She ached for Oscar, but knowing Andrew cared for him eased the guilt. She struggled to unfold the paper with her bound hands as Andrew added, "I don't know what I'd do without my parents with us."

"Your parents? You mean the Darlingtons are here?" Considering Richard Thorne was dead and Ma Frances at the other end of the jail, he could mean no one else. Anxiety fluttered in her stomach. What would they think of her?

He pulled the paper from her hands and unfolded it for her. "Yes, they arrived in Petersburg the day after Oscar and I did. They adore him already, and he's warming up to them faster than I thought possible." He looked at her and smiled before handing the paper back to her. "They're looking forward to meeting you too."

Worry about meeting his parents fled as she stared at the stick figure drawing. Created by Oscar's unskilled hand, the three people with heads bigger than their bodies took up most of the page, with some sort of four-legged animal squeezed in at the bottom.

Andrew pointed to the animal. "That's Oscar's attempt to convince me to retrieve Jack from Landkreis."

"Why can't you? It'd bring him such joy."

"Jack's still too young to leave his mother, and for now, we've nowhere to keep him. Besides, I'm not leaving town until you're by my side and we're heading home as a family."

Home as a family. The words made her sigh as she tucked in against him again. It didn't matter where that home would be so long as it was the three of them together and there were no Thornes to ruin their happiness. "I love you so much."

He pushed a matted knot behind her ear and caressed her face. "I love you too, Luella."

"I don't think I'll ever get tired of hearing you say that."

"What about this?" His lips captured hers for a moment and released far too quickly. "Do you think you'll ever get tired of that?"

"No. Although I wouldn't be opposed to something longer." She peered through her lashes and offer a coquettish smile.

His head bent around to her ear and his warm breath sent tingles across her skin. "I can arrange that, *Luella*." He said her name again, stretching it out in a teasing manner. Then his mouth traced kisses down her jaw until finally his lips reached hers.

He kissed her slow and long, like she was something to be cherished and savored. She wasn't a possession to him, and it wasn't all about his sole enjoyment. It was a kiss shared. Mutually enjoyed. A kiss that declared to each other the vows they'd taken under duress were now personal, genuine, and lifelong. He was hers and she was his. Until death did they part. As their kiss lingered, all the bitter taste of her past experiences gave way to a sweetness that made honey taste bland.

Far too soon, someone knocked on the other side of the wall.

Andrew grunted and rested his forehead against hers. "Twenty minutes went too fast."

"It did, but I can tolerate the wait until next time now that I know you love me."

"Never doubt it. I will love you until my dying breath."

Another, harder knock sounded on the wall.

"I'm coming." After one last, brief kiss, Andrew shuffled to the exit, as reluctant to leave her as she was him. "I'll be back as soon as I can."

Sheriff Shrode prodded him out the door, leaving Luella alone in the room. She removed her ring, examined the engraved letters, and smiled. *Hope.* Andrew couldn't have chosen a better word to encircle her finger and their lives. For the first time in her life, her hope was placed exactly where it belonged. In the hands and promises of a God who loved and made hearts new.

CHAPTER 41

City of Kansas, Missouri
December 24, 1884

THE EVENING WAS GROWING LATE when Andrew's carriage turned the corner of Cherry Street onto Seventeenth and stopped in front of the small iron-fenced yard. Home, finally. Light poured from the bay window of the quaint two-story frame home purchased just before he left a week ago. Andrew frowned as he realized the curtains weren't merely open—they were nonexistent. He'd told Luella to buy whatever she needed for the house while he was out of town, but apparently she hadn't considered those necessary.

He'd have to remedy that soon. The idea of anyone being able to spy on his family disturbed him. When he'd joined the Darlington household in 1860, the population of the City of Kansas had been under five thousand. Now the city numbered nearly eighty thousand, with more people pouring in every day. And with that booming growth came an influx of crime.

At least his parents only lived a few houses down. Even better protection was the surprise he'd brought back from his trip.

Andrew stepped down from the carriage onto the sidewalk. Behind him, Jack whined as if he knew Oscar was inside. There may not be snow for their first Christmas as a family, but there would be joy, laughter, and a tremendous amount of love. He paid the driver and walked to the door with a bag in hand and dog on leash.

Oscar's face appeared in the window. "Pa!"

His voice carried through the glass, and he disappeared from view.

Andrew grinned at the enthusiastic welcome. Wait until he saw Jack.

Oscar threw open the door and launched into his legs. However, his enthusiasm at seeing Andrew shifted the moment Jack barked. The reunion was everything Andrew hoped it would be. Jack jumped on Oscar, licking his face and barking happily. Oscar squealed as he fell back and tussled with the mutt. Andrew had to scoot them with his foot further into the hall so he could close the cold evening out. Oscar bounced between talking to Jack and making exclamations of "Look, Pa!"

Andrew set his bag down, ruffled Oscar's hair, and scratched Jack behind the ear. Warmth, the smell of dinner, and Oscar had all welcomed him home, but not his wife.

He straightened and glanced around for Luella. Halfway up the stairs, she watched them with a full-toothed grin and dancing eyes. The green velvet dress was new and completely distracting with the way it hugged her in ways he hadn't for too long. Praise God his days of traveling without her were over. He abandoned Oscar and Jack to continue their shenanigans and took the steps two at a time to reach her. He stopped a step below her, encased her waist in his arms, and drank in the joy teaming with mischief in her eyes.

"Welcome home. Are you going to kiss me or just stand there staring?"

That was all the invitation he needed. The lengthy greeting proved he wasn't the only one who'd been lonely.

He rubbed the soft velvet curve of her waist, fascinated by the feel of it. "Hello, beautiful."

She giggled and turned in a circle on the step. "Do you like it? Mother Elise helped me to pick it out for midnight services tonight."

"I love anything you wear." He pulled her onto his step, ready for another taste of her sweet welcome.

The skitter of paws and feet stole Luella's attention before he could succeed. "I can't believe you brought Jack back with you after you said dogs belong in the country."

"They do, but I'd be a monster to keep a boy from his dog." He led her downstairs to the parlor doorway to watch Oscar and Jack run around the lone sofa in the empty room. "Besides, I'll feel better having Jack protecting you when I return to my patrol duties next week."

Luella leaned against him and wrapped both their arms around her waist. "You're so good to us. Jack's the perfect Christmas gift. Look at how happy Oscar is."

Toys scattered across the floor as boy and puppy played chase. Despite wanting to keep the moment cheerful, his eyes wandered to the uncovered bay window and then over the empty room. "I thought I told you to buy anything the house needs."

"I did, but you already had most of the basics and the best-stocked kitchen I've ever seen. I just don't know what to do with the rest of the space. I've never lived with so few people." She twisted in his arms to face him, her countenance and tone suddenly somber. "How awful was it?"

The conversation must've recalled memories of the Thornes and thus the purpose of his trip. Andrew leaned into her caress and released a heavy breath. He'd hoped to avoid talking about it until after Christmas, but he should've known she'd be worried about him.

After a quick check to make sure Oscar was too preoccupied to listen, he lowered his voice. "It's over. Clint refused to see me before he hanged, and Pastor Newcomb said he rejected the gift of God's forgiveness. He's buried with Cyrus, Priscill, and Irvine now."

The same ache and disappointment he felt mirrored in Luella's face. "What about Ma Frances?"

That had been the hardest part of his trip. Sheriff Shrode allowed him one last visit with her before transporting her to the Indianapolis Insane Asylum. "You wouldn't recognize her. The entire time she rocked in the corner of her cell, curled in a ball. When I gave her the picture of Clint, Cyrus, Irvine, me, and her that I commissioned

Theresa to make, she clutched it to her chest and just muttered incoherently."

"Oh, Andrew, I'm so sorry." She wrapped her arms around his neck and held him.

Frances Thorne may not have been dear to him, but she had at one point been his mother. Knowing she would spend the rest of her life broken and mourning in a locked cell alone without the hope of Christ to bear her through hurt more than he would've thought. He soaked up Luella's support until he remembered happier news to share.

"Emma and Günter are married, and his family is helping to care for Widow Zachary. The woman's too stubborn to leave her house, but she's safe and cared for now."

"Thank you, Jesus."

Though Widow Zachary still refused to forgive Luella's part in her husband's death, Luella's concern and prayers for the woman had never wavered.

"And Mary? Is she well?" Luella asked.

"As well as can be. You know her. Determined to serve for however long God gives her, but she sends her love and prayers."

"When I learn to write, she is going to be the second person I write to."

"And who will be the first?"

"You, of course."

He brushed her cheek and stared into her endless pools of gray-blue. How he loved this woman.

Someone knocked.

"That should be your parents arriving with the surprise I have for you."

Mother Elise and Father Darlington entered with Christmas greetings and arms full of food. Interested by the smells emanating from the baskets, Jack came into the hall, quickly followed by Oscar.

"Did you bring cookies?" Oscar grabbed a basket from Father Darlington's hands and peeked under the towel. Disappointed, he tried to hand it back.

"Since you took it, you have to carry it to the kitchen." Luella shifted the rest of the food from Father Darlington's hands and glanced out the door. "Were you able to get them?"

"I was." Father Darlington smiled at Andrew. "I need your help to carry in a few things, Son."

Curious, Andrew followed him outside to a wagon holding an overstuffed chair and ottoman.

"Luella wanted you to have a special place to read to Oscar."

Andrew touched the chair and smiled. Luella truly had chosen the best gift. The only problem was he'd need to find a matching one so she could sit next to him too. After a few minutes of wrangling the chair over the iron gate and up the stoop, they placed it next to the sofa in front of the fireplace.

Oscar bounced up and down. "Sit in it! Sit in it!"

Tired from the long trip and now carrying furniture, he was more than willing to comply. Oscar climbed into his lap and Jack tried to follow suit. Luella must have anticipated the problem and entered with a blanket she piled on the floor and commanded the dog to lie on. Once his parents settled on the sofa and Jack seemed pleased to pass out on the blanket, Luella approached Andrew with a black leather Bible in her hand.

"I think you should christen the reading chair with its first story." She held out the tome with a shyness that surprised him.

When he flipped toward the book of Matthew, she stopped him. "Aren't you supposed to read books from beginning to end?"

Considering they'd been reading together from the New Testament for a while, something more than innocence laced that question. After squinting suspiciously at her for a moment, he opened to the cover page. Written in careful, but wobbly lettering, was a note to him.

I love you, Andrew.

Hope always,

Luella Darlington

The pride in Luella's face could only be surpassed by his own for her.

"Mother Elise helped me." She sent a thankful smile his mother's way and then sat on the arm of his chair. "You may now read from wherever you choose."

He was definitely going to need to find a second chair she could scoot close to him. "Since they'll read the Christmas story at services tonight, I have the perfect verses for our family."

With Oscar curled up on his lap, Luella leaning against him on the arm of the chair, and his parents sitting on the sofa next to him, he opened to Romans 8:24–25.

"For we are saved by hope: but hope that is seen is not hope: for what a man seeth, why doth he yet hope for? But if we hope for that we see not, then do we with patience wait for it."

Oscar's face screwed up in confusion, and Andrew simplified it for him. "Hope is trusting God's promise for our future. We can't see it yet, but because we know Him, we can look forward to heaven, no matter the struggles we face here." His gaze lifted to Luella's. "Although it's my hope we have a long peaceful life together here on earth first."

"That's my hope too." Her hand entwined with his.

"I hope we have cookies."

Oscar's food-focused stomach sent the family toward the kitchen for dinner. As everyone gathered at the table, Andrew's heart swelled with the abundant blessing of it all. His hope had always been to prove his worth. Yet now, as he sat at the head of the table with his wife's hand in his and Oscar already trying to sneak unwanted bites to Jack, he felt completely unworthy of all God had given him. And he was content with that. These last few months had taught him hope was never about him. Hope was always about the God who gave new life.

And this new life would never grow old.

Acknowledgments

As with every story I've written, God chose to grow me in ways I never imagined. Thank you, Lord, that I do not go through this process alone. May Your name always be glorified through my writing.

Without my family's support, there would be no book. Thank you, Travis, for all you do and sacrifice to make sure I get my writing time in. Thank you to Malaki, Nehemiah, Mom, Dad, Linda, Noah, Matt, and Ramey for always being my cheerleaders. I love you.

Thank you to Jennifer Uppencamp and Sandy McBeth at the Pike County Indiana Historical Society and Museum. Any misrepresentation of Petersburg is my own. These ladies were a wonderful help in bringing 1880s Pike County alive.

As always, I am grateful to my quad of besties: Angela Carlisle, Liz Bradford, Lucette Nel, and Voni Harris. Thank you for your friendship, writing support, and sisterhood.

Where would my books be without readers? Thank you to Casey Kohlman, Abigail Harris, and Charity Henico for all your enthusiastic support. It means the world.

Thank you to my Kregel team for believing in me, my agent Tamela Hancock Murray for encouraging and praying for me, and my amazing Kregel editors, Katherine Chappell, Janyre Tromp, and Lindsay Danielson. Thank you to all those on the Kregel team who design, distribute, and help market my book so well. God bless you all.

And thank YOU, reader, for choosing to read my book. I pray you were blessed by it.

Discussion Questions

1. Consider Lu, Andrew, Ma Frances, Clint, Priscill, and Cyrus and each of their connections to the theme of "counterfeit hope." Where did you see these characters putting their hope? How did putting their hope in places other than Christ affect their decisions and actions? How did putting their hope in these things fail them?

2. How did you see Lu grow and change over the course of the story? What about Andrew?

3. Andrew had grown up in a criminal family until his arresting officer took him in and gave him a new life. Andrew occasionally hinted that those first years were challenging for him and the Darlingtons. What challenges do you think he and the Darlingtons faced? How do you think they overcame them?

4. When Andrew discovered his former family was at the heart of the criminal dealings in Landkreis, his two lives collided. What are some of the complex emotions you saw Andrew face in regards to his former family? How do you think you would have felt in his situation? Could you have found forgiveness for each Thorne?

5. Andrew and Lu were forced into a marriage that neither of them wanted. In what ways did God use the situation for their good and His glory? How have you seen God work hard things for good in your own life or in the lives of those around you?

6. Do you believe Pastor Newcomb should have filed the marriage paperwork having known the circumstances surrounding Andrew and Lu's marriage? Why or why not?

7. In chapter 16, when Andrew confronted Lu about her stealing and her interactions with men, Lu said she didn't have a choice. Andrew countered by saying she always has a choice. Do you think this is true? Did Lu always have a choice? Why or why not?

8. One of the emotions Andrew struggled with after his family was arrested was guilt for not having shared his faith and not giving his family an opportunity to find forgiveness and hope through Jesus Christ. Do you feel it was his responsibility to do so? If he had shared his faith with the Thornes, how do you think they would have responded?

9. Widow Zachary refused to offer forgiveness for Lu's part in Sheriff Zachary's death. How did that refusal affect Widow Zachary and her daughter? Would you have been able to forgive Lu if you had been in Widow Zachary's position?

10. Andrew claimed Romans 8:24–25 as the verse for their family and explained to Oscar, "Hope is trusting God's promise for our future. We can't see it yet, but because we know Him, we can look forward to heaven, no matter the struggles we face here." How does having that hope in your life affect how you respond to difficulties in life?

HISTORICAL NOTES

Toxic Red Kidney Beans

This isn't a historical note per se, but a disclaimer. While doing research to find out what plant Ma Frances would use to make her family sick but not kill them, I learned something about kidney beans. While kidney bean powder is an excellent source of nutrition, one must be careful to soak and then boil the beans for at least ten minutes before consuming. Just four or five raw kidney beans can trigger extreme nausea, vomiting, diarrhea, and abdominal pain. I did speed up the timeline of the poison's effect for the sake of story pacing.

Miranda Rights and the Secret Service

Long before the Miranda Rights were established in 1966, the Secret Service had their own version that they were required to give every arrested criminal. Before they created their own version, it was a common practice for law enforcement agencies to grant freedom to criminals who spouted information at their arrests. However, Chief of the Secret Service Elmer Washburn (1874–1876) enacted a policy for the Secret Service which required operatives to inform arrested criminals that anything they did must be done "voluntarily and without any promises whatever." (See reports by Secret Service operatives as quoted in *Illegal Tender* by David R. Johnson [1995]). This policy was further emphasized by Chief James Brooks (1876–1888) in 1879, at which time operatives were instructed to warn suspects about their rights. Everything a suspect said would be documented and used against them in court, and they did not have to answer any questions until they had consulted a lawyer. Nearly ninety years before the rest of law enforcement agencies required it, Secret Service operatives were reading suspects their rights.

The Belmont Disaster

When looking for a reason why copies of Walt's reports wouldn't reach Andrew, I immediately thought of searching for an instance of a ship sinking on the Ohio River. It was a slim chance given my timeline, but God swiftly led me to the details of one that fit my story literally perfectly. On August 29, 1884, the *Belmont* ferry boat was hit by a tornado and capsized between Henderson, KY and Evansville, IN. Not only was this the exact location for my story, it also was within one week of my original timeline. All it took was shifting things by one week. Unfortunately, the *Belmont*'s story is one of tragedy as sixteen people, many of whom were women and children, lost their lives.

Turn the page for a peek
at the exciting final book in
Crystal Caudill's

COUNTERFEIT

FAITH

HIDDEN HEARTS
OF THE GILDED AGE
- THREE -

Excerpt From Chapter 1

"You'd best be minding your own business. Asking questions is dangerous. Just ask Mr. Farwell." Quincy forced his arm through hers in a mockery of gentlemanly behavior and propelled her down Fifth Street, away from the police station next to Independence Hall.

"What have you done to him?"

"You'll find out soon enough. I only wish I could be there when you find out his fate."

"If you've hurt him, I'll turn you over to the police."

"You should be more worried about yourself. I intend to make sure you understand the seriousness of your position." The fingers of his free hand stroked her arm as if she were a pet while his gaze wandered without appearing to see anything. "Maybe I'll start with catching flame to your skirts like the witch you always were." Quincy stopped walking, lost in the imaginings of his depraved mind. "Yes, that's what I'll do. Just a foretaste of what can happen if you open your yap."

There was no doubt he'd do it given the chance. He'd tortured animals that he'd claimed to adore. How much more delight would he take in harming his enemies?

"You wouldn't risk it. There are too many people around, and the police station's only a dozen yards away."

"You're right. It's too crowded here."

His free hand slipped underneath their arms to his pocket. The wooden handle of a knife emerged. In one swift movement, he shifted it into the fist beneath her pinned arm. He angled the blade's edge toward her and tugged her close. The point pierced through the wool of her coat and dress to scrape against flesh. Any movement contrary to his and she'd likely suffer a punctured lung.

"What say you? Shall we go for a ride?"

"I don't see as I have any choice."

"Maybe you got smarts after all." He guided her toward the cab-stand outside the Philadelphia Library.

When two men jogged down the library steps and turned their direction, Quincy angled his body toward hers and tilted his cap to shield his face from view. For a breath, the blond man's tortoise eyes met hers and hope for a rescue swelled within her breast. Then his gaze skittered away, and he walked past, talking to his companion, without a second glance. She should've known better than to hope. Heroes were in short supply in her life.

"At whose behest are you working, Quincy? I'll compensate you handsomely for telling me and then releasing me."

His derisive laugh declared his refusal. "Your pockets aren't deep enough. All you need to know is they've got eyes everywhere. No more questions. No need to worry. But if you speak one word to anyone, even your precious little girls, they'll know, and I'll get to have my fun."

He stopped at the first empty cab. "Christian and Carpenter Street." With a jab meant to remind her of the weapon he wielded, he released her arm and slid to stand almost against her back. "After you."

Getting in that cab meant submitting to torture—maybe worse, if he lost control. *My saviour; thou savest me from violence.*

"Get moving."

She'd move all right, but not inside. With one boot on the foot iron, she gripped the hansom's frame and drew in a deep breath. May these horses be as nerved as the ones that nearly trampled her. On a prayer, she rent a shrill scream that would either lead to her death or her salvation.

"A home run!"

—Misty M. Beller, *USA Today* best-selling author

HIDDEN HEARTS
OF THE GILDED AGE
— ONE —

COUNTERFEIT
LOVE

CRYSTAL CAUDILL

"Simultaneously well-researched and action-packed with delightfully flawed characters who will leave readers rooting for their redemption."

—AMANDA COX, Christy Award–winning author of
The Edge of Belonging

KREGEL
PUBLICATIONS